The characters and events in this book are fictitious. Any similarities to real persons, living or dead, is coincidental and not intended by the author.

T.R. FOLSOM

EYE WITNESS

A THRILLER

1

EMILY WARNER SHOULD HAVE DIED in the crash, but she survived.

A week before the accident that changed her life forever, Emily had turned fifteen, and her acne had just cleared up. She saw it as a good sign. She had a mad crush on Kevin, a boy from her school, and she'd caught him looking at her during class. However, her dreams of being kissed by him never came true. She never saw him again. In fact, she never saw any of her classmates and friends again. All because two cars collided at an intersection, one speeding through a red light, the other innocently adhering to the traffic laws.

The red traffic light was the last thing Emily saw, before the seatbelt cut into her chest, robbing her of her breath. Glass shattered all around her. The collision's sounds echoed in the night. The side impact knocked her unconscious. When she regained consciousness, she wondered for a moment whether she was dead. She felt numb, as if her body was gone. But then the pain receptors in her brain responded, and she realized she was still strapped in by her seatbelt, a sticky fluid covering her eyes. Sharp pain made her head ache worse than any migraine, while her body was tightly wedged between pancaked sheets of metal, plastic, and upholstery. She was trapped, unable to move.

Emily neither saw the blinking lights of the ambulances and the police cars, nor the flashlights of the first responders trying to assess the situation. She only heard the sirens and the police officers' and paramedics' voices, telling her to remain calm, assuring her that they would get her out. That she would be alright.

She wanted to believe them.

Emily felt movement and heard metal being bent or cut. Then somebody groaned, and she knew she wasn't the only one who'd survived. But before she could sigh with relief, a paramedic whispered low to a colleague, obviously not wanting Emily to overhear him, "The passenger has no pulse."

Her heart stopped in that instant. For an eternity, time stood still. But then her body reacted to the terrible news she didn't want to be true. Tears mingled with the viscous liquid in her eyes, the blood so thick that no light could penetrate. She tried to wipe it away, but her arm was stuck. She didn't know then that it wouldn't have made a difference. The blood remained where it was. No amount of tears could wash it away.

Deep down, Emily knew what it meant, even though she didn't want to acknowledge it at the time. Like a ragdoll, the paramedics pulled her out of the wreck. The morphine they gave her in the ambulance lulled her into a fitful dream, helping her push the memory of the crash out of her mind.

At the hospital, Emily heard the voices of the emergency physicians and nurses as they went to work on her. According to them, it was a wonder that she was alive.

She knew she should be grateful. But how could she be grateful for the nothingness that greeted her when she opened her eyes? Her future would be different from anything she'd dreamed of ever since she could remember. Nothing would ever be the same again. Her old life was over. A new one, one she hadn't asked for, had begun. And this new life was overshadowed by an absence of light that swallowed everything around her like a black hole.

Yes, she had survived.

But the miracle came at a price.

She was blind.

2

ERIC BOLTON PULLED HIS SILVER MERCEDES into a parking spot closest to the Emergency Department's entrance. He jumped out of his car and ran inside, not even locking it, his heart beating like a jackhammer, but he knew he wasn't having a heart attack. He was fit for his sixty-nine years, barely carried an extra pound around his midsection, and was as healthy as could be expected from an influential man who ate more meals in fancy restaurants than at home.

Inside the hospital, he oriented himself and quickly found a nurse's station. He had no time to lose.

"Where is my daughter? Madeline Bolton, she came in an ambulance."

The woman behind the counter looked at him. "What's your name?"

"Eric Bolton. I'm her father. Where is my daughter?" he asked hurriedly, leaning halfway across the counter as if that would make the woman answer any faster.

"Please calm down, sir," she said and typed something on her keyboard.

Calm down? How could he calm down? His daughter was hurt, badly hurt from what he could piece together from Lucia's frantic phone call. Madeline's housekeeper had cried, her words laden with sadness, alarm, and fear. It sent a shock through his body, and the resulting adrenaline pumping through his veins had somehow helped him drive back into the city and to the hospital without getting into an accident.

"Ms. Bolton was taken to trauma two," the nurse finally said. "Please take a seat over there." She pointed to the waiting room.

But Bolton didn't sit down. He couldn't. He needed to know what had happened, what state Maddie was in. He needed to be by her side, tell her that she would be okay, that her daddy was here to make sure she got the best care. So he ignored the nurse's suggestion and headed for the double doors that led to the trauma rooms.

"Sir, sir! You can't go in there!" she yelled after him.

But he ignored her, even as she called for security over the PA system. "Security to trauma center, corridor B immediately."

On the other side of the double doors, Bolton rushed along the corridor lined with a variety of medical equipment needed to monitor heartbeat, blood pressure, oxygenation and other vitals, as well as machines to shock a heart back into beating, and ventilators to take over a patient's breathing. He heard various beeping sounds and hastily spoken commands between the doctors and nurses. The sterile smell of disinfecting liquids hit him, reminding him that the last time he'd been inside a hospital was when Rita had given birth to Madeline. Back then, he hadn't minded the hospital smells or the sight of the many machines that helped sustain life. Today, the scene and its smells conjured up the worst possible outcomes.

A multitude of rooms, all with large floor-to-ceiling windows, some with closed curtains providing privacy, others with open ones, lay to his left and right. Many of the doors stood open, others were closed.

"You can't be in here," a firm male voice addressed him from behind.

Bolton ignored the reprimand and kept walking, reading the signs outside the doors. Trauma five, he read and headed farther down the corridor. But he didn't get far. The security guard's hand on Bolton's shoulder jerked him back, forcing him to stop and pivot.

"Sir, you have to leave, or I'll have the police arrest you," the tall black man wearing a dark-blue uniform warned.

"You don't understand," Bolton pleaded. "My daughter, she's here. She's hurt. I have to get to her." He tried to free himself from the man's grip, but couldn't. So he raised his voice. "Madeline, Madeline, baby, your daddy is here."

"Let's go," the security guard said and dragged him back toward the double doors.

Bolton didn't make it easy for him, using his weight against the man. "Damn it! Let me go! I have to see Madeline." He looked over his shoulder and called out toward trauma room two. "Madeline! Maddie!"

All of a sudden, a middle-aged black woman in scrubs appeared in the doorway. With the authority of a physician who'd seen it all, she looked straight at him. "Mr. Bolton?" Then her gaze shifted to the security guard, and she gave him a subtle sign by moving her head to one side.

The security guard let go of Bolton. Bolton made a few steps toward the doctor, then stopped. It was written on her face, the expression that meant that the news wasn't good.

She met him halfway. "I'm sorry." Her eyes brimmed with compassion. "Your daughter didn't make it."

All life drained from Bolton's body, and for a moment, the world stood still. The trauma surgeon was still talking. Words like cerebral hemorrhage and swelling of the brain echoed in the corridor. Bolton barely heard anything.

Madeline was gone.

Somebody led him to a chair where he sat numb from grief and pain. Everything seemed too quiet around him. And in the solitary pain of his grief, he realized that everything he'd achieved in his life, everything he'd worked for, meant nothing. He felt tears rim his eyes and forced them back. He couldn't break down now, couldn't allow himself to be weak. He had to be strong, for himself and his family. If he gave in now, if he allowed grief to swallow him, there would be nobody to comfort Rita, his wife of forty years.

But how could he comfort Rita when he himself felt more pain than he ever had?

He didn't know how long he'd been sitting there, somewhere in the hospital, when his cell phone rang. Automatically, he pulled it from his pocket and looked at it. He wasn't sure why he answered the call, when he could barely speak, but he did it anyway.

The familiar voice was cheerful. "Morning, Eric, how far out are you? The horses are saddled. We're burning daylight here."

"Mike," Bolton said, his voice breaking.

Mike Faulkner, the President's Chief of Staff had been his friend since they'd both been members of the same fraternity. While at first their career choices had taken them in different directions and to different locations, their friendship had only strengthened, until they'd both ended up in government, Faulkner in the executive branch, and Bolton as a defense contractor with ties to lobbyists, and as a major donor.

"Did you forget?"

"Mike..." Bolton collected all his strength to force the next words out of his mouth without breaking down. "Maddie... she's dead. My little girl is dead." A sob tore from his chest. It didn't matter that Maddie was thirty-two years old and lived on her own in a swanky townhouse in Georgetown. She would always be his little girl. And now she was gone. Her infectious smile gone. Her laughter gone.

"Oh my God, what happened?"

Bolton pushed another rising sob down. "I don't know. Lucia called me. She found her when she got in. They rushed her to the hospital, but it was too late. She's…" This time, reality sank in even deeper, and he couldn't get the word over his lips. The image was too raw, too painful.

"Eric, I can't even imagine what you and Rita are going through right now."

"Rita doesn't know yet. She's at home." His voice broke, but he pulled himself together. He took a breath. "I don't know what to do."

"I'm here for you, Eric. Whatever you need. You just let me know. You have to be strong for Rita, and I can be strong for you."

A sob tore from Bolton's chest. "Maybe there is something you can do. The police… they'll want to investigate what happened. And I need to know too. I need to know what happened and why. But I don't want the police to drag her name through the mud."

Even though he loved Maddie more than his own life, he wasn't blind. She'd been a wild child in her twenties, and had experimented with drugs. Her lovers spanned the globe. Not all of them decent men. He didn't want that to be her legacy.

"Don't worry about anything. You let me handle this. I'll make sure she'll be treated right. I'll send my own people in," Faulkner promised.

"The Secret Service? Can you do that?"

"Ordinarily, no. It's not within our jurisdiction. But I can call in some favors so DC Police won't take point on this. The Secret Service will make sure nothing leaks that you don't want the public to know about. And they'll be thorough. I promise you. That's the least I can do for my goddaughter."

"I don't know how to thank you."

"No need to thank me," Faulkner said. "Take care of Rita. She needs you now more than ever."

Before Bolton could utter another thanks, Faulkner disconnected the call, and shoved his cell phone into his pants pocket.

Faulkner stopped at the stable door. He'd looked forward to riding out with Bolton. He didn't get to ride his horses much anymore since he'd become President Robert Langford's Chief of Staff over two years ago. In fact, he didn't get to stay at his equestrian estate in rural Virginia much at all. Instead, Faulkner spent most of his days and nights in his house in Washington D.C. It was close enough to the White House so he could be in the Oval Office with fifteen minutes' notice, traffic permitting.

Sometimes he wondered why he'd taken the job. Was it because he liked the power the position afforded? The prestige? Or had he given in to the President's offer because they'd been friends since college? Like Bolton, the President had been a member of the same fraternity Faulkner had pledged to. Maybe it wasn't either of those reasons. Perhaps not remarrying after the unexpected death of his wife when their son was still a child had contributed to his quest for more professional challenges. He'd been no good at raising his rebellious and grief-stricken teenage son.

"Morning, Mr. Faulkner," the groom said.

Robert Woolf looked like a crusty old sailor, his face leathered from the time he spent outdoors whatever the weather, his hands calloused from the hard labor he performed without complaint. Faulkner knew a good man when he saw one. And Woolf was a good man, honest, reliable, invaluable.

"Morning, Robert."

"Has your guest arrived?" Woolf asked.

"I'm afraid he had to cancel. Something came up. And I have to return to Washington D.C. immediately."

Woolf sighed. "Hmm. The President sure rides you hard, if you don't mind my saying so. He never lets you enjoy a day off."

Faulkner let out a bitter laugh. "Normally you'd be right, but this time, I have to help an old friend out." He rubbed his hand over the horse Woolf had already saddled. "Perhaps you and Caleb can ride out instead. I'll call him and see if he has plans to come out."

Before he could reach for his cell phone, Woolf waved him off. "Don't think so. He was here yesterday."

"Caleb? Good!" Though his only son wasn't as much into horses as Faulkner and his wife had been, he occasionally did show some interest.

"He didn't take any of the horses out. He wasn't here long enough. I was ready to saddle Lucky for him, but he said he didn't have time."

Faulkner's forehead furrowed. "Then what did he do here?"

Woolf shrugged. "He said he forgot something last time he was here."

"Oh well, why don't you ride Lucky then? And maybe that boy who helps out here occasionally wants to ride the mare. I don't mind. He seems responsible enough."

"Will do, sir."

"Thanks, Robert."

Faulkner turned and marched out of the stable, pulled his cell phone from his pocket, and scrolled through his contacts.

3

THERE WAS NO PARKING outside the quaint Georgetown two-story townhouse when Detective Adam Yang arrived with his partner, Detective Simon Jefferson. It was to be expected. There was never any parking in this part of Washington D.C. to begin with. And today, it was even worse: a car was already double-parked.

Yang exchanged a look with Jefferson, his black partner of only two years. They'd both become members of the Washington Metropolitan Police Department in their early twenties and risen through the ranks, making detective within six months of each other. But that was where their similarities ended. Jefferson belonged to the black majority at DC Police, where roughly sixty percent of all officers were black, and only a little over two percent were Asian.

While Yang felt at home in the multi-cultural department, he was certainly the odd man out. Just like he was the odd man out in his extended Chinese family. His siblings, two sisters and a brother, as well as his many cousins, were professionals: lawyers, doctors, accountants. His parents had meant for him to follow in their footsteps, but he had no interest in medicine or accounting. The law had called to him, though not in the way his parents had hoped. A lawyer or judge in the family would have satisfied their ambitions for him, but Yang had chosen to join the police force instead.

"Just park behind the black car," Jefferson said with a shrug.

Normally, Yang would at least have made an effort to find a proper parking spot, but after an early morning phone call with his soon-to-be ex-wife in which they'd fought over the financial aspect of their divorce, which was dragging on for far too long, Yang didn't have any fight left in him.

Without a word, Yang switched off the engine and hopped out of the car. Jefferson was already on the steps leading to the entrance door, which stood open. Jefferson entered. In the well-appointed foyer, Yang caught up with his partner.

"Nice digs, huh?" Jefferson said in a low voice.

"It reeks of money." Just like half the city. Yet to Yang it was home. He couldn't imagine living anywhere else but inside the Beltway. There was something about living in the nerve center of the nation even though he wasn't part of its political fabric.

Hearing voices from a door, which was ajar, Yang headed for it. But before he and Jefferson reached it, a black man in a dark suit emerged from it and blocked the entrance.

Yang and Jefferson flashed their badges. "Detectives Yang and Jefferson, DC Police. And you are?"

When the man flashed his badge faster than a magician performing a trick, Yang already smelled trouble. The man's dark suit and his indifferent expression were a dead giveaway.

"Agent Banning, Secret Service." Banning pointed over his shoulder, still blocking the entrance to the living room. "My colleague Agent Mitchell and I have got this. You're not needed. Please see yourselves out."

"I don't think so. From what I've been told, this is a suspicious death, which falls firmly within our jurisdiction," Yang said without missing a beat. "So, unless this is a case of counterfeiting or bank fraud, I suggest you leave this to us."

Agent Banning didn't move. Behind him, Agent Mitchell came into view. He was a carbon copy of his colleague down to the boring tie, though his hair was shorter, and his shoulders broader.

"This is a case for the Metropolitan Police Department, not the Secret Service," Yang said.

"Guess you didn't get the memo," Agent Banning said with a smug face.

Yang opened his mouth to retort when his cell phone rang.

Agent Mitchell pointed to Yang's pocket, from where the sound originated. "I would answer it if I were you. Might be important."

Yang met Mitchell's gaze, then exchanged a look with Jefferson. Jefferson shrugged.

It was clear the agent knew something Yang didn't. He reached into his pocket and pulled out his cell. Pressing it to his ear, he answered, "Detective Yang."

"Yang, Lieutenant Arnold." Whenever his superior, Lieutenant Latochia Arnold, called, it was generally important.

Jefferson stepped closer so he could listen in.

"Lieutenant, ma'am. I was about to call you to—" He didn't get to finish his sentence.

"Have the Secret Service agents arrived yet?" she interrupted.

"Yes, how did—?"

Again, she interrupted him. "Good. Leave this to them. I'm pulling you and Jefferson off this case effective immediately."

"With all due respect, ma'am, this is our jurisdiction," Yang said as calmly as he could, while staring at the two Secret Service agents. "You can't just—"

"It wasn't my call, Yang. My hands are tied."

Yang grunted in displeasure.

"Listen, Yang," Arnold said with a little less force, "this comes from way above my pay grade. The victim's father has clout, and was able to pull some strings. The mayor leaned on the chief to let this one go. Something to do with the victim being in contact with members of a foreign government. Secret Service claims it's a matter of national security. It's total b—ahm, I don't like it either, but it is what it is. So, do me a favor, don't make a scene. Just leave, and let them deal with it."

"Alright," Yang said tightly and disconnected the call.

Trying to ignore the two agents' self-righteous facial expressions, Yang said, "It's all yours."

In the car, Yang turned to Jefferson. "Can you believe this crap? What the fuck was this all about?"

"Well, considering who the victim is… or was…" Jefferson said.

"What do you mean? Who was she?"

"Madeline Bolton. She belongs to D.C. high society." Jefferson shrugged. "Father is a big shot in politics or something like that. Apparently he's friends with the President."

Yang couldn't believe his ears. "How do you know that?"

Jefferson shook his head. "How *don't* you know that? I read the papers."

"Papers or gossip rags?"

"Either way, I keep up with what's going on in this town. Can't hurt knowing who's who."

Yang sighed and started the car. "Lieutenant Arnold wasn't kidding when she said this was above her pay grade."

"Arnold never jokes unless she's off-duty. Besides, do you really want to get involved in a case where the victim's family is going to be up your ass looking for any mistakes you might make? You know what rich people are like."

Yang grunted, still annoyed.

"You're just annoyed that Secret Service encroached on our turf," Jefferson said.

Yang cast him a glance. "I guess that's the difference between us: I want to solve cases, you want to close them."

Jefferson gave a short chuckle. "Those two things aren't mutually exclusive. You know that, right?"

4

EMILY FELT MOVEMENT return to her hands and feet as her body shook off the groggy feeling of the sedatives the IV had delivered into her vein. During the surgery, she imagined hearing sentence fragments of Dr. Milton Harland's steady voice giving orders to his small team. Most likely she was just dreaming, creating her own reality while her life lay in someone else's hands once more. There was comfort in that thought, and fear. Yet, she felt no pain, nor any sense of time having passed.

At some point, she heard the sound of a hospital bed rolling over the linoleum floor, and felt the movement of a nurse pushing the bed into the recovery room. The brakes being set made a grating noise and indicated that she'd arrived in a cubicle. The sleeve around her right bicep became tighter as it filled with more air. The pressure released slowly while a heart monitor beeped steadily.

"One forty-three over eighty-five," Tiffany, the nurse who'd helped prepare her for the surgery, said in a soothing voice. A warm hand touched Emily's. "Still a little high, but it all looks good, hon. The doctor will be with you soon. Just rest in the meantime."

Emily opened her mouth to thank her, but her throat was parched, and she couldn't form any words. Instead, she swallowed hard.

"I'll bring you some water."

Her lids were too heavy to lift, and she attributed the sensation to the sedatives she'd received. She was coming out of a sleep-like state and felt disoriented. Even if she could have opened her eyes, she didn't dare do so, worried about what would greet her. Darkness? Intense light? Nothing? She didn't want to speculate, because it would only add to her anxiety.

Emily felt cool water moisten her mouth and realized that the nurse had come back, pressed a cup into her hands, and led the straw to her lips. She couldn't remember accepting the water, nor could she feel how

Tiffany removed the cup from her hands, only that suddenly a different hand was touching hers lightly.

How much time had passed from the moment she'd taken a sip of water until a hand squeezed hers? She didn't know.

"It went well." The voice pulled her further out of her daze. It belonged to Dr. Milton Harland, the surgeon who'd performed the procedure. "Though it took longer than we anticipated."

Something about his statement sent unease through her body.

"What?" she managed to mumble.

Again, she felt a squeeze of her hand meant to reassure her. "Nothing to worry about. The stem cell patches have integrated well and appear to have repaired the optic nerve atrophy you were diagnosed with several years ago. We couldn't have done this even five years ago, but medicine has come a long way. As I told you in our pre-op discussion, this therapy is brand-new and still experimental, but I'm confident it's working. And with the donated corneas we implanted today, you'll eventually have 20/20 vision."

Emily picked up on the one word that belied the doctor's confident statement. She was good at that, at listening for words that didn't fit, because she'd had to rely on her sense of hearing more than ever after the accident. "Eventually?"

"Well, let's take a look, shall we?"

She felt the air between them move and realized that Dr. Harland was leaning in.

"Tiffany, dim the lights, please."

A warm hand touched her face, fingers brushed against her temple. Then the sound of an adhesive strip being pulled away from skin reached her ears, even though she didn't feel any discomfort. Until now, she hadn't even realized that her eyes were covered with something, a thin layer of gauze.

On her left side, Emily suddenly perceived a brightness she had almost forgotten existed. Her heart began to thunder in excitement while simultaneously the beeping coming from the heart monitor accelerated. Then an equal brightness appeared on the right.

"Now, slowly open your eyes," Dr. Harland instructed.

When she hesitated for several seconds, he added, "Don't be concerned. There are no harsh lights you have to be afraid of."

She couldn't delay any longer. It was time to face reality. For fifteen years, she'd lived in the dark. Today, she would find out if light would once again enter her life.

Emily released a shaky breath. "Okay then." Slowly, she lifted her heavy eyelids a tiny fraction of an inch. Something she hadn't seen in far too long streamed in as if the floodgates of a dam had been opened: light. With a gasp, for fear the light could burn her eyes, she squeezed them shut.

"Are you in pain?" Dr. Harland asked.

She shook her head. "It's so bright."

A soft chuckle rolled off the doctor's lips. "That's a good sign. We'll take it slow, alright?"

Slowly, she corrected him in her mind, her teacher side taking over for a brief moment. But then she immediately slipped back into her role as patient, a patient apprehensive about meeting disappointment. She'd been down this road once before. Back then, the operation had been a failure.

"Try it again," Dr. Harland encouraged her patiently.

This time, Emily forced herself to open her eyes wider, allowing more light to stream in. The brightness was overwhelming at first, but she called on all her courage not to give in to fear this time, and kept her eyes open.

"That's good." The doctor's voice was full of praise. Or maybe she was just projecting onto him what she was hoping for. "Just a little bit more."

Emily allowed her eyelids to swing open fully, braving the light as if she were a surfer taking a wave head-on. The reward followed only moments later. The light became more defined. Shapes formed, shadows appeared, and colors popped up from out of nowhere. The silhouette of a person separated from the bright background, still blurred, but becoming clearer with every second.

"Green," she murmured. "Your scrubs are green."

Somebody to the right of that shadow let out a relieved breath: the nurse, Tiffany. Emily turned her head slightly and focused on her. It took a few moments for the picture to sharpen sufficiently to recognize the shape of a petite woman dressed in pink. Emily swept her gaze upward and concentrated on the head and hair, but the area appeared as a dark black hole, a place devoid of light. Was there a problem with the corneas they'd implanted? Was there a tear, a blemish, an imperfection that suddenly caused the light to vanish?

"No," she muttered to herself, panic cutting off the air to breathe.

"What's wrong?" The doctor's voice made her snap her head back in his direction.

That's when she realized her mistake. There was no shadow on her corneas: Dr. Harland's silhouette appeared without shadows. To confirm her realization, she looked at Tiffany again. With every second, her eyes became more used to the light, and the shapes in front of her became more defined, revealing the nurse with more clarity, contrasting her dark skin from the pink scrubs she wore. Emily felt foolish not having realized that Tiffany was black. Instead, she'd falsely assumed the worst.

"Nothing... nothing is wrong." It was the truth. "I can see." She hesitated. She didn't want to complain or criticize, but her concern gained the upper hand. "Only..."

"You don't have a clear vision yet. It's still blurry," Dr. Harland guessed.

"How did you—"

"It's to be expected. If it had only been an issue about implanting new corneas, your sight would have been restored immediately. But with having to repair the optic nerve too, the process takes a little longer. Your brain has to form new synapses to process the signals the optic nerve is sending."

Relief washed over her. "How long?"

"It depends. In some patients, it takes a week, in others several. But in any case, your eyesight will improve with each day."

"Thank you." Emily turned her head toward Tiffany in order to include her. "I don't know how to thank you and your team." Tears suddenly welled up and clouded her blurry vision further. "And the donor's family too. I want to thank them."

"We're just glad we could take care of you," Dr. Harland said. "Right, Tiffany?"

"You've been a model patient, Miss Emily," Tiffany replied. "Now, let me call your ride to come so she can drive you home when you're ready."

"Thank you." But Tiffany was already turning and leaving her field of vision.

"And the donor's family?" Emily asked, looking back at the surgeon. She could now see that he had salt and pepper hair, but more details still escaped her. "I would like to call them."

Dr. Harland opened a folder, then sighed. "I'm sorry, Miss Warner, but the note from Transplant Administration says that the donor's family wants to remain anonymous."

"Oh..."

The news was disappointing, but in a way she understood. Perhaps they didn't want to be reminded of their recent loss. Emily knew what it meant. Unfortunately, she'd never had a choice whether to be reminded of it or not. Every single day of the past fifteen years she'd thought of what she'd lost: not only her vision, but also the person she loved most. She hadn't found it in her heart to show mercy to the person responsible. Instead, with all the anger of a fifteen-year-old girl, she'd made him pay.

5

"I CAN WALK," Emily said, but Tiffany forced her, gently but firmly, to sit in the wheelchair.

"Hospital policy," she insisted. "Now, I've already made your follow-up appointment with Dr. Harland. I noted the date and time on your discharge papers. Let me just get those for you."

Before Emily could ask more about the appointment, Tiffany pulled the wheelchair to the side and set the brakes, then walked behind the nurses' station and got busy looking for the folder.

"Damn it, Arleen, where did my patient's discharge folder go? I just put it down here a minute ago."

"Patient name?" one of the nurses, presumably Arleen, asked.

"Emily Warner."

"Don't have it here. Susan just grabbed a stack of files. Maybe she accidentally took it. She went into the back office."

With an annoyed huff, Tiffany marched off.

There was nothing else Emily could do, but sit there like a potted plant. As the chatter of the nurses died down, the sound of a TV mounted on the opposite wall drifted to her.

"... A memorial is being planned and will likely include foreign and domestic dignitaries and prominent members of the Washington D.C. society. The recent engagement announcement of incumbent Senator Puller's daughter to the son of his primary opponent Kurt Altman, has all of Washington's elite guessing whether the wedding can reunite these two bitter rivals. Stay tuned. And after the commercial break: Who was recently seen at the brand-new nightclub SWANK with his ex? You won't believe this."

"Here it is," Tiffany said from behind Emily.

Emily tore her attention from the TV and reached for the folder Tiffany pressed into her hand.

"So, the appointment is all set for late next week."

"What time of day? I teach until—"

"Don't worry, hon, I figured you'd say that. I arranged a late afternoon appointment for you."

"Thank you. Ordinarily I wouldn't mind... but I've already lost a few days this school year, and I don't want to short-change my students."

Tiffany clicked her tongue. "Nothing wrong with taking a few days off. An operation like this isn't to be taken lightly. You need plenty of rest."

"It's a long weekend for me. No classes on Monday. Dr. Harland said I can go back to work on Tuesday."

"Hon, Dr. Harland is a workaholic. Of course, he'll say you can go back to work after three days, because that's what he would do. I'm just saying if you feel you need more time to rest, take it. And don't forget to wear your sunglasses to give your eyes time to get used to bright lights. It can be jarring at first."

"I'll do that. I promise." Emily had no intention of jeopardizing her recovery. Besides, she felt comfortable behind dark glasses. For the better part of two decades, they'd been her defensive wall, a shield behind which to retreat when life became too overwhelming. And together with her cane and her seeing-eye dog, Coffee, they signaled to the world around her to get out of her way. Now, all that would change. And this change, though welcome beyond all imagination, was scary.

"Here we are," Tiffany suddenly said as she pushed the wheelchair out through the automatic doors of the hospital's main entrance. "Before I forget it: the pharmacy will deliver your meds to your home later today. Make sure you take them as prescribed. They'll make sure your body won't reject the corneas."

"I know. Dr. Harland explained before the operation." He'd warned her that her body might perceive the donor's tissue as a foreign entity and reject it, but that in the case of corneas such a rejection was extremely rare.

Emily let her gaze wander. Her vision was a little bit clearer now than right after she'd woken up from the procedure, but it still felt as if she were looking through a thick glass pane that distorted everything behind it.

"What does your friend look like?" Tiffany asked.

"She's Asian, dark hair, slim."

The only reason Emily knew this was because her neighbor Vicky Hong had described her appearance when Emily had moved into the quaint apartment building in the Columbia Heights neighborhood of Washington D.C. They'd literally bumped into each other when Vicky had rushed out of her apartment on the second floor while Emily had tried to unlock her apartment door—or what she thought was her apartment door. Unfortunately, she'd miscounted her steps and stopped in front of Vicky's apartment instead. For some reason or another, Vicky had befriended her immediately and taken her under her wing. Emily knew that at first Vicky's motives for helping her were steeped in pity and perhaps novelty of having a friend who was so very different from herself. But although they were as different as night and day—or maybe because of it—the quirky computer geek had become her BFF.

A dog barked, pulling Emily's attention into his direction. "Coffee!" She felt a smile curve her lips upward. Vicky had brought Emily's guide dog. "Come, boy!"

A big chocolate-brown lug of Labrador ran toward her. Emily reached for Coffee's head but fell short. Clearly, her depth perception wasn't up to snuff yet. But a second later, Coffee's wet nose nuzzled against her palm, and a tongue licked her skin, before he nestled his head in her lap.

"My good boy," she cooed, petting his head, rubbing behind his ears, while she looked into his eyes. He looked every bit as handsome as she'd always imagined.

When a shadow blocked out the light in front of her, she looked up. "Hey, Vicky." Her friend was dressed in a multitude of bright colors. It appeared that Vicky hadn't joked when she'd said that she liked to dress to be noticed.

"Hey, girl." A smile colored Vicky's words. "Ready for your new life to begin?"

Emily rested her gaze on Vicky's face and matched her smile. "I hope you didn't have to wait too long."

Vicky made a dismissive hand movement. "I used the time to catch up with old colleagues on the third floor."

"You worked here?" Tiffany said from behind the wheelchair.

"Yep, for about seven years. Admin and stuff. I'm working freelance now, medical transcriptions and computer work," Vicky answered. What Vicky dismissively called computer work was actually writing sophisticated computer programs for apps and websites. Vicky pointed toward Emily's lap. "Is that your discharge folder? I'll take that. My car is parked right there in the red zone." She looked over her shoulder, then grunted in displeasure.

"Oh come on, buddy!" she called out in the direction of her parked car.

Emily focused her eyes on the spot and saw a uniformed man standing next to the beat-up old Volkswagen Rabbit.

"It's Ambulance Parking only," the officer said in a rather stern and loud voice.

"I'm picking up a patient, for Christ's sake! Have a little compassion here. You can't just discriminate against a disabled American. There are laws." She motioned toward Emily. "Can't you see the girl is blind?"

Emily suppressed a chuckle. She'd been witness to Vicky's previous attempts at getting out of a ticket. Not all attempts had succeeded. In fact, only a few had. "I'm not blind anymore," Emily whispered.

Vicky turned halfway and whispered back, "Yeah, but *he* doesn't know that. You're wearing dark glasses and you have a guide dog with a vest saying so, so just play along. Maybe do a little Stevie Wonder, you know, the way he moves his head from side to side."

Emily had a hard time not breaking out in laughter, and even Tiffany let out a small chuckle.

"Some friend you've got," Tiffany said under her breath.

"Yeah, guess I was blind when I picked her."

"Very funny. Okay, let's move it," Vicky said and walked toward the car. "We're coming already."

"Coffee," Emily ordered her dog. "Forward." The dog turned and marched alongside the wheelchair while Tiffany pushed her in the direction of Vicky's car.

"I have to apologize for my friend, Officer," Emily said as they reached the car, where the policeman was still hovering. She reached out her hand, moving it from left to right, pretending not to be aware of the policeman's exact position. "Please give me the ticket. I'll pay it. She's only here to pick me up. It's all my fault."

The policeman shook his head. "It's alright, ma'am. I'm not gonna issue a ticket this time. Just make sure your friend doesn't do it again. Her car is no ambulance." He tossed a look at Vicky.

"Thank you, Officer, that's too kind," Emily said.

With a nod, he turned away.

The instant he was out of earshot, Vicky chuckled. "You've still got it."

Moments later, Emily was sitting in the passenger seat, Coffee was spread out on the back bench while Vicky switched on the engine and let it rev. Across the street, the police officer whirled around.

Emily put her hand on Vicky's arm. "Don't piss him off now."

Vicky stuck her head out the window. "Sorry, Officer, old car. I'm happy it still works." Before he could answer, she pulled out of the illegal parking spot and merged onto the street.

"One of these days," Emily started, but her friend interrupted.

"I know, I know, but when I see somebody with a stick up his butt, I just can't help myself. Good thing I have a get-out-of-jail-free card."

"Which is?"

For a second, Vicky took her eyes off the traffic. "A blind friend to evoke sympathy. Works like a charm every time."

"Yeah, about that." Emily pointed to her face. "Not blind anymore."

A genuine smile lit up Vicky's face. "I know. I'm so happy for you." Then she looked in the rearview mirror and pointed over her shoulder. "You gonna tell Coffee that you don't need him anymore?"

Emily shook her head. "I still need him. My sight isn't one-hundred percent yet. Besides, he's been with me for six years. I could never give him away. Guess he'll just have to spend his retirement with me."

"Seeing-eye dogs retire?"

"Sure they do. And Coffee deserves it."

She looked over her shoulder and gazed at her dog. He'd afforded her a certain independence, which a cane alone could never have provided. He was her second guide dog. Her first had given his life for her, saving her from being run over by a car. The teachers at the School for the Blind in Baltimore, where she'd spent several years, had warned the students regularly: It's not *whether* you're gonna get hit by a car, bus, or bike, but *when*. They couldn't have been more on the money.

"You okay?" Vicky asked.

Emily nodded automatically. "It's just a lot to take in. And I still feel a little woozy from the sedatives."

"It's okay if you want to close your eyes and nap a little." Seemingly without effort, Vicky navigated the car through busy traffic.

"I don't want to close my eyes. There's so much to see." She motioned to the buildings that seemed to whizz past the car, the people on the sidewalks, the cars coming toward them. "I thought Washington was a big city." Yet there were few tall buildings. It looked so quaint and had a small-town feel to it.

"It is, but every little neighborhood is like a village in itself. You'll see. You'll like it. We'll go exploring when you feel up to it."

"You're doing so much for me."

"Ah, it's nothing, it gets me out of the house. Besides, driving through D.C. traffic on a Friday is like contact sports for me. I love the challenge."

Emily had to chuckle. "You're strange."

"Strange good or strange bad?"

"No comment," Emily said.

She looked out of the passenger side window, but the speed with which the images moved past her made her dizzy, so she turned her head back to gaze through the windshield instead. Better, she thought and focused on buildings farther ahead, took in their shapes and their colors. A massive white building with a rotunda rose in the distance. She remembered it from pictures from before she'd become blind.

Emily pointed to it. "Is that the Capitol?"

"Yep."

"It's bigger than I imagined." Suddenly, something flashed in front of her eyes, blinding her for a short instant. She whirled her head in Vicky's direction. Her heart suddenly raced. "What was that?"

"What was what?"

She pointed straight ahead. "The flash."

"There was no flash," Vicky said slowly and with a good deal of concern in her voice. "Do you want me to take you back to the hospital?"

"No, no, don't. I… ahm, I'm fine, really. Maybe I just caught the sun reflecting in something shiny," she lied to Vicky, not wanting her to get worried and drive her back to the clinic.

Yet, she was certain that she hadn't seen light reflect on a shiny surface. She'd clearly seen the flash of a camera go off. Around the flash it had been dark, when right now it was daytime. What she'd seen was physically impossible. But what had flashed in front of her eyes had felt as real as watching the traffic around her.

Something was wrong, and that thought made her shiver despite the warm weather. An uncomfortable feeling akin to nausea settled in her stomach, which she couldn't ascribe to the medications she'd received today. No, this wasn't nausea, this was something else. Trepidation was rearing its ugly head.

6

After Vicky brought Emily back to her apartment and left after getting her settled, Emily walked into her bathroom. Sufficient light streamed through the small window, so she didn't need to switch on the overhead light. With hesitant steps she walked to the sink. This was the only place in her apartment that had a mirror. The small medicine cabinet that hung over the sink had already been there when she'd moved in. While she stashed the usual over-the-counter medications like aspirin, allergy pills, and salves for various cuts and burns there, she'd never used the mirror on its front. It had never been of any use to her. Until now.

Slowly, Emily took off her dark glasses and placed them on the counter next to the sink, where her personal beauty and hygiene products were displayed in an orderly fashion. She hadn't been a neat person as a teenager, but after losing her eyesight, she'd had to learn order. After reaching for anti-itch cream instead of toothpaste to brush her teeth, she'd learned her lesson quickly. Everything had its place now.

Emily put her hands on the edge of the sink, bracing herself for the truth. She knew she had scars from the accident. She could feel them with the pads of her fingers, could feel the tiny ridges, the bumps where once there had been smooth skin. In the months after the accident, she'd asked her doctors and nurses how terrible she looked. They hadn't been honest with her, claiming that the scars were barely visible. So she'd stopped asking. But she'd never stopped wondering.

It was time to see for herself. To face her fear that she was ugly. She knew it was shallow to worry about physical beauty, but it didn't stop her from feeling anxious. It was one thing to be overlooked by men because she was blind, and a whole other thing to be rejected because she was ugly.

"Time to face the music," she murmured to herself.

In one drawn-out movement, she lifted her head and looked straight into the mirror. It took a second or two for the reflection to come into focus. She stared into it, taking in what she could. There were no visible scars, none she could see anyway. Only when she leaned in closer, she noticed a few spots where her skin was darker, but a casual observer might think they were freckles. The skin around her eyes, while puffy and red from the operation, was otherwise unmarred. Her long dark-brown hair was straight and framed her face like a silk curtain.

Emily smiled at her reflection, relieved. She wasn't ugly. She stepped back a little for a different perspective. She remembered what she'd looked like as a young teenager. She'd held onto that image through regular visualization exercises they'd taught her in Baltimore. Just like she'd held onto other images, but over the years, the images had faded somewhat. And as she looked into the mirror now, she wasn't looking at the girl she'd once been. There were hints of her still left, but so much had changed. She'd matured.

Her long hair still had the same chestnut color as during her childhood, though now the color seemed even richer. Her irises were still brown, still unassuming, but different at the same time, more inquisitive, more thoughtful. *She* had changed. She had grown up, become a woman.

The reflection she gazed into now wasn't that of a stranger. It was a woman she knew and loved. She'd had no idea how much she now looked like her own mother at that age.

"Mom," she whispered and reached for the mirror as if to touch her.

The image blurred in front of her eyes, and she realized that tears were streaming down her face. "I miss you so much."

7

Adam Yang walked into the precinct's break room. Apart from Cindy, a rookie policewoman, it was empty. He wasn't surprised. Many staff members liked leaving early on Friday afternoons if their caseload allowed it. With a quick greeting, he acknowledged Cindy's presence and headed for the coffee machine. He poured himself a cup. Lately, afternoons spent doing paperwork had required more than just one dose of caffeine to keep him awake. He wasn't sleeping well. It was no wonder. His six-year marriage was over. Yet, the divorce was dragging on longer than his wallet could sustain.

Yang poured cream into his coffee and stirred it when he saw Simon Jefferson enter.

"Hey, there you are," Jefferson said and marched to the counter. "Oh, donuts." He snatched one and took a big bite, chewing. "You should try one. Arnold bought them."

Yang glanced at the donuts. "Fried sugar? You know that's pure poison, right?"

Jefferson shrugged. "Tastes good."

"No, thanks. What's the occasion anyway? It's not her birthday." It was tradition that police officers bought pastries or other sweets on their birthday.

"Don't know, don't care," Jefferson said between bites.

"Anyway, were you looking for me?"

"Yeah, my source told me that there are a few embassy gigs coming up where they need extra security. Are you still interested?"

Yang sat down his mug. This was excellent news. With dozens of large embassies in Washington D.C., there were lots of private security jobs available. However, only those who had connections got a shot at these lucrative deals. And Jefferson had connections in the right places.

"Hell, yeah!" Yang said before Jefferson could offer the jobs to somebody else. "I can do with the extra money. The lawyers are bleeding me dry."

"I thought you'd be done with them by now. I mean, you guys have no kids, nothing to fight over."

"Nothing to fight over? Tell that to Barb. Right now she's fighting me over my retirement. Can you believe that? I've got at least another twenty years before I can even think of retiring, and already she's got her hand out."

"She'll never win. You weren't married for that long. Come on, don't stress out over it."

Yang sighed. "It just gets to me sometimes. You think you know a person, and then they show you who they really are."

"Story of my life. It's easier being single." Jefferson took a second donut and bit into it. Then he glanced at the young policewoman who got up from her chair and headed for the door. "Hey Cindy, how you doin'?"

Cindy mumbled something unintelligible, her cheeks suddenly reddening, before she fled the room. Jefferson followed her with his eyes. Then he turned back to Yang, a grin on his face.

Yang shook his head. "Please! She's way too young for you."

"Come on, I'm just joking."

"I sure hope so."

Jefferson turned toward the door, when he almost collided with Lieutenant Latochia Arnold. By all accounts, she was a very attractive black woman with a curvy figure and a raucous laugh when she was off-duty. A single mother of two sons, both now in their early twenties, she'd risen in the ranks of the Washington Metropolitan Police Department through perseverance and hard work. However, rumors persisted that she'd benefitted from a connection in the mayor's office. It didn't matter to Yang how she'd gotten there. What mattered was that she was an effective leader.

"Lieutenant," Jefferson said and left the break room.

"Jefferson." She nodded and walked to the coffee machine. "Yang."

"Ma'am," Yang said.

She motioned to his coffee mug. "How about a donut with that?"

"You know me, I don't have much of a sweet tooth." Which couldn't be said for half the homicide branch.

"Good for you." She poured herself a cup then turned to the box of donuts. "Wish I could say the same."

There was no right answer to that statement. Yang was smart enough not to reply. Lieutenant Arnold was constantly fighting with her weight even though she didn't look overweight.

"Any news about the Bolton case that the Secret Service snatched from under my nose?" Yang asked instead.

She cast him a sideways glance, then looked at the donuts. After a couple of seconds, she sighed, and turned to him without taking a donut. "Why are you interested in it?"

Yang found the question peculiar. "Why wouldn't I be? It was within our jurisdiction, and if there was foul play involved, I would think our branch would be all over it."

"But we're not."

He couldn't let it go. "Because?"

"Like I said three days ago, it was the decision of the Chief of Police." Arnold took a sip from her coffee. "The Secret Service is perfectly capable of investigating Ms. Bolton's death. And there's no reason to assume that there was foul play."

"A thirty-two-year-old healthy woman dies alone in her home, and that doesn't look suspicious to you?"

Arnold's eyebrows lifted. "You looked into her?"

"On my own time, yes," Yang said quickly before she could accuse him of wasting police time. "There's plenty of information on her in the public domain."

"Well, then you probably also found out about Ms. Bolton's past."

He nodded. "Experimenting with drugs in her early twenties doesn't exactly make her a junkie. She got over that phase."

"Did she?" Arnold shook her head. "You can't know that."

"And you can't know that she didn't."

When she pressed her lips together tightly, then let out a slow breath, Yang saw something in her eyes.

"You do know, don't you?"

"This conversation is over," Arnold said. "If you think your caseload isn't sufficient, by all means, let me assign you more cases."

Arnold's stern look told him that he'd pushed his luck far enough.

"That won't be necessary."

"Very well, then," she said and left, snatching a donut on her way out.

Yang saw the fact that she hadn't resisted the sugary donuts as a sign that she too was frustrated by the situation.

Did he buy Arnold's explanation?

He shook his head. He'd never been one to take information at face value without doing a fact-check. And he knew exactly where to start.

Back in his cubicle, Yang looked around. Only half the officers in the homicide branch were in their respective cubicles. The others were out in the field. He couldn't see Jefferson anywhere. His cubicle next to Yang's was empty.

Yang picked up the phone and dialed the number for dispatch. Moments later, a bright young female voice answered.

"Is this Sophie? This is Detective Yang," he said cheerfully.

"Oh, hi, Detective. Yes, it's Sophie. What can I do for you?"

"I just wanted to get in touch with the officer who was first at the scene of the death in Georgetown on the 23rd, Madeline Bolton. Could you look that up for me please?"

"Sure thing, Detective."

He heard Sophie tapping on the keyboard.

"Here it is. Officer Cabbot. She was the first at the scene."

"Great, I'll talk to her. Thanks, Sophie."

"No problem. But you won't have any luck talking to Officer Cabbot."

"Why not?" Had the Secret Service barred her from releasing any information about the scene she'd been called to?

"She's on her honeymoon. Left yesterday. Tahiti, can you believe it?"

Yang forced a cheerful exclamation. "Wow, good for her. No worries, it can wait. Thanks again, Sophie."

He put down the receiver.

"What are you doing?" Jefferson suddenly popped his head around the partition between their two cubicles. Yang hadn't heard him come back.

"What do you mean?"

In a whisper, Jefferson said, "Don't play dumb with me, Adam. I heard you. Stop digging. It's not our case."

"Yeah, because the Secret Service took it from us."

"I'm sure they had their reasons."

"Aren't you the least bit curious why?"

Jefferson shook his head. "No. And you know why?"

"Why?"

"Because I want to get ahead in this job. And you don't advance if you start pissing off people in power. Easy as that."

"Well, in that case, I'll remain a detective forever, while you will one day become my superior."

"You're a hopeless case, you know that, don't you?"

Yang let out a mirthless laugh. "Nothing wrong with seeking the truth."

No matter what the truth might reveal.

8

THE SOUND BECAME LOUDER, more insistent. Emily's head was already hurting, and the aspirin she'd taken seemed to do nothing to dispel the dull ache. Dr. Harland had mentioned that a slight headache wasn't uncommon in the first few days after the surgery. After all, her brain had lots to process and was working overtime.

A knock, much closer this time, made her shoot up straight. She tried to find her bearings and realized that she'd been lying on the sofa. How long had she actually napped? Her gaze drifted to the windows, but the little light coming from there didn't tell her much about the time of day—the blinds were drawn, and she remembered now that Vicky had done this to help her rest. Besides, even if the blinds hadn't been drawn, she had no recent experience to distinguish midday sun from afternoon or evening sun.

Coffee sat up on his dog bed, suddenly alert.

Emily reached to the side table next to the sofa where a clock stood next to a burned-out lamp she'd inherited from the previous tenant. Her fingers found the correct button immediately.

"Four thirty-seven p.m.," a mechanical voice announced.

"Hello?"

Coffee jumped up.

Emily whipped her head in the direction of the male voice. A large dark shadow made her jerk back and, with the back of her knees, she knocked against the edge of the coffee table.

"Ouch!"

But the momentary pain wasn't her real concern. There was an intruder in her apartment. A burglar in broad daylight? Her heart pounded against her ribcage at a speed that mirrored her panic. How would she defend herself? Her path to the kitchen was cut off by the intruder. She couldn't make it to her knife drawer. She didn't own a gun, not even a baseball bat with which to fend off a burglar.

"What do you want?" she asked, her voice breaking, her knees shaking, ready to cave in. "Who are you?"

She focused on the shadow, sucked in a quick breath, prepared to defend herself with her bare fists, but the shadow was suddenly gone. Vanished into thin air. She took a breath, then another one.

"Miss Warner? Delivery," the same male voice called out.

Coffee barked and walked toward her. Finally, Emily realized where the voice was coming from: from outside her apartment.

She made a few steps toward the door and opened it. Outside in the hallway, a lanky teenager with a baseball cap stood waiting.

"You've gotta sign for it," he said, pointing to a spot on his clipboard.

"What is it?"

"Delivery from the pharmacy. They won't let me leave medication without a signature."

Only now, Emily saw the paper bag in his other hand.

She'd totally forgotten about the medication Dr. Harland had ordered for her. "Oh, sorry. I hope I didn't make you wait too long."

He handed her a pen, and she did her best to sign where he indicated. She had to close her eyes, which helped her recall how she'd learned to sign her name without looking, because watching the ink form words while she made loops and strokes only confused her and made her lose her place.

"Thank you," she said when she was done.

The young man handed her the paper bag with her medication. "Sure thing."

He sauntered down the hallway. For a moment, Emily just stood there, following him with her eyes until he disappeared around a corner. With a sigh, she pivoted—and froze instantly.

At the opposite end of the hallway, only a few steps away from her, the silhouette of a large man contrasted against the light coming from the window behind him.

Her heart stopped. Her nerves were frayed.

No, please, no. Don't let it happen again. Please, this time, don't let it end like this.

"Miss Warner, you okay? Didn't mean to startle you."

Relief at recognizing the super's voice washed over her. "Mr. Oberman?"

"Yes, sorry, I was just finishing the repairs in the apartment next to yours when I heard something."

"Just a delivery," she said, while he approached. And though she was trying to sound calm, in her own ears she sounded tense. The shadow earlier, and the flash on the drive home, had made her jumpy.

"Miss Hong told me she picked you up from the hospital today." Oberman pointed to her face. "It's gone well, I guess. You're looking straight at me. I believe that's the first time I've seen you without your sunglasses." He cleared his throat. "Sorry, I didn't mean to make you feel uncomfortable."

"You're not," she hastened to say. "It's just all so new."

He gave her a smile. "Well, you'll let me know if there's anything I can do for you."

"Thank you, Mr. Oberman. You're too kind."

But as much as Emily appreciated his well-meant offer, she was determined not to rely on the kindness of strangers anymore. From now on, she would strive to become truly independent. And no amount of unexplained shadows in her vision would stop her. Not this time.

9

IT HAD BEEN A STRESSFUL WEEK. In fact he'd never had a worse week in his life.

The killer sipped on the drink before him and leaned back in the armchair, while he stared out over the city lights. He preferred Washington D.C. by night rather than during the daytime. At night, everything seemed more beautiful and clean, less hectic. And darker. That's what he loved most about it.

He could slip through the night without being seen, without being recognized. And what he did was so much more enjoyable at night. His senses were heightened, his arousal at its peak, his needs at a point where he could barely wait for them to be satisfied. He enjoyed testing how long he could deny himself what he craved, because he knew that when he finally gave in to his desires, the fulfillment would be even sweeter. It always was.

Unfortunately, he'd overdone it a week earlier. He'd let himself get so crazed that he'd thrown all caution to the wind, and neglected to check that every door was locked before he indulged in his favorite game. He'd paid for it dearly.

Now, somewhere in Washington D.C. somebody knew his secret and could bring him down. The first days after the incident, he'd waited for the police to come knocking on his door to take him into custody, but nothing had happened.

His secret was still safe. But for how long? Would the person who was aware of his proclivities eventually find the courage to go to the police? Or would luck once again be on his side like it had so many times over the last years? The more time passed, the more he realized that he would be spared. After all, he'd cleaned up after himself. The one person who'd been close to exposing him, was dead, and while the other was still missing, he knew that person was too scared to take him on. He'd made sure of that. It was part of his game. He was clever that way, superior to everyone. He enjoyed the feeling of knowing that he was outsmarting everybody.

He emptied the glass and put it down, then took his car keys and left the building. It was time to take care of his needs, before the craving became too strong to control it. He couldn't afford another mistake.

10

THERE WAS REALLY NO EASY WAY to get from her apartment in Columbia Heights to the international school in Georgetown where Emily taught music. She had to take the metro to Shaw-Howard U, then switch to a bus to the quaint village-like neighborhood she only knew by its sounds and smells. A short, two-block walk brought her to the gates of the exclusive private school where daughters and sons of ambassadors rubbed shoulders with kids of rich lobbyists and politicians.

At first, Emily had been reluctant to apply for the position, thinking she wouldn't fit in, but when her career counselor had told her that the school had several blind students who would benefit from the guidance of a blind teacher, she'd sent off the application. She'd thought that all blind kids went to a School for the Blind, like she had in Baltimore, but it turned out that the District of Columbia had no School for the Blind and therefore integrated blind students into their regular classrooms. There was something to be said for this approach. After all, the children lived in a world of the sighted, so why not prepare them in the classrooms of the sighted?

Over the long weekend, Emily had stuck to her physician's advice and worn her dark glasses to protect her eyes from too much light, and had only ventured out with Coffee by her side, her collapsible cane in her handbag. She hadn't needed it. Her vision had become clearer with each day, but from time to time, shadows had appeared. Emily attributed them to exhaustion and had pushed them out of her mind.

Today, she felt rested and excited. For the first time, she would see her colleagues and her students, and wouldn't have to rely on only her auditory sense to recognize them. It felt like the first day of school all over again. However, knowing that the day was long, and tiredness would eventually creep in, she'd brought Coffee with her like she'd done every day since she'd started teaching. The kids seemed to like having the dog lie calmly next to her desk and observe the lessons, even though they weren't allowed to pet him. After all, Coffee was a service dog, not a pet.

At the gate to the school, Emily stopped. She moved her gaze to the fenced yard on one side of the elementary school, where kids from the ages of six to twelve were greeting their schoolmates, and exchanging news from their adventures during the long weekend. A few foreign languages drifted to her, and she recognized several of her students' voices. Finally, she would be able to connect faces to voices.

"Morning, Emily." The voice belonged to John Gonzalez.

She pivoted to watch him descend from his bicycle and lock it to the school's bicycle rack.

"Morning, John." Behind her dark glasses, she focused on him. His dark hair was short, his body stocky and muscular, his clothing casual. As a physical education teacher, his style fit. And considering that he also taught biology where he often got his hands dirty, the casual clothes made sense.

"You're early. I thought Tuesdays you don't have first period." Gonzalez unhooked his satchel from the bicycle's luggage rack and motioned toward her. "In fact, I thought you were off all week, after your... you know." He motioned to her eyes, then added, "It didn't get cancelled, did it?"

"No, no. It's all good." She walked straight toward him. "It worked. I can see. But I need to take it easy." She pointed skyward. "No bright lights for a few days."

He smiled. "Well, that's great." He opened the double doors and held them open for her.

She accepted the gesture and walked inside, Coffee marched slightly ahead of her, her hand on the handle connected to his harness.

"Morning, Miss Warner," the security guard who stood inside the foyer said with a nod.

"Morning, Todd," she replied to the hulk of a man and looked straight at him. He wore a blue uniform that identified him as security, though he wasn't wearing a jacket. His shirt was short-sleeved and exposed his impressive biceps and his dark-brown skin.

"Morning, Mr. Gonzalez," Todd greeted Gonzalez, who'd entered behind her.

Emily was already walking toward the teacher's lounge, Coffee guiding her automatically, allowing her to let her eyes roam and get to know the corridor she'd walked down for almost three years.

Emily opened the door to the teacher's lounge and entered the large, airy room where teachers escaped to in between classes or during their free periods to drink a cup of coffee, grade papers or prepare for their next class, and catch up on the news streaming from the old TV in the corner. It was also a great place to fill each other in on gossip concerning students, their parents, or other teachers. And considering the prominence of some of the parents, there was always gossip to be exchanged.

Several teachers were milling about the room. Some looked up when she entered, others continued with what they were doing without acknowledging her arrival.

"Morning, Emily." A beautiful redhead walked toward her, her voice identifying her as Isabelle Treadway. She would be an easy face to memorize. Her long red mane had a magnificent glow to it, and her face was pale like porcelain.

"Morning, Isabelle."

When Isabelle noticed Coffee, she said, "Oh dear, it didn't go well?" She quickly bridged the distance between them and put a hand on Emily's arm. "I'm so sorry."

Emily shook her head. "Don't be. It all went well." She pointed to her sunglasses, then to Coffee. "But I'm still healing, and until my vision is perfect, the doc said to wear my sunglasses and have Coffee by my side."

Isabelle let out a sigh of relief. "Phew! You scared me there for a moment."

A bell rang once. Five minutes until the start of first period.

Several of the teachers got up from their seats and packed up their belongings.

"Gotta go. Let's talk over lunch, okay?" Isabelle said and snatched her briefcase from a nearby table. Without waiting for Emily's response, she was already heading for the door.

Emily pivoted to head for her favorite spot, the sofa, when she caught a man staring at her. He sat at a table close enough to have overheard her conversation with Isabelle. Her vision was good enough to recognize the sneer on his face, but she had no idea who he was. He rose and grabbed his papers.

"Not disabled anymore, huh?" he said with a glance at her dog, already walking past her toward the door. The voice belonged to Carl Littleton, the English teacher. "Well, congratulations."

She knew he didn't mean it. Littleton had never liked her, never welcomed her. She'd found out why a few months after she'd started at the school. Isabelle had let her in on the big secret: Littleton's wife had also applied for the position as music teacher, but lost out to Emily. Littleton had claimed that the only reason Emily had been picked over his wife, was the fact that Emily was blind. Disabled. Littleton had claimed that because of affirmative action Emily had been chosen over his wife who now had to commute to a school in a rough neighborhood. And boy, had he let her feel that anger every single day.

At one point, Emily had spoken to the principal, Olivia Remmington, not to complain about him, but simply to ask why she'd gotten the position and not Littleton's wife.

. Principal Remmington, a woman in her early sixties, had smiled. "Emily, we weren't trying to fill a quota if that's what you're worried about. The Americans with Disabilities Act had nothing to do with us hiring you. But we have five blind students, and they have difficulty integrating. We figured if we brought in a blind teacher, they'll finally have somebody who understands them. And from what I can tell, the kids are doing better because of you. Because you listen to them. You're the better teacher for these children. So don't let anybody tell you that you don't deserve to be here."

A second bell interrupted Emily's memories.

She sighed and realized that the teacher's lounge had emptied out. She headed for the sofa, dropped her bag on it and took a seat. Coffee lay down at her feet. From her place in the corner, she could see the entire room. She familiarized herself with it visually. As teacher's lounges went, there was a certain chaos to it, and nothing seemed constant. She remembered the many bruises she'd gotten in this room, since somebody was constantly moving tables and chairs to accommodate whatever meeting was taking place at the time. It had taken months for her colleagues to realize that moving the furniture around willy-nilly was hazardous to their blind colleague.

Emily settled into the sofa cushions and pulled her cell phone from her bag. She pressed a button and said, "Play 'The Girl from Ipanema'."

Moments later, the hauntingly beautiful music performed by Stan Getz and Astrud and João Gilberto began playing quietly. She closed her eyes and took off her glasses, placing them beside her on the sofa. She rubbed the bridge of her nose and allowed the music to flood her senses. Music had been her escape for half her life and become as important to her as breathing. Bringing its beauty to young, impressionable minds was giving her a purpose, a purpose that had saved her from descending further into the dark hole that she'd retreated to after losing her sight. Music had lifted her up, given her hope, and sustained her. It had let her see beauty with her ears rather than her eyes. It had been a lifeline.

The loud slamming of a door startled her more than it should, and she whipped her head in the direction of the sound. Ever since the procedure to restore her eyesight, something felt off. She wasn't herself. She wasn't the composed, rational person anymore that she'd worked so hard to become over the last decade. Every little sound put her on edge, and every new sight scared her.

A janitor with a ladder trudged into the room. The ladder hit a chair and turned it over. He cursed. Then the janitor's eyes landed on Emily.

"Sorry, didn't know anybody was in here." He pointed to the ceiling. "Just gotta change out that fluorescent light. You don't mind, do you?"

"No, no, go ahead," Emily said and switched off the music.

"Don't let me stop you from what you're doing. I'll be out of your hair in no time."

He didn't waste time, positioned the ladder beneath one of the overhead lights and stepped onto the first rung. Then he seemed to have remembered something, because he stepped off again, walked to the door and flipped the light switch to turn all lights in the room off. There was still sufficient light streaming in from the windows.

"Don't wanna get electrocuted," he said with a look in Emily's direction, before proceeding with his work.

Emily continued watching him as he stood on the top step and reached his arms over his head to unhook the casing from the overhead lights. He pulled the burnt-out fluorescent light out and with one hand holding onto the ladder, the other gripping the fluorescent light, he slowly walked back down. All of a sudden, his foot jerked back as if a cramp was rendering his muscles useless.

Cold fear gripped her, and her eyes shot to the spot where he would fall. Instead of the wooden table that had stood at that place only a moment earlier, a lower table made of heavy glass with razor-sharp edges stood in its place. Terror made the blood freeze in her veins. The janitor would break his neck.

"Watch out!" Emily yelled at the same time as she jumped up from the sofa and charged toward the ladder. She didn't reach it in time. The glass shattered, the loud sound nearly piercing her eardrums. She squeezed her eyes shut, not wanting to see the tragedy, the blood.

"Miss? Miss?" Somebody was gripping her biceps and shaking her. "Is everything alright?"

Emily forced her eyes open and stared into the face of the janitor. In disbelief, she swept her gaze over his body looking for injuries. She found none.

"I'm okay. But the ladder..." She pointed to the object in question. "You fell."

He gave her a strange look, shaking his head. "I didn't fall." He released her from his hold. "Are you sure you're okay, Miss?"

Her eyes darted to the spot where the glass table had shattered. There was no glass. No shattered table, no sign of an accident, just a wooden table with several chairs.

And even while she said, "I'm fine," she knew she wasn't. Because she'd clearly seen the glass shatter from the impact of a person falling off the ladder. She feared what this meant. She was seeing things again. Things that weren't there.

She wanted to crawl into her closet, her chosen hiding space when things had started to fall apart after her accident fifteen years earlier. Just like then, she wanted to shut out the world around her, neither willing nor ready to face her fears. Only this time, it was worse. Back then, she hadn't known what was awaiting her. But this time, she knew what was in store for her.

11

"Here, this should help." Vicky handed her a glass of red wine.

"I don't really drink," Emily protested.

"Then it'll help even more. And you won't need as much. Trust me." She pressed the glass into Emily's hand, then reached for her own and took a seat next to Emily on the couch.

The moment Emily had returned from school, she'd knocked on Vicky's door, still shaken from the incident in the teacher's lounge, and told her about it. How she'd made it through five periods of teaching, she wasn't sure.

"Maybe you nodded off and dreamed it," Vicky said now, her voice more hopeful than convinced. "That's probably all it was. Believe me, I've had the craziest dreams, and sometimes they are so real that I could swear it wasn't just my imagination."

Emily took a reluctant sip from her glass of wine. "But I know it wasn't a dream. I saw what I saw. Somebody crashed onto the glass table and shattered it."

"The glass table that wasn't there?" Vicky sighed. "Emily, the last few days have been a huge change for you. What you're going through is stressful, even if it's the good kind of stress. Why don't you take an extra few days off? I'm sure Principal Remmington will understand."

"But it's not stress. I know it. I'm having hallucinations again." And that scared her, because she remembered all too well how it had ended the last time. She couldn't go through this a second time.

"Hallucinations? You're being a little harsh on yourself."

"But it's true." She looked directly into Vicky's eyes. "It's happened before."

"What? Like when?"

"The first time I had a cornea transplant, fifteen years ago."

Vicky's mouth dropped open. "You never told me you had a transplant before."

Emily sank deeper into the sofa cushions, leading the glass to her lips for a second time. This time, she took a longer sip. Actually, more of a gulp. In the silence that stretched between them, the memories of what had happened when she'd been just a little over fifteen years old, came rushing back like a tidal wave threatening to drown her. But she couldn't allow it. She had to deal with it, no matter how much it scared her.

"Shortly after the accident in which I lost my eyesight…"

"The accident that killed your parents?" Vicky asked. Emily had mentioned it early on when the question of family had come up.

She nodded. "Yes. When I was still in rehab for my other injuries, my arm and my leg, I was told that they could restore my eyesight. The transplant was scheduled, and all went well. Or so they thought." She blinked.

Vicky put her hand on Emily's forearm. "What happened?"

"I started hallucinating, you know, seeing shadows, seeing things that weren't there. I thought I was going crazy. The doctors believed that it was a side effect of the drugs they'd given me so I wouldn't reject the corneas. Or maybe that it was the trauma I'd suffered from the accident." Emily shook her head. "It was neither."

"Then what was it?"

Emily met her friend's concerned gaze. This wasn't easy to talk about, but she needed to get it off her chest. "I was going crazy. I couldn't distinguish between reality and fantasy anymore. It got so bad that they had to admit me…" She hesitated because the words she had to say carried a stigma. One she couldn't shake. Not even after fifteen years.

"Admit you? Where?"

When Emily remained silent, Vicky seemed to suddenly understand. "A psych ward? They put you in a nuthouse?"

Emily cringed. She regretted immediately having told Vicky about her brush with mental illness. But had it really been just a brush? Could mental illness really go away after a few years, or was this the sign that she hadn't overcome it?

"Calling it a nuthouse doesn't make it any less traumatizing, just so you know."

"Sorry, didn't mean it that way. But trust me, you don't belong in a… psychiatric hospital. You're as normal as I am."

"I didn't feel normal. And it didn't get better until…" She let out a long breath, not sure how to continue. It was true. She'd never felt truly normal. She'd covered it up by putting on a brave face, by trying to stay busy, by finding a purpose as a blind teacher. But had she only been masking the issue, hiding it under the veneer of a well-adjusted woman? "I've never talked about it."

"You can tell me. BFFs, right?"

Slowly, Emily reached for the memory she kept locked away together with other parts of her past. "One night, I couldn't take it anymore. The things I saw were too horrifying. I left my room, and in the corridor I saw somebody. I ran, and somebody chased me. I got to the staircase, to escape, you know…"

Even now, retelling what had happened was difficult, even though she left out the gory details, unable to put them into words. But she remembered everything as if it had happened only a moment ago. She'd seen a dark man chasing her down a hallway. She'd looked over her shoulder, trying to outrun him, but he was faster. And he was armed. The knife in his hand gleamed in the light of the dimly lit corridor, and the man's facial expression told her that he would use it on her, and he would enjoy hurting her.

"They found me at the bottom of the stairs a few hours later."

"Did you try to… I mean…"

She knew what Vicky was trying to ask. She couldn't blame her. The doctors had suspected the same thing. And even Emily herself couldn't say with certainty that she hadn't opted for the easy way out.

"Kill myself? End it? I don't know. I only remember the sensation of being chased. I don't know whether it was real or whether I made it all up. As for how it happened…" She shrugged. "I don't know whether I flung myself down the stairs or whether I slipped…"

Or whether the imaginary person chasing her had pushed her. She'd felt a hand on her shoulder, and knew that the man had caught up with her. "When they found me, I was bleeding from my head… from my eyes…" She paused. "My body was rejecting the donated corneas. I was going blind again. Only this time, it was worse: the fall caused more trauma. It damaged parts that couldn't be repaired, not back then. It made another transplant impossible. Not that I wanted one, not after what I'd been through."

Vicky nodded slowly, understanding coloring her voice, as she said, "You had to wait until medicine advanced sufficiently… and until you were brave enough to try again."

Emily acknowledged her friend's words with a nod. She took another sip from her glass. "I'm scared, Vicky. What if I'm not meant to see again? What if it's happening all over again?"

Vicky squeezed her hand. "It won't, you hear me?"

"I can't just wish these hallucinations away."

"That's exactly what you're gonna do. Don't let them control you. *You* are in control!"

"I don't feel in control right now."

Vicky put her fingers underneath the stem of Emily's glass to push it upward to Emily's mouth. "Let's drown those hallucinations."

"That's your solution?"

"Trust me, works for plenty of things."

"And if it doesn't?"

Vicky put her arm around Emily's shoulders. "Then you've always got me to chase away your imaginary monsters."

12

T HE EMBASSY OF ARGENTINA was located in an impressive building with an ornate façade only a block away from Dupont Circle and surrounded by numerous other embassies in equally beautiful mansions. Emily had been coming here for over two years, giving private piano lessons to the ambassador's ten-year-old daughter, Catalina. Ambassador Santiago Pacheco was a widower, charming at times, distant and withdrawn at others. It couldn't be easy to perform the duties of an ambassador while being a single parent to a child with special needs. Ambassador Pacheco could have chosen any music teacher for his daughter—money was certainly no object—however, the fact that Emily and Catalina had something important in common had made the decision easy for him. Catalina was blind and had been since birth.

After the death of his wife from cancer, Ambassador Pacheco had vacated his house in a ritzy suburb of Washington D.C. and moved into the residence that occupied the top floor of the embassy. In the afternoons and evenings, when Catalina was home from school, he often worked in his office in the residence so he could keep an eye on his child. Despite the fact that the nanny and the housekeeper took care of Catalina's needs, they weren't enough to give the child what she needed. A parent who was there for her.

"Time for Catalina's lesson, Miss Warner?" the security guard asked, reached for her bag, and put it on the TSA-style screening device, while Emily walked through the metal detector with Coffee ahead of her.

"Yes, time to catch up. I missed one lesson with her because I was off sick."

"I hope all is well now," the security guard said politely, but without much interest. "Enjoy your afternoon."

"Thank you," Emily said and walked toward the elevator.

She knew the drill. The security guard would remotely select the floor the elevator would bring her to, and the doors would only open once there so she couldn't reach the floors where the embassy staff worked and where confidential things were discussed. In the beginning, one of the security guards had always escorted her to the residence, but after a while, they'd stopped. She knew they'd run a thorough background check on her before she'd been allowed to teach Catalina, but had nevertheless insisted on keeping a close eye on her until they figured that one way or another she posed no threat to the ambassador and his daughter.

Arriving at the top floor, the elevator doors slid open amidst a soft pinging sound. Emily stepped into the small foyer that had only two doors. One was an emergency exit leading to the stairs, the other the door to the residence. It opened before she reached it.

Catalina stood in the doorframe, a smile on her face. "Miss Warner?"

"Hi, Catalina."

She ran her eyes over the girl. The pretty ten-year-old with the dark curls and the olive skin didn't hold a cane, having learned to navigate the ambassador's residence just like she'd navigated her previous home before that. Despite the things the child had been through, her own disability, her mother's illness and subsequent death, she was finally well adjusted and had blossomed from a withdrawn, grieving girl into a happy girl with a healthy dose of curiosity and eagerness to please.

"You brought Coffee," she said and looked in the dog's direction, homing in on him with her keen sense of hearing, something Emily had had to learn at age fifteen. Catalina, blind from birth, had never known any different.

"Yes, he's not used to being home alone. I hope that's alright with your dad... I mean, he's not really a service dog anymore..."

Emily entered the residence and closed the door behind her.

"Daddy doesn't mind. He said when I'm a little older, I'll get a guide dog too."

With surprising precision, Catalina found Coffee's head and petted him. Emily had never objected to her touching Coffee when they weren't at school where other kids could observe them. Coffee didn't mind. It seemed as if the dog knew that Catalina needed him just like Emily did.

"What did I tell you about petting guide dogs, Lina?" The male voice came from the end of a long corridor to Emily's right.

Emily turned her head toward the ambassador and watched him leave the shadows of the wood-paneled corridor and step into the light in the entry hall. He was younger than she'd assumed, his dark hair only showing a little gray sprinkling at the temples. He looked like he was in his mid-forties, which was considered extremely young for a man in his position. His wife, an American interpreter, had been younger, but it wasn't hard to imagine why she'd fallen in love with the handsome, tall man who looked like he owned the world. Only the fine lines around his eyes hinted at the pain he'd suffered.

"You said not to, Daddy," Catalina replied politely, but continued to pet Coffee. "But you see, he's not a guide dog anymore. I told you already." She pointed to Emily. "Miss Warner can see now."

Emily had announced the good news to her students on Tuesday, when she'd returned to the classroom to teach. Catalina had told her during a break that day that she was very happy for Emily.

Ambassador Pacheco unleashed a disarming smile and reached for Emily's hand, squeezing it for a moment. "I'm so happy for you, Miss Warner."

"Thank you, Ambassador." She motioned to Coffee. "I hope you don't mind that I brought him, but my doctor recommended I keep him with me until I'm completely healed."

"He's no trouble." He cast a warm look at Coffee, but didn't go as far as petting him. "Whatever you need is fine with me." He put his hand on Catalina's shoulder. "Lina, go run to the kitchen and let Maria know to bring a bowl of water for Coffee. He looks thirsty."

"Okay, Daddy." Catalina turned and walked off.

"Miss Warner?"

Ambassador Pacheco motioned toward the right, and Emily followed him to the living room, where a large Steinway piano was featured prominently. For the first time, Emily saw the quiet elegance with which the room was furnished. It was exactly how she'd imagined it. Her gaze was drawn to the portrait over the fireplace. The woman wore a long royal-blue dress and leaned with her back against a wall, one leg braced against it, her eyes beckoning the viewer to approach. Emily had never seen a more provocative painting in which the subject was fully clothed. Not that she'd been to a lot of museums before she'd lost her eyesight. Museums had bored her as a teenager. Back then, she'd never imagined that she would miss looking at beauty, at art.

Ambassador Pacheco seemed to notice Emily staring. "My late wife loved the Tango. It was how we met." It seemed as if he wanted to say something else, but then he changed the subject. "I wanted to have a quick word with you about Catalina."

"She's alright, isn't she? I mean…"

"I think so. But I just wanted you to be aware of something. Catalina is very fond of you, and now that you've regained your vision… well, I don't want to be insensitive… you have every right to choose what is best for you…"

"I don't understand."

For the first time since she'd met Ambassador Pacheco, Emily sensed an awkwardness in him that seemed unnatural for a man of his station.

"No operation in the world will ever restore Catalina's eyesight. I know she will ask you about it. She will wonder…"

"Wonder whether an operation would work in her case?"

To Emily's surprise, he shook his head. "No. She knows it won't. She was born without an optic nerve. And while I understand that damage to an optic nerve can now be repaired with an experimental stem cell treatment, there's no way yet to grow an entire optic nerve from stem cells." He let out a bitter laugh. "No matter how much I wish for it. For her sake. But Catalina is a smart kid, and I don't just say that because she's my daughter. No, she'll wonder whether you'll still be her friend, now that you can see. Now that you're not like her anymore." His gaze drifted to the portrait of his wife. "Catalina lost so much in such a short time. I hope she won't lose you too."

Emily let out the breath she was holding. "My friendships don't depend on me seeing or not seeing. I know what your daughter goes through every day, the challenges she faces with every step, even if those challenges might be over for me. I lived them for fifteen years, I'm not likely to ever forget what it's like to be blind." How could she? Blindness had informed all her choices, changed all her dreams about the future, made her into the person she was today. For better or worse.

"Thank you, Miss Warner. I'm sorry for being so blunt. I just worry that I'll never truly understand what it's like to walk in Catalina's shoes. Will you believe me if I tell you that for a day, when Catalina was staying with her grandmother, I wore a blindfold to put myself in her position, and by the end of the day, I was so frustrated with how difficult everything was, that I couldn't wait to tear the damn thing off?"

"I don't know many parents who would even try what you tried."

He let out a mirthless laugh. "My wife was better at these things." He paused for a moment, then looked straight into her eyes. "Catalina needs you. She can talk to you and know you'll understand her."

Emily nodded. There was a heaviness in the air she wasn't expecting. She'd never realized how much the ambassador understood that she wasn't just Catalina's private piano tutor, but also her confidant. She felt her eyes grow moist and blamed it on the fact that they were getting tired.

Before she could find anything to say, she heard somebody just outside the open door to the living room. Ambassador Pacheco looked past her, and Emily turned halfway. A young man in a business suit looked at them.

"Yes, Juan?"

"Sorry to disturb, Señor, Miss Warner," he said with a heavy Spanish accent. "But I need to respond to the Swedish ambassador regarding his upcoming ball. Will you be attending and bringing a guest?"

"Tell Ambassador Ingwaldsson I'll come, but alone. Thanks, Juan."

The ambassador's private secretary nodded and disappeared.

Ambassador Pacheco chuckled. "The music at the ball is going to be ghastly as usual. And it's not that Sven doesn't know. I keep telling him to hire an orchestra that plays a decent Tango, yet he insists on playing ABBA."

"I don't think ABBA is bad at all," Emily said, surprised about the ambassador's openness.

"It is when he sings along."

Emily couldn't help but chuckle. "You actually told him so?"

"Oh, yes, and not just once."

When Emily raised her eyebrows, he added, "We play golf together. He's not a bad guy, and he sure can drink—like all Swedes—but he has no ear for music." He motioned to the piano. "Maybe I can get you to play a Tango for him one day, so he can hear what he's missing."

Emily laughed, knowing that there was no way she'd ever get a chance to play for the Swedish ambassador.

Just then, Catalina appeared in the doorway, holding a precariously full bowl of water. When her father made an attempt to walk toward her to help her with the bowl, Emily gave a quick shake with her head and mouthed a silent no.

"Thank you for that, Catalina," Emily said instead, knowing that the girl didn't want any help, and watched her walk toward her with the bowl. "Coffee is already sitting to the left of your seat at the piano."

13

A LITTLE OVER AN HOUR LATER, Emily left the embassy and walked the short block to the metro at Dupont Circle to head home. Spending an hour with Catalina, who'd clearly been practicing her scales and the piece she was currently learning, had put her in a good mood. With her hand on the handlebar extending from Coffee's harness, she looked around and soaked in the atmosphere. A Starbucks at one corner, a few small stores at another, a large drugstore across the square. And the square itself, round with a grassy area, some trees and benches, as well as a statue in the middle. Ten streets culminated here. Traffic seemed busier than usual, and everybody on the sidewalks or crosswalks was rushing. Only Emily wasn't. She wanted to learn the route from the embassy to the metro station by sight.

Her cell phone rang. "Vicky Hong calling," the automated voice announced. Soon, she wouldn't need this feature anymore.

"Rest, Coffee," she commanded, then answered the phone. "Hey, Vicky."

"Hey," Vicky replied. "Are you on your way home?"

"Yeah, why?"

"I was thinking we could hang out tonight. You're not busy, are you?"

"No, I've got no plans."

"Great. It's a date."

"See you soon."

"Before you hang up, do you mind picking up some Chinese on the way?"

Emily closed her eyes for a moment. She should have guessed that Vicky had an agenda. "On the way?"

"Yeah, you're taking the Red Line to Gallery Place, aren't you? Chow's is only a block from there. And they have the best Chinese. I can call it in."

Emily chuckled. "You're lucky I'm hungry too."

"Great! I'll order us a feast, and we'll pig out tonight. See you shortly."

Emily shoved the cell phone back into her pocket and turned her head to Coffee. "Guess we're going to Chow's, boy. Forward."

Taking the metro from Dupont Circle to Gallery Place where she normally changed to get on the Green or the Yellow Line to Columbia Heights where her apartment was located, wasn't a problem. She'd done it almost daily in the last three years. But it was a different experience. People were rushing, pushing, and shoving, and she was glad that she still had Coffee with her and was wearing her dark glasses. Had she been without those particular accessories, Emily was sure she would have been trampled. Luckily, people did show some concern for a blind person. But eventually, she'd have to learn to navigate the metro and its crowds without those protections. The prospect seemed daunting, yet she knew she would master this too. After all, millions of people did it every day.

Once above ground again at Gallery Place, which was in the middle of Chinatown, she used her smartphone to find Chow's. Sure, she'd been here before, several times in fact, but always with Vicky, which was the reason she'd never bothered learning the route.

Chow's was a small restaurant with lots of colorful decorations, mostly in red and yellow. The dining room was packed, and several people were waiting in the foyer to pick up takeout.

Emily walked to the hostess table. Before she could ask for the takeout Vicky had ordered, the hostess barked, "No dogs in the restaurant."

"Oh, uh," Emily started and drew the woman's gaze, which had been fixed on Coffee, on her.

Only now did the woman seem to see her dark glasses and realize what they meant. For a moment she stared, then cringed. "Never mind. Dine in or takeout?"

"Takeout for Vicky Hong."

The hostess looked at her computer screen, then said, "Fifteen minutes."

Emily turned and walked to the chairs in the foyer, found an empty one and sat down. The hostess disappeared in the restaurant, and a moment later, a young Chinese man took over her station.

Emily waited patiently, Coffee at her feet.

Opposite her, two women were gossiping. She didn't mean to listen in, but listening was such an integral part of her life that she couldn't stop herself. Besides, the two were loud enough to be heard over the din of the restaurant. And had they not wanted to be overheard, they would surely have whispered.

"Did you read it?" the woman with the long dark hair asked, leaning closer to her friend.

The woman with the short brown hair made a dismissive hand movement. "Just another conspiracy theory. They've got nothing else to report."

"But don't you think it's odd that she died alone at home?"

"What's so odd about that? Even rich people die. Maybe she had a stroke, or a heart attack. The papers haven't exactly reported a lot of details yet."

The dark-haired woman shook her head. "She was healthy. Totally fit."

"You make it sound like you knew her." The short-haired woman tsked. "Which you didn't."

"We worked at the same place. I mean, I practically knew her."

"Just because you volunteer there a few times a month, doesn't mean you knew her."

"Doesn't mean that I don't care about what happened to her. It could have been a suicide. Why else would the papers not report the actual cause of death?"

"Papers? Plural?" Again, her friend shook her head. "*One* tabloid is spewing conspiracy theories. Doesn't mean anything. The same tabloid also claimed that the Speaker of the House is an alien from outer space."

The other woman lifted her hand. "Oh, which reminds me: did you hear that the Vice President's press secretary was seen coming out of you-know-whose brownstone very early on a Tuesday morning?" She chuckled.

"Nooo! Are you saying she was with that guy from—?"

The young Chinese guy calling out a name Emily didn't catch stopped the woman from finishing her sentence. Both leapt out of their chairs, and one snatched the order. Emily followed them with her eyes as they opened the door to leave.

"No, not a *him*. A *her*!"

A gasp was the last thing Emily heard before the door closed behind them. She had to chuckle inwardly. Washington D.C. was a caldron full of gossip. Considering the number of important people, many with political connections and money, or both, it was no wonder that everybody speculated about what everybody else was up to. Emily wasn't into gossip. Still, she got her fill of it anyway, because Vicky read pretty much every gossip column published in the capital.

"Vicky?" the male host called out.

Emily jumped up and took the plastic bag with the food. "How much?"

He gave her a strange look. "You already paid by credit card."

"Oh, uh, great, thanks."

Emily left the restaurant and headed back to the metro station. She managed to get on the next packed train to Columbia Heights. A middle-aged woman offered her a seat on the train, and even though Emily declined at first, the woman insisted. With a murmured thank you, Emily sat down. The rhythmic rumbling of the train made her doze off for a moment, when she suddenly heard Coffee growl. With a start, she was awake.

"Coffee? What's wrong?"

She followed her dog's stare, and her gaze landed on a homeless man who pushed his way through the throng of passengers, a "Spare some change" rolling off his lips like a broken record, his dirty hand held out. Everybody got out of his way, obviously not wanting his stench to transfer to their clothes. Emily could smell him too, and the unpleasant scent of urine and vomit became more intense when the man stopped right in front of her.

"Spare some change, Miss?"

He reached for her arm, but before he could touch her, Coffee reared up and let out a vicious growl, warning the man that he would pay dearly for accosting Emily if he tried. The homeless man virtually jumped backward, crashing against the woman who'd offered her seat to Emily.

"Get off me!" the woman yelled at him.

Before the homeless guy could do any more harm, two black youngsters intervened and grabbed him. The train was already slowing for the next station.

"Get the fuck out of here," one of them warned, while the guy struggled to free himself.

A moment later, the train stopped, and the doors opened. Several passengers got off and made space for the two teenagers to evict the homeless guy from the train. Then they jumped back inside, and the doors closed behind them.

"Don't thank us all at once," one of them said sarcastically.

"Thank you," Emily said.

Somebody started clapping, a second person chimed in, and in an instant, the whole train was applauding the two young men.

The woman who'd offered Emily her seat, said, "You've got a good dog there."

Emily nodded. "He protects me." She put her hand on Coffee's head and petted him. "Good dog, Coffee, good dog."

Shortly after, Emily emerged from the Columbia Heights Metro station and oriented herself. She strolled past several stores and fast-food places, and crossed Columbia Heights Civic Plaza where several stalls offered products like organic coffee and local crafts, and a band played rock music.

Normally, she would have stopped to listen for a while, but knowing that Vicky was waiting for the takeout, she continued on her way home. The next block was lined with more businesses, and Emily cast a quick glance at the displays in the windows. A jacket caught her attention, and she took a closer look. It was pretty, but it also looked expensive. Well, she didn't need a new jacket anyway.

Emily let her gaze sweep over the other items in the window, when a reflection in the glass startled her. A man in a business suit stood right behind her, looking over her right shoulder. He was taller than Emily by close to a foot, his short hair blond, his eyes a startling blue. He glared at her furiously, looking as if he wanted to attack her. A violent shiver went down her spine, while the man moved even closer. He raised one of his hands as if to strike her.

Ready to defend herself, Emily spun around, and froze. There was nobody behind her. In fact, the closest person, an elderly man with a cane, was at least ten feet away from her. Where had the blond man disappeared to so quickly?

Her heart beat excitedly into her throat. "Coffee?" The dog stood calmly at her heel, showing no sign of discomfort or perceived threat. No sign that anybody had come close to his mistress, or he would have growled to alert her, just like he had in the Metro.

She was certain then—the blond man in the suit was another hallucination, another trick her eyes were playing on her. Her gut filled with dread, and for a moment she thought she would burst into tears right there, but she choked them back. She had to be stronger this time. She wasn't a teenager anymore. Clearly, trying to ignore these hallucinations wasn't working. She had to deal with them, or she would suffer the same fate as fifteen years earlier. She couldn't let that happen.

When she suddenly felt a prickling sensation on her nape, she turned her head toward the square, but none of the shoppers there was looking in her direction. Still, she could have sworn that somebody was watching her.

14

WHEN THE DOORBELL CHIMED in the late afternoon, Rita Bolton wanted to ignore it at first. Her housekeeper had left to run an errand, her husband was making phone calls, and her oldest daughter, Natalie, had already left to return to her own house after helping with the arrangements for the memorial.

All Rita wanted to do now, was to bury herself under a warm blanket and cry until she had no tears left. Her grief knew no bounds. No mother should ever have to bury her child. Her own flesh and blood. Her little girl, her Maddie, the baby she'd longed for ever since she could remember. For years, she and Eric had tried to have a child, and for years, they'd failed. After her second miscarriage, Rita had finally agreed with Eric to adopt. Natalie had come into their lives as a 2-year-old who was already walking and babbling. She'd filled a void that Rita had felt for so long. Three years later, she'd finally found herself pregnant again. And this time, she'd carried the baby to term.

When the nurse had finally put Madeline on her chest, and the tiny baby had snuggled against her, Rita had fallen in love with the vulnerable creature and vowed to always protect her. She'd showered her with love. Could anybody really fault her for loving Maddie more than Natalie? She'd tried to love them both equally, but in truth, Maddie had always been her favorite. And now she was gone.

The doorbell rang again. She sighed. Perhaps it was just a delivery that needed a signature. Slowly, her feet carried her through the hallway of the enormous house to the entrance door. She opened it, ready to receive a package or an important piece of mail. But the person standing on her doorstep wasn't a UPS or FedEx driver.

"Caleb?"

The handsome young man with brown hair and an athletic figure wore a business suit. Today, his normally easy smile was absent from his face. He reached for her hand. "Mrs. Bolton, I wanted to come the moment my father told me about Maddie, but I stopped myself… I knew you wouldn't be ready to receive me."

Tears filled her eyes.

"But Maddie was my friend too. I wanted you to know how much she meant to me and everybody at the charity."

Unable to speak, Rita threw her arms around Caleb Faulkner, Mike Faulkner's son, and allowed the tears to flow, knowing that she could be herself with him. He'd always been a part of the family, had spent many summers with them when he'd been a child. He and Madeline had practically grown up together. And Natalie, too, she added belatedly.

Rita sniffled and withdrew from the embrace. "It's so good of you to come." She motioned to the hallway. "Please come in."

"Thank you, Mrs. Bolton."

He still addressed her formally even though she'd told him to call her Rita when he'd become an adult. But he'd declined, saying he'd feel odd if he suddenly called her by her first name. Calling her Mrs. Bolton was a sign of respect.

Rita led Caleb into the living room. "Would you like a drink?"

"That'd be great," he replied.

When she made a motion to walk to the cabinet where the alcohol was kept, he stopped her with that charming smile that had become his hallmark. Though today, it wasn't as cheerful as usual. There was sadness in it. He, too, was grieving for Maddie. "I know where everything is. Shall I make you one too?"

She nodded. "A sherry." She'd had far too much to drink in the last few days, but it was the only way she could make it through this tragedy. To feel numb helped drown out the grief and the pain.

When Caleb served her a glass of sherry and himself a glass of whiskey, he sat down next to her on the couch.

"To Maddie," Caleb murmured. "There was nobody more compassionate."

"To Maddie," Rita said, her voice breaking. She took a sip and swallowed. "Yes, she was compassionate, wasn't she? I was so happy when she started getting involved in the charity. I know people thought she only did it for the balls and fancy charity auctions, but she really loved helping those children. She wanted to make a difference, didn't she?"

She watched Caleb take a big swig from the tumbler. "More than we'll ever know. She was like a dog with a bone when it came to those kids. She never gave up, no matter the obstacle. She was too good for this world."

Rita choked back more tears at the glowing praise Caleb heaped on her daughter. "We have you and your father to thank for it. If your father hadn't asked her to join *No child abandoned* after he resigned and you stepped into his shoes, she might have never found her passion."

Caleb nodded. "Yes, it changed her life, didn't it?"

"She finally seemed content with her role in life. And now..." Rita couldn't continue, her eyes filling with tears again. She took a sip from her sherry. "Will you and your father come to the memorial next weekend?"

"Of course, we will," Caleb said immediately. "And if there's anything you want me to help you with, please let me know."

She smiled at him and nodded.

"I mean it," he insisted. "You should really take me up on it. You and your husband shouldn't have to carry this burden all by yourselves."

Rita squeezed his hand. "You are so kind. But your father already helped so much. We didn't have to deal with the police who might have dragged their heels with the investigation. It was so important to us... to Maddie... We wanted to follow her wishes..."

"It's tragic, all of it. My dad mentioned that they tried to save Maddie in the ER, and that her father was there at the end. Did he at least have a chance to say goodbye to her?" He looked into his glass. "I'm sorry, it's none of my business. It's just... I can only imagine how devastating it must have been to be there and..."

Rita put her hand on his forearm. "No... Maddie never regained consciousness."

Caleb sighed. "I'm so sorry."

Rita felt a little dizzy all of a sudden and swayed toward the coffee table as she set down her glass.

"Are you okay?" Caleb asked, his voice full of concern.

She motioned to the empty sherry glass. "I'm fine, Caleb. I'm fine. It just seems that every day seems so long now."

Caleb nodded. "It's understandable. You must be tired." He rose. "I should go and let you rest. I just wanted you to know that you're not alone with your grief."

Rita rose to her feet. "Thank you, Caleb."

When she took a step toward the door, he stopped her. "I'll see myself out."

"Goodbye, Caleb."

She followed him with her eyes and felt her heart ache. Maybe if Maddie hadn't been living alone, if she'd had a man like Caleb in her life and not that no-good lothario she'd been dating, the accident might have never happened.

A sob escaped from her chest. Every what-if scenario was playing in her head again as if on an endless loop. She needed to drown out those what-ifs that led nowhere. She walked to the liquor cabinet and opened it. She needed something stronger than sherry.

15

Dr. Harland flipped his head mirror up and rolled back with his stool. Today, a full week after Emily's transplant procedure, he wore a simple white coat over his dress shirt and pants, his name embroidered above the breast pocket. "It all looks good. There's no sign of scar tissue."

Emily edged forward on the broad faux-leather chair she sat on for the examination. "Are you sure there's nothing wrong?"

The surgeon wrinkled his forehead. "You don't seem happy about it. Should something be wrong?"

She fidgeted for a moment, her courage retreating. Maybe she shouldn't bring it up. If her doctor said that the procedure had been a success, then maybe she was wrong. Besides, if she told him what was happening to her, he would probably think she was crazy. Still, he was an expert who could perhaps find a logical reason for her hallucinations, or whatever she could call them.

"Miss Warner? Is there a problem? Are you experiencing any issues with your sight?"

She swallowed away her hesitation. "I see things."

"Well, you are supposed to see. That's the whole point."

"I mean, I see shadows…" When his facial expression changed, she continued, "I see things that turn out not to be there."

"Hmm." He rolled closer again. "Describe to me what you see."

She didn't know how to start. How to express what she was experiencing. "It's hard to describe. It's always something different. First it was just the shadow of a person that I thought was there, but wasn't." She reached for a description. "Like a Fata Morgana." She knew how silly it sounded, so she added, "Once I saw something that looked like the flash of a camera, only I was in the car with my neighbor, and there was no camera anywhere. I just don't know… it's unsettling." It was more than that. But she didn't want to influence the doctor's judgment.

"I think I might know what you're experiencing. It's actually quite common for patients whose eyesight is being restored after many years of blindness."

"It is?" She grasped for the hope in his words.

He nodded. "How can I explain this in laymen's terms? You see, for a very long time your brain wasn't processing any visual stimuli. So that part of your brain, those synapses that carried the electrical impulses, lay dormant. Now they're starting up again, and what happens sometimes is that there are delays."

"Delays? What do you mean?"

"Well, the impulse is being sent when your eyes perceive something, but the brain doesn't translate it immediately into something you can understand, or see. Think of it as a backlog in your brain. And once it works through that backlog, your brain sends you images that you saw earlier."

It made sense to a certain extent. But it didn't explain everything she'd seen. "Okay, so if I see a shadow of a person, then maybe I saw that person earlier?"

"That's right." He smiled, obviously pleased that his explanation had the right effect.

"But what about other things? I saw somebody shatter a glass table. And I know for certain that none of that happened since the operation."

For a moment, the doctor seemed to contemplate Emily's words. Then he said, "I think what's happening is that your brain might be mixing up things that you see on television or in a magazine, rather than what you're experiencing yourself. It can't yet distinguish between the two."

She thought about that for a moment. She had turned on the TV a few times for background noise, and also, when hanging out with Vicky, the TV was constantly running albeit on a low volume. "Maybe..." She wanted to believe it. "But how long will it take, until these, I don't know what I should call them, visions maybe, go away?"

"They can certainly take a few weeks, but I've found with other patients that sometimes it's a case of the patient resisting the change."

"Resisting suddenly being able to see? Why would I do that?"

"It's not a conscious choice. But change is stressful, even if it's good change." He turned to his desk and typed something on his computer, while he continued, "I'll refer you to Dr. Ian Sutherland. He's a great psychiatrist, who'll be able to help you work through that resistance and deal with the stress. You'll see—"

"But I'm not crazy. I don't need a psychiatrist." The word alone conjured up memories of her previous brush with that particular field of medicine. It would mean accepting that she was going crazy.

"Nobody is saying that you're crazy." He looked at her with kindness in his eyes. "But we're all stressed at one time or another."

"I'm doing fine." Though she knew she wasn't.

"I'm not saying you have to go see him if you don't want to, but I've put the referral through, just in case you decide you need a little extra help. How does that sound?"

She nodded, not wanting to alienate him any further. "Okay."

"And I'll see you back here in three weeks." He rose. "You can start taking off your sunglasses when you're outside. Only use them when it's really bright outside. On cloudy days or in the mornings or late afternoons, let your eyes get used to the light."

"Thank you, Dr. Harland."

He was already opening the door. "I'll send Jennifer in to set up your next appointment."

When the door closed behind him, Emily kept staring at it. Was it all that simple? Just a processing delay in her brain? She hoped that Dr. Harland was right. She wanted to believe him. Because the alternative was something she couldn't face again.

16

ADAM YANG OPENED THE GLASS DOOR of the refrigerator and grabbed a six-pack of beer before walking to the checkout of the convenience store. It was early evening, and he was the only customer at Patel's Market. He placed the six-pack on the counter.

"Evening," the Southeast Asian man with the name tag Sanjay greeted him.

"Hey," Yang replied, then pointed to the wall behind the clerk. "And a four-pack of AA batteries please."

Sanjay turned and selected the item, then scanned it and the beer. "Anything else?"

"That's it."

Yang reached into his pocket to pull out his wallet, when the door was ripped open. Instinctively, Yang's hand went to his shoulder holster, where he was still carrying his service weapon. He was off duty—as much as any policeman could ever be considered off duty—but was still armed. He was on his way home to watch a boxing game with his neighbors, but had remembered that the remote control was on the fritz, and he was running short on beer.

Yang didn't pull his weapon. The young woman who charged into the store wasn't brandishing a gun or any other kind of weapon.

"Help! Please help! Call 911!" she yelled, and gesticulated toward the street. "Somebody is being stabbed!"

Instantly, Yang was on high alert. "Where?"

"In the alley! Call 911!" she repeated and pointed to the left, adding, "I don't have my phone."

"I'm a cop," Yang said. To Sanjay, he said, "Call 911 for backup."

Without waiting for confirmation, Yang ran outside, his hand already gripping the handle of his gun. At the corner to the alley that the woman had indicated, he stopped, then peered around it, careful not to walk into a trap. A large trash container partially blocked his view. He listened for sounds of a fight, but apart from the traffic noise from the street behind him, he couldn't distinguish any such sounds. Had the perpetrator already fled?

His weapon pointing ahead, Yang stalked around the trash container, expecting the worst, a dead body, but hoping for the best, somebody who was injured only superficially. He hadn't expected to find nothing at all. No stabbing in progress, no body, no injured person. A few feet away, he noticed a door. He tried the handle, but it was locked.

"What the f—" he cursed, when he heard footsteps behind him.

He whirled around, ready to shoot. He let out a surprised gasp, then lowered his gun. The woman who'd stormed into Patel's Market stopped several feet from him.

"Is he dead?" she asked breathlessly, pointing at a spot behind the trash container, her eyes filled with horror.

Yang shook his head. "You sure it happened right here?"

The woman nodded emphatically and came closer, peering past him. "They were right there. Two white guys, a tall one stabbing a smaller one. I saw them. And they saw me."

For the first time, Yang looked the woman up and down, assessing her like he did with anyone who witnessed a crime. She was in her late twenties, early thirties, not beautiful in the common sense of the word, but attractive. Her chestnut hair touched her shoulders, her figure was athletic rather than skinny. She wore jeans and a pale-blue sweater and cardigan set that suggested a certain fragility and gentility in its wearer. It didn't quite fit with her face. There were hard lines around her mouth and her eyes as if she wasn't one to laugh often and easily. He recognized that look, had seen it often enough in family members of murder victims.

"You have to believe me. I saw them," she interrupted his musings.

"Okay. What's your name?"

"Emily Warner."

"Okay, Miss Warner," he said and put his weapon back into its holster. "Let's see if they left any evidence." He searched the wall and floor around the dumpster for blood spatter that indicated that a stabbing had taken place, using his cell phone's light to make sure nothing escaped his view. After a minute, he shook his head. "No blood." He met her eyes.

"That can't be," she insisted. Her expression was sincere.

He detected no hint of deception in her brown eyes. And he considered himself to be a good judge of character. It was the reason he was a good detective, one who knew when to believe a witness and when not to. Had Emily Warner come to the police station to report a stabbing, he wouldn't have hesitated to believe her. Everything about her spelled truth.

"Miss Warner," he said and glanced past her, when he suddenly noticed something: a security camera mounted on the corner of the building that housed Patel's Market. He pointed to it, then exchanged a look with her. "Come with me."

They quickly walked back into the store.

"Did you get them, officer?" Sanjay asked.

Yang shook his head. "Is that security camera out in the alley yours?"

"It is." He motioned to the small monitor behind the counter.

"Can you rewind the tape so we can see what happened out there?"

"Sure."

Moments later, Yang, Emily, and Sanjay looked at the monitor. The camera angle showed a large part of the alley, and was mounted so it covered the dumpster as well as the door.

"That's the back door to the store," Sanjay explained.

Yang looked over his shoulder to where a door led to the employee-only area of the store. "Do you keep it locked during the day?"

"Yes."

"Anybody back there?"

"Nope. It's just me."

Yang nodded and watched the security footage. He saw movement, a shadow. A moment later, Emily Warner came into view of the camera. She looked at a spot near the dumpster and suddenly recoiled, freezing in place for a second, before she took off running and disappeared out of view of the camera.

Yang turned to look at her.

"But I saw it," she stammered. "I saw those men."

Yet the tape showed nobody but Emily Warner running from an imaginary crime scene. She'd lied to him. Yang pulled his cell phone from his pocket and selected a number.

"Dispatch," the woman on the other end answered.

He gave her his name and badge number, then told her to call off the police cruiser that was on the way to the store. "False alarm. Thanks." He disconnected the call.

An uncomfortable silence stretched between them.

Sanjay broke it. "Just as well. We already had a stabbing out there a month ago. That's why we installed the camera."

"A month ago?" Emily echoed, looking distraught, crushed even.

Yang didn't know what to make of her reaction. Her gaze veered away, fixed on something in the distance. She had the look of a person who was remembering something, or trying to remember something. For a moment, he wondered whether she was under the influence of drugs. She didn't smell of alcohol, but she did have the look of a person who had trouble focusing.

"I'm sorry," she murmured. "I'm so sorry, Officer." Her face flushed with regret and genuine embarrassment.

"Are you alright, Miss Warner?" Yang wasn't sure why he felt concern for the woman who'd falsely claimed to have witnessed a stabbing.

"I'm sorry," she repeated and turned on her heel, rushing to the door, almost stumbling over her own feet to leave the store.

"Wouldn't have pegged her for a crazy," Sanjay said when the door fell shut behind her. "They normally wear tinfoil hats."

Yang sighed. "Guess you can't judge people by their appearance." And Emily Warner had appeared to be sane and normal. "Well…" He pointed to the beer and batteries.

Sanjay rang him up, and Yang paid with his credit card. While the clerk bagged the items, Yang thought of something.

"Ahm, do you still have the security tape of the stabbing from a month ago?"

"I'm sorry, but I only installed the camera after the stabbing."

"Never mind." Yang pulled out his business card and slid it over the counter. "If that woman shows up again with some other crazy shit, call me."

Sanjay took the card. "Sure thing." His eyebrows rose. "Detective Yang."

His purchases in hand, Yang left. He didn't make it a habit of giving out his card other than when he was working on a homicide, but for some reason he did it tonight even though he didn't exactly know why. It was just a hunch. That was the other reason he was a good detective. He followed his hunches. Sometimes they panned out. Sometimes they didn't.

17

SHAKING LIKE A LEAF, Emily accepted the drink Vicky had poured her. She was sitting on Vicky's couch, Coffee at her feet, Vicky's cat, Merlin, cuddling up to him. The dog looked at her, instinctively knowing that his human mom wasn't well. He knew her better than anybody, maybe even better than she knew herself.

Emily had been in the middle of cooking a meal for Vicky and herself, when she'd realized that she'd run out of cream. She'd left the apartment without Coffee who'd been dozing. Unfortunately, the corner store she normally went to had closed early due to a family emergency, so she'd been forced to walk a few more blocks to go to a different store. That's when she'd seen the stabbing.

"It was so real," Emily now repeated to Vicky. "It wasn't like the things I've seen before, not like the camera flash or the reflection of that enraged man in the window of the boutique. Not even like the glass table shattering. No, this was... real, you know? I saw them as clearly as I see you now."

Vicky sat down next to her on the sofa, leaning against the high armrest to look at her. "I'm so sorry."

Emily took a sip from the strong beverage. "The policeman looked at me like I was crazy." Tears welled up in her eyes, but she fought against them. "Because I *am* crazy. I'm going crazy." Again.

"No, you're not! Put those thoughts right out of your mind. They're not helping."

"I know that. They didn't help last time either." She pulled air into her nose, making an unladylike noise. "But I'll be damned if I don't fight it this time. I'm not a kid anymore."

"That's the attitude. You fight, girl!" Vicky praised.

"I mean it." Emily looked into her glass. "This time, I need to get to the truth. I need to know what's causing these visions."

"Didn't your surgeon say that in the first few weeks after the procedure it's quite common to see things that aren't there?"

Emily shook her head. "Not like this. Shadows, yes, quick flashes of something blurry maybe, but not whole reels of scenes that play out like a movie." Because that's how it had felt, like a movie where she was playing a part. "My doctor doesn't have the answers."

"Then what are you suggesting? Not the..." She made a circular motion with her finger.

"A psychiatrist? Hell, no. That didn't work when I was fifteen and impressionable. It's not gonna work now." If she told a psychiatrist what she was seeing, he'd put her on a medication that would make her feel like a Zombie. No, she didn't want to be drugged.

"Okay?" Vicky said shrugging. "Then what?"

"I need to find out who my donor is."

"Your donor?" For a moment, Vicky stared at her in confusion. Then the penny dropped. "You mean your cornea donor?"

"Yes."

"But how would that help you figure out why you're getting these visions?"

Emily sighed. "You'll probably think it's stupid, but..." And it probably was stupid, but she was grasping at straws now, because going down the same path as after her first cornea transplant wasn't an option. "I read this article a few months back... about organ transplants... you know I wanted to be prepared for the procedure. I read about all the things that could go wrong..."

Vicky sighed. "Hello, Dr. Google."

"Don't knock it. You would have done the same in my situation."

"Fair enough."

"Well, as I said, I read about organ transplants and how some transplant recipients could suddenly do things their organ donors could do, like playing an instrument for example. They called it cellular memory."

"And you think that you inherited some sort of cellular memory from your donor? Come on, Emily, I think that's a little farfetched. That's not even science. That's like buying snake oil from a car salesman."

"You're mixing metaphors," Emily interrupted.

Vicky rolled her eyes. "I wasn't going for a metaphor. I was just trying to show you how ludicrous the idea sounds."

"Be that as it may, but I have to find out who donated the corneas."

Vicky sighed. "I guess you could call your doctor and ask for the information. It should be in your medical file. And if it's not, you can always write to the United Network for Organ Sharing to contact the donor's family."

Emily forced a smile. "Yeah, not so much. The family wanted to stay anonymous, and even if I wrote to that organization, I doubt the family would reply. Besides, even if they did, it could take weeks. I can't wait that long."

Vicky made a resigned gesture. "If that's the case, if they want to stay anonymous, then you're out of options. It's not like you can hack into the network and look up your donor's information."

Emily cleared her throat. "No, you're right. I don't have those skills. I can pick a lock, but my IT skills are limited. So I thought—"

"Hold it! Did you just say you can pick a lock?" Vicky appeared stunned.

"Uhm, yeah?"

"How?"

"Well, it's been a while, but when I was a teenager, I learned it."

"You had classes in Lock Picking 101, or did they call it Burglary 101?"

Emily huffed. "No, of course not. It wasn't like that. I wasn't stealing anything. My father had a locksmith business, and I often spent afternoons at his shop to do my homework. Most of the time I was bored, so I watched him work. And occasionally he showed me a few tricks." She winked. "I'm a quick study."

Vicky shook her head in amazement. "That's quite something for a father to teach his daughter how to pick a lock. That's a pretty cool father, I'd say."

Emily ignored Vicky's last comment. Her father had been anything but cool. "It's not all that hard if you know what you're doing and have nimble fingers and the right tools."

"I bet you were popular in school. I could have done with a friend like that back then, breaking into teacher's offices to look at tests in advance."

"You're too bright. I doubt you ever needed any help to score high on a test. Besides, I never told anybody at school that I could pick locks."

"Why not?"

"Can you imagine if a teacher had found out? My parents would have gotten in trouble."

"Bummer!" Vicky said. "Picking a lock would have come in handy."

Emily grinned. "I didn't say that I never used my skill for my own purposes, just that I didn't tell the other students. I wasn't that great at physics, but the year after I learned to pick a lock, my grades picked up."

"You're hilarious! I wish I'd known you back then," Vicky said, smiling.

"Yeah, I wish I would have had a friend like you back then." Emily smiled, then sighed. "Better late than never, right?"

"I'll drink to that," Vicky said and clinked her glass to Emily's.

Both drank.

"So hypothetically, if *you* had an organ transplant, how would you go about looking for your donor?" Emily asked.

Vicky pressed her lips together, then sighed. "It's not exactly straightforward, if you must know. But the use of IT has made things easier."

"How?"

"For a few years now, all organs get assigned a barcode from the moment they are harvested until they are transplanted. So if you have the barcode, theoretically you could trace it to its origin."

"How do you know all this?" Emily asked.

Vicky smiled. "I might have known a guy who worked at the United Network for Organ Sharing."

Emily laughed. "You mean you were sleeping with him?"

Vicky winked. "Yeah, once or twice."

When Emily tilted her head to one side and gave her a *you're-shitting-me* look, Vicky added, "Okay, so it was all hot and heavy, and Terry wanted to continue, but he was a bit too clingy for me. He still writes me birthday and Christmas cards."

This information immediately gave Emily an idea. "So you're still friendly with him…"

Vicky stared at her, and slowly her facial expression changed to realization. Shaking her head, she said, "Oh no, missy! Not a chance."

Emily tilted her head to the side. "Come on. I'm sure if he's still keen on you, he'll do you a favor if you ask him."

"Sure, of course. Why haven't I thought of this?" Vicky paused for effect, then lifted her finger to her temple. "Oh yeah, that's right, because I'm not interested in visiting him in prison."

"He's in prison?"

Vicky rolled her eyes. "He will be, if he gets caught giving me confidential information."

Realization dawned, and Emily suddenly felt sorry for suggesting Terry get the information for her. "So you do still like him?"

"Enough not to ruin his life."

"I'm sorry," Emily said and meant it. "I'll figure out something else."

Vicky stared at her. "Please, Emily, don't."

But her mind was made up. She had to find her donor, no matter how.

"I know that look," Vicky said. "You're not gonna give up, are you?"

"Don't worry, I won't drag you into it."

Vicky shook her head. "You might know how to pick a lock, but that doesn't mean you know how to find your donor's info. You need my help."

Furrowing her forehead, Emily said, "But you just said that you don't want to ask Terry for a favor."

"And I won't."

18

ERIC BOLTON SAT BEHIND THE DESK in his opulent study overlooking a lush garden. He'd always considered the rich wood-paneling cozy and inviting, but now it felt oppressing. It was choking him with its dark tones that swallowed up all the light. He'd never felt so alone.

Footsteps echoed outside in the hallway, high heels that sounded just like Maddie's. For a short moment, he allowed himself to think that it had all been a terrible nightmare, or even that he was in a coma, and none of this was real. But he'd never been a man to spend his time spinning fantasies that bore no resemblance to reality. He knew whose footsteps he heard. And they weren't Maddie's.

"Natalie?" he called out.

A couple of seconds later, his daughter Natalie appeared in the door frame, dressed in a light jacket, her handbag slung over her shoulder, her car keys in her hand. "Hey, Dad."

She looked like the polar opposite of Maddie. While Maddie's hair had been a golden blond mane of curls, Natalie's was black and straight. Natalie kept it short in a Princess Diana style. It suited her. Whereas Natalie's face was classically symmetric, and she was considered a beautiful woman, Maddie's beauty had been of a different caliber. Maddie had inherited Rita's green eyes. It was those eyes that had drawn countless men to her. But it was her warm and inviting smile that had kept them enthralled.

"Are you leaving?"

Natalie nodded. "Paul just called. Finally, he'll be home a little earlier than usual. He's been working such late hours the last few months. His business dinner got cancelled, so I need to pick something up for dinner on my way home."

Bolton had never liked Paul Sullivan, Natalie's husband of only two years, but he tried not to show it. He didn't consider Sullivan an honest man, after all, he'd cheated on his first wife—with Natalie. Natalie had been Sullivan's mistress for three years, before he'd finally divorced his wife. How long would it take until Natalie would meet the same fate as Sullivan's first wife? How long until he cheated on Natalie? How long until he hurt her?

Maddie had never liked Sullivan either. There was no love lost between them. Only a month ago the two had argued in the foyer of a restaurant after they'd both attended Rita's birthday dinner. When Bolton had asked Maddie the next day why she and Sullivan were butting heads yet again, Maddie had claimed she didn't remember what the catalyst had been. But Bolton suspected that Sullivan had blamed Maddie for Natalie getting drunk at a girls' night where the sisters had hit the nightclubs with two girlfriends. The foursome had had far too much fun for Sullivan's liking. Natalie's husband had been livid when pictures of Natalie dancing provocatively had shown up in the tabloids.

Bolton tried to push the thoughts out of his mind. Natalie had made her choice, and there was nothing he could do to change that fact.

"Your mother will be disappointed that you can't stay for dinner," he said.

"I know, but I've spent almost every day here since…" She didn't finish her sentence, didn't have to.

"I know. Your mother appreciates it very much."

"Does she?"

Taken aback by Natalie's clipped tone, Bolton drew his eyebrows together. "Is something wrong, honey? Did you two have a fight?"

Natalie sighed. "A fight? No, of course not." She scoffed. "She's much more subtle than that. But then, I'm used to being compared to Maddie. Even now that she's gone, I can't do anything right in Mom's eyes."

Bolton rose and made a few steps toward her. "She's just grieving. We all are. Don't take it personally."

"Don't take it personally? Dad, she doesn't even see me! I'm invisible to her. I might as well be the maid. Whatever suggestion I make, be it the flowers for the memorial, or the type of casket, it's always: Maddie wouldn't like this, and she wouldn't like that." Anger and frustration rolled off Natalie.

Bolton had never seen her like this. "Please, Natalie, don't do this. Your mother loves you. She's just going through a very hard time."

"You think I don't know that? You think I don't know that Maddie was everybody's favorite, hers and yours? That I was always playing second fiddle? Maybe you should have returned me when Maddie was born." She pivoted, ready to leave.

Shock charged through Bolton. He grabbed her arm and forced her to turn back to face him. "Natalie, we love you. We wanted you."

"Don't lie to me, Dad. I was a placeholder until Mom got pregnant with Maddie. And now that Maddie is gone, suddenly you love me?" She stared at him, disappointment evident in her eyes.

Bolton shook his head at the revelation of how Natalie felt all those years. Had it really been so obvious that both he and his wife loved Maddie more than their adopted daughter? He'd always tried to share his affection for his daughters equally. Had he failed?

"I'm sorry I hurt you," he said. "I never meant to. You're my daughter, and just because you're not my flesh and blood doesn't change that. If anything happened to you, it would break my heart as much as losing Maddie breaks my heart."

He took Natalie into his arms, but she remained stiff. "Please be patient with your mother. Know that I'm here for you. Just like I'll always be here for you."

She finally put her arms around him. "I love you, Dad."

Relief washed over him. He needed Natalie's love more than she needed his. She was stronger than he could ever be. Natalie was now his shoulder to cry on, because he had to be Rita's rock, and there was only so much strength one man could muster on his own.

19

Mike Faulkner switched off the computer in his office in the West Wing. Most staff had already left for the evening, and he was finally ready to leave too. He stuffed a few files into his briefcase, when he heard a noise at the door. He looked up.

"Do you have a minute, sir?" Secret Service Agent Mitchell asked.

Faulkner nodded and motioned for him to enter. Mitchell closed the door behind him and stopped in front of Faulkner's desk. Mitchell was a tall, muscular black man in his early forties. He'd been assigned to the President's personal protection detail in the first year of Langford's administration before transferring to the investigatory branch of the Secret Service, but Faulkner had known Mitchell for far longer.

Their paths had crossed twenty years earlier, when Mitchell had been a Marine returning from a tour in Afghanistan and been framed for the rape of a fifteen-year-old girl, a crime he hadn't committed. Faulkner had acted as his defense counsel—pro bono—and been able to expose the true rapist, thus earning a not-guilty verdict for Mitchell. In return, Faulkner could always count on Mitchell's loyalty and discretion.

"Mitchell, you have news?"

"Yes, sir. About the Bolton case. We've determined that there was no forced entry; nothing was missing or disturbed, so we're ruling out a burglary. We've interviewed neighbors and acquaintances, and the housekeeper. Nobody saw anything unusual prior to Miss Bolton's death. Her head injury is consistent with a fall where her head struck the corner of the glass table. We're still waiting for the toxicology report. As you know, the Secret Service doesn't normally do investigations into deaths, and therefore isn't set up to do autopsies and toxicology tests. We had to farm all of it out. Hence the delay."

"I understand," Faulkner said.

"We expect an elevated blood alcohol level, given the report of the housekeeper that she found an empty wine bottle."

"Hmm. You're saying she was drunk?"

"Not sure how much she drank on a daily basis, but even if she had a good tolerance for alcohol, I'd say she was at least tipsy. It's entirely consistent with the assumption that she lost her balance and fell off the ladder while changing a light bulb. Though…" Mitchell hesitated.

"You don't believe it?"

Mitchell placed a bulky envelope onto Faulkner's desk. "We recovered Miss Bolton's cell phone and were able to get into it."

Faulkner raised an eyebrow. "No password? That's unusual."

"We found her PIN on a list of all her passwords in her handbag. According to the housekeeper, Miss Bolton had a problem memorizing passwords and PINs, so she wrote them down."

"Anything noteworthy on her cell?" He reached for the envelope and opened it.

Mitchell nodded grimly. "We found that she talked to somebody from the Russian embassy on the day before she died."

Faulkner stared at Mitchell. "Who?"

"The number is registered to Sergei Petrov, the cultural attaché."

Faulkner knew what this meant: Petrov could possibly be a Russian spy.

"Have you spoken to anybody about this?"

"No, sir. I figured it best to keep it under wraps. I checked with my sources at the FBI and the CIA to see if Petrov is under surveillance."

Impatiently, Faulkner asked, "And?"

"I'm afraid he's not. He was under surveillance when he first joined the embassy three years ago, but since they didn't unearth anything that indicated that he was a foreign agent, the surveillance was dropped after nine months. It appears he really is only a cultural attaché."

Faulkner pulled the cell phone from the envelope and entered the PIN on the post-it note that came with it. He opened the phone app and found Petrov's name instantly: it was the last call Maddie had made before her death.

"Given that Petrov has diplomatic immunity, how do you want me to proceed?" Mitchell asked.

Faulkner checked the length of the call. It had lasted less than a minute. What could Maddie have discussed with the Russian cultural attaché in under one minute? Nothing of substance, unless the call was a request to meet.

"Leave it with me. I'll think about how to handle this. We can't afford to cause an incident with a Russian diplomat in the tense situation we're in with the Russians right now. Any little thing could set them off and end negotiations regarding their discovery of a deposit of rare earth minerals in Siberia. We're not the only country keen on a steady supply."

"I'm fully aware of it, Mr. Faulkner. That's why only you and I know about this."

"Good work, Mitchell."

"Thank you, sir," Mitchell said and left the office.

Faulkner leaned back in his chair and stared at the phone in his hands. He scrolled through the recent call and message list.

20

"Y OU SURE ABOUT THIS?" Emily gave Vicky a long look. "You can still back out now."

"And what? Bail you out of prison when you get caught?" Vicky shook her head. "I don't have that kind of cash lying around. And neither do you."

Both were dressed in hospital scrubs and wearing lanyards with fake hospital IDs. Technically, only Emily's ID was fake, Vicky's had expired years earlier. It couldn't open any doors anymore, since the access rights embedded in the magnetic strip on its back had been revoked, but nobody could tell just by looking at the card. Vicky had used it as a template to print a fake ID for Emily and laminated it. It wouldn't stand up to close scrutiny, but it was good enough at a distance.

Vicky looked at her wrist watch. "Get ready. They should be coming out any moment now."

Emily looked around. It was early morning, and they were eyeing a door with a sign saying *Staff only*. It was one of the entrances to the hospital where Emily had received her transplant. The only way to open the door was with an access card. No lock to pick.

"Are you sure?" Emily asked.

"Don't worry. It's shift change."

"Why couldn't we just go in through the main entrance?"

"Because there's security at the main entrance this time of day, and they check IDs. Shhhh."

Emily heard the door creak, and a moment later it swung open and a man and a woman in scrubs came out. The two barely looked at Emily and Vicky as they passed. The door was already closing, but Vicky reached it and jammed her foot between door and frame. Emily glanced back at the two employees, but they weren't looking over their shoulders.

Quickly, Emily joined Vicky, and together they entered. In the corridor, several other medical staff members walked past them, some talking on their phones, others chatting, some yawning after working the nightshift. Nobody gave them a second glance, just like Vicky had predicted.

When the corridor intersected with another one, Emily heard a soft ping coming from the left. Yet Vicky was already turning right.

"The elevators are the other way," Emily said, stopping.

Vicky looked over her shoulder. "We're not taking the elevators." When Emily turned to walk alongside her, Vicky explained, "In an elevator, we're sitting ducks. People might look at our IDs, and realize that we don't work here."

A moment later, she opened a door. "We're taking the stairs."

Emily followed Vicky into the stairwell. Swiftly, they ascended to the fifth floor. Vicky opened the door to the hallway slowly and only a few inches, and peered through the gap, before opening the door fully and waving Emily to follow her.

The hallway was empty.

Emily was glad that Vicky was with her. Without Vicky, she might never have found her eye surgeon's office suite so easily. At the door to it, Vicky stopped, and Emily read the sign next to the door. Dr. Harland was one of four physicians listed.

"Now do your thing," Vicky whispered and pointed to the lock.

Emily pulled her tools from her handbag and took a step closer to the door.

"Looks professional," Vicky commented. "Where did you get it?"

Emily smiled. "Amazon Prime."

"You're shitting me!"

"Nope."

"I've gotta get me one of those."

With nimble fingers, Emily went to work, while Vicky turned around to watch the hallway. Emily concentrated on the task, trying to remember how to use the different tools to coax the lock into opening. She started to perspire, worried that she'd forgotten how to pick a lock. After all, it had been a while since she'd done this.

"What's taking so long?" Vicky asked under her breath.

"Not helping," Emily said with gritted teeth. She took a deep breath and relaxed her shoulders, then tried again. Finally, she heard a telltale click. She turned the doorknob, and the door opened. "Got it."

Vicky gave her an approving look, while they both went inside and pulled the door shut behind them.

The office suite was large. Behind a counter at the far end of the waiting room, there were several computer stations for the various medical assistants working in the clinic. To their right was a corridor that led to the physicians' offices and the exam rooms. Emily had been in one of the exam rooms not too long ago during her follow-up appointment with Dr. Harland. The clinic had been busy. Now it was quiet. While the clinic wouldn't receive patients until eight o'clock, the assistants would be here at seven thirty to man the phones and get the exam rooms ready.

"Okay, let's do this," Vicky said and headed to the assistants' workstations. At every station she touched the computer mouse and wiggled it to wake up the monitor. All four stations lit up with the logon screen, confirming that nobody had forgotten to log out. Vicky shrugged. "Would have been too easy."

She started rummaging through the desks.

"What are we looking for?" Emily asked.

"Login credentials. Check for post-it notes and the like."

Emily started at one workstation. "Do you really think that they are so careless as to leave their passwords lying around?"

"I don't think. I know."

When Emily tossed her a doubtful look, Vicky elaborated, "Hospital policy is to change passwords every month or so. Do you really think that everybody wants to memorize a new password that often? I mean, just think about it. For everything we do in our lives, we need a password. And most of the time it has to be complicated: a capital letter, a symbol, a special character, at least one number, a minimum of eight letters, and so on. Who can remember all that? People write it down."

"If you say so." Emily continued turning over everything on the workstation she was searching.

"Bingo," Vicky exclaimed.

Emily turned to her and saw her peel a sticky note from the underside of a keyboard.

Moments later, Vicky woke the computer again and signed in. Various icons appeared on the desktop, and Vicky clicked on one of them. A window popped open.

"You got your medical record number?"

Emily nodded, and pulled the piece of paper from her handbag, where she'd copied down the number from her last medical bill. "Here."

Vicky typed it in, and Emily's medical chart appeared on the screen. Vicky seemed to be familiar with the layout, because before Emily could even figure out what she was looking at, Vicky was already selecting a line to reveal the underlying information.

"Okay, this is the transplant info. Date of transplant, etc. etc. And here"—she pointed to a long string of numbers—"is the barcode of the donor organ. Now let's see who it belongs to."

She clicked on it. A short beep sounded simultaneously to a small window popping up.

"Oh fuck!" Vicky cursed.

Emily leaned in and attempted to read the message, but Vicky was faster.

"Access denied. You don't have sufficient rights to access this information. Contact an administrator."

"Oh crap," Emily said. "Now what?"

Vicky looked over her shoulder. "Time for the help desk."

"The help desk?"

Vicky looked at her wristwatch. "We might just have enough time. The help desk isn't staffed until seven. That gives us half an hour."

Confused, Emily furrowed her forehead, while Vicky was already logging off. "But if the help desk doesn't open for a half hour, how are they going to help us?"

"They're not. We're helping ourselves. Come. Hurry."

Vicky didn't explain any further, and Emily had to trust that her friend knew what she was doing. A few minutes later, they reached a door on the second floor at the opposite end of the hospital.

"This is the IT department. Get out your lock picks," Vicky said and motioned to Emily's handbag.

This time, Emily felt more confident in her skill, and she was able to pick the lock much faster.

"Done."

Moments later, Vicky shut the door behind them. They stood inside a large open-plan office with at least ten cubicles. To their left, an open door revealed a small kitchen or break room, and at the far end from the entrance there were two more doors that led into glass enclosed rooms. The entire office suite was empty.

"What now?" Emily asked.

"Same as before. We need to find somebody's password to get in. IT guys have access to pretty much everything." Vicky pointed to a cubicle. "I'll start here. You start at the other end. Look everywhere: underneath the keyboard, the mouse pad, the monitor stand, in drawers, underneath drawers... You know the drill by now."

Without a word, Emily went to work. Vicky did the same. Only the rustling of paper and the clanking of items being lifted and then set down on a desk could be heard. Emily worked as fast as she could. She left no item untouched, but her first cubicle was a bust. So was Vicky's. Minutes ticked by. The second cubicle Emily went through didn't yield any passwords either. Emily looked at the large clock on the wall of the room. Fifteen minutes to seven. Her heart started beating faster. She could feel the pulse along her neck drum as if it were a countdown. And maybe it was. Time was running out.

"Got it!" Vicky announced from behind Emily.

Emily whirled around and saw Vicky set a large coffee mug back on the desk.

"In the mug?" Emily asked.

"Underneath it. Pretty clever, particularly since the mug still has coffee from yesterday in it. Yuck!"

Vicky sat down at the desk and logged into the computer. The credentials worked, and she was looking for the right application, clicking on various folders, then closing them again.

With a look at the clock on the wall, which now showed that they only had seven minutes left, Emily said, "What's taking so long?"

"Not helping," Vicky replied, repeating Emily's own words from earlier back to her.

Emily understood, but it didn't make it any easier to be patient.

"Okay, I'm in the right system." Vicky looked at the piece of paper on which she'd written down the barcode number she'd found in the medical record.

The clacking of the keyboard echoed in the room. Emily noticed that it was the only sound she could hear. Both she and Vicky were holding their breath.

"Sesame open," Vicky murmured. A document opened on the screen.

Emily whipped her head in the direction of the door. Years of honing her hearing to compensate for her blindness, had made her hyper vigilant to sounds. There was no doubt. "Somebody's at the door." She could hear the soft scratching of a key against metal.

"Shit!" Vicky cursed. "Just another second." She hit a key on the keyboard. "Printing."

Somewhere in the room, a printer started whirring. Emily craned her neck. Where the hell was that printer?

"There!" Vicky pointed to an area close to the two glass offices.

Emily saw it, too. The printer was spitting out two pages, then stopped.

The door creaked open. Instantly, Vicky and Emily dove to the floor. Footsteps, then the door shut behind the person entering. Panicked, Emily stared at Vicky. Her friend put her finger over her lips, then crawled to the edge of the cubicle. Emily's heart beat into her throat and she watched in horror how Vicky looked past the partition.

Looking over her shoulder, Vicky made an 'okay' sign, then crawled in the direction of the printer. Emily wanted to jerk her back, when she heard sounds coming from the kitchen. The IT person was making coffee. Now she understood Vicky. They had a minute at best, before the person would leave the kitchen.

Vicky reached the printer, snatched the two sheets from it and hurried back. Keeping their upper bodies crouched low, Emily and Vicky rushed alongside the partitions which hid them from being seen from the kitchen. When they reached the end of the cubicles, Emily tossed a quick look at the open kitchen door. A man had his back to them, filling the coffee machine with ground coffee.

Vicky reached the exit first and opened the door soundlessly. Emily hurried toward her and followed her into the corridor, while Vicky quietly closed the door.

"That was tight," Vicky said.

"You think?" Emily's heart was still beating like a jackhammer.

Already motioning her toward the stairwell, Vicky folded the printout and shoved it into one of her pockets without looking at it.

Another two minutes later, and they were outside. Only then, Emily's heart seemed to find its normal rhythm.

When they reached the car, Emily couldn't contain her curiosity any longer. "Is the name of my donor on there?"

Vicky unfolded the paper and scanned it. Then she looked up, her eyes wide. "It is."

"Who is it?"

"You're not gonna believe this."

21

THE PRESIDENT'S LIMOUSINE, affectionately known as the Beast, rolled along the busy streets, two Secret Service agents in the front seats, President Robert Langford and his Chief of Staff, Mike Faulkner, in the back. While the two agents wore the usual dark suit, shirt, and tie, Langford and Faulkner were both casually dressed. It didn't happen often, but was warranted today. The new Prime Minister of Japan was an avid golfer and would be more easily convinced to agree to President Langford's trade proposal if the two met in a more relaxed environment.

"I hope you're right about this, Mike," Langford said with a glance at Faulkner. "It *was* your idea."

Faulkner lifted his hand. "Yes, and you can blame me for it if it backfires. Which it won't. I have it on good authority that the Prime Minister will do pretty much anything for a good game of golf."

Langford chuckled. "Which he wins, I assume?"

Faulkner gave a quick shrug. "Yes, but please don't make it too obvious. I'm sure his team told him what your handicap is, so it's best you don't lose by a lot. Just enough to make it a challenge for him."

"If you say so, Mike." For a moment, the president fell silent and looked out the window. "How is Eric doing?"

Faulkner sighed. "As can be expected. Such a tragic accident."

The President turned his face back to his Chief of Staff. "So it was ruled an accident?"

"It's but a formality." There was no need to tell the President about Maddie's contact with Sergei Petrov. He had enough to worry about. "Just a few more loose ends to tie up. But the way it currently looks, it most likely was an accident. There was no sign to the contrary, no forced entry, nothing stolen. I mean, we both knew Maddie…"

Langford sighed. "Yes, we did. So much promise, yet she could never get that wildness out of her. I suppose we all have our demons."

"Some more than others." Even Faulkner did. But he didn't like to dwell on it. Instead, he focused back on Madeline Bolton. "According to the housekeeper, Maddie was drinking that night. We'll know for sure when the toxicology report is back but she must have lost her balance when she was on the ladder to change a light bulb. The impact when she fell on the glass table caused a cerebral hemorrhage."

Langford blew his breath out through his nostrils. "It's odd, you know... I don't see Madeline as the type to do anything as mundane as changing a light bulb."

"True, she was somewhat of a princess the way her parents raised her, put her on a pedestal. It was impossible for Maddie not to disappoint them. Somehow I understand why she rebelled with drugs... and lovers."

"But I thought in the last few years she changed, didn't she? When she started to get involved in *No child abandoned*... what... two, three years ago?"

"She seemed more content. Still..." Faulkner sighed. "We'll never know what goes on inside a person. Even one we're so close to."

"What did you tell Eric about the Secret Service's investigation?"

"The truth." Though he hadn't mentioned Petrov to Bolton either. "But I promised him that the details will be kept confidential. Nobody needs to know that she was drinking. That's why I insisted on the Secret Service investigating the incident rather than DC police. Not that the media isn't speculating."

"That'll die down eventually. When's the memorial?"

"This weekend."

"I wish I could be there," Langford said, "but my presence will only draw more media to it and turn the memorial into a circus. Nobody deserves that, least of all Eric and Rita. You'll tell them that, won't you?"

"Of course."

"Are you planning to attend?"

Faulkner nodded. "One of us has to. Besides, I'm sure Caleb wants to attend too. He and Maddie were friends for a long time."

Langford smiled. "I remember you telling me when they were kids that you hoped they'd be an item one day."

Faulkner chuckled at the memory. "Things don't always work out the way parents plan. At least they got to spend a lot of time with each other at the charity."

"You can be very proud of your son, devoting his efforts to such a worthy cause."

"Yes, yes, of course. After all, I had to resign after you offered me this job."

"Do you regret it?"

Regret being one of the most powerful men in politics? "No, Mr. President, I don't regret it."

Langford chuckled. "I don't think I'll ever get used to you calling me Mr. President. Back in college, you called me all kinds of things. Do you sometimes look back at those days?"

Faulkner smiled. "Fondly. Everything was simpler back then. They called us the three musketeers. All for one, one for all."

Langford nodded. "And look at us now. We're still the three musketeers, albeit a little older, and a little grayer." He pointed to his own graying hair.

Faulkner shook his head. "I wish it were just the age and the hair."

"You still miss her, don't you?"

"Georgina is never far from my mind. No other woman could ever hold a candle to her."

Maybe if his wife were still alive, everything would be different. But she was gone, and had been for a long time.

22

"MADELINE BOLTON," Emily said in amazement.

She and Vicky had returned to Vicky's apartment together minutes earlier, where Vicky had made coffee, then booted up her computer.

"Everybody called her Maddie. She's pretty famous for somebody who's not a model or actress, you know," Vicky said. "At least in D.C."

"I'd heard that she died, but I'm not into all the gossip like other people."

"Ouch!" Vicky said in mock-pain.

Vicky consumed gossip and all gossip rags like stoners consumed weed.

"So, come on," Emily said impatiently. "What do you know about her?"

"Plenty." Vicky beamed proudly. "She comes from a very rich family."

"Figures." Even Emily had heard the name Bolton before.

"She was about your age, maybe a year or two older, and she was quite spoiled. Rumor has it that her father could never deny his daughter anything, so she always got whatever she wanted."

For a moment, Emily envied Maddie Bolton. She could only imagine what it was like to be adored by one's father. But that hadn't saved Maddie. She was dead, and there was nothing enviable about death.

"Of course, it wasn't all sunshine and roses. There were rumors of drug use in her late teens, early twenties, but when you have the kind of money the Boltons have, you can pay whatever it takes to get your rebellious offspring out of any situation. So after she'd experimented with drugs, sex was next." Vicky chuckled to herself. "Oh my! If I had a map of the world and stuck a pin into half the countries she had lovers from, I'd be running out of pins."

"You're joking! I mean there must be around 200 countries in the world."

"One-hundred-and-ninety-five," Vicky corrected her.

"You can't tell me Maddie had a hundred lovers!" No woman could possibly have slept with so many men. Her own list was much shorter. By a lot. In fact, she could count the men she'd slept with on one hand.

"Okay, so maybe I'm exaggerating a bit, but she had at least fifty," Vicky conceded. She made a dismissive hand movement. "What I'm trying to say is that she knew everybody: diplomats from various countries, politicians, celebrities, anybody who is anybody. And let's face it. She was very beautiful."

Emily looked at the computer monitor, where Vicky had pulled up a photo of Maddie. Gorgeous green eyes like those of a cat, blond curls spilling over her shoulders, clear skin, full lips, Maddie had it all.

"Yes, she was. Beautiful. Rich." She sighed. "And dead."

"There's more to her," Vicky continued. "You'd think that somebody like her would be shallow and arrogant. But that's not the case. Everything I read about her confirms that she had a big heart. She was warm and compassionate. She devoted a lot of time to that charity, what's it called? Something to do with rescuing trafficked children."

"Oh yeah, I heard about it. *No child abandoned*, right?"

"That's it."

"I think she organized charity auctions for them or something like that," Emily said, recalling a news report from months earlier. "What else do you know about her life?"

Vicky sighed. "Well, that's pretty much it. Except for how she died. They haven't reported much about it, only that she was found by her cleaning lady one morning. But apparently it was too late, and she died in the hospital. The authorities are still investigating what really happened, but rumors are that it was a household accident."

Emily furrowed her brow. "They're still investigating? But then how was I able to get her corneas? I mean, they probably did an autopsy that took a while. And once somebody is dead for a while, the organs become unusable." She'd done a lot of research about organ donation when she'd contemplated getting another transplant.

"That's true, but I have it on good authority"—she winked and Emily understood that she meant contacts from when she'd worked in the hospital—"that because she died in the hospital and was a registered organ donor, they harvested the organs before they ever got word that there would be an autopsy."

"They can do that? Is that even legal?"

Vicky shrugged. "It happens. I guess it would have been different had she already been dead when her cleaning lady found her. In any case, you can still do an autopsy after the organs are taken. There's still plenty of blood and tissue that can be examined and tested. And whatever else they do."

Emily tried to shake off the image of Madeline's body being cut open. "It's awful that she had to die."

"At least her death wasn't for nothing. Sick people received her organs so they can live. And you can see again." Vicky smiled.

"I know. And I'm grateful for it. But…"

"But what?"

"What if there is a price?"

"A price for what?"

"For my eyesight." Emily pointed to Maddie's image on the monitor. "What if she's reaching out to me? What if the visions I have are because of some unfinished business Maddie had?"

"If I didn't know any better, I'd say you're watching too many supernatural TV shows. Maddie is not a ghost."

"I'm not saying she is," Emily said. "But what if it's cellular memory?"

Vicky squinted then she shook her head. "That again? Really?"

"Like I told you already, there's a hypothesis that human cells have some kind of memory, and that people who received organ donations suddenly exhibit a skill that their donor had, like for example playing an instrument. I read on the internet that the theory is that memories are not only stored in the brain but also in other tissue. For example what if some of the things that Maddie saw left an imprint on her corneas, and now I see the same things?"

Vicky rolled her eyes. "You don't believe crap like that, do you? Just because it's on the internet, doesn't mean it's true. In fact, most of what you read on the internet is false."

"But it would explain my visions. It would also explain why I saw strange things after my first transplant. What if my donor back then wanted to show me something? What if Maddie wants to show me something now?"

Vicky sighed. "I know you want to get answers, but I think your doctor is right. Your brain isn't processing all images properly yet. Just be patient. Don't go down that rabbit hole." Vicky shook her head. "I should have never helped you find out who your donor is. It was a mistake. Look what it's doing to you."

Emily took Vicky's hand and squeezed it. "No, you did the right thing. I needed to know. And now that I do, I know that what I'm experiencing is somehow connected to Madeline Bolton. I can feel it."

"Emily, please—"

"I can prove it." It had just come to her. There was a way to prove to Vicky and to herself that her visions were Maddie's memories.

"And if you can't?"

"Then I'll never bring it up again, and you can say 'I told you so'."

"Deal."

23

SINCE YANG COULDN'T TALK to Officer Cabbot, who'd been first on the scene of Madeline Bolton's death, he decided on another route to get the information he felt he needed to seek in order to satisfy his inexplicable curiosity about the case. It didn't take long to find out who the paramedics were that attended to Madeline Bolton and transported her to the hospital. According to their supervisor, they were taking a short coffee break near Georgetown Waterfront Park.

Yang saw the parked ambulance, parked behind it, and got out of his car. Two EMTs, a man and a woman, sat in the back of the open ambulance, their feet dangling in the air. Yang approached them and pulled his shield from his pocket, flashing it at them when he reached them.

"Adam Yang, Homicide Branch," he said. "Are you Xavier Pabst and Keiko Takai?"

Both nodded.

"Yeah, what's up?" Pabst replied.

Yang put his badge back into his jacket pocket. "Just a quick follow up. The two of you were called to Madeline Bolton's house in Georgetown on the 23rd. Is that correct?"

"Yeah, we were," Pabst said and exchanged a look with his colleague.

"That was tragic," Takai, a pretty Japanese woman in her thirties added.

"So, homicide, huh?" Pabst asked. "Not an accident?"

"Well, that's not clear yet," Yang said in a casual, friendly tone, knowing that he got people talking more than they wanted, when he was friendly and open. "That's why I wanted to follow up on a few things with you guys. Since you were the first at the scene."

"Actually, a police officer beat us to it by a minute," Pabst clarified.

"You're right," Yang said quickly, then lied, "I already spoke to the officer, but I figured three pairs of eyes can see more than one, right? So could you describe the scene to me, please? Don't leave anything out. The smallest detail could be vital."

The two EMTs looked at each other and shrugged.

"Sure," Takai said. "The victim was in the living room. Pretty posh place, nicely furnished too."

Pabst rolled his eyes. "Keiko, I don't think the detective wants to hear what you thought of the wallpaper."

Takai shook her head at him. "Typical! You've gotta set the scene. Details. Background. You know." Then she looked at Yang. "Isn't that right?"

Yang scribbled in his notebook. "Please continue. What did you see in the living room?"

"We found her on the floor, lying on a bed of broken glass…"

"From the glass coffee table," Pabst interjected.

"Right. She was on her back and looking up at the ceiling. Her legs were at a strange angle."

Pabst nodded. "And a step ladder lay across her legs, you know, like it fell on her when she fell from it."

"Hmm," Yang murmured. "So it looked like she'd used the ladder for something. Were you able to see what she might have been doing?"

"Probably tried to change a light bulb," Pabst started.

"I saw a broken light bulb in her hand," Takai added.

"Yeah, I saw it too," Pabst said quickly, "but I'm not sure how she was gonna change the light bulb."

"Why not?" Yang asked.

"Well, the stepladder wasn't that high, and she wasn't exactly tall either. I doubt she could have reached the light fixture, you know with the ceiling being like nine or ten feet high," Pabst said.

"It was one of those older houses, totally renovated, but it had the high ceilings that you get in houses built at the turn of the century," Takai explained.

"As I said," Pabst continued, "she must have stretched to reach, and probably lost her balance." He shrugged. "Tragic really."

"Yes," Yang agreed. "And how did she look? Was there lots of blood? What kind of injuries did you see?"

Takai answered this question. "Not a lot of blood, a few cuts. Her head got the brunt of it, there was blood from a head wound. When we put her on the stretcher, you could see that blood had soaked into the carpet. Frankly, we were surprised that she was still alive. I mean, she must have been lying there for hours, before she was found."

"Yes, we're still working on the timeline from when she got home the night before and when she was found," Yang said as if he were involved in the investigation. "Can you tell me what she was wearing?"

"Businesslike," Pabst said, "you know, nice blouse and skirt."

"The blouse was red, and the skirt was black," Takai said. "Very nice quality. Not cheap."

"Did any of her clothing seem disturbed to you?" Yang asked.

"You mean like somebody was trying to undress her?" Pabst asked.

"Not necessarily. In the absence of having a picture of Miss Bolton at the scene, I'm just trying to get a picture of what she looked like."

Pabst and Takai exchanged a look. Both shrugged, then Pabst said, "She looked perfectly put together. As if she was ready to go to the office."

"Or just getting home from the office," Takai said. "I guess that doesn't really help you with figuring out when she fell off the ladder."

Yang smiled at her. "Trust me, all these details are helping me get a better picture of what might have happened."

Takai sighed. "It's such a shame. I've read about her. I recognized her the minute we got to her house. She looked just like in the tabloids, beautiful. And fashionable."

"That's the kind of stuff you notice," Pabst said to Takai. "Clothes and shoes."

"Well, those are all details," Takai added. "Besides, those shoes were Jimmy Choo's! That pair she wore cost six-hundred dollars easy!"

Yang stared at her. "Shoes? What kind of shoes?"

"Jimmy Choo's."

"What do they look like?"

Takai pulled out her cell phone and typed something on it, then turned the screen to Yang so he could see what she had pulled up.

Yang stared at the pair of elegant pumps with high heels that were at least three inches tall. How a woman could walk in them was beyond his comprehension. "She wore those?"

"Well, one of them," Takai said. "The other one must have slipped off her foot when she fell. I saw it on the carpet."

"Are you absolutely certain about this?" Yang asked.

"Of course, I know Jimmy Choo's shoes."

"I mean about Miss Bolton still wearing one of the high heels."

"She's right, Detective, I saw the shoes too. She was definitely still wearing one."

Yang flipped his notebook shut and put it and his pen away.

"Thank you so much for your time. You were of great help."

"Anytime," both said.

Yang turned back to his car and got in. Keiko Takai had provided him with vital information that led him to believe that Madeline's death had been no accident. Now the question was, would the Secret Service come to the same conclusion and treat Madeline Bolton's death as a homicide rather than a household accident? Or would they sweep the evidence under the proverbial carpet?

24

Emily hadn't been able to go back to Patel's Market right after her conversation with Vicky that morning. She had to teach the last three periods of the day, and those hours felt longer than they'd ever felt before. She could barely wait for the final bell to ring, and for her to pack up her things and leave the school behind, Coffee by her side.

When she entered the convenience store, she recognized the employee behind the counter. He was the one from the night before. She glanced at his name tag to make sure, and was surprised when she was able to read it. Clearly, her vision was improving, just like Dr. Harland had promised. Nevertheless, she was steadfast in her determination to find out why she was having strange visions, and whether they were connected to her donor.

Sanjay was waiting patiently while an older woman counted out coins to pay for her purchase. He didn't even look up to see who'd entered the store while he dealt with the customer. Emily browsed one of the shelves close by, trying to hide her own impatience, though Coffee seemed to sense her edginess, always attuned to her emotions.

When the older woman finally headed for the door, the plastic bag with her groceries in her hand, Emily walked up to the cashier's counter. The moment Sanjay caught sight of her, she realized that he recognized her. She wondered what he called her in his mind. Crazy? Delusional? It didn't matter. All she wanted was information he could, with some luck, provide her with.

Nevertheless, she felt her cheeks heat, no doubt as a result of her embarrassment the night before. Before she lost all her courage, she said, "Hi, I came in here yesterday evening." Of course he already knew that, but she had to start the conversation somehow.

He nodded. "Yes, Miss? What can I get you?"

Feeling bad that she hadn't come to purchase anything, Emily glanced at the items that were kept on the shelves behind the cashier.

"I'll take, uhm… a pack of AA batteries, please." It was something she could always use, and it would make her feel better about the commotion she'd caused the night before.

He reached for the batteries and set them down on the counter. "Will that be all?"

This was her chance. "Actually… I have a question."

He raised his eyebrows, but didn't say anything.

"You mentioned last night that there'd been a stabbing in the alley next door about a month ago?"

"That's right. What about it?"

"Was there a witness to it? I mean, did somebody see it go down?"

For a moment, Sanjay hesitated as if trying to remember the incident. Then he said, "Actually, there was a woman who saw everything and gave a description of the perpetrator to the police."

Emily's heart started to thunder. "Do you know who she was? I mean, do you remember her name?"

He gave her a curious look, looking her up and down, when his gaze trailed to Coffee. It seemed that he noticed the dog only now. Coffee was wearing his harness, which had Guide Dog inscribed on it. He tore his gaze away and met her eyes.

"Actually, yes, I remember the woman." He gestured to the rack of newspapers and magazines next to him, pulled a tabloid from it, and placed it on the counter. He pointed to the picture and headline. "It was her."

Emily stared at the newspaper. It took her a moment to focus her eyes.

"A real shame what happened to Madeline Bolton," Sanjay continued before she could read the headline. "She was really nice too. She waited here in my store while the police and ambulance were dealing with the stabbing victim."

Emily felt the excited drumming of her heart. She could practically hear the sound her blood made rushing through her veins. Relief flooded every cell of her body. What she'd seen happening in the alley the night before hadn't been a hallucination. It had been one of Maddie's memories. This meant several things. The transplant hadn't been a failure, and she wasn't crazy. She wasn't mentally ill or succumbing to hallucinations.

Emily recalled the events that had led to her first cornea transplant failing. She'd tried to ignore the things she saw back then. But now she realized that the unusual visions she'd had were memories of the organ donor. She had ignored them and paid the price for it: losing her eyesight a second time.

This time, she wouldn't make the same mistake. She wouldn't ignore Maddie's memories, because if she did, the same fate was waiting for her, she was certain. And this time, she wasn't going to let that happen.

Maddie was trying to tell her something. Maddie had given her the gift of sight. The least Emily could do was to find out what Maddie wanted her to see. No matter where it took her, and what it cost.

25

June 8ᵗʰ

ADAM YANG ENTERED HOMICIDE BRANCH, which was located in a three-story red brick building in Southwest Washington. From the outside, the building looked quaint. It had an almost small-town charm to it if one could forget that inside, police detectives worked on solving murders. What had really drawn him to a career in solving violent crimes, he wasn't quite sure. Nobody in his family had ever been a victim of a violent crime, let alone a murder victim. Still, he'd always loved solving puzzles, and to him, a murder was the ultimate puzzle.

A latte from a fancy coffee shop—which was much better than the swill they called coffee in the break room—in his hand, he walked toward his cubicle. Before he reached it, Jefferson already waved at him, his phone glued to his ear.

Yang approached and heard his partner's end of the conversation.

"Yes, Yang and I will be there in fifteen minutes." Jefferson disconnected the call.

"Simon, what's up?"

Jefferson rose from his chair and slipped on his jacket. "A dog walker found a dead body down at Fort Dupont Park."

"Let's go," Yang said as they both left the building.

"I'm driving."

Yang didn't object, and they got into Jefferson's car.

Fort Dupont Park was an almost four-hundred acre wooded park under the management of the National Park Service. It lay to the East of the Anacostia River, only a fifteen-minute drive from Homicide Branch on M Street. It provided about ten miles of hiking trails to the city's residents, and hosted many concerts and educational programs. It was popular with joggers and residents walking their dogs.

"What else do we know?" Yang asked, when they exited the parking lot.

"Not much. Just that the body is that of a naked female."

"Ah, fuck," Yang cursed.

"Ditto," Jefferson said.

They both knew what this likely meant: rape and murder. And the chance of finding the killer: virtually zero. Yet, none of them said so. They both would try their best to solve the case, whatever the underlying circumstances were.

"Forensics is already there," Jefferson added.

"Good." Yang took the last sip of his latte and placed the empty paper cup in the cup holder.

Jefferson motioned to it. "You'd better not forget to put that in the trash later."

"Don't get all bent out of shape. I know how you like to have a spotless car."

Before Jefferson could reply, a cell phone rang.

"Mine," Yang said, recognizing the ringtone, and answered it. "Detective Yang."

"Detective, this is Sanjay Patel."

"Uhm?" He didn't recognize the name immediately.

"From Patel's Market."

Now the penny dropped. "Oh yes, of course. What can I do for you, Mr. Patel?"

"You said to call you if that woman came back and behaved strangely."

"Emily Warner? The woman who claimed to have seen a stabbing?"

"I don't know her name, but yes, she came back yesterday evening. I was gonna call you right away, but then it got busy in the shop and I forgot. So I'm calling now. I hope it's not inconvenient."

"No, no, of course not. What happened? What did she claim to see this time?"

"Nothing. But she asked me about the stabbing that happened a month earlier. You know, I mentioned it when we talked."

"I remember."

"Well, she asked me if anybody witnessed the stabbing from a month ago, and I told her." There was a pause, and Yang felt that he was becoming impatient. But then Patel continued, "I even showed her a photo of the woman who saw the stabbing back then. It was the one who died recently. Madeline Bolton. It was all over the papers."

For a moment, Yang sat there, stunned. Jefferson shot him a curious look and mouthed 'what'.

"Are you saying that Madeline Bolton was a witness to the stabbing a month ago?"

"Yes, Detective. And that woman from two nights ago had a really odd look on her face when I told her. As if she saw a ghost or something. I hope it was alright to call you. I mean, you said…"

"Yes, Mr. Patel. Thank you very much for this information. I'll look into this woman to make sure she won't cause you any trouble."

"She didn't make trouble. Maybe she's not right in the head. Oh, and one other thing that was strange."

"What?"

"When she came to the store this time, she wasn't alone. She had a guide dog with her, you know the type blind people have. It said so on the dog's harness."

Surprise and bewilderment rose in Yang. Something clearly didn't add up. To Patel, he said, "Thank you again. If there's anything else, don't hesitate to call me, Mr. Patel." Then he disconnected the call.

Jefferson cast him a quick look then concentrated on traffic again. "What was that about? Are you still obsessed with the Maddie Bolton case? I thought you'd given up on that."

Yang sighed, not willing to tell Jefferson that he was still looking into the case. "Something odd just happened." He relayed his encounter with Emily Warner and the shopkeeper Sanjay Patel from two nights earlier as well as the conversation he'd just had with Patel. Yang made a mental note to look into the stabbing Madeline Bolton had witnessed. Perhaps Emily Warner had known about the incident and claimed to have seen it. Some crazies did anything to get attention.

"That's a little weird, I give you that," Jefferson said. "But that could be a total coincidence. I mean, D.C. is kind of a small town."

Yang tilted his head to the side and gave his partner a glance. "Yeah, not *that* small."

"Let it go, Adam. If the lieutenant finds out you're looking into something to do with Maddie Bolton, she's gonna have a fit. The Secret Service is on the case, and if there's something to find that's connecting this crazy chick to her, they'll find it."

"They might, they might not."

For a moment, there was silence between them, then Jefferson said, "You're gonna check it out anyway, aren't you?"

"Just for my own peace of mind."

"Don't let Arnold get wind of it."

"As long as you don't rat me out, she won't."

"My lips are sealed."

Moments later, they arrived at the park, where several police cruisers and a van belonging to the forensics team were parked. A uniformed officer led Yang and Jefferson to the spot where the body had been found. The area was wooded with lots of undergrowth that a regular jogger wouldn't have seen through. However, if a resident let his dog run off leash, which was illegal in the park, the dog would have been drawn to the scent of the decaying body.

When Yang and Jefferson reached the spot, they stopped and looked at the body.

The face was covered with dirt and leaves, but long, dark hair peeked out. She was white, petite, and slender. And completely naked. Not a stitch of clothing on her. Yang forced himself to study the body. The victim's soft tissue showed evidence of decay. He couldn't see what condition the dead woman's face was in, and he was glad for it. The body was already decomposing. Apart from the red marks around her wrists and neck, she had other injuries. Some, Yang guessed, had been inflicted before her death: cuts around her breasts and abdomen. Others that looked like bites could stem from animals who'd been attracted to the body by its odor. This woman had suffered greatly, he had no doubt about it. Yang swallowed the bile that rose, but he didn't have the option to look away. He was here to glean what he could from the scene to figure out how to best approach the case.

A female officer from the Crime Scene Investigations Division, who'd been crouching down next to the victim, rose and turned to them. Both Yang and Jefferson had worked with her numerous times before.

"Detectives," Lupe Serrano greeted them.

The thirty-four-year-old dark-haired Puerto Rican had a figure that many a man in the Police Department paid a second glance. Unfortunately, nobody had succeeded in catching Lupe's eye. Yang knew from personal experience that Lupe was only interested in women, a fact she didn't widely publicize. Not because she was ashamed of it, but because it was nobody's business, she'd told Yang. It had made the rejection easier to swallow for Yang, who at the time had just separated from his wife.

Jefferson motioned to the body. "Lupe, I see you're always getting the grisly cases."

She shrugged. "Are there any that aren't?"

"You've got a point," Jefferson said.

"So," Yang started, "what can you tell us so far?"

Lupe pointed to the victim. "White female, ligature marks around her wrists and ankles. Looks like she was bound for an extended period. Can't tell yet if she was raped, the autopsy will reveal that, but my guess? Probably."

"Cause of death?" Yang asked.

"None of the knife marks are deep enough to be the cause of death, and there's no gunshot wound... My best guess is strangulation."

Yang looked at the contusions on her neck and nodded. If Lupe was correct, then this was personal. Strangulation always was. Which could be a good thing, because it suggested that the victim knew her murderer. It would give them a starting point—as long as they could identify the victim.

"Find any ID?" Jefferson asked, clearly thinking the same as Yang.

Lupe shook her head. "Not a scrap." Then she pointed to the victim's hands. "She has defensive wounds on her hands and forearms. We'll get her fingerprints and see if she's in the system. We'll check her teeth, see whether we can determine anything from her dental work, if she had any done. DNA won't be a problem. But she looks very young, maybe not even eighteen. It's unlikely that her profile is in any DNA database, unless she has a juvenile record."

Yang felt a shudder run down his spine. So young. A girl whose life had been cut short. Were her parents looking for her?

"When can you get the autopsy done?" Yang asked.

"A day or two?" Lupe said. "At least the preliminaries. The tox screen will take longer."

"Thanks, Lupe, the sooner the better."

Because somewhere there had to be a family that missed this girl.

And the sooner they could identify her, the sooner they could find her killer. Without identification, they had nothing to go on.

26

DURING HIS LUNCH BREAK the same day, Yang logged into the system to look into the stabbing that Madeline Bolton had witnessed a month before her death. After searching for a little bit, he found the report he was looking for. It didn't take long to read it. The facts were pretty straight forward.

The perpetrator, a man named Roy Wozniak, whose priors were longer than Yang's arm, had mugged a tourist in the alley next to Patel's market. The man, Clay Kinsky from Pittsburgh, hadn't wanted to part with his possessions. That's when Wozniak had used the knife on him, stabbing him in the gut.

Madeline Bolton had just left her accountant's office half a block away and was walking toward her parked car, when she'd come across the mugging. She'd immediately yelled for help, alerting Wozniak.

Wozniak ran off with the tourist's wallet and watch, while Madeline Bolton had called 9-1-1 and helped the wounded man. Once the ambulance had arrived to take care of Kinsky, Madeline stayed at the scene to be interviewed by the arriving police.

By the time Wozniak was apprehended, he'd disposed of the wallet and watch, as well as the bloody knife and the clothes he'd worn during the commission of the crime. The tourist was too traumatized to be able to positively identify Wozniak. Only Madeline could say with one-hundred-percent certainty, that Wozniak was the culprit.

Yang wondered whether Wozniak, who was looking at another stint in prison, had decided to eliminate Madeline so she couldn't testify against him at his upcoming trial. It was a distinct possibility.

Yang read on. Wozniak hadn't been able to make bail, and was therefore held in jail until his trial. He couldn't have killed Madeline himself. But a man like Wozniak knew enough other ex-cons who could do the job for him.

However, two things made the assumption that Madeline was killed so she couldn't testify against Wozniak, very unlikely. Wozniak was hardly sophisticated enough to stage an accident such as the one Madeline had had. He was a smash-and-grab kind of criminal. The second reason was even more compelling. On the page where all evidence against Wozniak was listed, one stuck out: with her cell phone, Madeline had taken a photo of Wozniak in the act. Even with Madeline dead, Wozniak would still be convicted. He wouldn't gain anything by killing Madeline.

The entire file never mentioned any other witnesses, making it unlikely that Emily Warner had seen the same stabbing. Still, she could have easily read about it in the papers. However, it left him baffled as to why she would claim to have seen the stabbing two days earlier when it was easy to verify with the CCTV footage that there'd been no stabbing that day. He could only conclude that Emily Warner was a lunatic.

27

Sᴛ. Pᴀᴜʟ's Eᴘɪsᴄᴏᴘᴀʟ Cʜᴜʀᴄʜ was a historic church located in Rock Creek Parish in the Northwest of Washington D.C. The church had been built in 1775 and rebuilt and restored several times in the centuries that followed. Surrounding the church and amidst a rolling landscape lay Rock Creek Cemetery. It was a warm, sunny day. A large white canopy had been erected to shield the guests, many of whom were wearing black, from the rays of the sun. Underneath in the shade, rows of chairs had been placed, but there hadn't been enough. Numerous people stood at the back and the sides to attend.

Maddie had been popular, though Eric Bolton suspected that some of the people whose faces he didn't recognize were curious onlookers as well as reporters working for the tabloids. While they didn't carry large cameras, he noticed that some of them raised their smart phones to take pictures. No doubt, tomorrow, when this was over, many of the prominent mourners would find their faces pictured in the newspapers, and speculations about Maddie's death would continue.

Maddie's casket was draped with white lilies and a lone bouquet of Forget-me-nots. Bolton knew he would be true to the flowers' promise. He would never forget Maddie, never let a day go by without remembering his little girl. And each time, his heart would break anew. He had no idea how to get through the memorial without breaking down. As her father, he had written a eulogy, but it had become evident that he wouldn't be able to deliver it. Natalie had realized it too and offered to read his and Rita's words from the podium that stood in front of the rows of chairs.

When Natalie walked up on the platform that was raised about a foot so all guests could see her, the murmurs in the crowd ebbed and everybody fell silent. In her black shift dress that accented her slim figure, she looked out at the mourners, pulled the microphone closer to her face, and began.

"The words that I'm speaking are my father's and my mother's, but they might as well be mine, because they reflect my own feelings, my own grief..." She looked at Bolton and his wife and sniffled, before continuing, "Madeline might not have been my blood, but she was my family, and I loved her."

Bolton felt his eyes tear up. He was proud of Natalie, proud that she represented the family when neither he nor his wife could do it. She continued speaking about Maddie and what she'd meant to everybody, talked about Maddie's love for her parents and recounted stories from their childhood together. Natalie glossed over the difficulties Maddie had in her teens and early twenties and emphasized her joy of life and her dreams. Bolton lost himself in the good memories and pushed all others away.

Next to him, Rita wept silently, her eyes hidden behind large, dark sunglasses. Bolton held her hand and squeezed it, and she leaned into him. He put his arm around her and pressed her to him. It pained him to see his wife like this. He felt so helpless, because there was nothing he could do to ease her grief.

Natalie's eulogy was followed by Mike Faulkner's. The Chief of Staff had been Maddie's godfather. He talked about Madeline's achievements and her quick wit, relaying anecdotes from her life that made the mourners chuckle in spite of the solemn occasion. At the end, Faulkner conveyed President Langford's message of condolence. Bolton knew that his old friend Robert Langford wanted to attend the memorial, but knew that his presence would draw even more journalists, not to speak of the many locals and tourists who would show up to get a glimpse of the President.

The last speaker was the priest. He led the congregation in prayer. "The Lord is my shepherd..."

Bolton wasn't a religious man, but he hoped there was life after death, because if there was, he could hope that one day he would see Maddie again. One day, their family would be reunited.

After the prayer, three black women in white floor-length robes began to sing. Bolton had left the choice of hymns to Natalie. She knew music and went to church regularly—unlike the rest of the Boltons. He'd expected a religious hymn and was surprised to hear a song by a popular musician.

"Would you know my name if I saw you in heaven?" the women sang a cappella.

When he heard the first words, Bolton suppressed a sob. Eric Clapton's song, 'Tears in Heaven', a memorial to his son Conor, who'd fallen to his death as a four-year-old, was the perfect song to say goodbye to Madeline. Bolton looked to Natalie and met her eyes. He mouthed 'thank you' to her, before tears obstructed his vision.

The rest of the memorial passed in a blur for Bolton. The casket was lowered into the grave, and he just stood there, holding onto Rita, who seemed more fragile than ever before. To her other side, Natalie had taken her arm, supporting her mother in this difficult moment. Natalie's husband, Paul Sullivan, stood next to her, and to Bolton's surprise, even his eyes were moist, though he and Maddie had never truly gotten along. But he was family.

Bolton looked at the many faces that passed by the grave. The mourners tossed flower petals down onto the casket. A hole in the dirt, Bolton mused, a hole that would forever house the remains of his beloved child. No amount of beautiful flowers could disguise the fact that this was the end to a life cut short.

After everybody had had their turn, the priest approached Bolton and his immediate family and said a few words of solace and shook their hands before he and the three singers walked away. Some others left too, but many stayed, gathering in small groups to talk. Many of the mourners knew each other either from social functions, through connections at work, or because they were somehow related to each other.

Bolton spotted Faulkner and caught his eye. He gave his son-in-law Paul a sign and he came around to take Rita's arm, while Bolton met with Faulkner. He shook his old friend's hand.

"Thank you, Mike. We're all very grateful to you for speaking about Maddie."

Faulkner nodded. "I can't even imagine how you must feel."

Behind him, Caleb came into view. He approached.

"Uh, Caleb," Bolton greeted him. "Thank you for coming."

Caleb looked every inch the elegant young bachelor he was, the black suit accentuating his brown hair and fair skin. Caleb reached for Bolton's hand and shook it. "It's a loss for all of us. We all loved Maddie." He motioned to a group of people standing farther away. "Everybody from the charity came to pay their respects."

Bolton forced a smile despite the ache in his heart. "You'll tell them that Rita and I appreciate their kindness, won't you?" He'd seen the wreath the charity employees had bought.

"Of course, I will," Caleb said in a calm tone. Then he looked at his father, "I'll wait by the car."

Faulkner nodded. "I'll be right there."

Caleb walked to the group of charity employees and stopped there to talk, and Bolton turned his gaze back to Faulkner, when he saw a man approach from the other side. Bolton narrowed his eyes.

"How dare he show up here?" Bolton muttered under his breath.

"Who?" Faulkner looked over his shoulder, saw who was walking toward them, and put a hand on Bolton's forearm. "Take it easy. You don't want a scene."

Faulkner was right, he didn't want a scene with Diego Sanchez. But what was also true was that he didn't want the philandering lobbyist who'd dated Maddie besmirching this day.

But perhaps a scene was unavoidable. Diego Sanchez was steering toward Bolton. He was older than Maddie by almost ten years, which was strike one he had against him. Strike two was the fact that he was known to juggle women like a bartender handled bottles. The man was undeniably charming, a smooth talker if there ever was one. He had the looks for it too: tall, dark hair, olive skin, a typical Latin lover. Apparently women liked the type, but all Bolton had ever been able to see in him was a dishonest pompous ass.

Then there was strike three against him. He'd seduced Maddie and made her break off her engagement to a man who had worshipped the ground she walked on. That was the one thing Bolton couldn't forgive him. He'd hoped that Maddie would leave Sanchez once she realized what a mistake she'd made, but despite the fact that Sanchez would fly into a jealous rage every so often, whether in public or private, Maddie had always gone back to him. The tabloids had loved it. It was a constant 'on and off' relationship. Yes, Diego Sanchez was bad news.

Dressed in an expensive black designer suit with a violet tie, Diego Sanchez stopped in front of Bolton. He offered his hand. "My deepest condolences, Mr. Bolton."

Bolton ignored the proffered hand. "You shouldn't have come."

Sanchez retracted his hand. "I loved her. She would have wanted me to be here."

Bolton snorted. "I doubt that very much." He felt his heart contract painfully. "Because if you'd loved her, you would have treated her right."

Sanchez's jaw looked tighter when he responded, "Maddie and I had a complicated relationship. But we loved each other, and I grieve for her as much as you and your wife do." His voice grew louder and drew the looks of several mourners upon him. "My heart is broken, because I can never again tell her how much I love her. You're not the only one who lost her."

"Get out of my sight!" Bolton ground out, keenly aware that the reporters among the mourners were snapping pictures of the exchange.

Faulkner stepped between Bolton and Sanchez. "Mr. Sanchez, I think it would be best if you left," he said calmly. The two knew each other. Their paths had crossed many times.

Sanchez nodded. "If you would convey my condolences to Mrs. Bolton, please," he said before pivoting.

Sanchez almost collided with another mourner, Lars Nielson. Bolton noticed both of them freeze and stare at each other. For a moment, he wondered if Lars would take the opportunity to punch Diego, but he knew it wouldn't happen. Lars wasn't that kind of man. There was nothing violent in his personality. The tall blond man with the easy smile, the blue eyes, and the gentle demeanor was the polar opposite of the fiery Latino who'd stolen his fiancée without regret. Lars had pleaded with Maddie to come back to him, offered her to forgive her fling with Diego, but Maddie hadn't listened. Lars should have become Bolton's son-in-law, in fact, the wedding would have been this month, but instead of a wedding to organize, his family had to organize a funeral.

"Lars," Bolton said.

With a look of contempt directed at Sanchez, Lars walked past him to greet Bolton, "Eric, I'm so sorry. You and Rita must be heartbroken."

Bolton took his extended hand and shook it, then put his hand on the young Swede's shoulder and pulled him to his chest. "It's so good of you to come. Rita was hoping to see you." Over Lars's shoulder, Bolton saw Sanchez leave. He hoped he'd never have to see that man's face again.

28

"WHO'S THE MAN HUGGING MADELINE'S FATHER?" Emily asked breathlessly.

Emily had convinced Vicky to accompany her to Madeline Bolton's memorial service. When she'd found out that it was going to be an open-air event, she'd figured that it would be very hard for the family to control access to it. Surely, lots of curious people would attend, as well as people who were mere acquaintances, therefore Emily and Vicky wouldn't stick out as unusual. And it had worked. During the eulogies, Vicky and Emily had stayed at the fringes like many others for whom there weren't enough seats underneath the canopy.

Emily wore a sleeveless black shift dress with a black cardigan as well as sunglasses. She'd had to lend Vicky a navy-blue ensemble since Vicky didn't possess anything even remotely subdued, which she, too, had accented with dark glasses. Had Vicky worn any of her colorful clothes, they would undoubtedly have attracted attention—which Emily didn't want to risk. She was here to observe, to learn about Maddie, her family and friends. She hadn't expected to recognize somebody here. That was the reason for taking Vicky along. She knew who was who. Emily was still learning to recognize people's faces. But there was one face she had recognized immediately.

"The blond hunk?"

"Yes."

"That's Lars Nielson," Vicky whispered back. "He's a diplomat with the Swedish Embassy, some attaché or something, not sure. But Maddie and he were engaged. According to the tabloids, she broke it off."

"She did? Why?"

"Because of that guy over there." Vicky pointed to a Hispanic man stalking away from Bolton. It seemed the two had had an argument just before Nielson had joined them.

"Who is he?"

"Diego Sanchez. Apparently Maddie left this hunk"—she pointed to the blond Swede—"for that hunk." She motioned to Diego Sanchez. Vicky shrugged. "Frankly, I'd have a hard time choosing too. Both are kind of yummy."

"I saw him," Emily said.

"Who?"

"Lars Nielson."

"Where did you see him?"

Emily glanced around her to make sure none of the mourners were close enough to overhear her. "In one of my visions. Lars Nielson was the angry man that I saw in the reflection of a store window. Maddie showed him to me." At least that's what she had to assume. "I think Maddie wants to tell me something."

"Tell you what?"

"I don't know. There has to be a reason why he looked in the vision like he wanted to hurt somebody. I think I have to talk to him."

"And say what to him? Hey, hunk, I've seen you with Maddie's eyes?" Vicky said full of sarcasm.

Emily couldn't blame her. It did sound crazy. But somehow she had to speak to him. Maybe it would help her understand why she saw things that Maddie had seen. There had to be a reason for it. "I don't know what to say. Perhaps Maddie has a message for him. Perhaps she wants to apologize, you know? For dumping him? She could have unfinished business."

Vicky sighed. Emily had told her that Maddie had witnessed the stabbing in the alley next to the convenience store, the same stabbing Emily had seen in a vision. Reluctantly, Vicky had agreed that it was odd that Maddie had witnessed the incident and that Emily had had a vision of it in the exact same spot.

"Fine," Vicky said. "Let's talk to him."

They waited until Lars said his goodbyes to the Bolton family. In the meantime, Emily let her eyes wander, while Vicky pointed out this or that person she recognized from the tabloids. Clearly, Madeline had been popular, and her family knew everybody who was anybody in Washington D.C. But the connections and her popularity hadn't saved her from her fate. For an instant, Emily recalled how close she herself had come to death. She was grateful for having survived, even if the last fifteen years hadn't always been easy. Before drifting too far into the past, Emily nudged Vicky.

"I think he's leaving."

Together they made a beeline for Lars Nielson, though Emily had no idea what to say to him. It turned out she wouldn't have had to worry about how to start the conversation. A few yards away from Nielson, a man in a dark suit blocked their approach.

"Can I help you, ladies?" the man asked stiffly.

It wasn't a pick-up line, Emily understood immediately. The man was no mourner. He was security.

"Uhm, we just wanted to say hello to a friend," Vicky said and pointed in Nielson's general direction.

"Right," the man said. "Nice try, but Mr. Nielson isn't speaking to reporters."

"We're not reporters," Emily protested. She looked past the security guy's shoulder and noticed that Nielson was already walking toward a waiting car. Her opportunity to talk to Maddie's ex-fiancé was slipping away.

But the security guy wasn't budging. He narrowed his eyes. "I suggest you ladies leave the mourners alone," he said icily.

Vicky put her hand on Emily's arm. "That's just rude." She lifted her chin. "Let's go, Emily."

Reluctantly, Emily allowed her friend to pull her away. She would have to find another way to talk to Lars Nielson.

29

Yang had done his homework and researched who would be attending Madeline Bolton's funeral so he would recognize the faces. He was here on his own time. Something still bothered him about Madeline Bolton's death, and he wasn't ready to let it go. He'd come to watch the crowd, see who interacted with whom, who cried and who didn't, who made a scene, and who kept in the shadows.

Yang had dressed in a dark-gray suit so he could blend into the crowd. The funeral was well attended, comprised of friends, family, acquaintances, and people the deceased most likely knew from her involvement in a children's charity. Yang had watched the altercation between Eric Bolton and Diego Sanchez, and had noticed that the President's Chief of Staff, Mike Faulkner, had intervened so the situation didn't get out of hand. He'd also noticed several foreign dignitaries among the mourners, Maddie's Swedish ex-fiancé, as well as a few men who worked for the Russian embassy, though he didn't know their names. There were more foreign dignitaries among the crowd, evidenced by the presence of lots of security personnel. While the security personnel didn't wear uniforms, Yang could spot them a mile away. They moved differently than normal people, and their eyes roamed, always on full alert.

Whom he hadn't expected to see here was Emily Warner. He'd had to do a double take when he'd spotted her being stopped by Nielson's protective detail. She'd even brought reinforcements this time. The pretty Asian woman now pulled her away from the security guard. Was she as crazy as Emily Warner, or could she be her caretaker? Either way, Emily Warner and her companion shouldn't be here.

Nielson's security detail had made the right call in stopping her from approaching the diplomat. Yang would have done the same. She showed all the signs of a stalker. It was a shame, really, because if he'd met her under different circumstances, he would have found her attractive. But he was done with women who turned out to be crazy. His soon-to-be ex-wife Barb had turned his life into a shit show with her crazy claims of what Yang had supposedly promised her when they'd gotten married. Now she was using his amorous text messages against him during the divorce proceedings. Hence his tolerance for crazy women was at an all-time low.

He kept watching Emily and her companion as they walked away from the congregation. There was something about Emily. Her disappointment of not being able to talk to Nielson showed on her face. She didn't hide her feelings. She appeared truly sad, as if she'd failed in whatever task she'd set for herself. Odd, he thought. She didn't look tinfoil-hat crazy.

Yet she was attending Madeline Bolton's funeral as if they'd been friends. But had she been a friend, surely, she would have gone to greet Madeline's family and expressed her condolences like many of the other mourners did. The fact that Emily didn't even attempt to speak to the Boltons was even more reason to assume that she had no business being there. Yang tore his gaze from Emily and her companion. Just in time, he had to realize, because he now spotted two black men he recognized: Secret Service Agents Banning and Mitchell.

"Shit," he cursed low under his breath.

It wasn't unusual that law enforcement attended the funerals of those whose deaths they investigated. They had every right to be here. Yang, however, didn't. If the two agents saw him, they would recognize him. It would get back to his superiors, and he'd be in trouble for going against his lieutenant's express order to leave Madeline Bolton's case to the Secret Service.

Quickly, he ducked behind a group of mourners and turned in the other direction, before a copse of trees provided him with cover. From a safe distance, he peered back at the group of mourners and spotted Banning and Mitchell again. They were looking in his direction, but their gazes roamed, and Yang was certain they hadn't spotted him. Still behind the trees, he felt his cell phone vibrate. He pulled it from his pocket and checked caller ID.

"Hey, Simon," he answered.

"Where are you, Adam?" Jefferson asked.

"Running an errand," Yang lied. "What's up?"

"Autopsy on our Jane Doe is done."

"I'll meet you at the coroner's in half an hour."

"See you there."

30

SIMON JEFFERSON WAS ALREADY WAITING outside the large, glass-fronted building on E Street that housed the Office of the Chief Medical Examiner when Yang arrived. He was on his cell phone, finishing a call.

Jefferson looked him up and down, put his cell phone in his pocket, and motioned to Yang's suit. "Who died?"

"I had a meeting with my lawyer," Yang lied.

In the foyer, they showed their badges, signed in, and were directed to one of the autopsy rooms. Lupe Serrano, dressed in scrubs, was expecting them. She could have sent the autopsy report to their office, but she knew that Yang preferred seeing the body again and getting a verbal run-down of all pertinent issues found during the autopsy.

After a short greeting, Lupe motioned them closer to the female body on the stainless-steel table, a white sheet covering everything below the shoulders. The body had been cleaned up, including her face, which Yang now looked at for the first time. Her face was damaged by the elements and portions of flesh seemed to have been removed, exposing parts of the skull.

Lupe noticed Yang and Jefferson staring at the victim's face. "Bite marks from a wild animal. Most likely a raccoon," she explained. "In addition, the early, hot summer sped up the decomposition. It appears that her body was barely covered with anything, leaving her exposed to the elements. It'll make facial recognition difficult." She was very matter-of-fact, her voice not betraying any emotions. In the job that she held, it was a protective mechanism. Otherwise, dealing with death on a daily basis could turn into an emotional rollercoaster.

"How long has she been dead?" Jefferson asked.

"At least a month, possibly longer. Because her body wasn't covered adequately, I believe that whoever dropped her there was in a hurry. He wasn't taking time to dig a grave and instead just put her into a shallow ditch and tossed vegetation and brush over her. Entomology will help us determine date of death more accurately."

"You mean insects?" Yang asked.

"And the eggs they lay in a corpse. Depending on what state the larvae are in, we can tell—"

"Did I mention I just had lunch?" Jefferson interrupted. "No need to go into details."

Yang could only second Jefferson's sentiment. He wasn't fond of insects and their larvae either.

Lupe shook her head and sighed. Then she pointed to the victim's jaw. "Her teeth are intact. And they're helping me pin down her age."

"In which way?" Yang asked with interest.

"Well, the first two permanent incisors and permanent molars emerge between age six and eight, most of the remaining permanent teeth between age ten and twelve. But wisdom teeth only appear around age eighteen. X-rays showed that the victim's wisdom teeth haven't fully formed yet. Which suggests she's not eighteen yet."

"Can you narrow that down a bit?" Yang asked and exchanged a look with Jefferson. "NamUS will give us way too many hits if all we know is that she's a Caucasian female under age eighteen." NamUS was the National Missing and Unidentified Persons System.

Lupe raised her hand. "I'm not done."

"Sorry."

"I examined her reproductive organs and pelvis. It's likely that this girl wasn't menstruating yet. These days, the average age for menstruation is twelve years, though it can range from ten to fifteen years. Unfortunately, tests for estrogen were inconclusive due to the level of decomposition. Looking at the development of her breasts, however, which are rather small for her height, I'm also tending toward younger. My best guess is that she's between eleven and thirteen years old."

"A child," Yang murmured to himself.

Lupe nodded. "Yes, and one that had her innocence brutally taken from her."

Neither Yang nor Jefferson had to ask what it meant.

"There was significant damage to her genitals. She was raped, and not just once. I swabbed her for semen but given the state of decomposition, I'm not confident that we can get the rapist's DNA profile from semen. Considering that she was also bound by her hands and feet"—she lifted the sheet from the girl to show the ligature marks on the girls wrists and ankles—"I believe she was held captive somewhere. So she must have had lots of contact with the perpetrator. There's a chance that we can find touch DNA, but again, the elements as well as wild animals may have destroyed any trace."

"Damn. And the cause of death?" Yang forced himself to ask calmly, even though he didn't feel calm. He was enraged. Somebody had kidnapped, raped, and killed a child.

Lupe pointed to the girl's neck. "Strangulation."

"A rope?"

"No, no ligature was used. The perp used his hands. It takes a special kind of killer to squeeze the life out of a child, looking into his victim's eyes. She has defensive wounds on her hands and arms. She fought him."

"A psycho," Jefferson said.

"I leave that part to you, Detectives," Lupe said. "I'm just trying to tell you as much as I can about the girl so you can identify her. Which brings me to fingerprints. We've already run them through IAFAS. No hit, which didn't surprise me."

Yang understood. The Integrated Automated Fingerprint Identification System wouldn't contain the fingerprints of a twelve or thirteen-year-old girl unless she had a juvenile record.

"But," Lupe added quickly, "we did find skin and blood cells underneath several of her fingernails. They might be from her attacker. I've sent them for DNA testing."

"That's promising," Yang said. At least one good piece of news.

"Any other marks on her? Tattoos?" Jefferson asked eagerly.

Lupe shook her head. "No. Despite the cuts she has on her torso, which were most likely inflicted within the month before her death, I couldn't find any old scars. She still has her appendix. An x-ray confirmed that she's never broken a bone."

The fact that it appeared that the girl had had no operations made it impossible to cross-reference any hits from the missing persons register with local hospital records. They needed more information.

"Height? Weight?" Yang asked, grasping for any scrap that could be useful.

"Between four foot eleven and five foot tall, weighing between ninety and ninety-five pounds."

Yang pointed at the girl's hair. "Is that her natural hair color?"

"Yes, very dark brown, almost black. Her eyes are blue, a very light blue, though decomposition of the eyeballs has already clouded the lenses." She stretched her hand out to lift the girl's lids.

"Not necessary," Jefferson said quickly to stop her.

Yang echoed Jefferson's sentiment. It was one thing looking at a dead body, it was another to stare into a victim's dead eyes.

Lupe tossed them both a challenging look. "I hadn't pegged you for being squeamish."

"Big lunch, remember?" Jefferson said.

"Okay then," Lupe said. "I'll send the official autopsy report over when I get the tox screen and the DNA analysis back."

"That's great," Yang said. "Call us immediately when you get the DNA analysis back—I'm keen on finding out if we have the killer's DNA."

If the killer had previously committed a crime or been imprisoned, his DNA would be stored in CODIS, the Combined DNA Index System the FBI maintained, containing DNA profiles contributed by federal, state, and local participating forensic laboratories.

"Will do."

"In the meantime, we'd better slog through missing persons," Jefferson said.

"Let's get to work," Yang agreed.

31

Vicky would have called her crazy, that's why Emily hadn't told her about her plan. Casually dressed, and armed with her dark sunglasses, Coffee by her side, Emily pressed the doorbell of the small terraced house in the Anacostia neighborhood of Washington D.C. It was early evening but still light. The days were getting longer, and Emily was glad for it, because she loved taking strolls now that she could admire the sites of the city with her eyes.

The door opened, and a woman in her late forties said, "Yes?"

Emily recognized her from one of the newspaper articles Vicky had set aside for her. Lucia Garcia was the person who'd found Maddie Bolton and called 9-1-1. As Maddie's housekeeper, Emily hoped the woman could fill in some blanks when it came to understanding Maddie and what had happened to her. It had taken a little time to figure out where Lucia lived, but in the end she'd found the address.

"Lucia Garcia?" Emily asked, not directly looking at the woman. She had to play her part to get the woman to talk to her, and she'd found that people were much less likely to slam the door in the face of a person with a disability—which was also the reason why she'd brought Coffee. He completed the picture.

"Yes, that's me."

"I'm Emily Warner," she said. "I'm sorry to intrude, ma'am, but I volunteer for a podcast for the blind, and our listeners would like to hear more about Madeline Bolton." She sighed. "It's so tragic what happened to her. It must be very hard for you, having found her... I'm sorry, you're probably not comfortable talking to a stranger about her."

Emily made a half-hearted attempt at turning away from her as if she was planning to leave.

"No, please, stay. Would you like to come in?"

"Oh, that's so kind."

"Watch out, there's a step up," Lucia said.

Emily directed Coffee to lead her into the house, and Lucia gave her verbal instructions to get to the kitchen.

Once they sat down, Lucia asked, "Would you like something to drink?"

Emily shook her head. "No, thank you, you're too kind. Do you mind if I use my phone to record us? Unfortunately taking notes is—"

"No problem," Lucia interrupted.

Emily pulled her cell phone from her pocket and spoke into it. "Start voice recording."

"That's very fancy," Lucia commented.

"It helps a lot. Also with directions and all." While she said it, she felt guilty for misleading the woman. She appeared very caring and sweet, a good soul. But Emily also knew that she wasn't doing this to harm anybody. All she wanted was to find out what Maddie wanted her to know, what unfinished business she might have.

"The newspapers reported that you found Miss Bolton when you arrived for work that morning. That must have been awful."

"It was terrible. She was such a nice woman, so kind to me. She paid me well. She didn't like cooking or cleaning." She chuckled to herself. "I always made something for her and put it in the fridge to heat up in the evening or on the weekend. 'Cause I didn't work weekends." She sniffled. "And now..."

Emily felt the woman's grief. "It sounds like you were like family to her."

Lucia nodded. "Oh, I loved that girl. You know, I used to work for her parents when Maddie was younger, and then when she decided to live on her own, Mrs. Bolton said she wouldn't hold it against me if I went to work for Maddie." She smiled as if remembering something. "I think Mrs. Bolton wanted to make sure somebody looked after her."

"Like any mother," Emily murmured, remembering at that moment how much she missed her own mother.

"Yes, and Maddie was no good at housework. If I hadn't gone grocery shopping for her twice a week, I'm sure she wouldn't have eaten anything."

"You took good care of her."

Again, Lucia nodded. "That's why it was all so terrible. Finding her like that."

"The newspapers didn't say much about what actually happened to her, other than it was a household accident."

"It shouldn't have happened." Lucia sniffled, this time a little louder. She reached into her pocket and pulled out a crumpled-up handkerchief and blew her nose. "I'm sorry. But I didn't even know she knew where I kept the spare light bulbs."

"Light bulbs?"

"Yes, she was trying to change a light in the living room and fell off the stepladder." Lucia's eyes were rimmed with tears and a sob choked up her voice. "She hit her head on the glass table. There was so much shattered glass... Why didn't she wait for me? I would have done it for her."

A shattered glass table. Emily suppressed a gasp. The vision had shown her how Maddie had died. Emily waited, letting the grieving woman take a few breaths.

"She was so bright, you know, so smart when it came to book learning and all that, but when it came to doing things around the house, she wasn't brought up to do things for herself. There was always somebody to do everything for her... But why she would not have taken off her shoes when she stepped on the ladder, I'll never know."

Emily held her breath. "Her shoes?"

"Yes, those really expensive ones with the high heels. I don't know how she could walk in them. But to step on a ladder in high heels, who does that?"

Who indeed? No matter how inept Madeline may have been when it came to household chores, even a woman like Madeline Bolton would have known to take off her high heels before stepping on a ladder, even a stepladder. The risk of losing one's balance was so much greater without a stable footing.

"You're sure she fell off a ladder?"

"Yes. It was right there, lying across her legs. It must have toppled over when she fell."

"That's awful," Emily said with compassion. She felt a connection to Maddie, the kind of connection one would have to a sibling. Not that Emily knew from experience. She'd been an only child.

"She had some wine and must have lost her balance, you know, but she could hold her liquor." Lucia put her hand to her mouth and stared at the cell phone, which was still recording. "Please don't tell your listeners about that. She wasn't a drunk, she just enjoyed a glass or two in the evenings."

"Of course, I won't mention anything about that. I'll only take bits and pieces of this recording to give my listeners a good impression of Miss Bolton. Nobody wants to drag her image through the mud."

"Thank you."

Emily felt bad having to keep up the charade, but the ruse had loosened Lucia's tongue and revealed something crucial: either Madeline had been utterly careless by wearing high heels on a ladder, or somebody had made it look like an accident but had overlooked the shoes. A man, she thought, because a woman would notice details about another woman. And there was only one reason why somebody would stage an accident—to cover up a murder.

Was that what Maddie wanted her to see? Was that her unfinished business, getting justice for her untimely death? Was that what Emily's visions were all about?

There was only one way to find out. She had to continue digging. And Lars Nielson was the first man she needed to talk to. Maddie had called off their wedding because of another man. How had Nielson taken it? Had he decided that if he couldn't have Madeline, no other man could have her either? Was that why he'd looked so furious in her vision?

Another question remained: How could she get access to Nielson in order to talk to him?

32

YANG AND JEFFERSON had spent many hours going through the hits the database for missing children in the Washington D.C. area had spit out. They'd waded through the cases and thrown out all those that didn't fit the criteria Lupe Serrano had given them the previous day, eliminating those that clearly didn't fit the dead body. In the end, they'd narrowed the results down to three girls that all fit in terms of race, age, eye color, hair color, and height.

Yang and Jefferson were about to head out to visit the families of the three girls, when they got a call from Lupe Serrano.

Yang put the call on speaker. "Lupe, you got anything for us?" Yang asked, hoping for a piece of good news.

"We were lucky. The blood and skin cells under our Jane Doe's fingernails don't belong to her. We were able to get a full DNA profile. I've already uploaded it to CODIS. You should get the results shortly. I'll have it sent to your email as soon as I get it."

"Thanks, Lupe, that's great," Yang said.

The Combined DNA Index System enabled forensic laboratories to exchange and compare DNA profiles electronically. So even if the perpetrator was from out of state, they could get a match—as long as he was in the system. However, if he'd never been caught before, they were out of luck, and would have to identify the victim first and find a suspect the good old-fashioned way: through examining the girl's life, her family, her friends, and her routines.

"Oh yeah," Lupe added, "I ran the girl's DNA through the system this morning, and like I suspected, there was no match, not even a partial one."

Yang nodded to Jefferson.

"So, none of her relatives are in the system either?" Jefferson asked.

"No, sorry."

"Thanks, Lupe," Jefferson said, and Yang disconnected the call.

"You didn't really expect her DNA to be in the system?" Jefferson asked with a raised eyebrow.

"Occasionally, I like to be surprised." Yang grimaced. "Let's go and see whether we can give our Jane Doe a real name. We have three missing girls that match our Jane Doe's description."

Olga and James Zimmerman lived on the second floor of a duplex in Mount Pleasant, a middleclass neighborhood in the Northwest of the city. Their apartment was small but had high ceilings and a pleasant, airy feel. The rays of the late afternoon sun streamed in through large windows.

After showing their badges and asking to speak to them about the missing person report they'd filed, Olga Zimmerman invited them to come into the eat-in kitchen, where her husband joined them. Husband and wife looked to be in their mid to late forties. While the woman had a heavy foreign accent, her husband spoke with flawless American English.

"I'll make some tea," Olga said and reached for the kettle.

Her husband motioned to the chairs around the kitchen table, and Yang and Jefferson sat down.

"So you have news about Tatjana?" Zimmerman asked eagerly, glancing at his wife, who now joined them and sat next to her husband, clutching his hand.

"You found her?" she asked with a hopeful glimmer in her eyes.

Yang swallowed. This type of conversation was never easy. "You reported your daughter Tatjana missing six weeks ago?"

Olga nodded.

"She's not our daughter," Zimmerman interrupted.

Yang looked down at his notes. "It says here—"

"What he means is that she's not our real daughter." She looked at her husband. "What is it called again?"

Zimmerman squeezed his wife's hand. "She's our foster child."

"Why don't we start from the beginning?" Jefferson suggested. "When did she come to live with you?"

"About eight months ago," Zimmerman started. "See, Olga"—he looked at his wife—"is from Russia, and there was a need for Russian speaking foster parents. So we talked about it. I don't speak much Russian, but Olga is teaching me, so I can communicate better with Tatjana."

"So Tatjana is Russian?" Yang pointed to his notes. "It says here she's thirteen."

Olga sighed. "A sweet girl, but so troubled. She's gone through so much."

Yang nodded. Foster kids were often handed from one family to another, one bad situation to another. "So she's been in the foster system for a long time?"

"Oh no," Zimmerman said. "We're her first placement. She was trafficked, and then rescued by an organization who then worked with the foster care system to find a temporary home for her and the other girls until the biological parents could be found."

"In Russia," Olga added. "We knew that she wasn't going to stay with us forever, but we wanted to help. It's terrible what those people do to the girls. That's why they wanted somebody who at least spoke their language."

Yang exchanged a look with Jefferson.

Jefferson sighed. "That's very admirable of you to take her in and care for her. So what happened six weeks ago?"

"Yes," Yang added, "how did Tatjana disappear?"

Zimmerman looked at his wife, then sighed. "It's my fault. I was supposed to pick her up from her weekly group therapy session, but I got delayed at work, and by the time I got there, she was gone. We couldn't find her anywhere."

"And you reported her missing the same day?" Jefferson asked.

"Of course," Olga said. "No girl her age should be out alone at night. It's too dangerous. She's so young."

Though Yang had seen Tatjana's picture on her missing persons record, he asked, "Do you have a current photo of Tatjana?"

Olga produced her cell phone, and a moment later she laid it in front of Yang and Jefferson. "That's Tatjana."

Yang and Jefferson looked at the photo. The image matched the girl's photo on file. But was she the girl that they'd found a few days earlier? There were certainly similarities, but it was impossible to make a positive ID. They needed more information.

"Detectives," Zimmerman said into the silence, "you found her, didn't you?"

Yang met the man's eyes. "We found a girl matching her description, but we can't say for sure that it's her."

Olga put her hand over her mouth, forcing back a sob. "No, not Tatjana." Her eyes shimmered with unshed tears. The woman had grown to care about the girl.

"That's why we're here. Can you tell us if she had anything that would help us identify her?"

"On the day she disappeared she wore a pink T-shirt with a stitched T for Tatjana on the front," Olga said.

Yang slowly shook his head. "There were no…" He didn't have to finish his sentence. Olga's pained expression told him that she understood that the girl they'd found had been naked.

"How about scars? Or a tattoo? Or a birthmark or mole?" Jefferson suggested.

Zimmerman shook his head, but his wife contradicted him. "She had a scar." She pointed to her stomach. "Here. My husband wouldn't know. He's not seen her getting undressed. I helped her, you know. She had her appendix taken out, she told me."

Yang recalled Lupe's words that the dead girl had no visible scars, certainly not a surgery scar like the one Olga Zimmerman was describing.

Yang looked at her and gave her a reassuring smile. "The girl we found doesn't have a scar. It's not Tatjana."

Olga let out a breath, and a sob of relief escaped her. "Oh, thank you, thank you so much."

"You'll keep looking for her, won't you?" Zimmerman asked with a look at his wife. "We miss her."

Yang didn't have the heart to tell them that if the girl hadn't been found in six weeks, chances were that she'd never be found.

"We'll do all we can," he said and rose. It wasn't a lie. But it wasn't the truth either, because there wasn't anything he could do.

Back in the car, Jefferson said, "They seem like good people."

"Yeah. But that girl, Tatjana, it's tragic. First she gets trafficked, and then she goes missing from a good family that by all accounts cared for her. How much bad luck can somebody have?"

"You don't think she ran away?"

"My gut says no."

And his gut was rarely wrong, but finding out what had happened to Tatjana wasn't his case. And he hoped she'd never turn into his case, because it would mean that she'd turned up dead. But without a body, she was a case for missing persons, and would soon turn into a cold case.

33

THE SUN WAS LOW when Emily left Lucia Garcia's house. The woman had become very chatty and given Emily a good picture of what Maddie was really like. Not the flashy socialite who wore expensive dresses and went to parties with the rich, famous, and flamboyant. There was a different side to Maddie, one very few people got to see.

She cared about exploited children and abused animals, and she always carried cash in her jacket and pants pockets. Lucia had asked Maddie about the money when she'd accidentally washed her clothes without checking the pockets and then found the banknotes in the washing machine. Maddie had told her that she made sure to always have cash on her to give to any homeless person she encountered. She'd made Lucia swear not to tell her parents, because they didn't approve of giving money to somebody who might use it for booze or drugs instead of food. But Maddie didn't judge.

She also made donations to numerous causes, yet she made most of them anonymously. She didn't make them so the public knew how generous she was, but because she cared and wanted to help. She'd once said to Lucia that she didn't have many useable skills to truly make a difference, but at least she had money, and if she could change somebody's life for the better with her money, then at least she'd done something good.

Lucia had also elaborated about Maddie's other habits, how she always wanted the guest room to be made up and ready at a moment's notice, and how she liked to have berries in the refrigerator, and coffee ice cream in the freezer.

The ringing of her cell phone ripped Emily from thinking about her conversation with Lucia. She'd only recently changed the settings on her phone so it would ring rather than announce the name of the caller verbally.

"Coffee, rest," she ordered the dog. She pulled her phone from her handbag and looked at the display. "Catalina?"

"No, it's her dad."

"Ambassador Pacheco."

"I hope I'm not disturbing, but I need to change Catalina's lesson with you." In the background she heard Tango music.

"Wednesday's lesson?"

"Yes, would it be okay to shift it to Thursday at the same time? I know it's short notice, but I forgot that Catalina has a dentist appointment."

"Of course, it's not a problem. I'll come on Thursday then."

"Thank you, Miss Warner. Good night."

"Good night, Ambassador."

She put her phone back into her handbag and looked up. Coffee was still patiently waiting for her to command him to advance. She suddenly noticed that she was still wearing her dark glasses. She took them off and stuffed them into her handbag, before she said to Coffee, "Forward."

When she continued on her way to the Metro station, she recalled the tune that was playing in the background when Ambassador Pacheco had spoken. Something clicked, and an idea bloomed in her mind.

Before she could forget it, she pulled her cell phone out of her pocket again and called Vicky. She picked up after the second ring.

"Yeah?" Vicky said, chewing on something.

"Hey, I'm on my way home, and I just had an idea about how I can speak to Lars Nielson."

Vicky sighed and swallowed. "Okay, let me hear it."

"I'll tell you when I get home. Come over, and we can have some ice cream together. I'll get some on the way."

"Salted Caramel?"

"Yep."

"Deal."

Emily disconnected the call. After putting her cell phone back into her handbag, she looked around. She wasn't far from the Metro station, but since she'd left Lucia Garcia's house, the sun had disappeared behind some low clouds, and it had gotten darker. In the twilight, the area didn't look quite as inviting as it had earlier. In fact, the shadows falling onto the houses and cars made the area look ominous. She felt an unease travel up her spine. Her heart rate accelerated.

There were few cars on the street, and even fewer people. And the people she did see either rushed past her to get to where they had to go before night fell, or they lurked near an entrance to an alley or a building, smoking, perhaps waiting for something to happen.

Feeling uncomfortable, Emily urged Coffee to walk faster. When she'd been blind, she'd never felt this way. She'd never seen the dangers around her, had simply trusted Coffee to keep her safe, but now that she could see dubious figures prowling in the vicinity, she felt fear rising in her, and sending a shiver through her bones. Maybe she was paranoid, but she sensed somebody's eyes on her, but when she glanced over her shoulder, she couldn't see anybody. Still, the feeling didn't vanish. She wondered whether what she was feeling was related to Maddie. Was she having another vision caused by her donor's memories?

Emily knew she was close to the Metro station. She looked down at Coffee. His hackles went up. He, too, was sensing something. Not a vision this time, then. Her heart started beating even faster. She could feel it drumming into her throat, the sound so loud that she couldn't be sure that she heard footsteps behind her. Had one of the men she saw loitering decided she was easy prey? She clutched her handbag tighter to her body and held onto Coffee's harness, feeling that her hands were sweaty.

She finally spotted the sign for the Metro station. "Almost there," she murmured to Coffee and herself.

A few more steps, and the footsteps seemed to come closer. Of their own volition, her feet moved faster, falling into a slow jog. Coffee kept pace, but so did the footfalls behind her. Her breath became choppy, evidence of her lack of exercise and her fear.

Just a few more seconds, she urged herself. *You're almost there.*

A few moments later, she reached the station. There, Emily cast another quick glance over her shoulder, not sure what to do if confronted with a mugger. But to her surprise, nobody was following her. The sidewalk was empty. She could have sworn she'd heard footsteps following her, speeding up when she sped up. But maybe she was wrong. Could those sounds merely have been an echo of her own footfalls? Was she becoming paranoid, seeing dangers where there were none?

34

DIMITRY AND IRINA FEDOROV lived in a small house in the Southeast of Washington D.C. The property looked well cared for, and the small front yard featured colorful geraniums. Yang and Jefferson got out of the car.

"Are they Russian?" Jefferson asked.

"The names certainly are." Yang had studied the printout from NamUS while Jefferson was driving. "Their daughter is twelve years old. Sasha."

"Nice name," Jefferson said.

Yang nodded. "It's a short form of Alexandra. Eastern European I think."

"Well, let's see what they've got to say," Jefferson said and rang the doorbell.

A few moments later, they heard the sound of a chain, then a woman answered the door, opening only as far as the chain allowed.

"Mrs. Fedorov?" Jefferson asked.

She cast them a suspicious look. "Yes?"

Both Yang and Jefferson flashed their badges. "Metropolitan Police, may we have a word with you and your husband?"

Her eyes flashed with fear, then she turned away and said something in a foreign language. Yang recognized it as Russian. A few seconds later, the door closed, then the sound of a chain being removed could be heard. The door was opened, this time wider, by a man in his fifties. He had blond hair and brown eyes.

"Mr. Fedorov?" Yang asked.

"Yes, that's me." His accent was heavy and definitely Russian or Eastern European.

"We'd like to talk to you about your daughter Sasha. May we come in?" Yang asked.

First the man looked at Yang, then at Jefferson, before he nodded and allowed them to step into the foyer. His wife stood at the entrance to the living room, blocking it as if she didn't want them to enter. She was a corpulent, short woman with dark-blond hair and gray eyes. She seemed older than her husband, or maybe her life had been harder than his, and it showed on the wrinkles in her face.

"What is this about?" Dimitry Fedorov asked, exhibiting the same guarded air as his wife.

Yang exchanged a look with Jefferson, and his partner nodded. They'd worked with each other long enough to know what approach the other was suggesting. And considering the mistrustful behavior of the couple, Yang knew he had to be on his guard.

"Your daughter disappeared on April 15th. We're following up on your missing person report."

Irina Fedorov whispered something in Russian. Her husband looked at her, then turned back to Yang and Jefferson.

"Sasha came back. She ran away, you know. After an argument. But she is back."

Yang and Jefferson raised their eyebrows.

"You didn't report that she came back. The case file is still open," Jefferson said.

"Sorry. We were so happy she was back that we forgot to tell the police," Fedorov said quickly.

"May we speak to Sasha, please?" Jefferson asked.

For the first time, Mrs. Fedorov answered, "She's with her friend from school. Studying."

"Alright," Jefferson said hesitantly. "You need to report to the police that Sasha came back, so the case can be closed."

Fedorov and his wife quickly nodded. When Yang looked at them side by side, comparing their light hair and light complexion, he looked back at the printout from NamUS. The girl, Sasha, looked nothing like her parents. Her hair was almost black, and her eyes were a startling blue. There was no family resemblance.

Jefferson was already turning to the door, but Yang hesitated.

"One more question," he said. "Is Sasha your biological daughter?"

The pair looked at each other, then Mr. Fedorov answered, "She's a foster child."

Jefferson stopped at the door and turned around, exchanged a look with Yang, and said, "Was she rescued from traffickers?"

"Traffickers?" Fedorov asked. "I don't know that word."

"My colleague means was Sasha smuggled into this country for the purpose of sex?" Yang said.

Fedorov nodded. "Yes. She came from Russia. We took her in when we heard that this charity was looking for people who speak Russian."

Yang exchanged a knowing look with Jefferson. This was the second girl on their list who was a foster child from Russia. "What is the name of the charity you worked with?"

"*No child abandoned,*" Fedorov said.

The name rang a bell, but Yang couldn't immediately place where he'd heard it before. "Thank you. I guess we've got what we need. Have a nice evening."

He walked out with Jefferson. In the car, they looked at each other.

"How did you know that Sasha wasn't their real daughter?"

Yang tapped at the sheet of paper in his hand. "This girl looks nothing like the Fedorovs. Her hair is almost black, her eyes blue, and her facial features are totally different."

"You've got a good eye," Jefferson said. "Did you get the feeling that they didn't want to speak to us?"

"Yep. Don't you think it's odd that two out of the three girls that match our Jane Doe are Russian? And foster children?"

"Something is up. I think we should come back another time when the girl is home and talk to her."

"I agree," Yang said. "Let's go see the Veselak family."

"They sound Russian too," Jefferson said.

"Makes me regret never having taken Russian in school."

"At least you speak one foreign language." Jefferson started the car and pulled into traffic.

"To the chagrin of my mother, my Chinese isn't all it's cracked up to be. I can only speak it, not write it."

Jefferson glanced at the clock on the dashboard. "Oh, fuck, it's late. Let's visit the Veselaks tomorrow."

"Come on, it's not that late. Don't you want overtime?"

"I've got a date." He winked at Yang. "She's hot and—"

Yang lifted his hand. "Spare me. I know way too much about your love life already."

35

EMILY TOOK OFF COFFEE'S HARNESS and put it aside, glad to be in the safety of her home. She felt better now, and a little foolish for having been so paranoid earlier "Good boy," she praised Coffee. "Do you want dinner?"

Coffee wagged his tail excitedly. He knew what dinner meant, and walked to his bowl, put his paw on it and looked up at her. Emily took the bowl and prepared his dinner: kibble, fresh chicken breast from the refrigerator, and a little bone broth.

There was a knock at the door. "Emily, it's me."

"Come in, Vicky, it's unlocked."

While Vicky entered and closed the door behind her, Emily set the bowl in front of Coffee, and stroked her hand over his head. A moment later, he started gobbling up his food.

"Hey, your message light is blinking," Vicky said, pointing at Emily's landline.

"Oh, I didn't notice." She pressed the button, and let the message replay.

"Hi Emily, this is Kate Rosenstein. I don't know if you remember me, but I was your attorney fifteen years ago. Anyway, I thought I should let you know that your father is out on parole. He was released from prison three months ago. I was on a sabbatical, and apparently nobody else in the office passed the message on to you. Sorry. If you want to talk, call me."

She left a number, but Emily didn't even listen to it. All she had heard was that her father was out. He was free. She just stood there, bombarded by memories she had suppressed for all these years. Memories she'd forced into the darkest recesses of her mind where they could die a slow death. They resurfaced now, and all the pain she'd ever felt accompanied them.

All of a sudden, Emily couldn't breathe. Fear rose in her and choked off her airways.

"You told me your parents were both dead," Vicky said into the silence.

Emily didn't know how long she'd stood there, saying nothing.

"I told you that I lost my parents. It was the truth. I did lose them both. My mother died in the accident. My father went to prison for it."

"What?" Vicky stared at her, eyes wide, mouth open, her entire body a question mark. "For an accident?"

Emily shook her head. "It wasn't an accident."

"Back up." Vicky lifted her hand. "I get the feeling I need a drink for this."

"I think we both do."

Minutes later, after Vicky had brought a bottle of wine from her apartment and poured two glasses, Emily took a deep breath. After the trial, she'd never again spoken about the night she lost her mother and her eyesight.

Vicky put a hand on Emily's arm. "Tell me what happened."

"My mother wanted to leave my father. He accused her of having an affair, but I don't know whether that's true. It doesn't matter whether it was true or not. Mom just didn't want to live with him anymore. She said we'd be much happier without him. He was jealous and angry all the time. When something went wrong with his business, he always took it out on Mom." Emily felt her eyes moisten with unshed tears. "He never hit her, but Mom was a gentle, sensitive woman, and the verbal abuse hurt her just the same as if he'd given her a savage beating."

"I'm sorry…" Vicky murmured.

"I don't know when she told him that she was going to divorce him, but a week after my birthday he said the gift he'd wanted to give me was finally here. We just had to pick it up, and he wanted Mom and me to come with him. I asked him what it was, but he said it was a surprise. So Mom and I got in the car."

If only she'd told him that she didn't want a present, didn't like surprises. But like any fifteen-year-old, she'd believed that her father still loved her, even though he and her mother weren't going to stay together.

"He drove fast, reckless. He and Mom argued. Mom was begging him to stop. She wanted to get out. But he didn't stop. The light at the intersection was red. And even I could see the headlights of the car coming from the right."

Emily shuddered at the memory. Her legs trembled, and she put her hands on her knees to stop them from shaking.

"Your dad ran a red light?"

"Yes. The side impact killed my mother instantly. The firemen had to cut me out of the car. My dad only broke a few ribs and had some cuts and bruises. Nothing that didn't heal in a few weeks. He was sentenced to twenty years in prison."

"Twenty years for reckless driving and manslaughter?" Vicky asked. "I didn't realize… Was he drunk?"

Emily shook her head.

"Then why did he get twenty years? I mean… I've never heard of anybody getting such a long sentence for vehicular manslaughter."

"He was convicted of murder one."

Vicky stared at her. "Murder one?"

Slowly Emily nodded. "Because I survived and was able to testify against him."

Vicky said nothing, only waited patiently for Emily to continue.

"I told the police what Dad was saying while he was driving." Emily's throat went dry. She took a sip from her glass. "He told Mom that he would never allow her to leave him. She said he didn't have a say in it. She would leave him and take me with her. He said: *Nobody is going anywhere ever again, because tonight we're all going to die.*"

Vicky gasped. "Oh my God." She gripped Emily's hand. "He did it on purpose."

Emily nodded, tears brimming her eyes. "He'd planned it. He got us in the car on a ruse. He wanted us all to die together. But he survived. And so did I…" She tried to swallow away the pain, but couldn't. "I testified against him. I told them what he'd said to Mom in the car. I told them that he'd taken everything from me: my mother and my eyesight. The jury took less than an hour to come back with a verdict. When I heard the foreman of the jury say *guilty* on all charges, I cried with relief."

Vicky set her glass down on the table and put her arms around Emily, hugging her. That's when she realized that she was crying, just like fifteen years earlier when the jury had convicted her father of premeditated murder and attempted murder.

"It's all over, hon, it's all over," Vicky said in a soothing voice. "You're not that child anymore. You've survived. And you're stronger for it."

Emily hugged her friend tightly. "Thank you. Thank you for listening." She sniffled.

Vicky released her and looked at her. "Alright?"

"Better." Then she swallowed away the remaining tears. "But now he's out. He knows he would have gotten away with it if I hadn't testified. I made him pay for killing my mother, and for robbing me of my eyesight. And now he's back. He'll make me pay for testifying against him." And that thought sent a chill down her spine.

"He can't do anything to you. I know people like that. They're cowards. You've shown him that you won't be bullied. You stood up to him. He won't dare hurt you again."

"But what if he's here? What if he's come back to finish what he started fifteen years ago?"

"No! You think he's here in Washington D.C.? Why would you think that?"

"Lately, I've had the feeling that somebody is watching me, following me."

"Like how?"

"Tonight, I heard footsteps following me. I didn't see anybody, but I had this weird feeling. What if it's him? What if my father is watching me? What if he's trying to find an opportunity to kill me?"

"I doubt that very much. Fifteen years have passed. Prison changes people."

"Not for the better. I've never felt like that before. But after I went to talk to Maddie's housekeeper in Anacostia I sensed—"

"Anacostia? Are you out of your fucking mind?" Vicky almost yelled at her. "You don't hang around that neighborhood at night. Of course, you were followed! By a bunch of criminals. It's not safe there, not at night!"

"I had Coffee with me." Coffee lifted his head when he heard his name, then lay back down on the carpet.

"Yeah, well, Coffee isn't exactly an attack dog. He's no match for the criminals lurking around there at night. Have I taught you nothing?"

Emily opened her mouth to protest, but Vicky continued, "And what the hell were you doing talking to Maddie's housekeeper? How did you even find out where she lives?"

Emily pointed to the computer. "Internet? Which I believe you taught me."

"Not so you could play amateur sleuth!"

"But I had to talk to her. She was very helpful. And before you say anything else, I think I'm onto something. I think Maddie Bolton was murdered."

36

BRIGHT AND EARLY THE NEXT DAY, Yang met Jefferson in Yang's own neighborhood, Columbia Heights, where the parents of the third missing girl that matched their dead Jane Doe lived. Emil and Mila Veselak lived in a large apartment building.

After identifying themselves via the intercom system, Yang and Jefferson were buzzed into the building and took the elevator to the top floor. An attractive woman in her late thirties, early forties was expecting them at the door to the apartment.

"I'm sorry, Detectives, but my husband already left for work," she said in good English though her words were colored with an Eastern European accent. "I'm Mila Veselak."

Yang and Jefferson flashed their badges and followed her into the apartment, where she motioned them to sit in the living room.

"Are you Russian, Mrs. Veselak?" Yang asked. Considering that the families of the other two girls were Russian, he had a hunch.

She shook her head. "No, I'm Czech like my husband. But we met here in the United States. I studied here, and Emil came on a work visa."

Yang nodded. "My mistake. I guess I just assumed that you were Russian because of Annika."

A sad expression fell on her face. "Ah, Annika. Yes, she's Russian."

"She's not your biological daughter?" Jefferson asked.

"No, I'm afraid I can't have children," Mila Veselak said with a sad smile. "Annika is our foster child. We were hoping to adopt her if her parents can't be found. But then... she went missing. It's been ten weeks already..."

Jefferson gave Yang a look that said that this was odd. Three missing girls, all Russian, all in foster care. The chances of winning a small fortune in the lottery had better odds than this scenario. There were only so many coincidences Yang could accept at face value.

"Mrs. Veselak," Yang started, "how was Annika's English?"

"Not very good. That's why we were chosen to take her in. Both my husband and I speak Russian. It made it easier for Annika. She'd gone through so much, you must know."

"Tell us more," Jefferson said.

"Well, she fell in with the wrong people in Russia from what we could get out of her. And they sold her to a sex ring, and brought her to the USA. She was rescued, and a charitable organization helped place her, while they search for her parents. We heard about it in our church, so Emil and I decided to help."

"That's very admirable of you," Yang said. "Which organization did you deal with?"

"It's a charity. It's called... uh, something like abandoned children or so."

"*No child abandoned?*" Yang guessed and looked at Jefferson.

"Yes, that's the name."

By the expression on Jefferson's face Yang realized that his partner had expected as much. Yang made a mental note to call the Zimmermans to find out which organization their foster child Tatjana had come from.

Mrs. Veselak suddenly tipped her chin up as if steeling herself for bad news. "But you didn't come to ask me about where Annika is from."

Yang nodded slowly. "You're right." He hesitated, watching her reaction. She looked worried. "We found the body of a girl..."

She gasped and put her hand to her mouth.

"We haven't been able to identify her yet," Jefferson said quickly. "But she fits Annika's general description in age, height, eye color, and hair color."

"What my colleague is trying to say is that we need something to identify her by, either to confirm it's her or to rule it out."

Stiffly, Mila Veselak nodded. "I understand."

"Does Annika have any scars, any tattoos, anything that you can think of that would help us?"

Mila shook her head. "No scars, no tattoos. She has very beautiful eyes."

Yang exchanged a look with Jefferson. Neither of them wanted to take Mila Veselak to the morgue and have her look at the dead girl whose face was too damaged to make a visual identification easy. If it was indeed

Annika, Mrs. Veselak shouldn't have to look at her like that. She should remember her alive.

"It's her, isn't it?" Mrs. Veselak said, her voice shaking.

"It's possible," Yang said, "but we can't be sure until we've matched her DNA. Could you show us her room, please?"

Mrs. Veselak jumped up, and Yang and Jefferson followed her. The girl's room was bright and cozy. "This is Annika's room."

"Did she share a bathroom with you and your husband?" Jefferson asked. "We'll need a toothbrush or a hairbrush or anything else only she used."

Mrs. Veselak pointed to a chest of drawers. "Annika's hairbrush is in the top drawer, and I can bring you her toothbrush. We only have one bathroom."

Yang didn't want her to contaminate Annika's toothbrush, so he pulled out an evidence bag from his pocket and followed her, while Jefferson collected the evidence in the bedroom. "If you can point it out to me without touching it."

"Of course," she said and watched him touch the toothbrush with a clean tissue and drop it into the evidence bag, before sealing it.

He noticed her staring at the bag and met her eyes. There was something vulnerable about the way she looked at him.

"Mrs. Veselak," Yang said, searching for something to say to console her. But there was nothing. Their hopes at that moment were at opposite ends of the scale: Yang wanted the DNA to identify the girl, Mrs. Veselak wanted the evidence to rule her out so she could go on hoping that Annika was alive and would come back.

"When will you know?" she asked.

"In a few days."

Jefferson came out of the bedroom. "I've got everything we need." He lifted the evidence bag with the hairbrush. "Thank you, Mrs. Veselak. We'll be in touch." He was walking toward the door.

Already turning halfway toward the door, Yang felt her hand on his arm. He looked over his shoulder.

"The moment you know, please tell me. Either way. Yes?"

He nodded. "I promise."

Once in the car, Jefferson drove them back to the precinct, while Yang made a call to the Zimmermans and asked James Zimmerman, who answered the phone, which organization had placed Tatjana with them. When he got the answer, he thanked him and disconnected the call.

"And?" Jefferson asked.

"*No child abandoned*," Yang said. "You know what I think?"

"That we need to talk to somebody at *No child abandoned*," Jefferson answered.

"My thoughts exactly."

"Can you go alone? I've got to be in court to testify in the Hernandez case this afternoon."

"No problem. I can handle it."

Yang now recalled one other thing about *No child abandoned*, though he didn't mention it to his partner: Madeline Bolton had worked for the charity, though Yang wasn't sure in what capacity. Another coincidence?

37

LATER THE SAME DAY, Yang flashed his badge at the receptionist and demanded to speak to the person in charge at *No child abandoned*. The attractive twenty-something woman with long straight hair looked surprised and asked him to take a seat in the reception area, while she dialed a number and spoke in a hushed voice.

Yang looked around. For a non-profit, the place was rather swanky, making him wonder how much of the charitable donations that *No child abandoned* received actually ended up helping children, and how much was wasted on the offices located in a high-rent district of Washington D.C. The furnishings looked classy and elegant, not what he had expected from a charity that rescued trafficked and at-risk children. But then maybe having a classy façade brought in big donations from the capital's high society. Perhaps they didn't want to send their fat checks to a low-rent district. But then, what did Yang know about charities or high society?

It took several minutes until a man came out of one of the offices and approached Yang, hand proffered in greeting. "Detective Yang? I'm Caleb Faulkner. I'm the CEO."

Yang recognized him immediately. He'd seen him at Madeline Bolton's funeral, and knew that he was the son of the President's Chief of Staff, Mike Faulkner. He knew that Caleb Faulkner ran the charity, though Yang hadn't had much time to deepen his research into the charity. He made a note to do it later when back at the precinct.

"Mr. Faulkner, pleased to meet you," Yang said while Caleb ushered him to the office he'd just exited.

Once settled inside the office, Caleb behind the large desk and Yang in the comfortable chair in front of it, Yang pulled out his notebook and pen.

"Apologies for not making an appointment," Yang said though it was merely a platitude. He never made appointments when on a case.

"Not at all, Detective. How may I help you?"

Caleb Faulkner was friendly and open. Yang could imagine that he did well with rich donors, charming them out of their money—in a good way, of course. Yet, he also got the impression that Caleb was shallow and spoiled, which probably stemmed from the fact that his father was an important man in politics.

"Ahem, yes." He looked at his notebook where he'd written down all pertinent information. "I'm working on a case involving three Russian girls. Incidentally, all three were foster children and placed in Russian speaking families by your charity."

Caleb nodded. "Ah, yes, we often deal with Russian children here. Others, too, but the overwhelming majority of children we rescue are from Russia."

"I'm just trying to verify some of the information the families of the three girls gave me. Just background info to make sure we've got all pertinent details. I have the names right here." Yang pointed to his notebook.

"Sure. Go ahead and give me the names. I can pull their files up on my computer." Caleb nudged closer to the computer on his desk, his hands already hovering over the keyboard.

"The Zimmerman family took in a girl named Tatjana."

Caleb typed something, then nodded. "Got the file. Next one?"

Yang then gave him the families that Sasha and Annika had been placed with. He omitted that Sasha had come back to the Fedorovs, nor did he divulge that a body of a girl had been found, and that he suspected that one of these girls could be the dead body. It wasn't necessary for Caleb Faulkner to know. Besides, Yang needed information on all three girls. He was looking for anything they had in common.

"So, may I ask what these three girls are involved in? Did they get in trouble?" Caleb asked, looking up from the monitor.

"You could say that. They're missing."

Caleb raised his eyebrows and stared back at the screen, reading something. "Oh, now I see it." He pointed to the screen. "All three files have a note here that the girls were reported missing after they'd been placed with the families."

"Yes, my partner and I spoke to the families."

Caleb sighed. "It's not easy for these kids. They often come from broken families, or were trafficked… It's tragic. We do everything to help them make the adjustment." He shrugged, his expression serious. "But it happens that they run away. They can't adjust."

"I understand. Does the charity keep in touch with the families the kids are placed with?"

"Of course. We have employees who do welfare checks to make sure the children are doing well. We even require them to attend counseling regularly, both in group and individual sessions. Paid by the charity."

"Hmm. Interesting. So the families notified you that these three girls went missing?"

"Not me, per se, but yes, they all reported it to their case worker, and we made sure that the police were notified as well. It's standard procedure. And as I said, it happens with at-risk children. Some are very troubled. I'm assuming that's why you're here, Detective?"

"Yes, indeed. And these three girls, did you find that they were particularly, ahem, for lack of a better word, troubled?"

"Well, I'm not sure I've actually met them personally. See, I work mostly with donors, wining and dining them to keep money coming in, so we can take care of these kids, try to find their parents… if their parents want to be found."

Yang raised an eyebrow. "What are you saying?"

Caleb sighed. "We've had cases where children were sold to sex rings, because the family was in debt to unscrupulous people. In Russia we've seen particularly egregious cases. And often, when a child has to face that their family doesn't want them back, it's a blow to their psyche."

"Hence the counseling?"

Caleb nodded. "We have a contract with a psychiatrist whose focus is helping children."

"I was told by the three families that the girls barely spoke any English. Is that correct?"

Caleb looked into the screen, and after a while said, "Yes. That's correct."

"How do they communicate with the psychiatrist?"

"Oh, he's bilingual. He speaks Russian. We're very lucky to have him."

"What's his name?"

"Dr. Yuri Sokolov."

"Do we know what Dr. Sokolov discussed with the girls?"

"Hmm. It's patient doctor confidentiality, so you'll have to talk to him. But I can give you a printout of everything that's in the files that we have. Would that help?"

Surprised at Caleb's offer, Yang nodded. Not having to get a court order to access information was definitely a good thing.

"Thank you. That would be great."

Behind Caleb, a printer was waking up, and started spitting out pages. Meanwhile Caleb looked back at the monitor and moved his mouse, then stopped, startled. "Now, that's odd."

Yang leaned forward. "Is there a problem?"

"I'm not sure. Ahem." Caleb hesitated, but continued to look at the monitor. "It's just that I see here that all three girls were last seen at one of Dr. Sokolov's sessions." He looked straight at Yang. "If you hadn't asked me about Dr. Sokolov, I might not even have noticed it."

This was an interesting detail, just the kind Yang was looking for. He hadn't expected to find a gold mine like this. Before he could ask anything else, the phone rang. Caleb looked at it, then said, "Sorry, I need to take this. Just a minute."

Caleb answered the phone, but Yang didn't understand what he was saying. Caleb spoke a few words in a foreign language, before he put down the receiver. "Sorry about that."

"You speak Russian?" Yang asked, surprised.

Caleb chuckled. "Not that well anymore. I was quite fluent when I lived in Moscow as a teenager."

"That must have been quite an adventure. You were an exchange student?"

"No. Not in the way you're imagining. My father was the US Ambassador to Russia. We lived there for two years."

"Ah, that must have been quite something. What an opportunity."

"Hmm. I guess so. It was shortly after my mother's death. I don't think I could really enjoy it at first, and by the time I adjusted to Moscow, we were already leaving." He forced a smile as if pushing back painful memories. "Have you ever been to Moscow?"

"Can't say that I have."

The printer stopped spitting out pages, and Caleb turned to grab the stack, then handed it to Yang.

"I've got to go to a meeting," Caleb said, looking at his watch, "but if you need anything else, anything at all, please call me."

Motioning to the papers in his hand, Yang said, "You've already been a great help. I'll see myself out."

Yang decided to visit Dr. Sokolov immediately after his visit to the charity. When he reached the Logan Ambulatory Care Building on NW P Street where the psychiatrist had his office, the receptionist told him that Dr. Sokolov had left two days earlier to go hiking in the Italian Alps for a week, and couldn't be reached. Yang made a note on his calendar to connect with the psychiatrist upon his return.

38

EMILY DIDN'T LIKE USING CATALINA for her own selfish purpose, but she felt she had no other way of getting access to Lars Nielson, the Swedish diplomat Maddie had been engaged to. It was a long shot by any stretch of the imagination, but she knew that Ambassador Pacheco couldn't deny his daughter anything. Particularly not when he knew that it would make Catalina happy. Therein lay Emily's best chance.

Emily arrived at the Argentinean embassy as usual and started her lesson with Catalina while Coffee lay next to the piano, his head resting on his paws, his eyes almost closed. He seemed to enjoy the instrument's vibrations.

Earlier in the school year, Emily had introduced her students to popular folk music from several different countries, reflecting the heritage of the many foreign pupils in her class. She hadn't thought that this subject would be coming in handy in an unexpected way. All of Emily's students were enjoying the songs, and had participated enthusiastically. Several of them, including Catalina, had shown real talent, their voices a perfect match for capturing the spirit of the music.

Emily had planted an idea in Catalina's head the previous day at school, and now it was up to the girl to execute it. Emily knew that Catalina had already talked to her father the night before, which she'd reported to Emily in the morning, yet he hadn't given her a definite answer. It made Emily anxious, because the execution of her plan was time sensitive. The weekend was only a few days away.

The last notes of the piece Catalina was playing on the piano sounded.

"Bravo, Lina." Clapping came from the entrance to the living room.

Emily saw Ambassador Pacheco standing there, leaning casually against the door frame. How long he'd been standing there, Emily didn't know. But he appeared pleased with his daughter's progress.

"Thank you, Daddy!"

"You played very well today," Emily praised the girl. "I can tell that you've been practicing a lot."

Catalina beamed and rose from the bench, walking toward her father. "Daddy?"

"I'm here," he answered to indicate where he stood.

When she reached him, he took her hand, while Emily already slung her bag over her shoulder and reached for Coffee's harness.

"Can we do it, Daddy?" Catalina begged her father. "I asked the other students already, and there are already eight who want to do it."

Ambassador Pacheco looked at his daughter. "Why don't you let me talk to Miss Warner for a moment?"

"Okay." She turned around and headed in the direction of the kitchen.

When she was out of earshot, he approached her. Emily felt her heartbeat quicken. Would he tell her that her idea was out of the question? Had he sent Catalina away so that he could let her down easier?

"Miss Warner, Catalina came to me with this idea last night."

"Yes?"

He sighed. "She said she really enjoyed the folk songs you taught your class earlier in the year, and that she would love the opportunity to perform them—with some of her classmates... But there doesn't really seem to be any planned event at school..."

Emily nodded. "Yes, unfortunately the auditorium at the school is undergoing a renovation, so all school performances have been postponed."

"Yes, Catalina told me, and she also said you would lead your pupils if only there was another place to perform. So I was wondering..." He motioned with his hands. "And you can of course say 'no' if this is too much of an imposition, but there is one place where such a performance would be appreciated very much."

"You know of a different school that might lend us their auditorium?"

He shook his head. "Not a school. An embassy."

Emily opened her mouth. "Here?"

Again he shook his head. "No, but this weekend, the Swedish Embassy is having an event. And the kids could perform the folk songs there. Catalina said that one of them is a Swedish song."

"Oh, I mean that would be wonderful, but do you think the Swedish ambassador will like the idea? I mean, it's short notice."

"Are you saying that the kids might not be ready?"

"No, no, not at all. They're ready to perform at a moment's notice. But what about the ambassador?"

Pacheco grinned, and for that short moment, he looked fifteen years younger and a lifetime happier. "He already agreed."

Emily's heart leapt.

"All we need are the names of the students who'll perform, and maybe one or two chaperones, who will also need to be vetted. You're already cleared, so that's easy. If you can get the children's parents to give permission, I can take care of the rest."

"Oh my God, that's so wonderful. The kids will love it." Emily beamed.

"Anything to make Catalina happy."

Emily could see it in his eyes. Seeing Catalina happy made him happy. And although Emily had manipulated Catalina to score an invitation to the Swedish embassy party, nobody would be harmed by it. Catalina and her schoolmates would have a blast.

Ambassador Pacheco winked at her. "And maybe after the children's performance, you might play a Tango for me?" His eyes wandered past her.

Emily didn't have to follow his gaze to know that he was looking at the painting of his late wife, remembering the many Tangos he'd danced with her.

"Yes, a Tango just for you."

It was the least she could do.

39

Lᴜᴄɪᴀ sɴɪꜰꜰʟᴇᴅ ᴀɢᴀɪɴ, her red puffy eyes a testament to the fact that she too was grieving for Maddie. Bolton had never doubted her loyalty to his daughter, but the pain he saw in Lucia's eyes revealed that she'd loved Maddie like her own child.

Bolton had come to Maddie's townhouse to go through his daughter's personal belongings and make decisions about what should be kept and what should be disposed of. Lucia had insisted on helping him, and he was grateful for it. Her presence stopped him from wallowing in his grief every time he saw an item that had meant something to him and his daughter. And there were many such items: photos, gifts, and other keepsakes. Even Maddie's clothes conjured up memories of events where she'd worn them. But he didn't allow himself to dwell on anything too long.

He'd shed more tears than any man should, many of them locked away in his office or in his car, away from prying eyes, away from Rita, so he wouldn't ignite a fresh wave of tears in her. He had to be strong for her. That's why he'd insisted on clearing out Maddie's townhouse without her. She needed to rest. And he needed a purpose, something to occupy himself with.

"Mr. Bolton?" Lucia's voice came from behind him.

He pivoted. "Yes?"

"I found the key." She held a small key in her hand and lifted it up for him to see.

"What for?"

She stared at him with a look of concern. "For Maddie's jewelry box. Like I told you earlier."

Bolton nodded quickly. "Of course. I'm sorry, Lucia, I can't seem to concentrate."

Lucia cast him a gentle smile and pressed the key into his palm. "I understand. It's not easy. If you want to go home, I can continue here. I can sort through everything and make sure to put the important things into boxes for you and your wife..."

Bolton squeezed Lucia's hand. "No, no, I'll stay. It's my duty. I can't have you do all the work. You've done so much already." He motioned to the boxes Lucia had labeled to distinguish between important papers, items to donate to charities, items of sentimental value, and others. "You've done a good job. You knew her so well."

Again, Lucia sniffled. "If only I'd come earlier that morning. Maybe she would have made it."

"Don't, please don't. You're not to blame. You did everything—"

The sound of the doorbell interrupted him.

"I'll get it," Lucia said quickly and walked into the hallway.

Bolton heard the door opening.

"Mr. Faulkner," Lucia said.

Bolton walked into the hallway and saw Mike Faulkner enter.

"Thank you, Lucia," Faulkner said. "I hope I'm not disturbing." He looked past Lucia. "Rita told me you were here," he said to Bolton. "I was in the area, so I thought I'd quickly stop by."

Bolton motioned for him to enter. "Come on in."

Faulkner walked past Lucia, and gripped Bolton's hand. "How are you holding up?"

Bolton shrugged and motioned to the boxes. "As well as anybody can in this situation."

As they walked into the living room, Lucia asked from the door, "Mr. Faulkner, do you want something to drink? The kitchen still has—"

Faulkner turned to her with a smile. "No, thank you. Don't trouble yourself. I'm not staying long."

Faulkner turned back to Bolton, reached into his jacket pocket and pulled out a small plastic bag. Inside was a cell phone. "I just came to bring you Maddie's phone."

Bolton took it and looked at it. A post-it note was attached to the front of the phone.

"Her pass code, so you can access it. The Secret Service released it. They've taken everything they need from it."

"Anything helpful?" Bolton asked.

"They're still working through all the data they downloaded from it, but so far, nothing was helpful. I'm sorry."

For a second time, the doorbell chimed. Bolton looked past Faulkner to ask Lucia to see who was coming, but Lucia had anticipated him and was already opening the door.

"Oh, Mr. Sullivan," he heard Lucia say.

Bolton's son-in-law spoke in a low voice, when he greeted Lucia. "Better close the door quickly, Lucia," Sullivan said from the hallway, "or that reporter that was tailing me will come in. Can't go anywhere these days without being accosted by reporters."

"But don't you want to tell them what a nice woman Maddie was?" Lucia asked.

Bolton and Faulkner walked into the hallway.

Sullivan acknowledged their presence, but addressed Lucia's question. "Of course I want that, but reporters will just use my words and twist them around until they have a juicy story." He tipped his chin in his father-in-law's direction. "Isn't that so, Eric?"

Lucia looked at Sullivan and Bolton and seemed to contemplate something that caused frown lines to appear on her brow. "I don't think all reporters are like that. The woman who came to see me was very nice, and very respectful."

"A reporter interviewed you? About Maddie?" Bolton asked.

"She wasn't a real reporter, I mean, not for a newspaper..." Lucia appeared embarrassed.

"What do you mean?"

"Well, she was blind, you know, she had her guide dog and dark glasses. It was for a podcast for the blind. They can't read the papers, so this woman makes podcasts."

Bolton sighed. Everybody wanted to get the inside scoop on Maddie's life. "Lucia..." He shook his head. "What did she want?"

"She just asked me what Maddie was like at home, you know what she ate and things like that. I told her that she was nice to the homeless..." Her voice trailed off. "You don't think she would use my words to say something bad about Maddie, do you?"

Bolton exchanged a look with Faulkner, then looked back at Lucia. She was a good soul, but far too trusting. "Did she give you her card?"

"No, but she told me her name. Emily Warner. I wrote it down after she left. So that I can find the podcast. But so far I haven't found it."

Bolton let out a breath. How many people would be listening to a podcast meant for the blind? He doubted that the podcast's audience was large enough to even make a blip in the mainstream media. "Don't worry about it, Lucia. Just remember for next time to be careful what you tell others about Maddie. There are plenty of people who want to drag her name through the mud. We don't wanna give them any fodder."

"Yes, I'm sorry, Mr. Bolton." She sniffled and her eyes grew moist again. "I didn't mean anything by it. It was just so comforting to talk about Maddie." A sob tore from her chest.

"Now, now," Bolton said, "why don't you take a minute to wash those tears away, and maybe have a cup of tea or coffee, before we continue, hmm?"

Lucia nodded and walked to the powder room, but two heavy boxes blocked the door, so she went upstairs.

When she was out of earshot, Bolton motioned Sullivan and Mike to the living room. "She's a mess."

"Can't blame her," Sullivan said. "Finding Maddie... that image... it must have been a shock."

Bolton nodded. He didn't want to conjure up that particular image. It was bad enough to have to look at the bloodstain on the carpet where she'd fallen.

"So, what brings you here?" Bolton asked Sullivan.

"I'm hunting down the charity's audit files that Maddie took home with her the week before..." He didn't say the word, and Bolton was grateful for it. "She was supposed to review them before the board was gonna vote on them. We had to delay the vote..."

"There are documents in the hutch here, but I think they aren't related to the charity. Maybe upstairs? Let's have a look."

"I don't want to interrupt what you're doing. I can check upstairs," Sullivan said.

"It'll be faster if I help you," Bolton said and walked into the hallway. He was already on the stairs, when he heard two sets of footsteps behind him. At the landing, he turned toward Maddie's room. But at the door he hesitated. Entering felt as if he was violating her privacy.

Faulkner and Sullivan stopped next to him.

"You okay?" Faulkner asked and put a hand on his shoulder.

Bolton turned his head to his friend. "I'm still hoping that she'll come out of the bathroom and scold me for not having knocked."

"I get it," Faulkner said. "I've been there. With Georgina."

Suddenly the door to the guest bathroom opened behind him. Bolton pivoted, his breath catching in his throat. It was Lucia.

She looked at the three men before motioning to the open door to the guest room. "Is it okay for me to strip the bed sheets? The police asked me to leave it the way I found it that morning."

Bolton looked into the guest room. The bed wasn't made. He knew how diligent Lucia was. She wouldn't leave an unmade bed for longer than a day. "Did Maddie have a guest the night before her... before she..."

"I don't know," Lucia said. "It was my day off. But I found the bed like this. I told the Secret Service. And they said not to disturb anything."

Bolton nodded and looked over his shoulder into the room opposite, Maddie's bedroom. Her bed was made, which he knew had indicated that Maddie's fall had happened at night, not in the morning when she was about to leave for work. But he hadn't been aware that the guest room had been used.

He exchanged a look with Faulkner. "Did the Secret Service look into whether Maddie had an overnight guest?"

"They did. They got fingerprints that don't belong to either Maddie or Lucia," Faulkner said.

Lucia nodded. "They took my fingerprints." At the sound of a soft ping, Lucia said, "Laundry, excuse me," and hurried downstairs.

"Secret Service ran the prints they found in the room through the system, but there's no match," Faulkner added. "We have no idea how old the prints are. They could be from any visitor in the last year. My people also canvassed the neighbors, but nobody saw anybody other than Maddie enter the house in the two nights before..."

"Doesn't mean she didn't have a guest," Bolton said.

"True," Faulkner said. "But we have no confirmation either way."

"Did they look in her journal or calendar to see if she was expecting anybody?" Sullivan asked, as he walked into Maddie's bedroom and pulled out the drawers to her desk.

Faulkner followed him. "Trust me. The agents in charge of the investigation are thorough. They found no mention of an overnight guest anywhere."

"Ah, there's the file," Sullivan said and pulled a manila folder from the drawer.

Faulkner shrugged then looked toward the open door and lowered his voice a little. "Maybe Lucia forgot to make the bed after a previous guest left. It happens."

Bolton didn't contradict Faulkner, but he knew Lucia better. She was diligent. She would have never left the bed unmade after a guest had left, which meant somebody had slept in that bed before Maddie's death.

40

APPLAUSE FILLED THE LARGE BALLROOM in the Swedish Embassy as a dozen eleven- and twelve-year-old children bowed to the audience, their faces beaming with joy. Emily stood next to the piano and let her gaze wander over the crowd. She had donned a black cocktail dress she'd bought at the last minute so as not to stick out like a sore thumb. Still, she felt underdressed. The female guests wore stunning evening dresses in all colors of the rainbow, the men wore tuxedoes.

Ambassador Pacheco had greeted her and the children when they'd arrived with two chaperones in tow and ushered them into a smaller room so they could prepare for the performance. When she noticed him looking at his daughter, who was beyond excited, Emily realized just how much Ambassador Pacheco loved to see his daughter happy. He looked happy.

When the kids took their last bow, the two teachers who'd acted as chaperones, Isabelle Treadway and Olivia Remmington, the school's principal, approached the pupils and praised them for their performance.

The children talked excitedly, while music was piped in through the loudspeakers. Ambassador Pacheco had been right: the Swedish ambassador loved ABBA. And by the looks of it, many of the men and women who looked like they were Swedish diplomats, if their fair skin, blue eyes, and blond hair were anything to go by, loved the music and started dancing.

"This was such a wonderful idea," Olivia Remmington said to Emily. "How did you even get this done?"

Emily smiled. "It was Catalina's idea."

The principal chuckled and leaned in. "This is the first time I've ever been to an embassy party. I wish we could stay longer, but the kids need to go home, or we'll get in trouble with their parents." She looked at her wristwatch. "It's past their bedtime."

"Are you alright if I make my way home from here, rather than getting on the coach with them? My apartment is very close to here, and I'm a little tired," Emily said, though that wasn't the reason she didn't want to depart with the children.

"Of course, Emily! Don't worry, Isabelle and I will get the kids home. You've done enough. Get a good night's rest!" She waved to Isabelle, who was taking pictures with the children.

Emily noticed Ambassador Pacheco hugging his daughter, before he was pulled away by another man and disappeared in the crowd. It took a few more minutes until the children were ready to leave. Emily walked into the hallway with them, pretending that she, too, was leaving.

"I'd better visit the ladies' room quickly," she said to Isabelle and the principal. "See you all on Monday."

"Good night, Miss Warner," several of the kids said.

"Good night, kids," Emily replied and turned toward the ladies' room, but before she reached it, she pivoted. The children and their two chaperones had reached the exit and were walking past security.

Seeing that neither the kids nor the two chaperones were looking in her direction, Emily walked back into the ballroom. She'd spotted Lars Nielson briefly before the performance, so she knew he was in attendance, though he'd left the room before the performance had started. She had to try to find him. Emily snatched a glass of champagne from the tray a waiter passed around, not really interested in drinking it. But she knew she needed to look like she had a purpose here.

"Such a lovely performance," a woman in a long silver gown said to her and smiled.

"Oh, thank you," Emily said. "The kids enjoyed every second of it."

The woman nodded, then turned back to the two men she was talking to, and Emily walked past her, keeping her eyes open for a tall blond man. But with this being the Swedish Embassy, there were rather a lot of men who fit the profile. And with all men dressed pretty much the same, she had no other visual to go by.

She walked around the room, never staying too long in any position, not wanting people to realize that she knew nobody here. Ambassador Pacheco had disappeared, most likely drawn into a business conversation by another diplomat, or smoking a cigar in another part of the building. In a way she was glad for it, because she didn't want him to know that she hadn't left with the children, because she had an ulterior motive to attend tonight's event. She would hate for him to know that she'd used him and his kindness. But this was important to her, and in love and war, everything was fair. Though this was neither a matter of love nor war. It was a matter of preserving her own sanity. She had to do this for Maddie and for herself, so Maddie could rest in peace, and Emily could live free from the visions.

Emily felt her eyes getting tired. There were too many lights, too many people swirling around. She glanced to the dance floor, where several couples whirled around so fast, Emily suddenly felt as if the ground beneath her feet was moving. She quickly closed her eyes and took a breath, before turning away from the sight, and looked into the direction of the main entrance to the ballroom.

That's when she saw him: Lars Nielson, Maddie's ex-fiancé stood there, a glass in his hand. He was alone. This was her chance. As fast as she could, without running, she moved through the throng of people. She was in luck. Nielson hadn't moved from his spot near the door.

"Mr. Nielson," Emily said quickly, before her courage could desert her. "I'm Emily Warner."

He nodded politely and said, "I don't believe we've met, or if we have, please accept my apologies for forgetting your name."

His words were overly polite and formal, but given that he was clearly here to represent the Swedish government, it was understandable.

"No, we haven't met."

"Uh, I'm relieved that I haven't made a faux-pas then." He gave her a charming smile, and Emily understood why a woman like Maddie would be drawn to him.

"I'm here as a guest of Ambassador Pacheco from—"

"Argentina, yes, I know him well." Then he ran his eyes over her as if measuring her. "And you are… his… uh, friend?"

She shook her head. The idea that she was friends with the ambassador was almost funny. "I teach his daughter. Piano."

Nielson smirked and leaned in. "Of course you do. But may I say he's robbing the cradle, the old dog."

Emily felt herself blush. Nielson clearly thought that she was having a sexual relationship with the ambassador, which was preposterous to say the least. But maybe this assumption would help her in getting Nielson to talk to her about Maddie.

She smiled. "He's a very kind man."

"Very kind, and very tragic."

Nielson's words gave her an opening.

"I wanted to convey my condolences to you. What happened to Madeline... it's so senseless."

His demeanor changed. He took a sip from his glass. "It's hard to wrap one's head around it. Did you know her?"

"Yes, and no."

Nielson raised his eyebrows. "That's an odd answer to a very straightforward question."

"I never met her personally... but I'm grateful to her... for what she gave me." She had no idea whether to tell him about the fact that she'd received Maddie's corneas or not. Maybe it was stupid to reveal too much. She would come across as crazy if she told him the truth. "She was a very giving person."

"That she was."

"I know it's none of my business, but when she broke up with you... do you think she regretted it?"

He furrowed his brow.

"I mean, leaving you only months before your planned wedding... that..."

"Where did you get that from? The tabloids?" He shook his head. "Our split was entirely amicable. It was a mutual decision."

Emily's chin dropped. "But the fight you had with her..." Vicky had told her what she'd read in the press months earlier. It was in line with the vision she'd had in which Nielson had looked totally enraged.

Nielson scoffed. "It was an argument between friends." His chin tightened. "I warned her to be careful with that jerk... Diego Sanchez. He's as shady as they come. But she didn't want to listen, did she?" He sounded angry now and took a big gulp of his glass, emptying it. "And you're right, it's none of your business."

He stalked away, but instead of going into the ballroom, he went into the hallway and marched toward the main entrance of the embassy.

Emily sighed. She'd angered him, which hadn't been her intention. Nevertheless, she'd found out one piece of information: Maddie hadn't dumped Nielson. If their breakup had truly been a mutual decision, then Maddie would have no unfinished business with Nielson, no reason why she would want Emily to reach out to him. But Nielson's words about Diego Sanchez had caught her attention. What if Maddie was trying to show her that Diego Sanchez had something to do with her death? Was that why she'd showed Emily a vision of Nielson, so Nielson could tell her about Sanchez? It was worth a shot.

"Miss?" a male voice said from behind her.

She pivoted and found herself face to face with a man she recognized immediately, though his attire was different today. He was dressed in a black suit. Around his neck hung a lanyard with a label that identified him as security, while he wore an earpiece.

"Come with me, and don't make a scene."

41

ADAM YANG DIDN'T BELIEVE IN COINCIDENCES. Lars Nielson had approached him and asked to check whether the woman he'd been talking to was a reporter who'd infiltrated the embassy party, so she could grill him on his relationship with Madeline Bolton.

Yang had just relieved another security guard who'd been working the front entrance to the embassy, and had immediately checked the guest list. Emily Warner's name wasn't on it. Somehow she'd crashed the party. How, he had no idea. He hadn't considered her that clever, but clearly she'd found a way to get into the heavily guarded event. It didn't escape his notice either that she'd talked to Lars Nielson after being blocked from talking to him at Madeline Bolton's funeral.

This was the third time Yang had met Emily Warner, the third time her appearance was somehow connected to Madeline Bolton. First she'd shown up at Patel's Market, where Madeline Bolton had witnessed a crime a month earlier. A few days later she'd crashed—he was certain—Miss Bolton's funeral. And now she'd somehow infiltrated the Swedish Embassy party where she'd bothered Madeline Bolton's ex-fiancé. But to what end?

"Come with me, and don't make a scene," Yang said.

Emily Warner gaped at him. "You're the policeman..."

"Detective Yang," he said curtly and gripped her elbow. "Let's go."

"But I haven't done anything wrong."

"I don't know how you got into this party, but you weren't invited, Miss Warner. Or should I look for a different name on the guest list?"

"I was invited!" she protested, looking outraged. "I came with Ambassador Pacheco."

"Of course you did," he said unable to keep the sarcasm out of his voice. "And where's he now?"

She looked over her shoulder. "He was just here. Just a few minutes ago."

Yang steered her away from the open door to the ballroom, so nobody would hear her should she become hysterical.

"Why were you bothering Mr. Nielson?"

"I wasn't bothering him."

"You asked him about Madeline Bolton."

She had the decency to look sheepish. "I was just making conversation."

"Is that how you extract juicy stories for the tabloids?"

"The tabloids?" She huffed. "You think I'm a reporter?"

"Why else would you have approached Mr. Nielson and asked him questions about his ex-fiancée?"

"I'm not a reporter!" She almost spit out the last word.

If that was the truth, then she could only be a stalker, which made her even more dangerous. And crazy.

"Listen, Miss Warner," he said calmly, not wanting to rile her up even more, "let me give you some advice. Infiltrating an event hosted by a foreign government could get you in hot water—"

"But I didn't infiltrate the party!" she said exasperated. "I was invited to perform with my students. They sang folk songs, and I accompanied them on the piano."

He sighed. "Earlier you said that you came with Ambassador Pacheco."

"Yes, and that's true. He was the one who organized the performance so my students and I could attend. His daughter is one of my students."

Yang shook his head. The woman was getting more and more agitated, and it wouldn't take long before she drew the attention of the invited guests. "Please, Miss Warner, let's do this quietly."

He managed to usher her along the corridor leading to the main entrance.

"Why won't you believe me?" she said, her voice suddenly shaking.

When he glanced at her face, he noticed that tears brimmed in her eyes. For a moment, he considered that she might be speaking the truth, but he pushed that notion away. Too many things about this woman weren't adding up. If she wasn't a reporter here to get the inside scoop on the ex-fiancé of a dead woman, then she was most likely mentally ill, deranged, or just plain crazy. A shame really. She looked petite and graceful in her black dress. She barely wore any makeup, yet she looked prettier than most of the other female guests he'd helped out of their limousines upon arrival.

Not wanting to make her cry, Yang said, "I'll order an Uber to drive you home, alright?"

Arriving at the entrance door, he walked her outside. "I need to see your driver's license." He pulled his cell phone from his pocket and opened the Uber app. He wanted to make sure she didn't just give him a fake address.

"I don't have one."

He met her eyes. "You don't have it on you?"

She shook her head. "I don't have a driver's license."

Was she lying to him? He couldn't tell. Normally, he had a pretty good radar to figure out if a suspect was lying to him or not, but with this woman he couldn't tell. It was more than just a little unsettling.

"Fine," he said. "What's your address?"

"I can get my own Uber."

"I insist."

She sighed, then recited an address in Columbia Heights, not too far from Patel's Market and Yang's own apartment. He entered the address into the app and waited a few moments.

"The Uber should be here in a few minutes," he said and looked up.

But Emily Warner didn't look like she'd heard him. She was staring into the distance, her eyes wide, her mouth gaping open. Yang looked over his shoulder to see what she was looking at, expecting to see somebody. But there was nobody, just a large planter with flowers.

"Miss Warner?"

42

ONE MINUTE SHE WAS TALKING to Detective Yang, the next Emily's vision blurred. For a moment, she thought that her body was rejecting the corneas, but she was wrong. This was another vision, another memory from Maddie's life.

Perfectly manicured hands scrolled through the contact list on a phone, then tapped on a name. All Emily had time to read was the person's first name, Sergei. Then the reflection of a face appeared in a shiny armoire: Maddie. She held the phone to her ear. Emily couldn't hear what she was saying, nor could she hear whether Sergei replied or what he said. The call lasted just a few seconds. Maddie put the cell phone away then turned around.

That's when Emily realized that Maddie wasn't alone. The girl that stood in an elegant home, which she had to assume was Maddie's, couldn't be older than thirteen. She wore yoga pants and a big sweatshirt. Her feet were bare, her long dark hair wet as if she'd had a shower. Her blue eyes brimmed with tears. Her face and neck were covered in bruises. Her wrists seemed raw and red, as if something had irritated her skin. Emily tried to get a closer look, but Maddie's gaze swept upward, away from the girl's hands and back to her face.

The longer Maddie stared at her, the more Emily realized that the girl was frightened to death. She was shaking, her shoulders hunched forward, her chest quivering with sobs. Yet when Maddie put her hand on the girl's arm, which Emily could only interpret as a soothing gesture, the girl shrank back. She didn't want to be touched. Didn't trust anybody. Emily didn't need to hear Maddie's or the girl's words to understand that somebody had hurt the girl, and somehow Maddie was trying to help her.

Beneath the bruises and the tears, the girl was beautiful. Emily had never seen eyes like hers. They were captivating and drew the beholder to her. In a few years, the girl would bloom into a beautiful woman—if she could survive whatever hell she'd been through, whatever danger she was in. There was no doubt in Emily's mind that the girl had fled from something or someone.

Emily watched as Maddie's hand motioned the girl to follow her upstairs, where she opened a door to a bedroom. It was a cozy room with rich furnishings, a queen-size bed, an antique dresser, and a rocking chair with a reading lamp in one corner. The shades were drawn already.

Again Maddie exchanged a few words with the girl, but Emily couldn't hear their conversation, only see what Maddie had seen.

When Maddie turned and left the room, the vision suddenly stopped, and Emily found herself staring at a planter with flowers. For a moment, she didn't know where she was.

"Miss Warner? Are you alright? Do you need a doctor?"

Emily turned her head in the direction of the male voice, but the sudden movement made her sway. A firm hand gripped her elbow to help her regain her balance. She blinked and saw Detective Yang cast her a concerned look.

"I'm fine. Too much alcohol," she claimed even though she hadn't taken a single sip of champagne. It was better that Yang thought she was tipsy rather than crazy.

"Well, then let's get you home. The Uber is here," he said, and his voice was a lot kinder than when he'd accused her of having crashed the embassy party.

"Thank you."

She didn't need to stay at the party any longer. She'd talked to Lars Nielson. She didn't know whether she believed him when he'd told her that his split from Maddie had been amicable. However, Emily was surprised that he and Maddie had been an item in the first place. Nielson didn't strike her as the kind of man who was passionate enough for Maddie. Was Diego Sanchez different? Was he the kind of man who could fly into a jealous rage in a second? She should have asked the housekeeper about Maddie's relationship with him. But looking into Diego Sanchez had to wait. After what this latest vision revealed, it was more important to find out who the girl was, and how a man named Sergei was involved.

"And Miss Warner?" Detective Yang said as he opened the car door for her.

"Yes?" She got into the back of the Uber and met his gaze.

He seemed to hesitate. Then he reached into his pocket and pulled out a card. He handed it to her. "Next time you're tempted to crash a party, call me so I can talk you off the ledge."

"I didn't crash—"

"So you keep telling me."

"If you really think I crashed the party, then why don't you arrest me? I mean you're a real policeman, not just a security guard." What had gotten into her? Was it really smart to poke the bear?

"Quit while you're ahead, Miss Warner. Good night."

He closed the car door, and the Uber driver set the car in motion. Emily turned her head to look back at Detective Yang and noticed that he followed the car with his eyes. Then she looked down at the card he'd given her, but it was too dark in the car to read it. Instead, she placed it in her handbag and leaned back in the seat.

She was tired. Too tired to wonder why the detective had given her his card. It didn't matter. After all, she hadn't crashed the embassy party, and she sure had no intention of ever crashing one. Hence there was no need for Detective Yang to talk her off the ledge.

43

IT WAS MID-MORNING, when Jefferson parked a block away from the home of Dimitry and Irina Fedorov and killed the engine.

"You did what?"

Yang shrugged. "What would you have done? Arrested her? Remember, I wasn't there in my capacity as a detective. I was off duty."

"Which means exactly zilch." Jefferson cast him a deadpan look. "I mean, clearly there's something wrong with this woman. She has something to do with Madeline Bolton. You ran into her twice now."

"Three times," Yang corrected his partner, before he could stop himself.

"What? Not just at the corner store and the embassy?"

Yang pressed his lips together.

"Out with it," Jefferson demanded.

Knowing that Jefferson was like a dog with a bone, Yang sighed. "She and a friend also showed up at Madeline Bolton's funeral."

Mouth gaping open, Jefferson shook his head. "What the fuck were you doing at that funeral? What if Lieutenant Arnold finds out?"

"She won't. Not unless you tell her."

"I should!" Jefferson slapped his hand on the steering wheel. "How the fuck did you ever make detective?"

"Just the way you did, by not taking anything at face value and following my gut."

For a moment, Jefferson was silent. "Touché."

Yang grinned. "And here I thought you didn't speak a foreign language."

Jefferson rolled his eyes. "Just don't drag me into this. If anybody finds out you're looking into Madeline Bolton's death, I'll deny we ever had this conversation."

"Works for me," Yang said and got out of the car.

Jefferson did the same. "We should have brought a translator this time."

Yang shrugged. "If the girl knows anything, we'll ask her to come to the station and get a translator then."

They walked to the Fedorovs' house and rang the doorbell. There was the sound of footsteps, then the door was opened. It was Dimitry Fedorov.

"Remember us?" Jefferson asked.

Fedorov nodded. Behind him, his wife came into view. She looked frightened.

"We'd like to talk to Sasha to see if she can tell us something about the other two girls that disappeared," Yang said.

There was no mistaking the look the married couple exchanged. Yang had seen this look in lots of persons of interest before—when he'd caught them in a lie.

"Where is she?" He pointed to his watch. "There's no school today."

"We can do this the easy way, or the hard way," Jefferson added. "Trust me, you don't want the hard way."

Mrs. Fedorov suddenly burst into tears, and her husband drew her into his arms, while casting a pleading look at Jefferson and Yang.

"Don't hurt us. Please."

Yang's hand instinctively went to his service weapon. His senses were alert, and he scanned the hallway behind the couple. "Is anybody else in the house?"

"No," Fedorov said quickly. "No, just me and my wife."

"Do you mind if we come in?" Yang asked. When Fedorov made a motion to invite them, Yang nodded to Jefferson, before they both entered.

Yang quickly checked every room on the first floor, while Jefferson did the same on the second floor.

"It's just the two of them," Jefferson confirmed, when he came back downstairs and joined them in the living room.

"What's going on?" Yang asked the couple. "Where is Sasha? And don't say she's studying with a friend."

Mrs. Fedorov continued crying, but her husband replied, "She not here. She did not come back."

Yang exchanged a look with his partner. "You're saying she disappeared again?"

Fedorov shook his head. "She did not come back like I told you. She still missing." He looked fearful as if he was expecting to be punished.

"You lied to us? Why?"

"You police. We did not want to get in trouble. If we get in trouble with police, immigration will not give us green card."

"Fuck," Yang cursed.

Jefferson shook his head. "Jesus Christ! You thought you'd be in trouble if you admit that Sasha hadn't come back? Let me tell you something, you're in trouble now because you lied to us." Jefferson's voice got louder with every word he spoke.

The Fedorovs both shrank back, clearly scared.

Yang put his hand on his partner's arm. "Don't. I know where they're coming from. Russia isn't exactly known for ethical policing." Then he addressed Fedorov. "You were afraid we'd tell immigration that a girl disappeared in your care, and you thought you'd be punished for it?"

Fedorov nodded.

"But then why did you report her as missing in the first place if you were so scared about the police?" Jefferson asked.

"It was the school," Fedorov said. "The school made report. We had to speak to police."

Yang nodded, understanding. Had they lived in fear all this time, waiting for immigration to knock on their door?

"Okay, I get it," Yang said. "But you have to do something for us now."

The couple's eyes widened.

"I need you to come to the station with us to give a DNA sample, Mr. Fedorov." Then he motioned to Mrs. Fedorov. "And we need to get Sasha's DNA. From her toothbrush or hairbrush. Do you have that?"

Fedorov said something in Russian to his wife. She nodded and motioned to the ceiling. "Upstairs."

"I'll go up there with you," Jefferson said.

Reluctantly, the woman walked to the door, and Jefferson followed her.

When they were out of earshot, Yang took a step closer to Fedorov. "I want you to understand something, Mr. Fedorov. Nobody will hurt you or your wife or jeopardize your immigration status, if you've got nothing to do with Sasha's disappearance. But if you do, I won't rest until you pay for your crime. Do you understand that?"

Fedorov nodded, his big frame trembling.

"Good," Yang said. "So you'll come to the station voluntarily?"

"Yes, Detective. I give my DNA. And you will see I did not hurt Sasha."

Yang studied the man's face. Too much fear was written on the Russian immigrant's face for Yang to be able to tell if he was lying or telling the truth. Science would have to give an answer to that question.

44

EMILY FIDGETED. Maybe this was a bad idea. What was she even expecting to find out? Wasn't she drawing attention to herself by being here? And what would she even say? Perhaps she should've at least discussed this with Vicky. But then again, had she told Vicky what she was planning, her friend would undoubtedly have talked her out of it.

"Yes, can I help you?" The woman who'd opened the door wiped her hands on her apron.

This wasn't Mrs. Bolton. Clearly, people like the Boltons had domestic staff.

"Uh, yes, I... uh." Emily cleared her throat. "I'm here to see Mrs. Bolton."

Suspiciously, the housekeeper looked her up and down. "Do you have an appointment?"

"Uhm, no, but—"

The feisty-looking woman put her hands on her hips and thrust her chin up. "Mrs. Bolton is not to be disturbed."

"But, I need to talk to her—"

"Can't you reporters give the woman a break? She's grieving!"

Clearly, the housekeeper was loyal to her employer and protective of her. But Emily couldn't give up now.

"I'm not a reporter! Maddie gave me a gift," Emily said quickly. "And I want to thank Mrs. Bolton for it."

"Just leave!" the woman said in a loud voice, ready to slam the door in Emily's face.

"What's going on, Trudy?"

The voice came from behind the housekeeper, who now turned and revealed Mrs. Bolton approaching. Emily recognized her from the funeral. She was petite and looked fragile in her black dress. Her hair was perfectly done in a low bun, her make-up impeccable, yet it couldn't conceal the paleness of her face and the hollowness of her eyes. This was what a grieving mother looked like.

"Mrs. Bolton," Emily said quickly, "I need to thank you for what Maddie gave me."

"I'll take care of it, ma'am," the housekeeper said. "This reporter won't disturb you again, I promise."

But Mrs. Bolton looked past her employee and stared at Emily. Their eyes met for a long second.

"What about Maddie? What did she give you?"

"My eyesight," Emily said, still holding Mrs. Bolton's gaze. "She gave me her corneas."

Mrs. Bolton's lips began to tremble. Trudy fell silent.

"Please come in, Miss?" Mrs. Bolton said after what seemed an eternity.

"Warner, Emily Warner."

Moments later, Emily sat down on the sofa in the elegant living room, while Mrs. Bolton took a seat on the armchair across from it.

Trudy stood at the door, hesitant to leave her employer. "Ma'am?"

"Leave us, Trudy."

Grunting something unintelligible, Trudy left, but didn't close the door behind her.

"I'm sorry to intrude like this," Emily said.

Mrs. Bolton nodded. "I knew that Maddie was an organ donor, but I thought that my husband made sure that her name was withheld..."

"It was a clerical error," Emily lied. She felt bad about having to lie to this woman who had gone through so much.

Again, Mrs. Bolton nodded, but didn't say anything.

"I was blind for fifteen years, and never thought that I would be able to see again. But your daughter's gift..." Emily felt her eyes moisten, sensing Mrs. Bolton's grief physically. She felt bad about disturbing her in her time of grief.

"I wish I could say that I'm happy that something good came of it... I do..." Mrs. Bolton forced a smile to her lips. "But I can't... I just want my daughter back."

"I can feel your grief. I lost my mother fifteen years ago, in the same accident that robbed me of my eyesight..." She sniffled. "I still grieve for her today, and I always will. But I pray that I'll never have to grieve for a child... that I'll never have to feel the pain you do."

A lonely tear loosened from Mrs. Bolton's eye and ran down her cheek. She didn't wipe it away. "Thank you, Miss... Miss Warner. I appreciate your words. Hundreds of people expressed their condolences to me and my family, but they were just words, hollow words. But you, a stranger, you seem to understand what I'm going through…"

Emily swallowed hard. "I feel a connection…"

Mrs. Bolton's forehead furrowed. "I'm not sure I follow."

"I know this might sound strange. I don't quite understand it myself, but ever since the transplant I've been seeing things…" She took a deep breath. "Memories… memories that aren't mine."

Mrs. Bolton's frown deepened.

"I see things that your daughter saw and did."

Mrs. Bolton shook her head. "No, no, that's not possible."

She understood Mrs. Bolton's reaction. Had somebody come to her to claim the same, she wouldn't have believed it either. She wished she didn't have to probe any further and open up fresh wounds, but she needed to find out what the flashes of Maddie's life meant.

"I thought that too at first, but I can't shake the memories. It's as if Maddie is asking me to do something for her… I know it sounds crazy."

Mrs. Bolton rose from her chair, her body rigid. "Because it is crazy. If you're trying to get money from me—"

"I'm not here for money," Emily interrupted and rose too. She hadn't meant to upset the grieving woman. For a moment she toyed with the idea of simply leaving before she upset Maddie's mother even more. But she couldn't leave. She needed to get to the bottom of this. And she also realized that she only had a few moments left before Mrs. Bolton would throw her out. "I'm here because I think Maddie was murdered and wants me to help her find her killer."

Mrs. Bolton gasped.

"She's showing me things through her corneas that I think have something to do with her death. I need to do this for her. So she can be at peace." And so Emily could be at peace too.

"I don't understand, Miss Warner. Why are you doing this to me?"

"Because we both need answers. Maddie's death wasn't an accident. I can feel it. Why would Maddie have stepped on a ladder in three-inch heels?"

"How do you know this? I didn't even know… Nobody told me about the shoes…"

From somewhere else in the house, Emily heard voices.

"Maddie wants me to find who did this to her. I need your help. Please, Maddie needs your help. She showed me somebody. A man. She talked to him before she died. I think he's either involved or he knows something." Emily guessed that the latter was the case and that it had something to do with the bruised girl, but she didn't want to upset Mrs. Bolton even more. She didn't need to know about the girl. Not yet anyway.

"Diego?" There was a glint in Mrs. Bolton's eyes. "I never liked him. He wasn't good for her."

"It wasn't Diego. And it wasn't Lars either. She called him Sergei. I think she needed to see him. And it was urgent." That was her best guess, even though Emily hadn't heard the conversation.

"Sergei? But why would Sergei..."

"You know a Sergei?"

She nodded. "Sergei Petrov from the Russian embassy. But he never had a relationship with Maddie."

"Are you sure?"

"He's gay. He wasn't one of her lovers. They barely knew each other. I can't imagine why she would talk to him."

"But—"

"Who the hell are you?"

Emily whirled around to the female voice coming from the door. She recognized the young woman with the black pixie haircut and the slim figure. She'd seen her at the funeral: Natalie, Maddie's older sister.

"I'm just here to—"

But the woman marched toward her, an angry expression on her face. "Leave my mother alone! You people have nothing better to do than bother others in their time of grief. If you don't get out of here this minute, I'm calling the police!"

"Natalie," her mother said.

"Can't you see that my mother is in no condition to talk to anybody?" Natalie continued and tossed Emily an angry glare. "Trudy?"

The housekeeper appeared in the door. She'd clearly been waiting there for her cue.

"Show this woman out!" Then Natalie narrowed her eyes at Emily. "If you ever approach my family again, I'll have you arrested."

Emily had no choice but to leave. "I'm sorry," she said with a last look at Mrs. Bolton who now looked distraught. She meant it. She was sorry for upsetting Maddie's mother, but Emily knew she was doing this for Maddie, and ultimately for Mrs. Bolton. Because once Emily could find who was responsible for Maddie's death, her mother would finally have closure. As would Emily.

45

It was already late afternoon, when Yang and Jefferson had to make another visit to one of the foster parents.

"This is the part of my job I hate most," Yang said.

Jefferson, who stood in the elevator next to him, nodded. "Ditto."

The elevator dinged, and the doors opened on the top floor. They'd been here four days earlier. Yang felt a heavy pit in his stomach. He hated to be the bearer of bad news, but there was no way around it.

The door to the apartment was already open. Mila Veselak stood there. This time she wasn't alone. Her husband, Emil, stood next to her, an arm around her waist as if he guessed why Yang and Jefferson were back. Her look was one of trepidation.

After a quick greeting, and introducing himself and Jefferson to Emil Veselak, they entered.

In the living room, Jefferson motioned first to the couple, then to the sofa. "You might want to sit down."

A sob tore from Mrs. Veselak's chest. "It's Annika, isn't it?"

Yang sighed. "I'm sorry. We got the DNA analysis back. It matched the samples we took from Annika's toothbrush and hairbrush."

Mrs. Veselak burst into tears, and her husband pulled her into his arms, letting her cry on his shoulder.

He looked at Yang and Jefferson. "We wanted to adopt her… if her parents couldn't be found." He choked up, then cleared his throat.

Yang watched his body language and listened to the tone of his voice. His training kicked in just like it had to. Because having positively identified the victim meant that now Yang and Jefferson could look at suspects. And knowing what he knew about rape and murder told him who had just become the main suspect: Annika's foster father. It didn't matter that the man looked almost as grief-stricken as his wife. Many criminals were gifted liars and actors. Yang would be neglecting his duty if he didn't consider Emil Veselak a person of interest and take the appropriate steps.

Yang exchanged a look with Jefferson. They'd discussed this on the way here and prepared for what they needed to do.

"We need to ask you a few questions. May we sit down?" Jefferson asked.

Mila Veselak peeled herself out of her husband's embrace and wiped her tears on the sleeve of her blouse, seemingly unconcerned about wrinkling the silk. "Please, I'm sorry, please, Detectives, take a seat."

When they were all seated, Jefferson pulled out a small notepad and pen.

"Tell me how she died," Mila Veselak said, her voice breaking. Her husband reached for her hand and squeezed it.

"She was strangled," Yang said.

Mila's lower lip quivered at the news. "She had to look into her killer's face... oh my God... how long did she struggle.... my girl... Annika..."

"Don't do this to yourself, Mila," her husband said, but she shook her head and looked at Yang instead.

"That's not all he did, is it?"

Yang held her gaze and waited for Jefferson to reply.

"We believe that she was bound and held somewhere. She was raped."

Another sob tore from Mila's throat.

"Multiple times," Jefferson added. "We have DNA that we believe to be from the perpetrator."

"Then you can find him," Mila said, lifting her chin. "And punish him."

Yang nodded. "There was no match in the national database."

"But you have to find him," Mila insisted.

"We will. And now that we've identified the d... the victim, now that we know it's Annika, we're collecting DNA from every male she was in contact with."

Slowly, Emil dropped his wife's hand and turned his gaze to Yang and Jefferson. He swallowed. "You're talking about me."

Mila turned to look at her husband, then back at Yang and Jefferson. "You can't be serious. Emil would never touch Annika. Never."

Emil reached for his wife's hands and captured them. "Don't, Mila. They're just doing their job. Aren't you, Detectives?"

"We can do this one of two ways," Jefferson offered. "If you're willing to give us a DNA sample right now, there won't be any need for you to come to the station, at least not now. But if you refuse, we'll get a warrant—"

Emil lifted one hand. "That's not necessary. I don't want you to waste your time investigating me when you could be out there looking for the killer." He cast his wife a quick look. "What is it you need? Blood?"

Yang shook his head and reached into his jacket's inside pocket. He pulled out a clear plastic evidence bag. "Just a swab of the inside of your cheek."

Emil nodded.

Yang donned gloves so as not to contaminate the DNA sample. He used the long cotton swab in the evidence bag and rubbed it against the inside of Emil's cheek a few times to make sure he got a sufficient sample, before he dropped the swab into a vial, closed it and dropped it into the evidence bag. Then he sealed it with a label, wrote Emil Veselak's name on it, and dated it.

He handed Emil the pen. "Please sign across the label to confirm that this is your sample."

Emil did as he was asked, before handing everything back. "What now?"

Jefferson answered in Yang's stead. "We'll be in touch."

"How long is this going to take?" Emil asked, pointing at the DNA sample Yang held in his hand.

"A few days," Jefferson answered. "And you'll both need to answer more questions about the circumstances of Annika's disappearance."

"Can I see her?" Mila asked.

Yang sighed. "I don't think that's a good idea right now."

Mila's eyes filled with tears anew. "How bad does…" She couldn't finish her question.

"Give it a few days, Mrs. Veselak… for your own sake," Yang said. He understood that she wanted to see the body to get closure, but he feared that seeing Annika's body would only make her pain worse. Yet ultimately it wasn't Yang's choice to make.

In the elevator, Jefferson turned to Yang. "Let's get a uni to keep an eye on Emil Veselak, while we wait for the DNA analysis."

"You think he's involved in Annika's murder?"

"It's possible. The wife is genuinely distraught. Hard to fake that. She loved that girl. But he?" Jefferson shrugged. "I've sat across from cold-blooded killers who sounded more honest than Mother Teresa. Sure, he appeared sad, and he was willing to give us the DNA sample voluntarily, but that means nothing. He could be packing his bags as we speak and getting ready to leave the country…"

"I agree. Let's get an officer here right now to watch him," Yang said and pulled out his phone.

46

IT WAS EVENING, when Eric Bolton rushed into the house. He'd been in meetings all afternoon, while Natalie had tried to reach him. When he'd finally been able to return her call, she'd told him that Rita had had a visitor who'd left her distraught and in tears.

Bolton found his wife in the living room. A bottle of Scotch sat on the coffee table. Rita held an almost empty tumbler in her hand, while she stared into the distance. He knew that look and knew that he had to pull her out of the dark hole she'd descended in.

"Rita," he said and sat down next to her, while he gently pried the glass from her hand.

She turned her head to him. "Eric…" She rested her head against his shoulder, and a sob tore from her throat. "Maddie was murdered. Our baby was murdered."

"What?" Bolton gripped his wife by the shoulders to look at her. "Did that woman say that?"

She nodded amidst tears. "She said she got Maddie's corneas in a transplant, and now she sees things that Maddie saw."

"That's ludicrous!"

"But then how would she know things that I didn't even know?" Rita wailed. "She saw Maddie talking to Sergei Petrov from the Russian embassy."

"Sergei Petrov?"

"Yes, just before her death."

"Impossible. I don't even know who he is."

"She knew him. They met at a couple of events in the last few months."

"Who is this woman who told you all that crap?"

"She said her name is Emily Warner. And she was blind for fifteen years before she got Maddie's corneas."

Fury charged through Bolton. "The organ donation was made anonymously. That woman doesn't even know whether she got Maddie's corneas or somebody else's."

Rita shook her head. "She said there was a clerical error, and that's why she knew."

Bolton's jaw tightened. "That's total bullshit. That woman is probably part of some scam to get money out of us. Probably some fake psychic trying to get you to fall for her tricks! It's unconscionable trying to exploit you in your grief."

"But what if she's right? What if she does see what Maddie saw? What if she knows who the killer is?"

"Nobody is saying that Maddie was murdered. Mike's people are still investigating. And they haven't found anything yet that points to murder. I'm sorry, honey, but this woman was just trying to con you. I'll make sure she'll never do anything like that again."

Rita stared at him, fear in her eyes. "What are you gonna do?"

He pulled out his cell phone. "I'm calling Mike. He'll take care of it." He tapped on Mike Faulkner's number and let it ring. On the third ring, Faulkner picked up.

"Hey, Eric, what's up?"

"There's been an incident."

"Hold on, let me put you on speaker. I'm in the middle of getting dressed for a dinner at the White House." Bolton heard some background noise, then Faulkner said, "Okay, tell me what happened."

With the cell phone on the dresser in his bedroom in the Washington townhouse where he'd lived for the past two years, ever since he'd become Chief of Staff, Faulkner reached for his cufflinks and continued dressing for the formal event the President had requested he attend.

"Some woman came to see Rita today. She claimed that she got Maddie's corneas. And she said she sees *things*."

"What things?"

"Things that Maddie saw. As if she now has Maddie's eyes. How can she even know that she got Maddie's corneas, when the organ donation was made anonymously?"

Faulkner sensed Bolton's frustration and anger. "What's her name?"

Faulkner heard Rita's voice saying something to her husband.

"Rita said she introduced herself as Emily Warner. It's probably not even her real name. The name sounds familiar. I could swear I've heard it before, but I can't remember where."

"Eric, put Mike on speaker." A moment later, Faulkner heard Rita loud and clear. "She said she was blind for fifteen years. I don't know why she would do this. Why she would want to hurt me like that by pretending she could communicate with Maddie? As if Maddie was telling her to expose her killer."

"Her killer?" Faulkner dropped one cufflink. "She claims she knows that Maddie was murdered? The Secret Service hasn't made that determination yet. We don't have any evidence of that at this point."

"Let me handle this, Rita. I don't want you to get even more upset," Bolton said. "Mike, you need to do something. That woman who holds herself out to be some sort of psychic is obviously crazy and could be a danger to Rita. I want to make sure she doesn't come back."

Faulkner grabbed a pen from the dresser and said, "What's her name again?"

"Emily Warner," Rita said.

Faulkner scribbled down the name on a notepad. "Got it. I'll make inquiries into her. Anything else you can tell me about her?"

"She's around thirty," Rita said. "And… uh… Eric, there was something else she said… I forgot now…" Rita sounded frazzled.

"Sergei?" Bolton asked.

"Yes," Rita said eagerly. "She also claimed that Maddie spoke to Sergei Petrov before her death."

"Sergei Petrov?"

Shit! How could this woman know about Maddie's call to Petrov? This wasn't good. There had to be a leak somewhere. But he trusted the Secret Service agents on the case and knew for certain that they wouldn't have mentioned the phone call to Petrov to anybody. Faulkner hadn't even mentioned it to Bolton.

"Yeah, from the Russian embassy. Do you know him?" Bolton asked.

"I've heard the name." And that was all he could say. "I'll look into it."

"And if we have to get a restraining order against this Emily Warner, we will," Bolton said.

"Let me check her out first. She's probably just a run-of-the-mill fake psychic trying to drum up some business. I've seen cons like that before."

"Thanks Mike, I appreciate it," Bolton said.

"I'll be in touch," Faulkner said and disconnected the call.

Outside in the hallway, he heard the old wooden floorboards creak. The door of his bedroom was open, and he called out, "Caleb?"

Footsteps approached, until his son came into view. "Hey, Dad, sorry didn't want to disturb you while you were on the phone."

"I didn't expect to see you tonight. Or did I forget we were meeting for dinner?" Faulkner motioned to the tuxedo jacket that hung on the outside of the closet. "I'm expected at the White House."

"No, we didn't arrange anything for tonight. I was in the area, and figured I'd stop by on the off chance that you've got time for a drink. Don't worry, maybe this weekend?"

"I'd like that," Faulkner said, still distracted from the phone call with Bolton.

He was wracking his brain about how this woman could know about Maddie's phone call to a Russian cultural attaché, when only a handful of people knew about it. What else did she know?

47

"The Embassy of the Russian Federation. How may I direct your call?" The woman's accent was heavy.

"Sergei Petrov, please," Emily said with butterflies in her stomach.

It had taken her only a minute to find the embassy's telephone number. It had taken her much longer than that to muster all her courage to make the call. She had no idea what to expect, or how to even explain to the Russian diplomat that she needed to talk to him about Madeline Bolton.

"Mr. Petrov isn't in today. I'll put you through to his voicemail."

Before Emily could say anything else, the woman transferred her, and a recording played. It was in Russian and then repeated in English. "You've reached Sergei Petrov. Please leave a message, and I'll return your call."

"Mr. Petrov, you don't know me, but… uh, I need to speak to you about Madeline Bolton. It's important. Please call me back as soon as you can. I'm Emily Warner." She recited her cell phone number before disconnecting the call.

What now? She was stuck. Maybe Vicky had an idea about how to proceed. Emily had already filled her in on her latest vision in which she'd seen Maddie with a pre-teen girl while contacting Sergei. However, she hadn't told her friend about her visit to Mrs. Bolton. Vicky would only chew her out for having been so brazen.

When she heard music from Vicky's apartment next to hers, she knew that Vicky was home.

"Coffee, come, let's visit Vicky."

The dog got up and wagged his tail. Coffee loved Vicky, because she always had treats, and because Coffee loved to play with Vicky's cat, Merlin.

The moment Emily entered Vicky's apartment, Coffee was begging for treats, and Vicky's cat jumped off the couch and greeted Coffee by rubbing its body against Coffee's legs.

"So, did you call him?" Vicky asked, while pointing to a coffee cup.

Emily nodded, giving the mug a thumbs up. "He wasn't in. I left a voicemail."

Vicky handed her the coffee mug, and they sat down on the couch, while their pets played on the floor.

"Well, that's all you can do."

Emily shrugged. "I feel like I'm spinning my wheels. I have this odd feeling that the girl I saw in my vision is in danger."

"You can't know that," Vicky said. "I mean Madeline worked for that charity, right? *No child abandoned?* So it's probably just a vision from her work at the charity. I looked at their website, and it says there that they rescue children who have been trafficked. So that makes total sense that Madeline would have had contact with a child like that."

"Yeah, except, I don't think Madeline was involved in the day-to-day running of the charity. From what I've heard, she was doing fundraising and PR for them. She might not have had contact with the children."

"And where did you hear that?"

Emily shrugged. "I think her housekeeper mentioned something like that." Though now Emily wasn't sure about it anymore. "Maybe I should check with the charity directly."

Vicky shook her head. "And say what? You can't just call them and say you'd like to know what Madeline Bolton did there."

"Well, we'll just have to go there under some pretext."

"We?"

"Yeah, we could go there and we can casually ask what Maddie's job there involved."

"Casually? Emily, they'll throw us out."

"Us?" Emily grinned. "So, you're coming with me?"

Vicky rolled her eyes. "At least if I'm with you, I can drag you out of there before you do anything stupid."

"You're the best!"

"The jury's still out on that."

Forty-five minutes later, Emily and Vicky stood in the reception area of the charity's offices.

Emily smiled at the female receptionist who couldn't be older than twenty. Her make-up was flawless, her hair long and straight, and her manicured nails so long that Emily wondered how she could even type without hitting random keys.

"How can I help you?" the receptionist asked with a smile.

"Uh, yes, my friend and I..." Emily started. "We'd like to volunteer for a charity. So we figured, we'd stop by and see if you have any need for volunteers."

"Yes, we're always looking for volunteers." She reached for two clipboards and pinned a form on each one. "I'll have you fill in the application form."

Emily reached for the clipboards and handed one to Vicky.

The receptionist motioned to the comfortable armchairs in the reception area. "Take a seat, and when you're done, just hand the forms back to me."

Emily and Vicky sat down on the chairs, the clipboards on their laps.

"Well that's not helpful," Vicky whispered.

Emily nudged closer. "Once we give her our forms, we'll ask a few questions. I'll figure out something." She gave her friend a confident look even though she didn't feel very confident. She had to come up with something, or this visit would be a bust.

Emily's gaze wandered. The wall opposite of the seating area was decorated with photos. She leaned closer to Vicky. "That guy in the photo looks familiar."

Vicky looked up and followed Emily's gaze. "Oh, yeah, that's the President's Chief of Staff. You saw him at the funeral."

"Yes, you're right. Why do you think his photo is on the wall?"

"He was the CEO and Chairman of the charity before he became Chief of Staff," Vicky whispered back.

Emily thought back to the funeral where she'd seen Mike Faulkner giving his condolences to the Bolton family. It gave her an idea.

"Are you done with the form?" Emily asked Vicky who nodded. "Okay then, let's do this."

She took both clipboards and together they walked back to the reception desk and handed them to the young woman.

"Here you go. I have a quick question about what kind of volunteering opportunities you have," Emily said with a smile.

"It really depends," the girl said vaguely.

"It's just that I spoke to Rita the other day… I mean Mrs. Bolton… you know Madeline's mother?" Emily fished.

The girl sat up straighter. "Oh yes? You know the Boltons?"

"Yes, that's really why we're here. Since Maddie is gone, we figured there's a void we need to fill. We were so impressed with what Maddie did here that we really wanted to help out and carry on her work, you know? She always talked about the children. She really loved being with them and helping them."

The receptionist's forehead furrowed. "But Miss Bolton didn't have a lot of contact with the children directly. Not on a day-to-day basis anyway."

Emily quickly let out a chuckle. "Of course, I know that. But the way she talked about them always made us feel like she spent a lot of time with them."

"Maybe you should talk to Mr. Faulkner directly," the receptionist said and reached for the phone.

"Oh, is that the time?" Vicky suddenly exclaimed and grabbed Emily's arm. "We have to get to the reception at the embassy. It would be rude to be late."

"Oh, you're right," Emily replied and tossed the receptionist a regretful look. "We'll have to talk to Mr. Faulkner another day."

Emily and Vicky rushed out through the glass doors. At the elevators, Vicky impatiently pressed the button, while Emily glanced over her shoulder. Through the glass doors she saw a man approach the receptionist's desk and exchange a few words with her. Just as Emily heard the elevator ding and the doors open, the man pivoted and looked in her direction.

This wasn't Mike Faulkner. It was a younger man. He looked familiar too. She'd seen him at the funeral.

Emily rushed into the elevator with Vicky, and the doors closed.

"Phew, that was tight," Emily said with relief.

"You think?"

Emily turned to look at her friend, but instead a reflection in the stainless-steel interior of the elevator caught her attention. She saw somebody entering a luxurious bathroom. The mirror picked up her reflection, confirming that it was Maddie, who now bent down to the cabinet beneath the sink and opened its white doors. Inside, there were a few cleaning utensils and toilet paper rolls neatly stacked two rolls wide and three rolls high. Maddie slid an envelope between the second and third row of toilet paper. Then she closed the doors and rose. Her face reflected in the mirror above the sink. Worry was written on it. Then she took a deep breath before she turned away.

Emily's vision blurred, and she suddenly felt Vicky's hands on her shoulders, shaking her.

"You saw her again, didn't you?"

Emily nodded. "And I think I know now what I need to do."

48

After finishing his work for the day, Yang didn't go straight home. Instead, he drove to the apartment building where Emily Warner lived. He found the door to the building open.

He'd done his homework and performed a quick background check on Emily Warner. Her claim that she had no driver's license was indeed true. While this was the case for a small number of people who lived in big cities with good public transportation and who didn't need or want to drive, Emily Warner's reason was unexpected. Her social security records identified her as blind.

He hadn't been able to investigate any further to see how Emily Warner was connected to Madeline Bolton. Not only did he not have a justifiable legal reason to snoop around in her life, if Lieutenant Arnold got wind of the fact that he was still looking into the Bolton case, she'd discipline him. Nevertheless, he couldn't ignore his gut feeling.

Yang entered the building and walked up one flight of stairs and found Emily's apartment immediately. For a moment, he stood in front of the door. He could still turn back now, and nobody would be the wiser. But his internal voice urged him to follow his gut feeling. He knocked.

A dog barked in response. Then he heard the sound of footsteps getting louder. A moment later, the door was opened.

Emily Warner froze the moment she laid eyes on him. Yang couldn't help but notice her wary look. The chocolate-brown lab next to her appeared relaxed.

"Miss Warner, do you remember me?"

She nodded and swallowed hard. "Detective... uh, Yang."

She met his gaze, a clear indication that she could see him. She wasn't blind.

"Yes. I'm sorry to disturb you, but I wonder whether I might come in for a quick word?" He added a smile to his question, trying to diffuse the tension between them.

Her shoulders relaxed somewhat, and she motioned for him to enter. "Please, come in."

Then she addressed her dog. "Coffee, go to bed." The dog trotted to a comfy looking dog bed next to the sofa and lay down.

Yang entered and closed the door behind him. He let his eyes roam, absorbing things that gave him a better picture of who Emily Warner was. A harness with the words "Guide Dog" and a sturdy handle hung on a peg near the door. It was the kind guide dogs for the blind wore. There were no pictures or paintings decorating the large living room with the open plan kitchen. A piano stood against one wall. There was no sheet music anywhere on or near the piano. No magazines or books on the coffee table. He saw speakers with a dock for a smart phone.

"What is it you wanted to talk to me about?" Emily said, interrupting his observations.

When he looked at her, he noticed that she seemed to have gotten over the initial shock of seeing a police officer on her doorstep. But he also recognized the stiffness with which she held her body. He'd seen the same kind of stiffness in people who'd already received bad news and were expecting more of the same.

"I just wanted to follow up with you after the other night at the embassy event."

"Oh, of course, I can reimburse you for the Uber." She made a motion toward the kitchen counter, where her handbag lay.

"No, no, please, I'm not here to get reimbursed. I just wanted to make sure that you're feeling okay. You seemed distraught the other night."

She hesitated, before she answered, "I didn't think a homicide detective visited members of the community to check if they're alright."

He gave her a disarming smile. "They don't, normally. But they normally don't work private security jobs at an embassy either." He shrugged. "I just get the feeling that you and I were supposed to meet for whatever reason."

"You mean because we ran into each other twice now? DC is a small town," she said lightly.

"Three times," he corrected her. "I saw you at Madeline Bolton's funeral."

"Oh!" Her surprise was genuine, as was her sheepish facial expression. "I didn't see you there."

"I kept at the fringes… like you. I didn't have an invitation. And I'm guessing neither did you nor your friend." He kept his tone light, not wanting to sound as if he was accusing her of anything.

"Did you come to arrest me for crashing a funeral?"

"No. I'm just curious. You claimed to see a stabbing that actually happened a month earlier, you crashed Madeline Bolton's funeral, and you crashed the embassy event and talked to Madeline Bolton's ex-fiancé. Why?"

"I already told you that I didn't crash the embassy event. I was invited by Ambassador Pacheco." She pointed to the piano. "I teach his blind daughter music."

Yang lifted his arms in surrender. "Okay, let's say you were invited. It doesn't change the fact that all three events tie back to Madeline Bolton. According to Sanjay Patel, Miss Bolton witnessed the stabbing that you claimed to have seen. What is your fascination with this woman? Were you stalking her when she was alive?"

"I wasn't stalking her or anybody else!" Emily said in a raised voice, sounding outraged.

"Then what? Why can't you let her rest in peace?"

"Because I have her corneas." She almost yelled at him.

He froze, trying to digest the news. "So it's true. You were blind. And now you can see, thanks to Madeline Bolton."

Emily nodded. "Yes, thanks to her and an experimental stem cell treatment. I'm grateful for my eyesight." She hesitated.

"I sense a *but* coming…"

"You have good instincts, Detective. But I'm afraid you won't believe me if I tell you. So unless you're planning to charge me with crashing a funeral, you should leave."

"Trust me, I've heard my fair share of weird stories. What is the *but*?"

She cast him a long look, and he held her gaze as if they were engaged in a game of chicken.

"Very well, Detective. My eyesight came at a price. I see snippets of Madeline's life. Visions of things she's done, people she's met. Her corneas are showing me things that she saw. Things that I think are related to her death."

"That's impossible." The words shot out of his mouth, before he could stop himself.

She scoffed. "Like I said: you wouldn't believe it."

And why would he? Psychic visions? There was no evidence they existed. There had to be some explanation for it. "Maybe you just read things about her and now think you're seeing those things."

"Yeah, that's what my surgeon thinks too. But I know what I saw. I saw the stabbing that Maddie witnessed. I saw the glass table shattering when she crashed onto it."

Yang sucked in a breath. That particular detail hadn't been released to the public. Only the police and EMT personnel as well as Madeline's immediate family knew about it.

"And I saw Maddie with a child," Emily continued, her voice agitated, "a girl no older than thirteen, beaten, in fear. I saw her with that child. She called somebody, maybe because she needed help. I don't know why. I can't hear her, I can only see what she saw. The number on her cell phone belonged to a Russian diplomat. Sergei Petrov. I don't know how he's involved, whether he's a friend, or whether he's the one who killed her."

Surprised at Emily's claim, Yang just stood there, mouth gaping open. He too was suspecting that Madeline Bolton's death was no accident. But why did Emily believe it was murder?

"You don't believe me," she said into the silence.

"It's not that—"

"Don't treat me like an imbecile," she said, interrupting him. "I know what I've seen. Madeline is trying to show me something."

Yang was wrestling with himself, trying to line up the pieces of information with his own clandestine inquiries into the Bolton case. But he couldn't tell Emily that. This was police business. And it wasn't clear how Emily had obtained this information. Perhaps she had overheard somebody discussing the case. Or maybe there was a leak. But he knew one thing for sure: Madeline Bolton was not sending messages from the grave.

"I'm sorry, Miss Warner. Let me give you some well-meaning advice. Please forget about what you've seen. You don't want to get mixed up in something that you can't handle. If Miss Bolton's death was truly no accident, the investigation will show it. But you can't be involved in this."

She pressed her lips together. "Fine."

In that moment, she reminded him of his soon-to-be ex-wife. He'd learned from her—the painful way—that when a woman said *fine,* it meant anything but. But he had no right to dictate anything to Emily

Warner. All he could do was give her advice so she wouldn't be drawn into something that was way over her head.

"I'm sorry to have disturbed you," he said and made his exit.

49

YANG STARED AT THE COMPUTER SCREEN in his cubicle, thinking about his conversation with Emily Warner the night before. Could there be any truth to what she claimed she'd seen in a vision?

In it she'd seen Madeline Bolton with a beaten child, while calling a Russian diplomat. Did it have something to do with her job at the charity? After all, *No child abandoned* rescued abused and trafficked children, many of whom were Russian. Caleb Faulkner had confirmed it. Perhaps there was a simple explanation for why she'd called Petrov. He doubted that Madeline spoke Russian. Maybe she'd called Petrov to translate for her so she could communicate with the child.

But why not go and ask Caleb Faulkner to help her communicate with the girl? He spoke Russian. It would have been easier. No, there had to be another reason why Madeline needed to speak to Petrov. Was it just coincidental that during that phone call the beaten girl was with her? Or could it be that Emily Warner was wrong altogether? Had she combined two unconnected visions into one? Not only that, there was no way to tell when this incident had taken place. It could have happened months before Madeline Bolton's death.

Yang ran his hand through his hair. Why the hell was he even wasting his time with this nonsense? There was no such thing as visions. Emily Warner was either crazy if she believed in these visions, or she was spinning a story from bits of information she could have come by via any number of means in order to gain attention. There was no reason to believe that anything she'd told him was true.

But trying to forget what she'd said wasn't as easy as that. It bugged him. Maybe there was something to it. But how could he figure out what? Maybe he should talk to Emily again to see if he could dig deeper and find out where she really got her information from.

"Just got the DNA results back for Fedorov," Jefferson said over the partition that divided his cubicle from Yang's.

Yang looked up from the files for the three missing girls that he'd combed through for any similarities. He rolled his chair back and scooted closer to his partner. "Tell me it's him."

Jefferson made a face. "Nope. No match."

"Damn, I really didn't like that guy."

"You and me both," Jefferson said and shrugged.

"How about the DNA results for Annika's foster father?"

"Emil Veselak's? Not back yet," Jefferson said with a regretful look. He motioned to the file in Yang's hands. "Find anything?"

"All three girls were last seen at their sessions with the psychiatrist several weeks apart, just like that guy from the charity mentioned." Yang tapped on the file. "The first girl to disappear was Annika, on March 30th, then Sasha, on April 15th, and then Tatjana, on April 27th. At the time of their disappearance, the girls' foster parents were all interviewed, as were the teachers at the schools—they all went to different ones."

"No suspects?" Jefferson asked.

"They interviewed Sokolov each time. I've read through the witness statements he's made after the disappearance of each girl, and I find the coincidence that each girl was last seen at one of his sessions a bit too suspicious. His staff claims that he was still in the building when the girls disappeared, and the detectives who looked into him couldn't find anything to connect him to the abductions."

Jefferson took a sip from his coffee cup. "Any other witnesses to the disappearances?"

"They looked at a homeless guy who was hanging around outside the shrink's office, but there was no evidence that he was involved. However, in Annika's file I found that the homeless guy claimed to have seen a well-dressed guy in an expensive car hanging around there sometime after Annika's session ended, though he couldn't give an exact time. Nor a description of the man or the car. He was high on something."

Jefferson shrugged. "He could have just been making shit up. Drug addicts make shitty witnesses."

"True. But what if he really saw something? Sokolov could have come back later to pick up the girl. He could easily have told her to wait for him. In the meantime, he could have made sure that the staff in the building knew he was still there, thereby establishing an alibi. I think he's our strongest suspect. He's the one person all three girls have in common. He should be back from his European vacation."

"Well, then what are we waiting for? Let's pay the shrink a little visit," Jefferson suggested and rose.

On the car ride to the psychiatrist's office, they discussed their approach. Having been partners for two years, they were on the same page.

Upon arrival at the medical office building, where Dr. Yuri Sokolov had an office, Yang flashed his badge at the receptionist.

"Detectives Yang and Jefferson. We're here to speak to Dr. Sokolov."

"I'm afraid he's on a coffee break," the young man with the pale face and overly long eyelashes said.

"Perfect timing," Jefferson said, "then he's not with a patient right now. If you could show us to his office please?"

The receptionist sighed. "He's not in his office. Otherwise it wouldn't be much of a break, would it?" When Yang tilted his head and gave him a stare, he added, "You'll find him downstairs at Starbucks. Most likely in the armchair in the far corner."

"Thank you," Yang said.

The psychiatrist was indeed sitting in an armchair in the corner of the large coffee shop on the first floor of the building. There were hardly any other customers. Sokolov sipped on his coffee and took a bite from a scone. He was tanned, which was consistent with him having hiked in high altitude recently. And he looked relaxed. Time to rattle his cage, Yang thought.

When Yang and Jefferson approached and stopped a few feet in front of him, he looked up.

This time, Jefferson took care of the introduction. "Dr. Sokolov?"

The doctor nodded.

"Detectives Yang and Jefferson, DC Police, Homicide Branch."

A flicker of dread flashed in Sokolov's eyes, but it disappeared quickly. Yang noticed that the man kept his emotions on a tight leash.

"How can I help you, Detectives?" he asked politely and leaned back in his chair.

Yang and Jefferson pulled chairs from the adjacent table closer and sat down.

"We'd like to talk to you about three Russian girls in foster care that went missing after attending therapy sessions with you," Jefferson said.

"Hmm," Sokolov said, "I'm afraid I don't have any new information. I already spoke to the police about Annika, Sasha, and Tatjana weeks ago."

"So you remember their names?" Yang asked.

He tipped his chin up in a show of defiance. "Wouldn't you? It's part of my job. I care about my patients, so of course, I know about the girls that disappeared."

"One of them turned up." Yang made a deliberate pause. "Dead."

"Oh, I'm sorry to hear that."

"You don't seem too surprised," Yang fished.

"I'm not. I'm aware of the statistics when it comes to missing children. If they aren't found within the first forty-eight hours, the chances of finding them alive are virtually nil. But I'm sure you're familiar with crime statistics. So, how may I help you?"

Yang and Jefferson exchanged a look. Yang knew exactly what his partner was thinking. Sokolov had something to hide and tried to disguise that fact by acting as if the questions didn't concern him personally.

"The girl we found has been positively identified as Annika."

"Poor Annika, she was such a sweet girl."

The doctor sighed, and for a moment it looked like he cared about the girl. But it could all be an act. Besides, as a psychiatrist he was well schooled in showing empathy for his patients even if he didn't feel such an emotion.

"How did she die?"

"We're not at liberty to disclose the details," Jefferson said. "Let's just say the manner of her death was violent in every sense of the word."

Sokolov took another bite from his scone.

"We've been going through a list of all men who've had contact with her before her disappearance and are trying to eliminate as many as possible so we can narrow our investigation," Yang said.

"Well, I suggest you talk to the detective who interviewed me after Annika disappeared. I'm sure he'll tell you that I had an alibi for that time."

"We've already done that," Jefferson said.

"Then I'm not sure what else you want from me," Sokolov said.

"For the purpose of elimination, we'd like you to provide us with a DNA sample," Jefferson said.

Sokolov tossed him a look. "I'm happy to give you a DNA sample." He paused. "Once I see the warrant." He stretched out his hand.

Neither Yang nor Jefferson could produce a warrant. No judge would sign off on it, given that they had no other evidence to link him to Annika.

"Ah, I see. You don't have a warrant." He smiled knowingly. "Then I'm afraid I can't help you. Enjoy the rest of your afternoon, Detectives." He reached for his iPad and began reading.

"We'll be back," Yang promised.

Yang and Jefferson pivoted and exited the coffee shop through the same door they'd entered it.

"Around the corner?" Jefferson asked the moment they were out of earshot.

"Yep. It's only a matter of time."

They walked through the entry hall of the building, then exited. Once outside, they hurried around the far side of the building, then circled it, before they reached the corner that was occupied by the coffee shop. They stood only a few yards away from Sokolov. They had a clear view of his back, with only the glass separating them. They stood in the shadow of a tree, watching him.

The moment Sokolov emptied his cup of coffee and stood up, Yang said, "Give it a second."

Yang's heart raced as he watched Sokolov walk away from the armchair.

"Now!" Jefferson said.

Just as Sokolov exited through the door that connected the coffee shop with the building's entry hall, Yang and Jefferson charged into Starbucks through the main entrance door from the street. A barista was already walking to the table where Sokolov had left his coffee cup and half-eaten scone. She was about to touch the cup, when Yang stepped between her and the table.

"DC Police, we'll need to confiscate this," he said to the startled woman.

She gasped, and her eyes widened, a protest on her lips.

Yang flashed his badge, and she stepped back.

"It's all yours, Officer," she said and walked away.

Jefferson already handed him an evidence bag, and gloves, and together they bagged the paper cup and plate, and the half-eaten scone.

Jefferson grinned triumphantly. "That'll teach him not to leave his trash on the table next time."

Yang chuckled. "If we're lucky, there won't be a next time for him."

50

THERE WERE STILL LOOSE ENDS to tie up, the killer realized now. It irked him to no end. But it couldn't be helped. Somehow two people knew more than they should. While he didn't know exactly how much they knew, and how they'd come by that information, he couldn't risk them exposing him, or sticking their noses into his business and uncovering all kinds of things he didn't want anybody to know.

Emily Warner was just a schoolteacher, yet somehow she'd realized that Madeline Bolton's death wasn't an accident. And he'd been so careful staging the scene. Not only had he made it look like Madeline had fallen off a stepladder and sustained fatal injuries, he'd even placed a light bulb in her hand so it looked like she'd tried to change it.

He'd removed the glass he'd used to drink wine with Madeline, while he'd left hers in plain view. On top of it, he'd emptied the entire bottle of wine into the sink so it looked like she'd had too much to drink. And so far, it had worked: the Secret Service had found no evidence of foul play, and he hoped it would remain that way. It meant he had to make sure that Emily Warner never got a chance to report to the authorities what she suspected. It was bad enough that Madeline's parents knew that somebody suspected that their daughter had been murdered.

It was time to get rid of the troublesome music teacher. All he needed to do was follow her and take care of her, preferably in a dark alley. He could make it look like a mugging gone wrong, and nobody would be the wiser.

Good riddance, Emily Warner. You should have stayed out of my business.

51

IT WAS AFTER MIDNIGHT, and the streets had started to empty out. Emily felt a shiver run down her spine and involuntarily cast a look over her shoulder. Even though the weather was mild, she felt a cold breeze at her neck. She knew the feeling wasn't caused by the weather, but the fact that she was nervous. Still, she had to do this. She had to break into Maddie's townhouse.

She saw nobody on the quiet side street in Georgetown. The restaurants were closed, and only a few bars were still serving customers. But the townhouse Emily approached was far enough away from the main street and the bars.

She wore black jeans and a dark green trench coat over her black T-shirt. Her handbag was slung across her torso. In addition to its usual contents, it held a small flashlight and her lock picks.

Emily was glad to see that the entrance to Maddie's townhouse was covered with a small portico that helped partially conceal her when she reached the door. Casting another look over her shoulder and seeing nobody, despite the fact that the small hairs at her nape stood up, Emily donned a pair of surgical gloves and went to work. Her fingers trembled slightly when she inserted one of the lock picks into the tumbler and tried to get the second one to follow.

Her heart beat into her throat, and sweat started to build on her brow. Shit, she wasn't made for a life of crime. She was too nervous, too scared that somebody would see her and call the police. But she had to do this, for Maddie, and for her own sanity. She took a long steadying breath.

"Come on," she murmured to herself. "You can do this."

Emily closed her eyes, and found that it was easier to feel the machinations of the lock when she didn't look at it. Instead she felt the grooves and notches and sensed how to move the lock picks to get the lock to open. A few more seconds, and she knew she was on the right track. A soft click, and it was done.

Emily turned the knob and pushed the door open. She slid inside the dark interior and pulled the door shut behind her. She stood in the hallway and didn't move. The house was quiet, except for the soft movements of a pendulum clock. She had half expected, half dreaded to hear the beeping of an alarm system, but heard nothing of the sort. She expected that Maddie had an alarm system in the house. What single woman living in a house by herself didn't? But she had hoped that after her death nobody had set the alarm. After all, over three weeks after her death, her family had surely started to remove all valuables from the property.

She pulled her flashlight from her bag and switched it on, making sure to direct the beam of light to the floor and far away from any windows. The first room to the left was a living room. A few steps farther, a flight of stairs led to the second floor. Emily did a quick sweep of the first floor, but except for a small powder room with a pedestal sink, no other bathrooms were on this floor, only a large kitchen and dining room.

She walked upstairs and heard the creaking of the old wooden stairs beneath the thick carpet that covered them. Upstairs, she saw two doors. Both were open. She entered through the first door and moved the beam of light around the room. This had been Maddie's room.

A king-size bed was framed by bedside tables and an ottoman at its foot. In front of the window stood an antique desk that Maddie seemed to have used both for putting on make-up and jewelry as well as doing paperwork. Emily didn't dare shine her light onto it too closely, worried that the beam might be seen through the window. Instead, she turned and walked through the short hallway flanked with closets into the en suite bathroom.

There was no window in the bathroom. Emily moved the beam of her flashlight until she found the vanity. It had two sinks. She quickly bent down and opened the doors beneath the first sink, but only a few bottles of shampoo and bodywash were inside it. No toilet paper, no envelope. She closed the doors again, then moved to the second sink and opened the cabinet below.

There, she found a plunger, and a few cleaning products. No toilet paper.

Surprised, she straightened, then found the light switch and flipped it. It took a moment for her eyes to adjust to the light, but once they did, she realized her mistake. The bathroom she stood in wasn't the bathroom from Maddie's memories. This bathroom's color palette was a mix of soft cream and warm accents. The bathroom from the vision had had bolder, colder colors, blues and grays.

Maddie hadn't hidden the envelope in her own bathroom.

Shit!

A sound behind her made her whirl around. Emily almost lost her balance and felt dizzy for a fraction of a second, before her eyes perceived the person who'd snuck up on her. Her heart stopped for a moment, only to beat at double its normal rate a moment later. She shrank back and hit the countertop behind her, her escape route cut off by the man in front of her.

He'd come to kill her.

52

"I'M NOT HERE TO HURT YOU."

Emily's heart beat like a jackhammer. She didn't believe him. And why would she? He'd tried to kill her once before.

Prison had aged him, and not in a good way. Emily recognized him nevertheless. How could she ever forget the face of the man who'd robbed her of everything she'd loved?

"What do you want? Haven't you done enough bad to last a lifetime?" She couldn't get the word *Dad* over her lips.

"We have no time to discuss that right now. We've gotta leave." He reached for her arm, but she recoiled from his touch.

"I'm not going anywhere with you!" Despite her firm words, she trembled with fear.

"You don't have a choice right now," he said.

She detected no malice in his face. Maybe prison had taught him to hide his feelings.

"You tripped an alarm when you broke in. The police will be here in three minutes tops."

"I would have heard it," Emily protested. Her hearing was excellent, and had an alarm system started to beep she wouldn't have missed it.

"It was a silent alarm. Now, let's go, or we'll both land in prison. And trust me you wouldn't like it one bit."

She was torn. She didn't trust him, but he could be speaking the truth. Maddie, a woman living alone, who had valuables like jewelry in the house, would have had an alarm system. Emily just hadn't expected it to be a silent alarm.

"Fine," she said finally. "Let's go."

Her father turned around, and Emily switched off the light in the bathroom, and used her flashlight to guide her way. In the upper hallway, her eyes fell on the second door. Shit! She wasn't done yet. She had to check if there was a second bathroom on this floor.

Her father was already putting one foot on the first step, when Emily headed for the guest room.

"What are you doing, Emily? We've gotta get out, now!"

But she ignored him. She hadn't come this far to leave empty-handed. Quickly, she rushed into the guest room, where she found a second door that led into an en suite bathroom. She shone her light inside and found the single sink vanity. She crouched down.

"Damn it, Emily!" her father grunted. "We don't have time for whatever you're doing."

"I need to do this!" She opened the cabinet below the sink. But instead of finding toilet paper, she found only a toilet plunger. "Fuck!"

Where had Maddie hidden the envelope if not in her own house?

"Let's go," her father ordered and grabbed her biceps, forcing her to rise and come with him.

"I can walk by myself!" she hissed.

"Then move it!"

He hurried to the stairs, then raced down, Emily on his heels, but walking slower. When they reached the foyer, her father suddenly stopped in his tracks.

"Shit! They're already here," he uttered under his breath.

A moment later, Emily saw what he saw. Through the small glass pane over the entry door, lights flashed red and blue, though the police hadn't put their sirens on, intent on surprising the intruders.

Oscar Warner had been right about the silent alarm. She shouldn't have been surprised. He'd had his own locksmith shop before he'd gone to prison, and knew enough about locks and alarms to have spotted whatever telltale signs Maddie's townhouse exhibited.

"This way," her father said and ushered her to the back of the house.

"Where are you going?" she asked.

He looked over his shoulder. "Out the back."

She followed him through the kitchen, which had a door leading into the tiny, narrow yard that even on a sunny day would probably not get a single ray of sunshine. A fence and shrubbery provided cover, but Oscar Warner seemed to have no trouble finding a way through them. He squeezed through a gap between the old fence—which was missing a panel—and a thick bush, and disappeared before her eyes. Then his hand appeared from where he'd disappeared, and despite her hatred for him, Emily reached for his hand, and allowed him to pull her through.

She found herself in the overgrown yard of the house behind Maddie's. Her father motioned to the left and put his finger over his lips to urge her to remain silent. She nodded and followed him until they reached a rickety gate. Oscar Warner who was almost half a foot taller than his daughter, peered over it. Then he pulled the wooden gate open and stepped outside.

"It's clear," he whispered and made a motion for her to follow him.

Emily complied and stepped out onto the pavement. Several cars were parked on the quiet side street that had only narrow sidewalks.

"This way," Emily's father said and pointed up the gentle slope to the street that ran parallel to the street on which Maddie had lived.

Just as they reached it, and her father turned to the right, Emily cast a look back. She couldn't see the police cruiser on Maddie's street, but she saw its flashing lights reflect in various windows of adjacent buildings.

Emily quickly joined her father on the parallel street. After another block, he stopped and pointed across the narrow street. An old, beat-up Toyota was parked there. "Hop in. I'll take you home."

Emily froze. The last time she'd gotten in a car with him, she'd lost her mother and her eyesight. "No." She shook her head. "I can get home by myself. It's not far," she lied.

"You can't walk all the way to Columbia Heights, and the Metro has already stopped running."

Instinctively she took a step back, widening the distance between them. "How do you know where I live?"

He hesitated, then ran a hand through his thinning hair. "The same way I knew that you were breaking into a house. I followed you. I've been following you for a while now, a few weeks." He looked down at his shoes. "Didn't have the courage to approach you."

Her father admitted that he didn't have the courage to approach her? He didn't sound like the man who'd planned to kill his family fifteen years ago. But it could be an act. Just like he'd lured Emily and her mother into the car so he could execute his plan.

"What for?" she asked, her tone clipped.

"Because I wanted to talk to you. To... to ask you—"

"For money?" She practically spit the words out.

A surprised look appeared on his face. "No. I don't want any money. I have a job."

"Then what do you want?"

"Forgiveness."

His simple one-word answer hit her like a freight train she hadn't seen coming. Instinctively, she shook her head. There was no forgiveness in her heart. Her blindness she could have forgiven him for, but her mother's death?

"Mom is dead because of you. There is no forgiveness for that. You may have served your time in prison and maybe society considers your debt paid, but I don't. I loved her. I needed her, and you took her from me!" She couldn't stop the tears that had started running down her cheeks. "You shouldn't have come!"

She glared at him. How could he ask for forgiveness and thus dredge up the past, the past that was filled with so much pain, so much hurt, and a loss that she would never get over?

"I've changed," he claimed. "I'm not the same man anymore. I was an angry man back then, always blaming your mother for everything that went wrong, when I only had myself to blame. What I said back then in the car... I was so angry with your mother for wanting to leave me... I should have just gone to a bar and gotten drunk instead of... instead of... doing what I did. I deserved to be in prison for what I did. If I could go back in time to fix this, I would."

"There's no going back..."

"I know that. That's why all I can do is ask you to forgive me. I understand that you're not ready for that." He sighed. "When I found out that you could see again, I was so happy."

Were those tears rimming his eyes? That couldn't be.

"I know you'll need time. I just wanted to let you know that I'm here for you. Whatever you need me to do for you, I'll do it. I want to be part of your life again."

"You have to leave. Don't follow me anymore."

"Fine, I'll stay away to give you space, but I'll be back. I won't give up. I will make it up to you. I'll earn your forgiveness."

"I can't..." She pivoted.

"Emily, please—"

But Emily began running. How could he be so cruel to remind her of what she'd lost?

Of her mother's death.

And of the lonely days and nights Emily had spent as a teenager and young woman growing up amidst strangers.

And of the fact that she was alone in this world.

Alone and scared that she could lose her eyesight once more.

When she'd put enough distance between her father and herself, she pulled out her cell phone and called Vicky.

"Emily?" Vicky asked, sounding wide awake despite the late hour.

"Can you come and pick me up, please? I'm in Georgetown."

53

Y ANG HAD JUST COME BACK from a late lunch, when Jefferson stood up from his desk and motioned for him to approach.

"Simon, what's up?" he asked.

Jefferson put the receiver down. "That was Lupe. Emil Veselak's DNA results are back."

"Got a hit?"

"Nope. He's not a match." He shrugged. "Not that I thought he would be. He and his wife struck me as genuinely grieving."

"Yeah, I had the same feeling. Did Lupe say when she'll have the shrink's DNA results back?"

"All she said was she's put a rush on it for whatever that's worth. Maybe in a day or two?"

"Do you think it would be worth trying to get Zimmerman's DNA too?"

"Tatjana's foster father? We don't really have anything to connect him to Annika, other than that the girls all came through the same charity and visited the same shrink."

"If Zimmerman picked Tatjana up from the shrink's office after group sessions, he might have run into Annika—and Sasha."

"Guess it's worth a try. We can swing by in the evening."

"We're not gonna get a warrant that fast," Yang mused.

"With the little evidence we have linking him to Annika, I doubt we'll get a judge signing off on it. Let's just use our charm to get him to give us a sample voluntarily."

"Works for me." Yang looked at the large clock on the wall. It wasn't even 3p.m. yet. "I doubt Zimmerman will be home before six."

"I guess that gives me enough time to go for a coffee and soak up a few rays of sunshine," Jefferson said, and reached for the jacket hanging over his chair.

"Yang, Jefferson, my office!" Lieutenant Arnold called out from the entrance to her office.

Jefferson exchanged a look with Yang. "Or not."

"Yes, Lieutenant," Yang quickly replied and walked toward her office, Jefferson on his heels.

"I wonder what we've screwed up now," Jefferson murmured under his breath for only Yang to hear.

Arnold wasn't alone. When Yang and Jefferson entered, a man in a dark suit was sitting in one of the chairs across from Arnold's desk.

"Close the door," Arnold ordered. Then she introduced the man in the suit. "Detectives Simon Jefferson and Adam Yang, this is Nikolai Belsky. He's the Chief of Security of the Russian Embassy."

Yang exchanged a surprised look with Jefferson, before greeting the Russian. "Pleased to meet you." Then he looked back at Arnold, who motioned to the empty chairs.

Yang and Jefferson sat down.

"There's been an incident this morning, and the Russian Embassy has asked for our assistance—and our discretion," Arnold said, then nodded at Belsky. "Mr. Belsky?"

"Lieutenant Arnold assured me that you're her best homicide team," the man said in heavily-accented but perfect English and gave them an intense look.

Yang didn't show his surprise at the praise Arnold had heaped on him and his partner. "How may we help you?" he asked instead.

"This morning, one of our diplomats was jogging along the Potomac just south of Georgetown University. He was shot twice at close range. He would have bled out if it hadn't been for a woman walking her dog finding him and calling an ambulance immediately. He's currently in the ICU at George Washington University Hospital. He's in a coma."

"Was there any evidence that this was a mugging gone wrong?" Jefferson asked.

Belsky shook his head. "He still had his watch and his ring as well as his keys and phone. According to his friends, he never took a wallet with him when jogging. Nothing was taken. And we don't believe this was random."

Yang raised an eyebrow. "Did he receive any threats?"

The Russian hesitated, before he continued, "The embassy staff regularly receives threats for all kinds of reasons."

The answer felt evasive. Yang rephrased his question. "Were there any specific threats against this person?"

"Not that we know of."

"Okay," Yang said, "what can you tell us about the incident and the background of the victim?"

Belsky reached for a slim file on Arnold's desk and handed it to Yang. "I've put together a dossier. In it you'll find everything you need to know. The bullets the surgeons removed from him, as well as his clothing, have been handed over to your forensics team for analysis. We're relying on your discretion. We haven't released any details about this attempted assassination to the press, and have urged the witness who found him not to speak to the press. We don't want the perpetrator to know that the cultural attaché survived. Or he might try it again."

"We understand," Jefferson said. "We can provide the victim with police protection at the hospital."

"That won't be necessary. I've already got two of my best men stationed outside his room."

"Very well," Jefferson said. "We'll get right on it."

"Thank you, Detectives," the Russian said and rose. "Lieutenant," he added with a nod to Arnold. "My direct cell number is in the file. Please communicate directly with me, nobody else."

Arnold nodded. "Rest assured my team will make this a priority."

With another nod, Belsky left the office. When the door closed behind him, Arnold leaned back in her chair, relaxing somewhat. Then she motioned to the door. "Get to work. This takes priority over your other cases."

Yang exchanged a look with Jefferson. "Over the Annika murder case? That Russian is still alive, Annika is dead."

Arnold narrowed her eyes at him. "I'm aware of that. But we don't always get to choose what we want to do. Dismissed."

Yang and Jefferson turned and left the office.

Outside and out of earshot, Yang said, "Pressure from above?"

Jefferson nodded. "Looks like it."

Arriving at their cubicles, Yang opened the file, and they both started reading. Yang didn't get far. On the first line, the name of the Russian attaché was disclosed.

Yang instantly recognized it. The man who'd been shot twice while jogging was the same man Emily Warner had mentioned. According to her, Madeline Bolton had called him.

And now, Sergei Petrov was in a coma, unable to reveal if he knew anything that could shed light on Madeline Bolton's death.

This couldn't be a coincidence. He had to question Emily Warner. The sooner, the better. But he couldn't tell his partner, not yet anyway, because Jefferson had made it clear that he didn't want to get involved in a case that Lieutenant Arnold had clearly asked them to stay away from. Therefore, he'd never told Jefferson that he'd visited Emily Warner at her home.

54

SERGEI PETROV had been an easy target.

The killer had figured out pretty quickly that the Russian cultural attaché liked to run in the early morning hours before starting his day at the embassy. As a rather low-level diplomat, he didn't have personal security with him, which had made it easy to take him down.

He'd dressed up like a runner, with shorts and a sweatshirt with a hoodie and a front pouch, in which he'd hidden the gun. He'd waited in the thicket for a while, making sure that there were no other runners who might be able to see him and later describe him. Luckily, at five-thirty, few joggers were around, and the path was practically deserted. And he wouldn't be missed either. He could show up at work at his usual time, and nobody would be the wiser.

Once he was sure that he was alone, he emerged from the bushes and started running after Petrov. He caught up with him very quickly, then ran past him. At the next curve of the path, he'd stopped abruptly, pulled the gun from his pouch and waited for Petrov.

The Russian saw the gun too late, and didn't even have time to scream. He fell like a dead tree. He was about to check Petrov's pulse, when he heard a dog barking in the distance. Not wanting to take any chances, he ran in the other direction instead. Petrov was dead. One bullet had hit him in the chest, the other in the stomach. He wasn't a particularly good shot, but at a distance of only a few yards, not even he could miss.

One problem was solved. Whatever the Russian knew, whatever Madeline had told him before her death, died with him.

One down, one to go.

Now it was Emily Warner's turn. She'd thwarted his efforts the night before, though he doubted that she was aware of that fact. He'd followed her and had been surprised to see that she was breaking into Madeline Bolton's house. From a concealed entry to a business across the street, he'd been contemplating whether to kill her inside the house, but he'd hesitated. If her body was found inside Maddie's house, the police would connect her to Maddie, and this time, DC Police would for sure get involved and dig up whatever connection she had to Maddie. It would blow up the case, which he couldn't afford.

So he'd waited for her to emerge from the house, and planned to kill her far enough away from Maddie's house so her death wouldn't be connected to Maddie. However, another man had entered shortly after Emily, and less than two minutes later, the police had arrived, lights flashing. He'd ducked into an alley and hightailed it out of the area, not wanting to be seen by the police. It had pissed him off.

But tonight, he was in luck. He'd followed Emily in the Metro without being seen, which was easy during rush hour. As a precaution, he'd donned a fake beard and glasses so nobody would recognize him.

Emily Warner had stopped at a hair salon, where she'd spent an hour getting her hair cut. He'd waited impatiently across the street. When she left the salon, she stopped at a supermarket, where she took her bloody time. He was getting impatient, and the gun in the pocket of his sports jacket felt like a hot iron. His hand was itching to get on with it. By the time Emily left the supermarket and headed in the direction of her apartment, the sun had set. To his delight, Emily Warner took one of the many side streets rather than staying on the busier main road.

This was his chance. The moment he turned into the street Emily had taken, he sprang into action. Shielded by trees and other shrubbery in the front yards of some of the homes, he pulled a balaclava from inside his jacket and slipped it over his head.

55

IT WAS DARK, and Emily felt a chill creep up her spine to her neck. She could have blamed the fact that her hair was shorter now, and didn't fully cover her nape. While blind, she'd never realized that her heart-shaped face would look better when framed by hair that only reached to her chin. She was a woman now, not a teenager, and needed a grown-up haircut.

But her new haircut wasn't the cause for the chill she now experienced. Schooled by fifteen years of relying on her auditory sense, she felt that somebody was following her. For a moment, she thought that her father hadn't given up, and was still shadowing her, but this felt different. She inhaled the air around her, but didn't smell anything in particular.

She wished Coffee were with her, but she'd left him at home after his appointment with the vet, where Coffee had received his annual vaccine. Her trusted guide dog had looked tired, and since she felt that her eyesight was becoming clearer and more defined with each day, she'd opted to let Coffee rest at home.

Coffee would know if somebody was truly following her, or if she was just being paranoid.

Another sound, this time that of a small pebble or piece of gravel being crushed underneath the sole of a shoe, sent a shot of adrenaline through her body. She stopped breathing. For an instant, she closed her eyes, concentrating. She was right in her suspicion. Somebody was following her.

She sped up, and the bag of groceries in her right hand suddenly felt heavy. At the next corner, she quickly turned right. As she made the turn, she glanced to the right to where she'd come from, and saw a dark figure. For a fraction of a second, the light of a streetlamp fell on the person's face. But she couldn't see the face, because it was hidden behind a black ski mask.

Emily's heart stopped. The person in the black clothes and mask looked straight at her. He knew that she had discovered him.

Panic struck her. She started running down the street as fast as she could. When she glanced over her shoulder, she saw the stranger come around the corner. He was running too, but he was faster.

Desperate to get to safety, she charged around the next corner. The moment she was out of her assailant's line of sight, she tossed her shopping bag behind her. She heard the glass jar of jam break on the sidewalk, and imagined that the apples and bananas rolled out of the bag and onto the asphalt, creating a tripping hazard. She didn't stop to look, but continued running.

A curse from behind her told her that the would-be attacker stumbled, but when she quickly glanced over her shoulder, she realized it had barely slowed him down. And now, she saw something in his hand, something that reflected in the beam of a streetlight: a gun.

"Help! Somebody help me! Police!" she screamed at the top of her lungs, while she kept running.

The man chasing her was catching up. Her lungs burned from exhaustion, and fear cut off her air supply. Her legs were hurting from the exertion.

A gunshot rang out.

Emily screamed. She didn't feel anything, no pain. Was she shot? She didn't know. She just kept running. But at an unevenness on the sidewalk, she stumbled and fell forward. She braced her fall with her palms, biting back the pain, and scrambled to get up. A glance over her shoulder made her blood freeze in her veins. The assailant was less than fifty yards away, the gun pointed in her direction.

At this distance, she was sure the bullet would find its target.

She whirled around to run, when a second gunshot sounded. She tumbled, while she heard a thud as if the bullet had embedded itself somewhere close. This time, Emily hadn't slipped or stumbled, but somebody had tackled her from the side. Together, they landed in the tiny front yard of an apartment building, shrubbery obscuring the shooter's sight. The person who'd tackled her was covering her with his body.

"Stay down," he ordered, and lifted himself off her with the agility of a dancer. Even without seeing his face, she recognized him.

Detective Yang pulled a gun from his holster and peered around the bushes at the entrance of the yard, his gun pointed in the direction of the assailant. He ran down the street, out of her line of sight, but moments later, he was back, breathing hard.

"He got away."

"If you hadn't been here…" She shuddered at the thought. She would be dead now.

He reached down to help her up, and she was glad for the assistance. Her knees were wobbly, and her breath uneven.

"It was pure luck," Yang said. "I was on my way to you."

"You were? Why?"

He took her elbow, steadying her. "Let me call this in. Then we'll talk."

56

IT HAD BEEN SERENDIPITY that Yang had decided to stop by Emily Warner's apartment on his way home. Had he not been so suspicious about how she knew of Sergei Petrov and decided to talk to her about it without letting his partner know, Emily would be dead now. The intention of the assailant in black clothes and a balaclava of the same color had been clear. Luckily, the first gunshot, which had alerted Yang just in time to come to Emily's rescue, hadn't found its target.

He reported the incident so the area could be searched for the bullets or any other evidence to identify the would-be killer, but since there were no traffic cameras in the area, nor any businesses, which might have had cameras pointing to the sidewalk, the chance of finding the assailant this way was non-existent. Emily's statement didn't help either. She couldn't describe him. But when she'd realized that somebody was following her, she'd acted quickly and tossed her shopping bag into the assailant's path, most likely buying herself a few crucial seconds. He admired that. It showed quick thinking and ingenuity.

While a couple of uniformed police officers still searched the area for the bullets and shell casings, Yang took Emily home. She didn't protest. She knew as well as he did that she'd just escaped certain death. It showed on her face.

When Emily unlocked the door to her apartment and opened it, her brown Labrador was already waiting for her with his tail wagging.

"Good boy, Coffee," she cooed and petted the dog.

Coffee licked her hands before he looked past her to Yang.

"Hi, Coffee, do you remember me?" Yang crouched down, and Coffee instantly greeted him with a friendly poke before he licked Yang's ear. He looked up to Emily. "Guess he remembers me."

"He likes you. He's not friendly with everybody. He's trained to protect me." Emily ushered him in and closed the door behind him.

"That's good," Yang said.

"I have to thank you. I don't think I would be here if you hadn't—"

He lifted his hand, stopping her. "—if I hadn't been suspicious of you."

"What?" Her chin dropped. "I don't understand."

He sighed. "It's about our previous conversation where you mentioned Madeline Bolton's corneas and what you saw."

She crossed her arms in front of her chest, her jaw tightening. "Of course you didn't believe me."

"It's not that," he protested, even though she was right. He hadn't believed the tales of the visions she'd claimed having. But now, with everything that had happened in the meantime, he was willing to consider that maybe she wasn't lying. Or crazy.

"Of course not." Sarcasm dripped off her like water out of a leaky faucet.

Yang shoved a hand through his thick hair. "Listen, I shouldn't even be here, but there's something that makes me think that what you seem to know about Madeline Bolton may be connected to another case that landed on my desk today."

"Another murder?" she said, her voice but an echo.

"Attempted murder, from what I can piece together so far." Then he looked straight into her eyes, before he added, "Sergei Petrov from the Russian Embassy was shot this morning. He's in a coma."

Emily gasped. Her shock was real. No doubt about it. "No, no!" She shook her head. Then her eyes seemed to focus on something in the distance. It took a few seconds, before she continued, "That means he's not her killer. But he knows something. And that's why somebody wants him dead. The same person who tried to shoot me."

Automatically, Yang shook his head. "There's no way." Though the moment the words rolled over his lips, he wondered whether there could be a way these two incidents were connected.

Emily started pacing. "It has to be. I mean… we're connected because of Maddie. He knows something that can help us figure out who killed Maddie, and clearly the killer thought it was information that could expose him, and that's why he shot Petrov. And…"

"There's no evidence that Madeline Bolton was murdered."

"There is!" Emily protested. "The high heels!"

Stunned, Yang stared at her. He'd made the same observation. No woman in her right mind wore high heels when stepping on a ladder to change a light bulb. "How do you know about the shoes? One of your so-called visions?"

"I'm gonna pretend you didn't insult me just now. It wasn't a vision. I spoke to Maddie's housekeeper. She told me that Maddie still wore one of her high heels when she supposedly fell off the ladder." She sighed. "The 'supposedly' is my interpretation, not the housekeeper's."

"How did you get her to speak to you?"

Emily shrugged. "I might have said that I was doing a podcast for the blind…"

Yang couldn't help but admire the woman's ingenuity. Still, if she was right about her theory that Petrov knew something related to Madeline Bolton's death, and was shot because of it, Emily Warner could be in danger too. Hell, if the shooter tonight was the same, he'd already figured out that Emily might be able to expose him as Maddie's killer.

"Listen, if you're right, if the person who shot Petrov is the same as the one who aimed at you tonight, then you'll have to stop playing amateur sleuth. Or it'll get you killed."

"You don't understand! I need to find Maddie's killer. I need to do this for her." She hesitated. "And for me. Or I'll lose my eyesight once more."

He furrowed his brow. "What's that supposed to mean?"

"You won't believe me."

"Then make me believe you. Tell me the truth."

She hesitated, then she said, "Shortly after I first lost my eyesight at age fifteen, I got my first cornea transplant. I could see again, but I started seeing things that weren't there. The doctors thought that I suffered from PTSD and they committed me to a… a mental institution for a few months. But the visions didn't stop, until one night when I thought I was being chased. I ran and fell down a flight of stairs. When they found me, I was blind again. My body had rejected the corneas."

"I'm so sorry," he murmured.

"I didn't get another transplant back then because the fall had damaged my optic nerve. But now, fifteen years later, medicine has advanced far enough. I got a stem cell treatment to repair my optic nerve, and then I received Maddie's corneas." She looked at him, meeting his eyes. Her gaze was plain and honest. "The visions started almost immediately. I don't know how I know, but I feel that if I don't help Maddie expose her killer, I will lose my eyesight again."

Yang nodded. He understood so much more now. And he felt for her. He had the overwhelming need to put his arms around her to comfort the fifteen-year-old girl hiding behind the façade of an independent woman. But he didn't act on it.

"I understand why you're doing this. But I can't condone it. You're putting yourself in danger." He motioned to the door. "You could have gotten killed out there tonight. You have to leave this up to the professionals." He realized that he'd raised his voice.

Emily glared at him. "No! I won't! The papers still call Maddie's death an accident, when I know it wasn't! Clearly, nobody except for me even suspects that her death wasn't an accident!"

Surprised at Emily's firm tone and loud voice, he tried to calm her down. "Please, it's not your job! It's mine."

"Then do your job!" She fairly shouted. "Or who knows what will happen to the girl that I saw with Maddie when she called Petrov." She let out a breath. "I tried to figure out how she's connected to Maddie, and all I can come up with is that she knows the girl from the charity where she works."

"You mean *No child abandoned?*"

"Yes. I went there, but they told me that Maddie didn't have much contact with the children. So—"

"You did what?" Stunned, Yang could barely get the words out.

"Well, Vicky and I pretended that we wanted to volunteer there so that we could ask questions," Emily said during his silence.

"You can't go back there."

"Well, I'm not planning to," Emily huffed.

"Good." Because snooping around would only get her into trouble, and next time he might not be there to save her.

"So what are you gonna do about Maddie's murder and how it relates to Petrov?" She tipped her chin up.

"I'll look into it." Even though the case was the Secret Service's. But clearly Agent Mitchell and Agent Banning hadn't gotten very far yet. They only saw part of the picture, but Yang now had more pieces of the puzzle, and somehow Petrov and the charity were part of it. "Miss Warner, you have to promise me something. Stop investigating on your own. Leave it up to me. Can you promise me that?"

A sound at the door to the apartment made him snap his head in its direction. It sounded like somebody was scraping against the lock with something sharp. He cast a quick look back at Emily, who had heard the sound too. Was the shooter here to try it again?

Yang pulled his gun from his holster, then motioned for Emily to move into the hallway. Emily motioned to her dog, and the two silently hurried away.

The scraping continued. Yang pressed himself against the wall next to the door, gun at the ready. Three more seconds, and the lock clicked and the door was opened. A long kitchen knife was the first thing Yang saw, then the person entered.

Yang put the nozzle of his gun to the intruder's head. "Drop the knife, or I'll shoot."

The intruder screamed, and the knife clattered to the floor.

"Don't shoot!" the woman yelled.

"Vicky?" Emily cried out from the hallway and came running. "Don't hurt my friend!"

Yang cursed. "Shit!" He lowered the gun and stepped away from Vicky. When she looked at him, he recognized her as the woman who'd accompanied Emily to the Bolton funeral. "Fuck! Why the hell are you breaking into Emily's apartment?"

"I'm not breaking in," she ground out and held up a key. "I heard raised voices and came to check up on Emily." Now she looked at her friend. "Are you okay?"

Emily nodded. "I'm fine."

Vicky pointed to Yang. "And who's the gunslinger?"

Yang flashed his badge. "Detective Adam Yang, DC Police."

Vicky stared at the badge and then at Emily. "You're dating a detective? When did that happen?"

Emily's cheeks reddened. "It didn't."

57

AFTER VICKY'S EMBARRASSING QUESTION, Yang made a rather hasty exit, but not without warning Emily not to put herself in danger any longer and letting her know that he would send a uniformed officer to watch her apartment building. While Emily appreciated his concern for her safety as well as the armed guard he promised to send, she had no intention of complying with his request. She had to continue following the clues Maddie was sending her.

"So you're not dating him, but he's in your apartment in the middle of the night," Vicky said, interrupting Emily's musings.

"It's not the middle of the night. It's barely nine o'clock," Emily deflected.

"That's neither here nor there. So, what happened? Why was that cute detective here?"

Vicky wasn't wrong: Detective Yang was good looking and seemed to have her best interests in mind, not to speak of the fact that he'd risked his own life to push her out of the way of a bullet.

"He saved my life," Emily started and filled Vicky in on what had happened after she'd left the hair salon.

Vicky let herself fall on the couch. "That's bad, really bad."

Emily flopped down next to her. "Yes, I was counting on speaking to Sergei Petrov because I think he knows something about Maddie and the girl I saw in my vision. But the detective just told me that Petrov was shot this morning, and he's in a coma."

Coffee squeezed himself in between them, indulging in pets from both of them.

"Oh fuck," Vicky said. "You think it was the same person who tried to kill you?"

"The detective thinks so." She sighed. "Petrov knows something, I can feel it. What am I gonna do now?"

"I don't see that there's anything you can do. It's out of your hands."

"But I have to do something."

"You're not gonna listen to the detective, are you?" Vicky asked and tilted her head to one side.

Emily shrugged. "If the police haven't figured out by now that Maddie was murdered, they don't want to find out. I have to do it."

"But you're putting yourself in danger if you continue looking into this. I mean, some asshole tried to kill you tonight. Doesn't that scare the shit out of you?"

It did. "I can't just give into that fear. Or the killer will have won."

"Your stubbornness will get you killed."

"I hope to get to the truth before that can happen."

For a moment they were both silent. Then Vicky said, "So what do you want me to do?"

Emily turned on the couch, and pulled one leg beneath her to face Vicky. "Since you're asking: could you talk to somebody at the hospital to see what Petrov's prognosis is?"

"They're not allowed to tell me. Besides, you don't even know which hospital Sergei Petrov is at."

"I can guess though. A gunshot wound? And he's a diplomat. Trust me they would have taken him to the hospital with the best trauma center."

"George Washington University Hospital," Vicky said.

"Exactly. Where you used to work. And you told me yourself not too long ago that you still have friends there. Please…"

Vicky let out a breath. "Fine. I'll go there tomorrow and see who's willing to gossip. But you have to do something for me in return."

"Anything," Emily said automatically.

"You need to watch Merlin and hang out at my place while I'm gone. He hates being alone."

Vicky's cat would probably enjoy a few hours of solitude, but Emily wasn't going to contradict her friend.

"And I've got the cable guy coming. You know what it means when they say they're coming between eight and twelve."

Emily rolled her eyes. "It means they could come whenever it pleases them."

"Right. So, give me your phone."

"What for?"

"I'm gonna give you all the details and the reference number in case you need to call them."

Emily rose and went to get her handbag, then unlocked her cell phone and handed it to Vicky.

Vicky took it. "Hey, do you still have ice cream in the freezer?"

"Always."

"Cool, I'll take two scoops."

Emily walked into the kitchen and opened the freezer. While she prepared a small bowl for Vicky and herself, she said, "So you really think Detective Yang is cute?"

Vicky chuckled. "He's a dish. I'd date him, but he didn't even give me a second look. He was totally into you, though."

"No, he's not." Emily shook her head, though the thought of Detective Yang being interested in her gave her an odd sense of confidence that she'd never felt around men. "He thinks I'm crazy."

"Good crazy or bad crazy?"

Emily walked back to the couch.

"Right now I think he's tending toward *bat-shit crazy*."

Vicky placed Emily's cell phone on the coffee table and took the ice cream bowl. "Trust me. Most men will easily look past the crazy as long as the girl is pretty. And you are pretty. Especially with your new haircut. It looks very sophisticated."

Emily smiled. "Thanks! I should have done this years ago, but I just didn't know what I would look like with shorter hair."

Vicky winked at her. "Better late than never." She ate a spoonful of ice cream. "Now let's figure out how you can land a date with the detective."

Emily almost choked on her ice cream. Her best friend had a one-track mind. But right now Emily would indulge Vicky, because she needed to forget that she'd almost gotten killed tonight. And what was the harm in fantasizing about a date with a good-looking man? A date that would of course never happen.

58

IT WAS MID-MORNING, when Mike Faulkner looked up from his desk. One of his many staffers was standing at the door. "What is it, Abby?"

Abby Kline, a nearly thirty-year-old political science graduate who'd started working for him about a year earlier took a step into the office and pulled the door shut behind her. "I was just informed by my liaison in the Russian Embassy that one of their diplomats, an attaché, was shot yesterday morning."

"How come I'm only hearing of this now? A death of a diplomat on U.S. soil has to be handled with the utmost care."

"I was only just told about it myself," Abby protested.

"Fine. Let's get the Russian ambassador on the line so the President can express his condolences and assure him that we'll do everything in our power to assist them in investigating this unfortunate incident. You know the drill." He made a dismissive hand movement.

"But, sir, Mr. Faulkner, the attaché, a Sergei Petrov, isn't dead. He's in a coma at George Washington University Hospital."

"Oh," he said, stunned now. "Do we know what his prognosis is?"

Abby shook his head. "No, not yet."

"Make sure you inform me the moment he comes out of his coma, if he comes out of it. We need to stay on top of this. Understood?"

She nodded. "Yes, sir."

Faulkner stared down at the papers on his desk, thinking. What would Petrov be able to reveal if he woke up from his coma? Had he recognized the shooter? And would he reveal what he and Maddie had spoken about before her death?

When Faulkner didn't hear the door open, he looked up again. His staffer was still standing there.

"Anything else?"

"Your son called to say he won't be able to meet you for dinner tonight."

"Just as well. I've got too many things to do anyway. Can you cancel the reservation?"

"Certainly, sir."

"And, Abby, cancel my five p.m. appointment with the house minority leader. I need to leave earlier."

"He won't be pleased. It took him almost a week to get on your calendar."

"Yeah, well, he'll just have to wait. I've got more important things to do than hear him whine how badly he feels treated by the president. Just tell him I have an urgent dentist appointment or something like that. You figure it out."

He made a shooing motion, and Abby left his office. When she closed the door behind her, he let out a long breath.

59

ERIC BOLTON LOOKED UP from the desk in his study and saw his wife walk into the room, still wearing her bathrobe, a newspaper in one hand.

"I thought you wanted to sleep in, honey," he said and rose to kiss her.

"I couldn't sleep," she said.

"You should have Dr. Hinkelstein give you something. You haven't slept properly since..." He didn't have to finish his sentence. They both knew that neither of them had had a good night's sleep since Maddie's death.

Rita lifted the newspaper. "Did you read this?"

"Read what?"

She spread the newspaper out on his desk and pointed to a column on page five. He had to lean in to read the small headline.

Russian diplomat shot while jogging, he read.

He lifted his eyes to look at Rita and shrugged. "I'm not sure what you're getting at."

"It says that the man who was shot was Sergei Petrov."

The name sounded familiar, but Bolton couldn't immediately place it. Ever since Maddie's death, he was having trouble concentrating, his thoughts constantly drifting to the girl he'd lost. He had to force himself to read the short article that only consisted of two paragraphs. According to the article, Sergei Petrov had been shot in the early morning hours of the previous day. It was unclear if he'd survived the shooting or not. Neither the police nor the Russian Embassy was commenting.

"Is this somebody we met at an event recently?" he asked, rubbing his nape.

"We met him a few months ago at a charity event," Rita said. "But—"

"It's sad, but I barely remember him. I guess we can send a condolence card to the Russian Embassy?" he offered, though he was baffled why Rita cared. She was dealing with enough, grieving for their daughter.

"That's not why I'm telling you this. It's about that woman who was here. The one who got Maddie's corneas."

Anger churned up in Bolton. That woman had upset Rita with her visit. "Did she bother you again? I swear, I'm gonna have a restraining order put—"

Rita interrupted him by putting a hand on his forearm. "No, Eric, listen. She hasn't come back. But I remember what she told me that day."

"All lies! Don't go down that road, Rita. It'll just hurt you even more."

But Rita shook her head. "Eric, please. That woman said that she saw Maddie call Sergei Petrov before she died. I dismissed it because I didn't think that Maddie had much to do with him. After all, he's gay, so he was certainly not one of her beaus. But now he got shot. It must mean something. It could somehow be connected to Maddie's death."

"But that makes no sense. We don't even know if they knew each other, let alone if they spoke on the phone."

"Please, Eric, I need to know. I need to know what happened. Mike's people haven't found anything yet. I need closure. I need to know whether this Sergei had anything to do with Maddie."

Eric closed his eyes and sighed. He wanted closure too, but he didn't want Rita to go down another rabbit hole.

"Miss Warner said that Maddie called Sergei to ask for help. I need to know why. Please, Eric, please talk to the police or the Russian Embassy. Find out whether Maddie was in contact with him and why."

Tears started to well up in Rita's eyes. He couldn't bear to see her cry again. It hurt too much.

He took her by the shoulders and squeezed them. "I'll talk to the police and find out who's working this case."

"Thank you, Eric, thank you." She pressed herself against his chest.

"But you have to promise me something."

"Anything," she said and looked up at him.

"Talk to Dr. Hinkelstein to give you something so you can sleep again. You need to rest, or you'll get sick. And I need you to be here for me, just like I'm here for you. We need each other now more than ever before."

"I promise, Eric."

"I love you," he said.

"I love you," Rita said, and the words she hadn't spoken since Maddie's death warmed his heart.

60

AFTER THE REVELATIONS from the previous night, Yang had gotten in early to pore over the files of the Annika murder case, and re-read the thin dossier Belsky had given him on Sergei Petrov, as well as the notes he had made about Madeline Bolton. Somehow all three cases were connected. But how? He needed to brainstorm, but hadn't had a chance to speak to Jefferson yet. His partner had called to say that he was going to the dentist for an emergency root canal and wouldn't be in until after lunch.

When his phone rang an hour before lunch, Yang saw it was an internal call and picked it up. "Yang here."

"Detective, you have a visitor. A Mr. Eric Bolton," the receptionist said.

Yang instantly sat up straighter. "Ask him to wait in interrogation room two. I'll be right there."

What did Madeline Bolton's father want from him? Had he somehow found out that Yang was looking into his daughter's death behind the Secret Service's back? Just as well that Lieutenant Arnold was in a leadership meeting across town. With some luck, Yang could keep Bolton's visit quiet.

Yang entered the interrogation room and closed the door behind him. Eric Bolton, who'd been standing and looking at the two-way mirror, now pivoted.

"Mr. Bolton? Detective Yang." He reached out his hand, and Bolton shook it.

"Good morning, Detective."

Yang pointed to the chair on the other side of the small table. "Please take a seat."

Once they both were seated, Yang asked, "How may I help you?"

"I'm really sorry to take your time, Detective, I'm sure you've got more than enough work." Bolton sighed. "But I understand that you're assigned to the Petrov case."

Yang raised an eyebrow. Nobody except for a few high-ranking police officers like the Lieutenant and her superiors knew that the division was handling the attempted assassination of Sergei Petrov. "I'm afraid I can't talk about the case, nor can I deny or confirm that such a case exists."

Bolton nodded. "I understand. But let's just say I know from one of your superiors that you're handling the case and would like to give you some information. Wouldn't you want that information?"

Yang looked at Bolton's face, trying to determine the older man's intention. "Well, that depends on the information."

"My wife asked me to come," Bolton started. "She recently spoke to somebody who believes that my daughter, Madeline, spoke to Sergei Petrov before her death."

Yang was suddenly all ears.

"But I looked at her cell phone, and I can't find any record of the call, nor that she even had his phone number. Maddie probably knew him from one event or another, but I don't know why she would have talked to him." He reached into his pocket and pulled out a cell phone with a post-it note on it. He slid it toward Yang. "That's her cell phone, and that's the PIN. The Secret Service gave it back to me."

"What did the Secret Service find out?"

Bolton shrugged. "From what they told me, there was nothing useful on the cell phone. But maybe you could take a look?"

Yang nodded. Having access to Madeline Bolton's phone was an unexpected boon. "Mr. Bolton, I'm of course aware of what happened to your daughter. In fact, my partner and I were supposed to investigate her death, but then the Secret Service claimed jurisdiction. Apparently the Chief of Police was told the case had something to do with national security."

Bolton appeared embarrassed. "I'm sorry. I was very distraught when I got the call about Maddie. I was still in the ER when I spoke to Mike Faulkner... you know... the Chief of Staff, and I needed to find out what had happened to my little girl..." His voice broke, but then he caught himself and continued, "So when Mike said he'd have the Secret Service investigate, I agreed. I didn't mean to cause any strife between the police and—"

"No need to apologize, Mr. Bolton," Yang interrupted. "I'm very sorry for your loss." He cleared his throat. "So, you're saying Madeline might have been talking to Sergei Petrov?"

Bolton nodded. "Yes, and my wife is wondering whether somehow Petrov's death and my daughter's death are connected."

Yang realized immediately that Bolton had no idea that Petrov had survived the attempt on his life, and he had no intention of correcting him. The fewer people that knew that Petrov was still alive, the safer the diplomat was.

"It's certainly something I can look into, but considering that your daughter's death is being investigated by the Secret Service, who won't share any information with us, I would like to ask you for help."

Bolton nodded instantly. "Of course, anything you need."

Yang took the pen and notepad that lay on the table between him and Bolton. He wasn't going to waste time, and concentrated on those questions that he hadn't been able to get answered by other sources. This was his chance to collect more pieces of the puzzle.

"My understanding is that your daughter worked for a charity? Can you tell me more about that?"

"Yes, I was so pleased when she got involved with *No child abandoned*. She had her troubles, you know, but when she was finally able to focus her energies on something good, something worthwhile, she bloomed." A smile appeared on Bolton's face. "She was good at what she did, convincing people to donate to a good cause. She knew how to pull at potential donor's heartstrings. The money rolled in, and the charity could do so much good with it. Even more than when Mike was running it."

"Mike?" Yang interjected.

"Oh, Mike Faulkner. He founded the charity years ago."

Yang remembered now that he'd read it on the charity's website, but he didn't interrupt Bolton.

"He ran it, but then had to resign when he became the President's Chief of Staff. His son, Caleb, took over for him. Caleb and Madeline were such a great team."

"Were they romantically involved?"

"Oh no, we'd hoped, my wife and I, but no, Caleb never showed any interest in Maddie in that way. In fact, he doesn't date much. He's very dedicated to his job. I guess that doesn't leave him much time for a relationship."

"Hmm. Did your daughter have contact with the children the charity rescued?"

"I don't believe so. She was really at her best when wining and dining donors. I mean, yes, occasionally there would be events where the children that had been rescued were in attendance, so the donors could see what their dollars had made possible. Maddie could have had a seat on the board, like my son-in-law, but she wanted a little bit more involvement than only attending board meetings and signing off on financial documents and audits."

"Your son-in-law is on the board of *No child abandoned*?"

"Yes, ever since Mike Faulkner stepped down as CEO and Chairman. In fact, they knew each other from before Natalie married Paul."

"Just for the record: that's Paul Sullivan, right?"

"Yes." Bolton shrugged. "He sits on a lot of boards."

"So he and your daughter Madeline had lots of contact?"

"As little as was necessary," Bolton said cryptically.

"Meaning?" Yang asked with interest.

"They butted heads a lot."

"About?"

Bolton gave a shrug. "I never interfered. They just didn't like each other, and being involved in the same charity didn't improve their relationship. They often disagreed on how to run the charity."

"Hmm." Yang made a note to look into Paul Sullivan. After all, most murders were committed by people the victim knew. "As for Sergei Petrov. Do you know him personally?"

"I'm not sure."

Yang raised an eyebrow.

"Listen, I meet a lot of people in my line of work, and I go to a lot of events hosted by one government or another. I'm sure our paths have crossed at some point in the last few years, but truth be told, I wouldn't be able to pick him out of a lineup."

"I understand. So what makes your wife think that your daughter spoke to him before her death?"

Bolton sighed, and Yang realized immediately that Bolton felt uncomfortable answering the question. "You probably think it's stupid, but … for lack of a better word… a psychic came to see her and told her things that my wife found credible."

Yang knew exactly what Bolton was trying to say, but he didn't let on that he knew who that so-called psychic was, though he needed to confirm his suspicion. "Did this psychic have a name?"

"Emily Warner, though I'm not sure if it's even her real name."

Yang nodded. His suspicion turned out to be correct. Emily had spoken to Mrs. Bolton, and while he wasn't happy about the fact that she was interfering with police work, her action had resulted in Eric Bolton coming to him for an interview.

"I will look into her," Yang claimed. "Is there anything else you can think of that may help us connect your daughter to Sergei Petrov?"

With a regretful look, Bolton shook his head. "I wish I could give you something else, but that's all I know. I know it's not much, but…"

"It's a lead," Yang assured him. "If there is a connection between your daughter's death and Mr. Petrov, I'll find it."

They both rose and shook hands.

"Thank you, Detective."

Yang showed him out, then went back to his cubicle with Madeline Bolton's cell phone in his hand. He looked at it, contemplating his next move. Bolton had given him enough information to suspect that the Russian diplomat knew something related to Madeline's death.

Yang opened a file, looked for a phone number, then dialed it.

The call was answered after the first ring. "Leave a message," the voice with the Russian accent said followed by a beep.

"Detective Yang from DC Police. I need to know if Sergei Petrov knew Madeline Bolton and called her before her death. It's important."

61

EMILY POURED HERSELF A SECOND CUP of tea while Coffee and Merlin were chasing each other around the coffee table in Vicky's apartment. Vicky had left over an hour earlier to go to the hospital on her reconnaissance mission. So far, Emily hadn't heard back from Vicky. For the fifth time, Emily checked to make sure her cell phone wasn't set to silent. She was anxious. Reality was only just setting in. The previous night too much adrenaline had pumped through her veins for her to realize the severity of her situation. Somebody was trying to kill her because she was following the clues Maddie was giving her.

Was she really prepared to continue on this path, even though her actions were turning her into a target? What if she couldn't find out who murdered Maddie?

She stopped herself, suddenly realizing something. The fact that somebody was trying to kill her had to mean that she was on the right track. She was making the killer nervous. It meant she was close to figuring out who was behind all this. Why else would Maddie's killer find it necessary to eliminate her? Her and Sergei. Perhaps it meant that both Emily and Sergei had pieces to the puzzle, and if they put their heads together, they would find out who the killer was. That's why it was crucial for Sergei to wake up.

The doorbell suddenly rang, the sound so loud that Emily jumped involuntarily, spilling some of her tea on the coffee table. Her heart beat into her throat, and with trembling hands, she set down the mug.

She took a breath, and walked to the door. A killer wouldn't ring the doorbell. Besides, this was Vicky's apartment. Emily pressed the intercom.

"Yes?"

"It's the cable company for Victoria Hong."

"Come on up." She pressed the button to buzz him in, and relaxed.

She sensed Coffee behind her, and pivoted. He was staring at her, clearly having sensed her uneasiness. She petted his head. "I'm alright, Coffee. Good boy."

Merlin was inserting himself between Emily and Coffee, his soft bushy tail brushing against Emily's legs.

"Yes, you too, Merlin. Now go play."

But Coffee didn't move, even when Merlin went to the couch and jumped up. Coffee was still alert, knowing that the doorbell meant that somebody was coming.

Emily heard a sound outside the door and looked through the peephole. She had a hard time training her eye on the man outside, even though her eyesight was getting better each day. But she had to squint.

She opened the door, and looked at the man. He wore a T-shirt with the emblem of the cable company, and carried a toolbox.

"Victoria Hong?" he asked with a smile. "I'm Jamie."

Emily didn't correct him. He didn't need to know that she wasn't Vicky. "Please come in." She pointed to the living area. "The cable box is there."

He entered and stepped past Emily, when Coffee blocked his way. The dog let out a low growl.

Jamie stopped. "Does he bite?"

"No, no. Sorry, he's just a little on edge," Emily said and took Coffee by the collar. "It's all good, Coffee. Easy. That man is just here to repair something, okay?" She spoke in a soothing voice, indicating to her trusted guide dog that everything was okay.

"Thanks. I'm not much of a dog person." He forced a smile. "I guess dogs can sense that, can't they?"

"Animals are very intuitive," Emily said. And knowing that Coffee didn't like Jamie made Emily feel a little apprehensive too, even though the man didn't do anything to warrant her unease.

He walked to the TV and put down his toolbox next to it. "How long have you had the pixilation issue?"

"Uh… just a couple of days…" Emily guessed. Had it been longer, Vicky would certainly have gotten a repairman out sooner.

"Well, let's have a look then."

While he got several tools out of his box and started working on the cable box, Emily bent down to Coffee and petted him. "Be a good boy, Coffee." The dog leaned against her legs, his body more relaxed now. "Go play with Merlin."

"I think there's a loose connection somewhere," Jamie said, looking over his shoulder. "Mind if I move the TV stand?"

"No, no, go ahead, whatever you need to do."

Her cell phone rang, and Emily walked over to the kitchen counter where she'd left her phone. She picked it up and looked at the number. *Spam Risk* it said, so she pressed the button to decline the call, when a loud bang sounded behind her and made her whirl around. A metal bowl with decorative wooden fruit clattered to the floor. Coffee barked, and Merlin suddenly jumped off his perch on the couch and onto the coffee table, hissing at Jamie.

"Fuck, sorry!" Jamie said and lifted his hands, but Merlin jumped at him, scratching him. Several magazines fell off the coffee table and landed on the floor.

"Merlin, off!" Emily yelled, but the cat didn't listen, and kept hissing at the cable guy.

"I'm sorry," Jamie said and motioned to the bowl. "I hit it with my shoulder when I moved the TV stand."

Coffee kept barking and ran to Merlin's side, as if to defend his friend.

"Don't worry," Emily said. "It didn't break."

"I'll help you," he said, attempting to reach for a decorative banana, but Coffee and Merlin didn't stop barking and hissing.

"I'll do it," Emily said. "Sorry about Coffee and Merlin. They just got startled."

Jamie forced a smile. "Guess I'm not a cat person either."

"Coffee! Enough." Her dog instantly turned quiet and looked at her. She pointed to the couch, and Coffee walked there and jumped up. When he was seated, Merlin turned away from Jamie and joined Coffee, snuggling up against him.

Emily sighed, then she started picking up the pieces of wooden fruit and placed them back in the bowl, before collecting the magazines from the floor. One of them had fallen open, and Emily was about to close it, when she caught sight of the glossy picture on the right page. She gripped the magazine and pulled it closer, focusing her eyes on the picture of a bathroom. She'd seen this bathroom before—not in real life, but in a vision. This was the bathroom where Maddie had hidden an envelope.

Emily looked at the other pictures in the magazine that seemed to highlight a luxurious condo. In one of the pictures a handsome man with an olive complexion stood in front of a fireplace, in another, the same man posed sitting on a chaise longue.

She'd seen this man before. She needed a few seconds, before she could read the headline.

At home with Diego Sanchez. A look at contemporary living in a historic building.

Emily's heart fluttered. "Oh my God." Maddie had hidden the envelope in Diego's condo. It could only mean that she trusted Diego with whatever information it contained.

62

SHORTLY AFTER LUNCH, Yang sat in his cubicle and put the receiver down, stunned at the information he'd just received, when he saw a movement from the corner of his eye. He turned his head and saw Jefferson strolling in.

Yang motioned to him. "Finally!"

Jefferson approached and furrowed his forehead. "What?" His voice sounded as if he had a gag in his mouth.

"We've gotta go and arrest Sokolov." He called out to the desk sergeant, "Send a couple of unis over to Dr. Sokolov's office in the Logan Ambulatory Care Building on NW P Street to make sure he doesn't leave. But don't have them go up. Have them cover all exits. We'll be there in a few minutes."

"We got him?" Jefferson asked.

As they hurried outside, Yang said, "I'm driving. You're probably still out of it."

"I'm fine," Jefferson protested.

Moments later, they were in the car and heading toward Sokolov's office building. Finally, Yang could fill in his partner on what he'd found out. "We got a DNA match."

"That fucking bastard killed Annika? No wonder he didn't wanna give us his DNA."

"He didn't kill Annika."

"What?" Jefferson shot him a confused look.

"His DNA was a match for a 22-year-old rape case in Illinois. That's why he didn't volunteer. He must have realized that once his DNA was in the system, it would link him to that rape."

"Fuck me!" Jefferson said.

"Yeah, that was a stroke of luck. Not that it gets us much further with Annika's case, but at least we get one asshole off the street."

"How the fuck did he ever get a medical license?" Jefferson growled.

"Guess he was never a suspect in that Illinois case. He probably moved out of state shortly after he committed the crime," Yang said, shrugging.

"And forensics is sure that he's no match to the DNA found on Annika's body?" Jefferson asked.

"Hundred percent."

Jefferson sighed. "Sucks."

"Yep."

They fell silent for the remainder of the drive. Yang decided to fill Jefferson in on what he'd learned from Eric Bolton later. Right now they had to arrest a violent offender.

At Sokolov's office building, a squad car was already parked in front of the entrance. Curious office personnel were exiting the building on their way to lunch, while a uniformed police officer stood at the entrance door to watch whether Sokolov was leaving.

Yang walked up to the uniformed police officer and flashed his badge. "Detective Yang and Jefferson. Is Sokolov still inside?"

"He hasn't left while I've been here. My colleague is at the back exit."

"Good. Stay here. We'll go up."

Side by side, Yang and Jefferson entered the foyer and walked toward the elevators, when one of the elevators opened, and Sokolov stepped out of it. Their gazes met. Yang reached for his gun, and Sokolov's eyes widened. He knew the jig was up.

Sokolov spun around and ran in the opposite direction. Yang and Jefferson chased him.

"Dr. Sokolov! Police! Stop now!"

The idiot didn't listen, and Jefferson caught up with him a moment later, tackling him to the ground, while Yang pointed the gun at Sokolov's torso. "One wrong move, and you'll find out how much a bullet wound hurts."

Sokolov panted. Jefferson had him pinned down, while he pulled out his handcuffs.

"Yuri Sokolov, you're under arrest for the rape of Sharon Engels in Cicero, Illinois on June 10th 1999," Jefferson said, while cuffing his hands behind his back. "You have the right to remain silent. You have the right to an attorney, and if you cannot afford an attorney one will be appointed for you. If you waive these rights and talk to us, anything you say may be used against you in court."

Jefferson pulled Sokolov up.

Defiantly, Sokolov glared at Yang. "You have nothing on me, nothing!"

Yang smiled then motioned to the coffee shop in the foyer of the building. "And you should have bussed your table and not left a half-eaten scone behind."

Jefferson grinned. "You'll have plenty of time to learn to clean up after yourself in prison."

Sokolov grunted, but his facial expression changed. He knew he was caught.

Yang felt satisfaction engulf him. A moment like this was why he loved being a cop. He couldn't imagine doing anything else with his life.

63

Emily was ready to leave her apartment, when she realized something. The uniformed police officer that Detective Yang had assigned to protect her was still sitting in his cruiser outside. She couldn't risk him following her where she was headed. Yang wouldn't approve of what she was doing: still snooping around to find Maddie's killer. For a moment, Emily thought whether there was a way to distract the officer so she could sneak out without being seen, but Vicky wasn't home, so she had to come up with another idea.

She walked down to the first floor, but instead of leaving through the front door, she headed in the opposite direction and turned left when the corridor ended. A few steps farther, a door led outside to the tiny yard, were Oberman, the super, kept the large trash containers for the building. She glanced around and found a gate at the far end of the yard. There was a gate that led alongside the building, connected to the building next to Emily's, which according to Vicky belonged to the same landlord.

Emily entered the yard of the neighboring building, found the door to its lobby unlocked and went inside. She walked through the lobby, then peered outside. Several bushes obstructed the view from the building's entrance door to where the police cruiser was parked. Emily went outside, and just before she stepped on the sidewalk, she looked in the cruiser's direction. It was parked so the driver would only see her if he looked in his rear-view window.

As quickly as possible without running, Emily rushed along the sidewalk and turned into the next side street. Relieved that the police officer hadn't spotted her, she let out a breath.

Finding the building Diego Sanchez lived in wasn't a problem at all. The article that had appeared in the glossy magazine a few weeks prior to Maddie's death had given Emily sufficient information to figure out the address. What was more difficult was to collect all her courage to ring the doorbell. Whether Sanchez was home or not, and whether he would invite her inside, was out of her hands.

"Yes?" a male voice came through the intercom.

"Mr. Sanchez? I'm a friend of Maddie's, and I wanted to talk to you about something she told me before her death." It was a lie, though the gist was the truth. She had something to tell him about what Maddie had *shown* her *after* her death.

There was silence, and it stretched for several seconds.

Sanchez wasn't falling for the ruse. Perhaps too many curious reporters had tried this trick before. Emily sighed. Maybe she would have to break into his condo like she'd broken into Maddie's house. It would be more difficult though, because she didn't know when Sanchez wouldn't be home.

"Top floor," the same voice suddenly said. Simultaneously, Emily heard a buzzing sound, and pushed the entrance door open.

Nervously, Emily stepped into the elevator and rode up to the fourth floor. She wasn't afraid of Diego. Maddie had trusted him enough to hide information in his place, so Emily didn't believe that he would present a danger to her. Still, Sanchez didn't know her, and eventually he'd figure out that she wasn't a friend of Maddie's. Emily could only hope that she had enough time to search for the envelope before Sanchez threw her out.

When the elevator pinged and the doors slid open, Emily stepped into the hallway. A door at one end was already open. In its doorframe stood Diego Sanchez. He was dressed in jeans that rode low on his hips, and a T-shirt that showed off his muscular physique. He looked so different from when she'd seen him at Maddie's funeral. It was easy to see why Maddie had fallen for him. He oozed sex appeal. Paired with his penetrating dark eyes and his fit body, it wasn't hard to imagine that women swooned the moment he walked into a room.

"Mr. Sanchez," she greeted him, smiling at him in the hope that her smile would portray her as a confident woman.

"Diego," he said and offered his hand. "I'm afraid I don't know your name."

"Emily Warner."

"Please come in."

The condo looked just like the pictures in the magazine, albeit a little messier. The kitchen counter was littered with dirty dishes, and the living room had books and newspapers strewn around.

Sanchez caught her gaze. "Excuse the mess. I wasn't expecting anyone."

Emily turned to him. "I'm sorry to intrude." Her hands suddenly felt clammy, and she wiped them on her jeans.

He seemed to notice her nervousness if the look he gave her was anything to go by. "You said you were a friend of Maddie's. I'm afraid she never mentioned your name."

Before Emily could come up with a response, Sanchez continued, "You're not the kind of woman Maddie was friends with. In fact, she didn't have many female friends."

His words sounded like a challenge.

"I know. Maddie and I really had nothing in common. And under normal circumstances, we probably would have never met. But we both care about the truth."

Sanchez raised his eyebrows. "The truth about what?"

Emily hesitated and cleared her throat. Could she trust Sanchez with the truth? Could she confide in him? Unable to answer, she did the only thing she could. She stalled. "Excuse me, do you mind if I use your bathroom?"

For a moment, she thought he would refuse her request, but then he motioned to a corridor and said, "The guest bathroom is through the second door to the left."

She nodded. "Thank you."

"Shall I make you a drink in the meantime?"

Emily forced a smile. "That would be great."

While Sanchez walked to the refrigerator, Emily headed down the hall. She opened the door he'd indicated, but immediately realized that this wasn't the bathroom from her vision. Without making a noise she pulled the door shut again and snuck farther down the corridor, glad that the plush carpet swallowed up the sound of her footsteps.

The corridor made a bend to the right, and Emily followed it. The door greeting her was closed. She pressed down the handle and opened it. This was the master bedroom. A massive king-size bed dominated the room. The décor was decidedly masculine with bold colors and no frills. She walked into the room and immediately headed for the open door to the en suite bathroom. She looked at the double sinks and the large shower. Yes, this was the bathroom Maddie had shown her in the vision.

Not wasting any time, Emily crouched down and opened the cabinet doors below the first sink. Inside, toilet paper was neatly stacked two rows high, not three like in the vision. She understood immediately why

Madeline had hidden the envelope there. Over time, Diego would use the rolls until he would have found the envelope. Emily's heart began to pound. She removed the top row of the rolls, and there it was: the envelope that Maddie had hidden. Emily reached for it when a sudden sound behind her made her whip her head to look over her shoulder.

Sanchez stood in the open door and glared at her. "Who are you really, and what the fuck are you doing here snooping around?"

Emily swallowed hard. "Shit."

64

AFTER BOOKING SOKOLOV and notifying the U.S. Marshall Service and the Cicero Police Department that the rape suspect was in custody and ready to be transferred to Illinois, Yang took his partner aside and filled him in on his conversation with Eric Bolton.

They were in one of the interrogation rooms so nobody could overhear them.

"You're shitting me," Jefferson said, his jaw dropping. "You think Madeline Bolton's death is connected to the assassination attempt on Petrov?"

"It's possible." What Yang had left out was that Emily Warner was the person who'd put that particular bee into Mrs. Bolton's bonnet. There was time to go into the details later.

"But you just said that there's no record on Madeline Bolton's cell phone that the call ever happened."

Yang sensed that Jefferson wasn't buying it. "I'm waiting for Belsky from the Russian Embassy to confirm that there was indeed a call between them."

"Yeah, good luck with that. Belsky isn't exactly an oversharer. His file on Petrov was rather thin."

While Yang was worried about the same thing, he didn't voice his concern. Instead, he said, "If he wants us to find out who shot Petrov, he'd better cough up some information. I don't like being hogtied during an investigation."

"Hmm," Jefferson grunted. "So how is Petrov doing anyway? Any news?"

"Still in a coma as far as I know."

There was a knock at the door, before it opened, and one of the uniformed officers entered.

"Detective Yang, sorry to interrupt."

"What is it, McBride?"

"You asked me to let you know the minute the ballistics report was back. It's on your desk now."

"From the bullet they dug out of Petrov?" Jefferson interjected.

McBride stared at him. "No, one of the ones that missed Emily Warner last night. They dug one out of a fence post, but couldn't find the second bullet."

Before Jefferson could ask anything else, Yang quickly thanked McBride and motioned for him to leave. When they were alone again, Yang met Jefferson's inquisitive stare.

"Wanna tell me what else I missed?" Jefferson said.

Yang shifted his weight from one leg to the other. "I was gonna tell you, but then you had to go to the dentist and…"

Jefferson tilted his head to one side. "Sure you were." His voice dripped with sarcasm. "What the fuck happened?"

"Miss Warner was attacked last night. She lives in my neighborhood, and I happened upon her just as somebody was shooting at her. I managed to get her to safety before she could get hurt."

Jefferson ran a hand through his hair and shook his head. "You happened to run into her? Really? Don't bullshit me."

Yang ground his teeth. "Fine. So I was on my way to her. I just wanted to follow up on what she'd told me before. Just to see if she's really crazy."

"Which she probably is," Jefferson interrupted.

"That's what I thought too—before somebody was trying to kill her. It might all be connected."

"Connected how? You mean Petrov's shooting and that woman's? But they have nothing in common."

"They do: Madeline Bolton. She's the connection for all three cases."

"But—"

Yang's cell phone rang, and he looked at the display. "It's Belsky."

He answered the call and put it on speaker phone. "Yang."

Belsky didn't bother with a greeting. "You're correct about the phone call. Madeline Bolton called Petrov the day before her death, but only left a message."

"How do you know that they didn't actually speak?"

"Petrov was out of the country during the time of the call and got back a day after Ms. Bolton's death."

"Could he have called her back from a different number?"

"No."

Yang exchanged a look with Jefferson, who shrugged.

"And what did the message say?"

"That's all I can tell you."

"You mean that's all you want to tell me."

"You catch on quick, Detective. Have a good day." Belsky disconnected the call.

"That confirms it," Yang said.

"Okay. But then why is there no evidence of this call on Madeline Bolton's cell phone?"

"I believe that somebody erased all traces of it."

"You have a theory who might have done that?"

"The cell phone was in the possession of Madeline, her father, and the Secret Service. Her father asked me to check if I could find any evidence of the call and gave me the phone. So he certainly wouldn't have erased it. That leaves Madeline herself and the Secret Service."

Jefferson grimaced. "My money is on the Secret Service."

"Mine too. For some reason they didn't want anybody to know that she was in contact with a Russian diplomat."

"Yeah, but why? You think she spied for them?"

"Doubt it," Yang said.

"You have a better theory?"

"Not sure how it all fits together, but listen to this: Madeline Bolton was an organ donor. Emily Warner received her corneas."

Jefferson's eyebrows rose.

"Yep, she was blind for the last fifteen years. And now she can see. She claims to have visions of things her donor has seen. She was the one who alerted the Boltons to the fact that Madeline called Petrov. And then Petrov gets shot one morning while jogging, and Emily gets shot at the same night. Coincidence? I think not."

"But—"

Yang lifted his hand. "That's not all. As you know, Madeline Bolton worked for *No child abandoned*, the same charity that placed three Russian girls who all disappeared. We found Annika's body. But we might have a chance to save the other two: Sasha and Tatjana."

"They could be dead too. I mean, they disappeared weeks ago."

"Yes, but I think at least one of them is still alive."

"Is that one of your hunches?"

"More than that. In the vision where Emily saw Madeline make a call to Petrov, she also saw a girl."

"We both know that psychic visions aren't real," Jefferson said, shaking his head.

"Normally I would agree with you. But Emily was right about the phone call. I think we have to follow that lead."

Slowly Jefferson nodded. "Let's bring her in."

65

HER HAND STILL GRIPPING THE ENVELOPE, Emily jumped up. Diego Sanchez didn't look as friendly and charming anymore as he had when he'd invited her into his condo. Right now he looked furious, and she now understood what the tabloids meant when they reported that he would fly into a jealous rage now and then. The Diego Sanchez that glared at her, hands on his hips, was furious and looked like he was capable of killing her if she didn't come up with an answer he liked.

"I received Maddie's corneas. She's the reason I'm not blind anymore. I owe her to find out who killed her," Emily said, barely pausing between the sentences. "I see glimpses of her life, and I saw that she hid a letter in your bathroom. I think it will explain…" Her voice trailed off when she noticed Diego's expression change and his gaze zero in on the envelope in her hand.

He made a step toward her and reached for the envelope. She looked at it and noticed that a name was written on the outside. When she looked up, she met his gaze. "I think it's addressed to you."

"That's Maddie's handwriting. How did you know?" He shook his head, clearly trying to wrap his head around the whole situation.

"I think we should read what she wrote. It might tell us who killed her," Emily said.

"You don't buy the accident theory either, do you?" he asked, his voice calm, almost detached.

Emily shook her head.

Slowly, he nodded. "Come. I think we could both do with a drink right now."

In the living room, Diego poured himself a glass of whiskey, while Emily opted for a glass of mineral water. When they both sat down on the large sofa, Diego held the unopened letter in his hand for a long while.

"Despite all the things you might have heard about my relationship with Maddie, I loved her." He gave her a sideways glance. "Yes, we fought, but we always made up."

"She must have trusted you, or she wouldn't have hidden this letter in your place."

"Do you know what's in it?"

"No. But I suspect that it will somehow lead me to her killer."

"Will you open it for me?" he asked. "My hands are shaking." He took another gulp from his drink. "I've been drinking too much ever since she died."

Diego rose and went back to the kitchen counter, where she heard him open the bottle and pour himself another glass.

With her back to Diego, Emily took the envelope and ripped it open. Inside was one sheet of paper. She unfolded it and read:

"Dearest Diego,

I don't know whom else to trust but you. A Russian girl came to me to ask for help. I recognized her as Sasha, a girl the charity rescued but who later disappeared. I couldn't get much out of her due to her broken English and the trauma she's suffered, but I know she's been abused, most likely raped many times. I'm trying to protect her, but nobody can know that I'm hiding her until I can get help for her. I think she'll be able to identify the man who abused her. If you find this letter and I've disappeared, then talk to Sergei Petrov from the Russian Embassy. He'll know what to do. You can trust him with your life.

I love you,

Maddie."

Emily looked up from the letter just as Diego returned with his second glass of whiskey. She met his eyes. Now everything made sense.

"Oh Maddie," he murmured and looked away, perhaps to hide the tears that rimmed his eyes.

"I think I understand what happened," Emily said.

"I don't. Tell me what you know." He sat down next to her.

"In my vision, Maddie was with the girl, Sasha, when she tried to contact Sergei Petrov from the Russian Embassy. I think she called him because the girl was Russian and didn't speak English very well. But I believe she only left a message for Petrov. He was shot yesterday morning."

Diego whipped his head to her. "Are you saying the person Maddie wants me to contact is dead?"

"No. He's in a coma, but until he wakes up, we won't know what all this is about. But I have a theory."

"Let me hear it."

"Maddie must have tried to figure out who hurt that girl, and maybe the man who raped Sasha found out that Maddie was snooping around, and he killed her."

"By staging an accident?"

Emily nodded. "Yes, and then he must have realized that Petrov knew something, so he shot him. And the same day that Petrov was shot, he came after me. Luckily a police detective saved me."

"Back up," Diego said. "What happened?"

In as few words as possible, Emily explained why she believed that Maddie was murdered, and what she'd done to find out why.

When she finished, Diego said, "Did this Detective Yang believe you?"

"I don't know. Some bits yes, but others, I'm not sure he believes all of it."

"That's understandable. Frankly," Diego said, "I have a hard time myself believing what you told me." Then he pointed to the letter. "But this letter was definitely written by Maddie. And you knew where she hid it."

"I think it was her insurance policy."

"I think so too." He took the last swig from his tumbler. "Do you think that girl, Sasha, is still alive?"

"Yes. Maybe she ran when that man killed Maddie."

"We need to find her. She might be the only eyewitness to what happened to Maddie."

"I agree," Emily said, when her cell phone suddenly rang.

She pulled it from her pocket and looked at the display. "It's Detective Yang. I should tell him what we found."

Diego put his hand on her arm. "Don't mention the letter."

"Why not?"

"If the killer was able to get to Petrov and to you, it's best if nobody knows about the girl."

"But Detective Yang already knows about the girl in my vision. This is just confirmation that I was right."

Diego sighed. "Just be careful who you trust with this information."

She nodded at Diego's odd comment, but didn't say anything in reply. She trusted Yang. He'd saved her life. Taking a breath, she answered the cell phone. "Detective?"

"Miss Warner, I need you to come to the precinct."

Surprised, she asked, "Uh, for what?"

"The ballistics report came in."

"And?" she asked curiously.

"Let's discuss it when you get here. Have the uniformed police officer who's stationed outside your apartment building drive you to the precinct."

"Okay, give me a half hour. I just stepped out of the shower and need to dry my hair," she said to buy herself some time to get back to her apartment. She disconnected the call and got up from the couch.

On her way out, Diego handed her a card. "This is my cell phone. Call me later. We need to figure out how to find Sasha."

Emily put his card in her handbag. "I'll call you."

For the first time since the visions had started, she felt confident that she would get justice for Maddie, and that she wouldn't suffer the same fate as after her first cornea transplant.

66

YANG WAITED IMPATIENTLY for Emily Warner to arrive at the precinct. Even Jefferson was now on board with Yang's theory that Madeline Bolton lay at the center of three cases: the attempted assassination of Sergei Petrov, the attack on Emily Warner, and the murder of Annika.

When Emily arrived at the precinct it was late afternoon. A police officer accompanied her to one of the interrogation rooms. Yang and Jefferson entered right after her.

"Miss Warner, this is my partner, Simon Jefferson," Yang introduced her.

After a short greeting, Yang asked her to take a seat. He and Jefferson each took a seat opposite her, and Yang placed the files he'd brought with him on the table between them.

"What did you want to talk about?" Emily asked, giving Yang an inquisitive look.

"The ballistics report came back. We recovered one of the bullets meant for you, and it matches the one that was taken out of Sergei Petrov. They were fired from the same gun."

Emily swallowed hard, and he could see that she was trying to remain calm. She nodded. "What now?"

Jefferson cleared his throat. "My partner filled me in on everything you told him about your connection to Madeline Bolton and what you've claimed to have seen."

"Claimed?" she snorted, then looked at Yang. "You still don't believe me?"

"I do," Yang replied and exchanged a look with Jefferson. "Especially because everything you've told me has turned out to be true. I was able to confirm that Madeline Bolton did indeed call Sergei Petrov. But he didn't get the message until after her death because he was out of the country."

"Then you must know why Madeline called him. I mean you know what the message was about?" Emily asked, a glimmer of hope in her brown eyes.

"The Russian Embassy won't disclose what the message was about," Yang said with regret.

"But why? They can't just withhold information like that."

Jefferson looked at Yang. "Now I see what you mean. She's stubborn."

Emily huffed. "I'm sitting right here, Detective Jefferson. And I don't appreciate being talked down to."

Jefferson looked at her. "I'm not talking down to you. I'm admiring your tenacity."

Emily let out an unladylike grunt under her breath. Then she looked at Yang. "I'm not sure why you wanted me to come here when you could have told me over the phone that the ballistics are a match."

"The ballistics just confirm what you've already suspected. The real reason you're here is because you told me that there was a girl with Madeline Bolton. I want you to identify her."

He opened the Annika murder file and pulled out a photograph of Annika, then slid it across the table to Emily. "Is this the girl you saw?"

Emily instantly shook her head. "She looks similar, but no. It's not her."

That's what he wanted to hear. She'd passed his test. He knew that Annika couldn't have been the girl with Madeline, because Annika had been dead for at least a month before Madeline had called Petrov. He exchanged a look with Jefferson, who nodded.

Jefferson grabbed the file beneath Annika's and removed a photo from it, then slid that one toward Emily. "How about this one?"

Again, Emily shook her head. "No."

"Okay," Jefferson said. "One more." He fished a photo out of the last file.

The moment Emily saw the photo, she said. "That's her."

Yang leaned closer. "Are you sure?"

She nodded excitedly. "That's her! That's Sasha."

Yang did a double-take. "I never mentioned her name to you. How do you know it?"

Emily's eyes widened, and a sheepish expression spread over her face. He could tell that she was contemplating whether to tell him the truth or lie to him.

"Miss Warner, if you know something that might help us, you have to tell us," Yang said.

Emily hesitated, then sighed. "You have to promise me that you won't tell anybody outside of this room."

Yang raised an eyebrow.

"Miss Warner," Jefferson said in a stern voice. "Tell us the truth."

Finally, Emily Warner spoke. "I think Sasha is in danger. I found a letter Maddie hid before her death. In it, she says that this girl, Sasha, asked her for help. She wrote that the girl had been abused and raped, more than just once. And that if anything happened to Maddie, to go to Sergei Petrov, because he would know what to do."

Yang's jaw dropped. "Where's the letter?"

Emily fidgeted on her seat.

"Miss Warner," Yang urged her. "Where is the letter?"

"Diego Sanchez has it. I found it in his condo."

"How the fuck—" Jefferson cursed, but Yang interrupted him.

"Continue. How do you know Sanchez?"

"I don't, not really. But I had to get into his place to look for the letter."

"Let me guess," Yang said. "You had a vision."

Emily nodded. "And when I realized that Maddie had hidden the letter in Diego's condo, I went there to talk to him." She lowered her lids for a moment. "I found the letter, and then Diego caught me snooping around. The letter was addressed to him. We read it together."

Yang let out a long breath and exchanged a look with his partner.

Jefferson looked back at Emily. "The three girls whose photos you just saw all disappeared in the last few months. They're all Russian, and they were all placed into foster homes after being rescued by the charity Madeline Bolton worked for."

"*No child abandoned*," Emily said.

Jefferson and Yang nodded.

"That's the connection, isn't it?" Emily asked, and Yang could see the wheels in her head turning. "Sasha was probably in Maddie's house when Maddie was murdered. She might have seen the killer."

Yang took a breath. "Yes, she might be an eyewitness."

"That's why she's in danger," Emily said. "Please don't tell anybody that Sasha might have been there. If the killer finds out that Maddie called Petrov, and that I'm looking into her death, he'll find out about Sasha too. We can't let that happen. We have to find her before he does."

"I agree with you, Miss Warner, except for one thing," Yang said. "You're not part of *we*. My partner and I will investigate. You're in too much danger already."

"But—"

Yang raised his hand to stop her. "Over my dead body."

67

THE KILLER COULDN'T BELIEVE that Sergei Petrov had survived. He should have put a bullet in his head just to make sure, but when he'd heard sounds in the distance, he knew he had to get away quickly.

Emily Warner had had dumb luck. How she'd heard him when he hadn't even heard his own footsteps was beyond him. Nevertheless, the second bullet would have struck her after she'd stumbled if a man whose face he hadn't seen hadn't appeared on the scene and pushed her out of the line of fire.

But he wouldn't give up so quickly. He had to try again. And Petrov was first on his list.

Dressed in a white doctor's coat over green scrubs, he walked along the corridors of the hospital. In addition to a white cap that hid his hair, he also wore a surgical mask. Nobody would recognize him or even give him a second look. While walking past an unmanned nurse's station, he picked up a clipboard with empty forms and turned right at the next bend.

He passed two orderlies, who didn't even look up. Pleased with his disguise, he had no problem navigating the many corridors of the hospital and finding his way to the intensive care unit. Two men in dark suits stood outside one of the rooms: Russians. He knew the type. They were here to protect Sergei Petrov. He'd half expected them, but had hoped he'd only have to get past the medical personnel. He had to come up with plan B.

He turned well before he reached Petrov's room, walking in the same confident manner as before, as if he didn't even notice the two security guards. A few yards farther he found a door leading to a supply room open. He peeked inside and found it empty. Quickly, before somebody could see him, he snuck inside. The shelves were stacked with neatly folded linen. He looked around when he saw the smoke detector on the ceiling.

It gave him an idea.

He left the room and walked down to the end of the corridor. There, he found the fire alarm. He looked over his shoulder, making sure nobody saw him. The coast was clear. He pulled the fire alarm. A moment later, he heard a blaring noise.

Suddenly people were running in different directions. He rushed back to where he could see the door to Petrov's room.

With trepidation, the two Russians watched the medical personnel buzz around the floor. He saw them exchange a few words, before one of them left his post and marched toward the nurse's station, presumably to inquire about what was happening.

This was his chance.

He gripped the syringe in the pocket of his white coat and walked closer, passing hospital personnel and the odd visitor. He rushed toward the Russian in front of Petrov's room.

"I got an alarm that the patient's ventilator is malfunctioning," he said to the Russian. "Quickly, help me, we have to work manually."

The Russian opened the door and ran into the room. The killer followed and kicked the door shut with his foot. Before the security guard realized that Petrov's ventilator was working perfectly, he jabbed the syringe in the Russian's neck. The Russian reared back, but the substance in the syringe worked fast, and he collapsed.

The syringe meant for Petrov was empty. But he'd come so far, he couldn't give up now. He pulled the syringe back, filling it with air, then grabbed Petrov's arm and pushed the air into the IV port. He removed the syringe, and already rushed toward the door, not waiting for the heart monitor to give the confirmation that Petrov was dead. He had to get out of this place before somebody realized that he didn't belong here.

68

I︎T WAS DARK, when Vicky parked her car half a block away from Maddie's townhouse in Georgetown. Emily had left her apartment building via the adjacent building again, then joined Vicky two blocks away, where she was waiting in her car, thus avoiding being seen leaving by the police officer sitting in his cruiser outside the building. Normally, Emily wouldn't have minded him watching her, he'd done so when she'd gone to school to teach, but this was different. Besides, she was with Vicky, and Diego would meet them at the house, so she was hardly in danger of being killed today.

"Thanks for doing this," Emily said.

"I can't really let you do this alone. You don't know this guy. And from what I've read in the tabloids, he's got quite a temper."

Emily tilted her head and smirked. "Or might it be that you think he's handsome?"

"Handsome? He's not handsome." Vicky smirked. "He's sex on a stick."

Emily rolled her eyes. "Case in point."

They got out of the car and walked up to the brownstone. As they walked up the three steps to the entrance door, Emily reached into her handbag and pulled out her lock-pick set.

"Make sure that nobody sees me," she told Vicky.

Before she could insert the pick into the lock, the door opened inward. Emily froze and gasped.

"Were you trying to break in?" Diego said, opening the door wider.

"Uhm, yeah, I mean how else would we get in?" Emily said.

"With a key, of course," he said and motioned for her and Vicky to enter.

"You have a key to Maddie's house?" Emily asked.

"Of course, just like she had a key to my condo."

For a moment, Emily let the news sink in. Diego could easily have entered Maddie's townhouse and waited for her to come home so he could kill her. Weren't most murders committed by the victim's partner? But Maddie had trusted him. She wouldn't have hidden the envelope at his place if she thought that he would hurt her. Had Maddie made a fatal mistake?

"And the alarm?" Emily asked.

"I know the code. But the alarm wasn't set," Diego said.

Then he looked at Vicky, and Emily realized that she hadn't introduced the two yet. "Vicky, this is Diego Sanchez. Diego, this is Vicky Hong."

"Nice to meet you, Vicky." He shook Vicky's hand. "Please call me Diego."

"Nice to meet you too." Vicky ran her eyes over him for longer than Emily thought was polite. Then she purred like her cat, "Diego."

"Okay," Diego said, "where shall we start?"

"We're searching for anything that indicates that Sasha was here and where she might be hiding now," Emily said. She motioned to Sanchez. "You know the house better than Vicky and I. Are there any hiding places?"

He motioned to the stairs. "There's a small attic area that you can only access from the closet in the guest room."

Emily nodded, and they all trotted up the stairs. Emily now saw the house by daylight and it looked even more luxurious than when she'd broken in. She'd decided not to mention the break-in to Diego.

The bed in the guestroom had been stripped. Diego pointed to it. "Maddie's housekeeper was very good. The bed was always made in case of any last-minute visitors."

"Perhaps the girl slept here the night before Maddie died," Emily mused.

"I wish we could confirm that, but with the sheets gone, who knows?" Vicky added.

Diego opened the closet and walked inside. He was tall enough to push the attic access open. "Can you grab a chair so I can have a look up there?"

Emily had already anticipated his request and took the chair from the small desk and handed it to Diego. He put it into position and stepped onto it. His head and shoulders disappeared in the attic.

"It's dark," he said.

"Use your cell phone," Vicky suggested.

"Good idea." He pulled his cell phone from his pocket and used it to illuminate the attic.

"Anything?" Emily asked.

"No. There's a lot of dust up there, but nothing seems to be disturbed." Moments later, he stepped down and pulled the access panel back in place. He dusted off his shoulders.

Together the three searched the bedrooms of the townhouse, but there was no sign of anybody but Madeline having stayed there: no clothes a twelve- or thirteen-year-old would have worn, no shoes that weren't Maddie's size. The kitchen didn't reveal anything either. The refrigerator had been emptied, most likely by the housekeeper, and all trash was gone.

When it was time to search the living room, Diego said, "I can't go in there."

Emily looked at him.

"That's where she died," Diego said.

Emily's heart began pounding. The press had never released any information as to how and where exactly Maddie had been found, and from where they were standing in the hallway, Diego couldn't see the red stain on the carpet.

"How did you know?" she asked.

He turned his head to look at Emily. "When her father didn't return my calls, I spoke to Lucia. Maddie's housekeeper."

Emily nodded. She herself knew how chatty Lucia had been to her, a stranger. To Diego she would have been even friendlier.

"Besides, you can see the bloodstain looking down from the second-floor landing. It's a good spot to watch what's going on," Diego added.

Emily realized that too. "Vicky and I will look through this room," Emily said.

But the living room didn't reveal any clues either. Besides, the forensics team had most likely searched this room thoroughly for any evidence. Emily had to admit that the search of Maddie's townhouse had been a long shot from the beginning.

"I found something," Diego said from the hallway.

Excited, Emily and Vicky joined him in front of the coat closet.

"What?" Emily asked.

"I checked all of Maddie's jackets and coats, and not a single one has any money in the pockets," Diego revealed.

Vicky furrowed her eyebrows. "So?"

"Maddie always carried cash in her pockets to give to the homeless," Diego said. "She was a sucker for a sob story. I told her many times that the money she gave to people would just go towards booze and drugs, but she never listened to me."

"So you think somebody emptied her pockets?" Emily asked.

Diego nodded. "Sasha. She must have taken all the cash she could find."

"You don't think that Sasha robbed and hurt Maddie?" Vicky said, shaking her head.

"No," Diego protested. "But if she saw what happened, she would have been frightened—"

"—and taken all the money she could find," Emily said, "so she could flee."

Diego nodded eagerly. "She would need money to hide somewhere."

"Why not go to the police?" Vicky asked.

"She's Russian, and many Russians don't exactly have faith in authorities," Diego explained. "Maybe she couldn't trust the police and thought they wouldn't believe her anyway."

"Then where would she go?" Vicky asked. "Whom would she trust?"

Emily thought about it for a moment. "Maybe a church? There's a Russian Orthodox church here in Washington D.C. Perhaps she sought sanctuary there."

"That could be it. She would go somewhere, where they speak her language," Diego added.

"Let's check that church. And if she's not there, we can search all the others," Emily suggested. "There might also be a Russian cultural center somewhere. We should check with them too. And the Russian Embassy."

"What if she's injured?" Vicky added. "A girl her age out on the street, scared and panicked could easily have been attacked."

"We should split up so we can cover more ground," Diego suggested. "Vicky, can you call the hospitals in case they have a patient that fits her description?"

Vicky nodded. "Sure."

"Diego," Emily interrupted, "how much money did Maddie normally have in her pockets?"

He looked back at the jackets and coats. "Maybe a total of a hundred to a hundred and fifty? Why?"

"That's not a lot of money. Maddie died almost four weeks ago. If all Sasha had was the money she found in Maddie's pockets, she would have run out of it pretty quickly," Emily mused. "So how does a girl like that survive if she's out of money?"

Diego shrugged. "I don't know." He sighed. "I'll speak to my contact at the Russian Embassy, and then I'll check with the Russian Orthodox Church. Can you start inquiring with the other churches in the city, Emily?"

"Yes. But there are so many."

"Concentrate on those closest to here, and then work your way outward. Sasha would have had to rely on public transportation to get away," Diego added.

"It's getting dark soon. We should leave," Vicky said. "Can we drop you off somewhere, Diego?"

"No, thanks. I'm parked around the corner. We'll talk later." He reached in his pocket and gave Vicky his card. "That's my number. What's yours?"

Vicky recited her number, and he saved it in his cell phone, before Vicky and Emily left the house.

69

It was almost 9 p.m. when Yang found a parking spot a block away from his apartment building. After Emily Warner had left the precinct, he and Jefferson had pored over the files of the Petrov shooting and the Annika murder, as well as the files of the two missing girls, Sasha and Tatjana. They came up with theories of how everything was connected to Madeline Bolton, but in the end they had to realize that there were still too many missing pieces.

Tomorrow, they would look over everything again with fresh eyes.

Yang felt tired. He got out of the car, and locked it. He crossed the street and walked along the sidewalk, until he got to his apartment building. The light over the entrance door wasn't on. Maybe it had burned out, but Yang was too tired to alert the building superintendent.

When he walked up the steps to the entrance door, he sensed that he wasn't alone anymore. Slowly, without making any hasty movements, he reached for the gun in his holster and pulled it out. An instant later, he whirled around and pointed his weapon at the person who'd snuck up on him.

Immediately, the young woman raised her arms. "Don't shoot, Detective Yang."

He kept his weapon trained on her. "Who are you?"

"I work with Sergei Petrov at the Russian Embassy. I've waited for you for several hours."

He perused her. She wore a black skirt and a dark cardigan over a white blouse. Her dark blond hair was tied into a bun, making her look like a strict school principal, even though she couldn't be older than thirty. He couldn't see a weapon on her, nothing bulged under her clothing, though it was possible that she had a knife or gun strapped to the inside of her thigh. But even if that was the case, it would take her too long to draw her weapon to be a danger to him.

"How do you know who I am and where I live?"

"You don't really think that all the Russian diplomats stationed in Washington D.C. issue visas for Americans to visit Mother Russia, do you?"

No, he wasn't that naive. Slowly, he lowered his gun. "What do you want?"

She motioned to her hand, and only now he saw that she held a manila envelope in it.

"You can lower your hands."

"Thank you, Detective."

He put his gun away. "What is it?"

"It might help you find out who shot Sergei. This is what Sergei has been working on for the last few months. I summarized and translated it into English for you. I think what's in this dossier is the reason why Sergei was shot." She handed him the envelope. "Nobody can know that I gave you this."

"Not even Belsky?"

"It's highly classified. If he finds out I gave you this, he'll send me back to Russia, and I will be tried for treason. Siberia is too cold for my liking."

Yang wasn't surprised that Belsky hadn't given him whatever information was in this envelope. The file on Petrov had been a little too thin to be complete. "Then why take this risk?"

"Because I don't want the guilty party to get away. He has to pay for what he's done. Sergei is a good man. And I think you're a good man too. You'll do the right thing."

Her confidence surprised him. Had she looked into his background before showing up here? "If I have any questions about what's in this envelope, how can I contact you?"

"You can't." She whirled around and ran around the corner, disappearing into the darkness.

There was no use following her. Most Russian diplomats were likely trained as spies and knew how to disappear. Yang unlocked the front door and entered the building. When he reached his apartment, he unlocked the door quietly and opened it. He listened for any sounds, before he turned on the light and stepped inside. He closed the door behind him and flipped the deadbolt. He was alone.

Only three sheets of paper, neatly printed, were in the envelope. Yang began reading.

According to the dossier, Sergei Petrov was charged with investigating the disappearance of numerous Russian girls who were trafficked and ended up in foster care in Washington D.C. The summary outlined that Petrov suspected that the charity *No child abandoned* served as a front for a child sex ring, though he hadn't been able to find any evidence of it yet.

Yang turned to the next page, where Petrov reported that he had an inside contact at the charity who was trying to get Petrov access to internal files. While Petrov didn't name his contact, Yang had to assume that Madeline Bolton was the person who'd been helping Petrov. It made sense, since Madeline's letter had said to contact Petrov if anything happened to her. And even though Yang hadn't seen the letter himself, he believed Emily. Tomorrow, he'd contact Diego Sanchez and request to see the letter in his possession.

On page three of the dossier, Sergei's assistant had summarized a case involving the family of a fourteen-year-old girl living in Moscow. The girl had been brutally raped and nearly strangled to death. But the case had never made it to the courts. The reason became clear in the next paragraph: the family had received a large amount of money to keep quiet about the sexual assault.

At first, Yang didn't understand what this case had to do with Petrov's investigation of the charity, but then he read on. With every sentence everything became clearer. His chin dropped at the revelations Petrov's assistant was sharing with him. When he reached the end of the page, he sat there, stunned and shocked.

He understood now why Belsky hadn't shared this information with DC Police. It would cause an international incident.

Yang pulled his cell phone from his pocket and called Jefferson. It rang once, before his partner picked up.

"Haven't we spent enough time together today?" Jefferson asked.

"I had a little visit from somebody from the Russian Embassy."

"Belsky?"

"No. Petrov's assistant. She told me that Petrov was investigating the disappearance of Russian girls who were rescued by *No child abandoned*."

"You're shitting me."

"That's only the tip of the iceberg. She gave me details on a case from years ago, where an American national paid off the parents of a 14-year-old girl who was brutally raped and nearly strangled to death. The man in question was the American ambassador to Russia. Mike Faulkner."

"What? Not the—"

"The President's Chief of Staff."

"The Chief of Staff is a fucking pedophile?"

"Yep. And I think he raped and then strangled Annika."

70

THE NEXT MORNING, Jefferson picked up Yang from his apartment so they could drive to the precinct together and talk without being overheard by anybody at the station. Yang had shown Jefferson the contents of the envelope the Russian operative had handed him.

"I looked into Mike Faulkner, and the dates of when he lived in Moscow track with the dates of the assault the Russian family reported."

"I wish we had financial records to confirm the payoff," Jefferson said.

"No judge is gonna sign off on that, not if we don't have anything else to tie him to the missing girls. That's why I dug deeper last night. And guess what, not only was Mike Faulkner the CEO and Chairman of *No child abandoned*, before he had to resign when he became Chief of Staff, he founded the charity. Guess when."

Jefferson raised his eyebrows.

"Right after returning from Russia."

Jefferson tossed him a stunned look. "You think he did that so he could have access to vulnerable children?"

"We have to assume it. It's an odd thing to do after paying off a family so they wouldn't go to court. Can you imagine the scandal? An American ambassador being dragged into a Russian court?"

"He would have had diplomatic immunity," Jefferson threw in.

"True, but there would have been a scandal nevertheless. The papers would have reported it, and the U.S. would have been disgraced in front of the whole world."

"You think somebody at the State Department was aware of what happened?" Jefferson asked.

"I don't know. It's possible. Though I have a feeling that it was all hush-hush. After all, before Mike Faulkner became Chief of Staff, he would have been vetted. And if the State Department was in on the cover-up, it could have come out then."

"So we have to assume that nobody, apart from Faulkner himself and the Russians, knows about this." Jefferson nodded to himself. "How are we gonna connect him to Annika's murder and the disappearance of the other two girls? All we have so far is that he paid off a Russian family after the rape of a 14-year-old girl, and that he founded the charity—which of course gives him access to the charity's records so he knows where the children are. But that won't get us a warrant to get his financial records or his DNA."

"Don't forget: he was the one who talked Bolton into using the Secret Service to investigate Madeline Bolton's death. It leads me to believe that Madeline was onto him, and that's why she had to die. And since they knew each other well, Madeline would have let him into her house. Hence there was no evidence of a break-in. And Faulkner has the Secret Service in his pocket. If there was any evidence linking him to Madeline Bolton's death, he's probably swept it under the carpet by now."

"Makes sense," Jefferson agreed, "but that still doesn't get us a warrant to get his DNA so we can compare it to the DNA Lupe found under Annika's fingernails. Heck, as Chief of Staff he can probably get the President to claim executive privilege and shut down our investigation completely."

"That doesn't make sense," Yang protested. "Sure, they can claim it's a political witch hunt, but executive privilege? No way. And the Metropolitan Police isn't under the President's purview."

"The President can lean on the mayor, who then leans on the Chief of Police, and they'll make our lives miserable."

"Hmm." Yang knew his partner was right. "But we need Faulkner's DNA. I can sense that he's behind the disappearance of those girls. Once a pedophile, always a pedophile."

"I agree, but there has to be another way to prove that it was him. And frankly, without the DNA, all we've got is circumstantial evidence, rumors, and statements from the Russians that could turn out to be totally fabricated."

Yang sighed. "Damn it! There must be a way. I mean we got Sokolov's DNA even though he didn't consent to it."

"You're suggesting getting Faulkner's DNA on the sly?" Jefferson shook his head. "We can't just waltz into the White House and snag his coffee mug. He's too well protected. It's not like he's the average Joe who goes to coffee shops and restaurants. Or gets his DNA tested on one of those genealogy sites to find out where his family is from."

"What?"

"Yeah, you know those test kits from 23andme or ancestry.com."

"That's it!" Yang exclaimed.

"What? You're gonna send him a test kit under some pretext? Yeah, good luck with that."

"No. We won't need to do that." Yang pulled out his cell phone and dialed a number and put it on speaker. The call was answered after the second ring.

"Morning, Lupe," Yang said.

"What's up?" Lupe asked.

"Just a question. If I can't get a DNA sample of a suspect, but I could get one from a relative of the suspect, would that help confirm that the suspect is the perpetrator?"

"Not confirm, no, but it would make it very likely that if there's a partial DNA match that you've got your man. Ever heard of the Golden State Killer?"

"Sounds vaguely familiar."

"His name was Joseph James DeAngelo Jr. He committed murders and rapes in the 1970s and 80s all over California. He was finally apprehended in 2018. Well, the reason they caught him was because one of his relatives did a DNA test for some genealogy site. The person was a partial match to the rape kits of the victims. So all the police had to do was look into the male relatives of that person and boom, the Golden State Killer was caught."

Jefferson was pulling the car into the police parking lot and killed the engine.

"Thanks, Lupe! That's all I needed to know."

"Anytime."

Yang disconnected the call and exchanged a look with Jefferson.

"And that's what I call out-of-the-box thinking," Yang said, grinning.

Jefferson opened the car door. "You're gonna be fucking annoying all day, because you came up with the solution, aren't you?"

Yang got out of the car. "Just like you would if you had come up with the idea."

Inside the precinct, they didn't get a chance to sit down at their desks, because Lieutenant Arnold called them into her office.

She had a sour look on her face, making Yang wonder if she'd somehow found out about Bolton's visit the day before.

"Shut the door," she ordered.

When Jefferson closed the door, Arnold let out a breath. "Sergei Petrov is dead."

"Fuck!" Yang cursed.

"Didn't make it, huh?" Jefferson said.

"He would have if somebody hadn't injected air into his IV port."

"What?" Yang exclaimed.

"Somebody caused the fire alarm to go off yesterday early evening, and lured one of the Russian security guards away from outside Petrov's room, and then attacked the other security guard and injected him with something, knocking him out immediately."

"Is the security guard dead?"

Arnold shook her head. "Had it happened anywhere else, and not in the hospital, he would be, but the ICU staff was able to revive him. He's still in the hospital. I need you to go there and interview him, and review the security tapes to see if you can find out who did this."

"We're on it," Jefferson said.

"You can count on us," Yang added.

"And, Detectives, Belsky is breathing down my neck. You'd better come back with a lead."

Nodding, Yang and Jefferson left the office.

Now that their prime witness was dead, it was even more important to get Faulkner's DNA. And to protect Emily, before the killer tried again.

71

AT THE HOSPITAL, the Russian security guard, Ivan Lipovsky, was awake. He looked pale, but was able to sit up. Yang and Jefferson flashed their badges at the security guard who stood at the foot of the hospital bed.

"Belsky told us you were coming," the man said. "Come in."

"Mr. Lipovsky," Yang started. "Are you feeling up to answering a few questions?"

Lipovsky answered in a hoarse voice. "Yes."

"What can you tell us about the person who attacked you and killed Sergei Petrov?" Yang asked.

"Not much," he said in heavily accented English. "It was a man. An American. He said that Petrov's ventilator wasn't working. He said I needed to help him so Petrov could breathe." He cast a look at his colleague.

The security guard who stood at the end of the bed said, "The alarm went off, and people were running around, you know, trying to evacuate…"

"Your name is?" Jefferson asked.

"Alexander Gurin."

"Mr. Gurin, did you see the man who attacked your colleague?" Jefferson asked.

"No. I went to the nurse's station." He motioned toward the door. "I wanted to know what was going on." He glanced at Lipovsky. "I shouldn't have left my post. It's my fault."

"Mr. Lipovsky, can you tell us what the man looked like?" Yang asked, addressing the patient.

Lipovsky shrugged. "Not really. He wore scrubs, you know, green ones, and a white coat like a doctor."

"How about his face? Was he young, old, what color hair did he have?" Yang asked.

"I don't know. He wore a mask. A surgical mask. And something on his head." He looked to his colleague.

"A cap, like in the operating theater," Gurin helped out.

"Right," Lipovsky agreed. "I couldn't see his hair. The cap covered it fully. He was a tall man, and not fat. Uh, slim."

Yang looked at Jefferson. "It's not much."

Jefferson turned back to Lipovsky. "So when the man asked you to help him with Petrov because the ventilator didn't work, what did you do?"

"I opened the door and went inside. He came in after me and closed the door. Then I felt pain in my neck. Here." He pointed to the right side of his neck. "He stuck a needle in me. I tried to pull it out, but everything went dark."

Jefferson looked at Yang. "Right-handed?"

Yang nodded. "Most likely." Then he addressed Lipovsky, "Do you know what you were injected with?"

"Don't know. The doctors took my blood after they revived me. They are testing it now."

"Can you notify us when the results come in?" Yang asked.

Gurin answered in Lipovsky's stead. "I will send the result to you when we get it."

"Thank you," Yang said. "If either of you remembers anything else, please call us immediately."

The two Russians nodded, and Yang and Jefferson left the room and headed for the security office of the hospital. Their visit had already been cleared with the chief of hospital security, and a technician was waiting for them in a dark room with a wall of a dozen monitors.

"I've queued the tapes up for you, Detectives," the quirky young woman with the purple hair said. "This is the view of the doors leading into the ICU."

Yang took the seat next to the technician, while Jefferson stood behind them. "Okay, let's see it."

As the technician played back the tape, she narrated what they were seeing. "So this is right when the alarm starts. You can see people suddenly rushing around." The doors opened, and several medical personnel left the ICU. A moment later, a tall man with a clipboard and dressed like a surgeon entered, but the camera lost him.

"This might be your man," the woman said.

"Why do you think that?" Yang asked.

"Because I know most doctors and nurses on that floor, and I've never seen him."

"Are you sure? I mean you can't see his face," Jefferson interjected.

She turned her head to him. "True, but everybody has a certain gait. I don't know anybody with this particular gait."

Yang was impressed. "You're very observant."

"That's why they pay me the big bucks," she joked.

"Is there another camera inside the ICU?" Jefferson asked.

"No. Patient confidentiality, sorry."

"Okay," Yang said, "how about any cameras in the corridor from where that person came?"

"Yep. Give me second."

She found the right camera angle and made the tape show in reverse. Yang and Jefferson watched as the suspect moved around the hospital to the point where he'd pulled the fire alarm. The next camera showed him entering a staircase, where the camera lost him, only to reappear on a lower floor. But no matter which camera caught sight of him, his mask prevented any identification, and he never lifted his head high enough for the camera to catch a good view of his eyes.

The last camera that caught him just before he left the hospital via an employee exit, recorded him as he took off his mask and his cap and tossed it in a trash bin. But all the camera caught was the back of his head.

"Is that brown hair or is it lighter?" Yang asked.

"Hard to tell," the technician said. "That exit isn't very well lit."

"But he made a mistake," Jefferson said and pointed to the trash bin. "He tossed his mask and cap in there. Maybe we can get some DNA off it."

"Good idea," Yang said.

"Ahm," the technician said, "sorry, but the bins get emptied every night. Our janitorial staff is pretty diligent."

Yang sighed. "Let's check it anyway." He rose. "Thanks for your help. Would you mind sending us the snippets that captured the suspect?"

She nodded. "Sure thing."

"Just email it to me." Yang handed her his card, and left with his partner.

72

E<small>MILY DISCONNECTED THE CALL.</small>

"That was Diego," she said to Vicky, who sat, laptop on her lap, on Emily's couch. "Sasha didn't go to the Russian Embassy for help. And the Russian Orthodox Church hasn't heard from her either."

"That sucks," Vicky said. "I've called all the hospitals in the area, and nobody matching her description has been admitted."

"How did you even get them to give you that information? I mean, HIPPA and all…"

"I told them that my daughter ran away, and I'm worried sick." She grimaced. "Some people fall for any sob story."

"Maybe she wasn't admitted, but only went to the emergency room or an urgent care center where she was released after being treated?" Emily asked.

"I checked that too. Still, no sign of Sasha." Vicky sighed. "How many churches have you spoken to?"

"Too many to count."

Emily felt discouraged. She'd visited the churches in the immediate vicinity of Maddie's townhouse, but when she realized how much time she was wasting, she called those that were farther away. Still, Sasha hadn't shown up anywhere.

"I don't know where else she could be," Emily said and plopped down next to Vicky.

Coffee immediately got up from his spot on the floor and nestled his head in her lap. It was amazing how attuned he was to her moods. She petted his head and scratched him behind his ears. "You're a good boy, Coffee. I wish you could help me find the girl, but you're not a bloodhound."

Vicky put her laptop on the coffee table. "Not even a bloodhound could help us. So, any idea what your detective is doing to find the girl? I mean you identified Sasha for him, right?"

"He's not *my* detective."

"He could be," Vicky mused. "But seriously, what is he doing to find her?"

"I don't know. He was all like"—she changed her voice to mimic Yang's—"my partner and I will investigate. You're in too much danger already. And over my dead body." She changed her voice to normal again. "You know how men are."

Vicky chuckled. "He's just trying to protect you. It's kinda sweet."

"I don't need sweet, I need to find Sasha." Though maybe Vicky was right. Maybe Detective Yang really wanted to protect her. "She's the one in danger now. What if the killer finds out that she might have witnessed what he did to Maddie? What if she was right there in the house?"

"Well, we don't know whether she was," Vicky said. "There was no evidence that the girl was staying with her. But then again, the police had already gone through the place, and the housekeeper probably cleaned everything, stripped the sheets, and all. So there's nothing for us to find." Vicky shrugged.

"The sheets! Damn it! Yes, of course!"

Vicky stared at her. "What about the sheets?"

"Lucia would have stripped the sheets if she saw that they had been used. That means somebody did sleep there before Maddie's death. I could talk to her and confirm so—"

"No!" Vicky interrupted. "You're not going to do that. By now that woman probably knows you're not a reporter for a podcast for the blind."

"Fine, then how about Diego? She knows him. He could ask her."

Vicky looked like she wanted to protest, but then thought better of it. "Actually, that's not a bad idea. I'll call him." Vicky was already dialing his number, and her cheeks were turning a pretty pink.

"Oh my God, you've got the hots for him," Emily said.

"I don—oh hi, Diego, it's Vicky." She let out a girlish laugh. "Yeah, I'm fine. Listen, Emily and I were talking and we wanted to confirm that Sasha was staying at Maddie's." She listened, then continued speaking. "Yes, I know, but the sheets were stripped from the guest room. Could you call her housekeeper and find out if the bed had been used?" She paused a moment. "That's great, thanks. Talk later."

She disconnected the call. "He'll do it. He'll call me back the moment he's spoken to her."

Only five minutes passed, and Vicky's cell phone rang. "Hi, Diego," she answered, then listened, before saying, "Thanks so much. I'll talk to you later."

Emily gave Vicky an expectant look when she disconnected the call. "And?"

"Lucia said that the bed was used, but that Maddie never mentioned to her that she was expecting an overnight guest."

"That means Sasha slept there."

Vicky's facial expression suddenly turned serious. "I hate to say this, but what if she's dead?"

"Dead? No. She can't be dead. We need her to identify the killer."

"I know that, but what if she saw everything, and the killer discovered her before she could hightail it out of there? What if he killed Sasha and then removed the body?" Vicky asked.

Emily contemplated her friend's words. "You mean so that Maddie's death would still look like an accident? Because if both Maddie and Sasha had been found dead in the house, it would have looked like murder no matter how well the scene was staged."

"Exactly," Vicky agreed. "Now the question is: how can we figure out if Sasha was murdered in Maddie's house? I mean, it's not like there was a big blood stain other than where Maddie died."

"I have an idea. I need to log into my Amazon account."

"Okay?" Vicky grabbed the computer. "What do you need?"

"Luminol."

73

WITH INVESTIGATING SERGEI PETROV'S DEATH and the attack on the Russian security guard, Yang and Jefferson had their hands full all day interviewing hospital personnel who, according to the surveillance tapes, had run into the killer. Unfortunately, everybody was too busy with their own work, as well as concerned about the fire alarm, that they barely noticed the man. Nobody could give a description of the suspect.

The trash bin the killer had tossed his mask and cap into contained several items, including several surgical masks, but no cap, which confirmed that the bin had been emptied by the janitorial staff prior to Yang and Jefferson searching it.

When it was clear that they couldn't gain any further insights at the hospital, they knew they should head back to the precinct. But they also knew that they had to catch Caleb Faulkner and somehow get his DNA so they could prove that his father, Mike Faulkner, had raped and killed Annika.

Jefferson parked half a block away from the offices of *No child abandoned* from where they had a good view of the entrance doors.

"I can't let him see me. He would recognize me," Yang said to his partner.

Jefferson drummed his fingers on the steering wheel. "We could be sitting here forever. We don't even know whether he's still at the office."

"That's why you'll call them and tell the receptionist that the car service for Caleb Faulkner is downstairs, and see what she says."

"That's dumb."

"You have a better idea?"

Jefferson grimaced and pulled out his cell phone. He dialed the charity's number and put it on speaker.

"*No child abandoned,* how may I direct your call?" a cheerful young woman answered.

"Yeah, hi, ma'am. This is Executive Limos. Please let Mr. Faulkner know that I'm downstairs waiting to take him to the airport."

Yang shot his partner a what-the-fuck look, but Jefferson simply shrugged.

"The airport? But he's not going to the airport."

"Are you sure, ma'am? Can you check his schedule? Because I got this booking a few days ago, and my office is pretty diligent in their record keeping."

"I'm telling you..." The clacking of a keyboard could be heard through the phone. "There, I'm right, he's not going to the airport. He has a dinner reservation at the *Brick and Mortar* at 7p.m. So, I'm afraid your office is wrong."

"Thanks, ma'am, I'm gonna have a word with the office. Sorry to bother you."

Jefferson disconnected the call. He grinned. "And that's what I call a smooth operator."

Yang smirked. "I think you should take a date to dine at the *Brick and Mortar* tonight."

"I was thinking the same thing. Let's see if the chick from traffic is free tonight." He already scrolled through the contacts in his phone. "What are you gonna do while I'm wining and dining my date?"

"I guess I'll have to get a job as a kitchen porter."

Two hours later, everything was in place. Yang had arrived before the restaurant opened, flashed his badge and asked to speak to the manager, telling him that he needed access to the used dishes, cutlery, and glasses of a specific customer, without giving any details as to who and why.

At first, the manager had been less than cooperative.

"If word gets out that I allowed the police to spy on my customers, nobody will want to dine here anymore. I'll lose business," the heavy-set man with the goatee said.

"Don't you want to help put a criminal behind bars?"

"I wish I could help you, Detective, but unless you come back with a warrant, I can't do anything for you."

Yang was standing near the entrance to the kitchen, when the door opened and several voices drifted to him. He recognized two different foreign languages.

On a hunch, he said in a friendly voice, "I get it, I totally understand, I do. I guess it would be different if I worked for immigration, right? They don't seem to need a warrant."

The manager's face froze, and Yang realized he'd hit a nerve. He guessed that half the kitchen staff didn't have a visa to work in the U.S.

The manager forced a smile. "I'm sure we can work something out, Detective. Everybody knows that I love supporting our hard-working police force."

"That's great," Yang said. "And don't worry, your guests won't even get a glimpse of me. Now all I need is for you to provide me with a kitchen porter uniform and apron. I need the suspect's table number. That table's food order will go through me, and when the dishes come back, they'll only be handled by me."

"Is that really necessary? I can just have the waitress separate that person's dishes."

"I don't want your front house staff to know what's going on. They might act differently and tip off the suspect."

"But then how will you know which plate your suspect ate from?"

"Don't worry, I've got it covered."

"Whatever you say, Detective." He pointed to the door leading into the kitchen. "Let me show you where you can get changed."

By the time the restaurant opened and started filling with guests, Yang had called Jefferson and informed him which table Caleb Faulkner would occupy. Jefferson and his date arrived shortly after Caleb Faulkner and a male guest were seated at table seven. Jefferson bribed the snooty host to get a table from which he could observe Caleb.

I'm in place, Jefferson texted to Yang.

Good, Yang texted back.

It didn't take long until the food order for Caleb's table reached the kitchen. Yang memorized the items, glad to see that Caleb and his guest were only ordering main courses, no appetizers.

When the kitchen plated the two entrees, Yang reached into his pocket and pulled out two sheets with colored stickers in the form of small dots. He lifted the plate with the duck and stuck a red dot onto the bottom of the plate, then placed a blue sticker onto the bottom of the steak entrée. Then he placed the plates on the counter for the wait staff to take.

Immediately after the waitress took the dishes to serve her customers, Yang texted a message to Jefferson.

Food is on the way.

He's having the duck, Jefferson texted back a few seconds later. *And a glass of red wine. The other guy is drinking a beer.*

That was good news. The two glasses would be easy to tell apart.

It seemed to take forever, until Caleb and his companion were done with their main courses.

Jefferson alerted Yang by text message the moment the waitress took the dishes. Yang snatched them after she placed the dirty dishes on the counter in the kitchen and lifted the plates. The dots were still in place and, now wearing gloves, Yang placed the plate with the red dot into a large plastic evidence bag together with the utensils.

They're ordering dessert, Jefferson texted.

While this meant they'd have to stay at the restaurant longer, it also improved the chances of forensics finding usable DNA. Yang and Jefferson repeated their procedure for the dessert course. Yang placed the dots onto the bottom of the plates, and Jefferson texted which dessert Caleb was getting.

When the two finally finished and paid their bill, Yang was able to bag Caleb's dessert plate and spoon, as well as his wine glass.

Got everything, Yang texted to Jefferson. *Enjoy the rest of your evening.*

Oh, I will, Jefferson texted back.

Ten minutes later, Yang was back in his street clothes and in his car. From there, he called Lupe's cell phone.

"Yang? What do you want? It's late."

"Sorry, but it's extremely urgent. Can you run some DNA off of used dishes?"

"Yeah, I can. But it'll have to wait till tomorrow."

"Can I drop it off with you so you can do it first thing?"

Lupe sighed. "Fine. And what do you want me to do with it when I have the result?"

"Compare it to the DNA you found under Annika's fingernails."

"Why didn't you lead with that?" Suddenly Lupe sounded a lot more alert. "I'll text you my address. I'll go in early tomorrow. I'll put a rush on it. Let's get this bastard."

That was Yang's sentiment too. Soon, Mike Faulkner would trade his White House office for an eight-by-eight cell.

74

IT WAS LATE AFTERNOON, and Faulkner sat behind his desk in the West Wing poring over boring files, when his assistant Abby entered after knocking briefly.

"Secret Service Agent Mitchell is here to see you."

"Show him in," he said eagerly.

Moments later, Mitchell entered with a manila file folder in his hand and closed the door behind him. "Sir."

"Mitchell, what news do you have?"

He knew Mitchell well enough to know that the man didn't waste anybody's time. If he didn't have any news, he wouldn't have shown up in person, nor would he have closed the door to guarantee their conversation remained private.

He placed a file folder on the desk in front of Faulkner. "The toxicology report for Madeline Bolton. Like we suspected she had alcohol in her blood and something else."

"Something else?" Faulkner opened the file folder.

"A drug called Midazolam. It's a benzodiazepine used in surgery settings. It has a paralyzing effect."

Shit!

Faulkner continued looking at the page in front of him, not wanting to meet Mitchell's gaze. "That would support the theory that this was an accident. Perhaps she mixed alcohol and this drug to sleep better. And when she stepped on the ladder, she was drowsy and lost her balance. Don't you think?"

Having recovered his composure, he looked at the agent.

"That's certainly possible, sir, though it's not exactly a drug you can buy in a store."

"Neither is ecstasy, yet Maddie got her hands on it when she was younger." He shrugged. "Who knows about this report?"

"Apart from the lab that ran the tox screen? Only you and I, sir."

"And your partner, Agent Banning?"

"He's out in the field and hasn't seen the report yet."

"Let's keep it that way. I need to look into something first."

"Can I be of assistance, sir?"

"No. It's something I'll have to do myself. Thank you," Faulkner said, dismissing Mitchell.

When the door closed behind the Secret Service agent, Faulkner stared at the toxicology report without reading a single word of it.

He'd failed. He knew what he had to do now, and he dreaded it. But it had to be done. It was his responsibility now.

75

THE BOX WITH LUMINOL had arrived at Emily's apartment soon after she returned from teaching her last class. It was already early evening when Emily unpacked the small container of Luminol powder, poured it into a larger spray bottle, then added distilled water, before screwing the lid back on the bottle and stashing it in her bag.

Originally Vicky had planned on accompanying her back to Maddie's townhouse, but Vicky had left because one of her clients had a major server issue and Vicky needed to fix the problem on site. Vicky had asked her to wait until the next day, but Emily didn't want to wait. She had to know whether Sasha was dead or whether there was still a chance of saving her.

Again she snuck out of the house via the back, so she could avoid being seen by the policeman out front. He was a nice guy and had given her a ride to and from school. She felt bad for him, because he would probably get in trouble if Yang found out that she'd ditched him yet again. But if all went well, he'd never have to find out about it.

At least this time, Emily didn't have to worry about the police showing up at Maddie's place, because the alarm hadn't been set when she'd been at Maddie's house with Diego and Vicky. She could have asked Diego to lend her his key, but for some reason she felt odd about it. She couldn't put her finger on it, but she preferred to use her lock picks to enter Maddie's house. And this time, it was easier than when she'd done it the first time. Practice truly made perfect.

Emily didn't use the Luminol in the living area, since she already knew that there was blood because it was where Maddie had died. Instead, she started with the powder room. She sprayed the floor and part of the walls, then closed the door behind her without switching on the light. If there were traces of blood, the Luminol would make the area glow blue in the dark. But there was no blue glow in the powder room.

She did the same in the kitchen and laundry area, though it was a little more difficult there, because she had to pull the shades in the kitchen, and the room didn't turn quite as dark as she'd hoped. However, except for a small area around the set of knives that were displayed in a wooden block, there was no blue glow anywhere else in the kitchen. The blue glow around the knives wasn't unusual. Everybody cut themselves once in a while when chopping food.

Upstairs, Emily worked her way through the two bathrooms and two bedrooms. But she couldn't find any blood. Nothing on the carpets or the wall, nothing on the mattresses or any of the furniture. She even sprayed the closets, but there wasn't a trace of blood anywhere. She was relieved, because it gave her hope that Sasha was still alive. But where had this girl run to? Where was she hiding?

Emily opened the shades in Maddie's bedroom again, before she returned to the guest room. As she pulled back the curtains, she looked out over to the houses on the other side of the street. It had gotten darker since Emily had arrived at the house. With Maddie's house sitting on a slight incline, Emily was able to look over the roofs of the neighborhood. Only a few blocks away, a building rose two stories higher than most of the houses in this neighborhood. But the building looked abandoned, maybe ready to be demolished. Many of its windows were boarded up.

She focused her eyes on the windows that weren't boarded up, and thought she saw a light. Were people squatting there? Perhaps some homeless were taking shelter there. Nobody would bother them there, and they would be protected from the elements.

Had Sasha looked out this window when she'd slept here? Had she seen the abandoned building? Emily tried to figure out what was going through Sasha's mind the night Maddie died. Had she seen the killer and recognized him as the man who'd hurt her? If she'd recognized him, she would have been scared. And being a victim of sex trafficking probably meant that she didn't trust any adult.

Emily understood why Sasha wouldn't have run to the police. In her eyes, they were probably just as corrupt here as in her own country. She would have sought the help of people who were like her: mistreated, abused, and homeless. Those were the people she could trust.

76

HE'D COME TO KILL HER. He'd been thwarted twice, but this time he would succeed. She deserved it too. Emily Warner was an annoying busybody who stuck her nose into things that didn't concern her. She had to go, before she figured out how he'd killed Maddie, and, more importantly, why.

And this time, she was making it easy for him. Emily was in Maddie's house, and she was alone. Nobody would come to rescue her this time. And once she was dead, he could sleep easier and go back to his life, unafraid of being caught.

Though he didn't like the idea of killing her in Maddie's house, he had no other choice. But he had a plan. He wouldn't leave Emily's body here. He'd take it to another place where the police couldn't connect her death to Maddie's. He'd parked his car in a side alley, and once the streets had emptied out, he would put the body into the trunk of his car and dispose of it.

From his hiding place in the coat closet on the first floor, the killer listened as Emily walked around in the bedrooms, and opened and closed blinds. He wasn't concerned about her snooping around in Maddie's home. There was nothing for her to find to pin on him. All he had to do was to wait. He still had the gun he'd shot Petrov with. This time he would make sure that his victim died on the spot. Having to finish the job in the hospital had been risky. He didn't want to repeat this.

He suddenly heard Emily's voice coming from the top of the stairs. It appeared that she was talking to somebody on the phone. He held his breath and listened.

"Vicky, damn, why are you not picking up? There was no blood other than where Maddie died. Anyway," she said, "I know where Sasha is. I figured it out. I'm gonna go there now. It's not far from Maddie's house. And as soon as I've got her, I'll call you, and then we can take her to Detective Yang together, and she'll be safe."

He put his gun back into his pocket. On second thought, there was no rush in killing Emily Warner. She could lead him to Sasha, and all his troubles would be over. That little bitch had escaped him, and he'd been unsuccessful in finding her. The day after her escape, he'd feared that the police would turn up at his front door any moment, but with every day that had passed, he'd realized that Sasha hadn't gone to the police, because she didn't trust anyone in power. She wasn't wrong. Few men could be trusted in Washington D.C.

He'd almost given up on finding Sasha. This was a fortunate turn of events. He would kill two birds with one stone. Emily Warner he'd kill quickly, but Sasha, she would have to suffer. She would have to pay for escaping and putting him through an emotional rollercoaster.

He smiled to himself. Emily would lead him right to Sasha.

Tonight's gonna be a good night.

The melody suddenly began playing in his head, and it made him feel like nothing could go wrong now.

77

Emily put her cell phone back into her pocket, when she suddenly heard a sound from the stairs. She turned around and saw Diego walk upstairs. She froze, surprised at seeing him.

"Oh, Diego."

"Hey Emily, I thought I'd stop by to help you," he said with an easy smile.

"Oh?"

"Yeah, I spoke to Vicky a little earlier, and she said you were coming here with"—he pointed to the Luminol spray bottle in her hand—"Luminol to check if there's blood that might belong to Sasha. Did you find any?"

She shook her head, her voice failing her. Being alone with Diego suddenly made her feel uneasy. Weren't the crime statistics pretty clear about the fact that most murder victims were killed by somebody they knew and trusted? Maddie had trusted Diego. And he had a key to her place. Plus, he knew her routine.

"Yeah, no blood anywhere," she pressed out.

"You okay?" he asked and gave her a concerned look.

"Yeah, I'm fine. Just a little tired." He didn't seem to believe her. Had he overheard the message she'd left for Vicky?

"Have you had any luck with the search for Sasha?"

"No, no. Nothing at all. It's as if she's disappeared from the face of the earth." Emily motioned to the door. "I think I'm done here."

He let her pass, then followed her down the stairs. "Maybe we should just canvass the neighborhood, see if anybody has seen the girl," Diego suggested when they reached the first floor.

She was glad that she had her back to him so he couldn't see her alarmed facial expression. She was certain now that Diego had heard every single word of her message to Vicky. He would follow her so she could lead him to Sasha. Somehow Emily had to get rid of him and get Sasha to safety before Diego could hurt them both.

But how?

"Oh you know, I think I saw something in the kitchen that I found odd," she said, turning to him. "Maybe you can explain it. I mean you've probably spent a lot of time in this house, so you might know whether it's out of place or not."

"Sure, what is it?"

She motioned for him to walk into the kitchen, and he turned and walked through the door.

"Under the sink," she said and followed him, until she could grab a thick glass cookie jar that stood on the kitchen counter.

"Down here?" he asked and opened the cabinet under the sink.

Just as he cast a quick look over his shoulder, she swung and hit him over the head.

Diego let out a painful grunt and put his hands up to shield his head, but she swung again and he went down.

Emily dropped the jar, which surprisingly was still in one piece, and ran as fast as she could. She slammed the door shut behind her and sprinted across the street, glad that there was little traffic.

Her heart was pounding, and her lungs burned from exhaustion. But she couldn't stop and allow Diego to follow her. She had to find Sasha and get her to safety.

78

YANG RUBBED THE BRIDGE OF HIS NOSE, tired from staring at his computer monitor. For the umpteenth time, he watched the tape of the hospital's security cameras that had caught Petrov's killer. But no matter how long and how often he looked at the man, he couldn't identify him. He even put a photo of Mike Faulkner on the split screen to figure out if his eyes and forehead matched, but the video was too grainy and the killer never looked directly into the camera and was too far away to make a positive identification.

He minimized the video and instead, opened the list the security technician at the hospital had compiled for him. It consisted of the names of all hospital personnel that had encountered the killer. The technician had been very thorough, and even noted down the time stamp of where and when the hospital staff had crossed paths with their suspect.

In the cubicle next to him, Jefferson was speaking to one of the people on the list.

"Thanks for your help. If you remember anything else, you have my number."

Yang pushed his chair back and popped his head past the cubicle divider. "Anything useful?"

Jefferson met his gaze. "Nothing. Everybody is very friendly and wants to help, but nobody really noticed the guy. Not only did he pull the fire alarm, this happened around shift change, where everybody was running around frantically anyway."

"He probably timed it that way, knowing that with people coming and going, nobody would notice him."

Jefferson nodded. "Yeah, that's my guess too."

"Where are you on the list?" Yang asked.

"I've already called the first seven from the top."

"Okay, I'll start on the bottom then. This'll be a long night."

"I've gotta stretch my legs." Jefferson rose. "You want coffee?"

"Not the disgusting swill from the break room."

"I'm talking real coffee. I'll go across the street."

"Then I'll have a latte, thanks."

Jefferson left, and Yang dialed the cell number of a nurse who was listed as the last person on the staff list to cross paths with the killer. He only reached her voicemail. It was possible that she was sleeping, or in a part of the hospital that required her cell phone to be turned off. Yang left a quick voicemail, then moved on to the next person.

This time, the staff member, a janitor, picked up. But while the janitor remembered the man because he found it odd that he was carrying a clipboard with blank paper, he couldn't give a good description. He recalled, however, that the man was at least six feet tall.

At least this detail confirmed that Mike Faulkner could be their man. He was just a little over six feet tall, though a lot of other people were too.

The next person on the list was a hospital administrator. She hadn't even noticed the man, too concerned about the fire alarm and her duty as a fire marshal for her unit.

Yang was about to dial the next person on the list, when an email notification popped up on his monitor. It was from Lupe and marked urgent.

"Finally," he mumbled under his breath.

He opened the email and read it. At the same moment, Jefferson was back with two paper cups from the fancy coffee shop across the street.

"Here's your coffee."

But Yang didn't reach for his cup. He continued staring at the screen. "You're not gonna believe this."

"What?"

"The DNA result is back. We have a match."

Jefferson leaned in to read the email. "You're fucking kidding me."

"Time to get a warrant," Yang said.

"I'll write it up," Jefferson offered, placing the cups of coffee on the desk.

"I'll call the judge."

"I can't wait to put the cuffs on him," Jefferson said.

"You and me both."

79

By THE TIME Emily reached the abandoned building, it was dark. She'd run most of the way to put as much distance as possible between her and Diego. She couldn't believe that she had trusted him. And worse, that Maddie had trusted him. And paid for it with her life.

"I'll get justice for you, Maddie," she murmured to herself.

A chain-link fence surrounded the property, and *No trespassing* signs were posted everywhere. It took Emily a few minutes to find a spot where the fence had been pulled back for a person to slip through to the other side.

Overgrown weeds covered the narrow strip of bare ground that surrounded the building, which took over most of the massive corner lot. By the looks of it, it had been an office building or some other type of commercial enterprise. Some of the windows were boarded up, others had glass panes that were still intact or had been blown out. It looked like the building might have sustained fire damage at some point in the previous years.

There were several entrances into the building, and the trampled ground leading to a makeshift door made of mismatched plywood and without a lock indicated that more than just a few people had taken this path inside. Most likely the place was swarming with homeless people. For a moment, she wished that she'd brought Coffee with her. With her dog by her side, she would feel safer, but there was no time to go home and fetch him. Sasha was in real danger, and Emily needed to find her before Diego did.

When Emily entered the dark building, she picked up myriad smells. There was dust in the air, the faint smell of a wood fire, and the putrid smell of rotten food, urine, and excrement. She recoiled from the smell, then steeled herself. If Sasha had managed to hide here since Maddie's death, the least Emily could do was to deal with the minor inconvenience of disgusting scents.

She heard sounds coming from one of the upper floors, some clanging, some shuffling, hushed voices. Emily pulled out her phone and used the light from the display to find her way to the stairs. Debris was scattered on the stairs: empty bottles, broken glass, and other trash. When she spotted a hypodermic needle, she knew she had to be careful. Not only could drug addicts be unpredictable, there was a real danger that she could accidentally be jabbed with a needle containing remnants of heroin.

Setting one foot in front of the other, she walked up to the second floor, careful to steer clear of any dangers. On the landing, she oriented herself and listened for the sounds she'd heard. They came from the left. She followed the short corridor, still using her cell phone to guide her farther into the interior of the building. When she came to the first opening, where at some point there had been a door, she peered into the space. It appeared the room had once been a large open-plan office. Some of the cubicles were still there, but it was evident that a lot of the plywood from the old office furniture had been used as firewood, if the charred floor was anything to go by.

Near the entrance, Emily spotted a person lying on the ground, covered with a blanket. She walked closer, when the person rolled to face Emily, and quickly jumped up. Before Emily knew what was happening, the person was brandishing a knife.

"Thief!" the teenager with the dirty face said. "Don't touch my stash!"

He couldn't be older than sixteen, but the hard lines in his face attested to the hard life he was leading.

Emily lifted her arms. "I'm not here to steal from you."

He looked her up and down. Then he scoffed. "Social worker? Yeah, don't bother. I'm not going back." He spit, hitting her cardigan. "I can take care of myself."

"I'm not a social worker," she said, trying to remain calm, even though her heart was beating into her throat. "I'm trying to find a girl. She's in danger."

The boy gave her a mistrustful look and still kept the knife pointed at her.

"She's Russian. Her name is Sasha. She's twelve or thirteen, long dark hair, blue eyes. Is she here?"

The boy shrugged. "I don't rat on people."

"Of course not," she said quickly. "But a bad man is after her, and I've come to help her get away before he finds her."

He shrugged again. "The world is full of bad men."

There was a flat tone in his voice that sounded like resignation, like somebody who'd lost hope.

"That's true. That's why I know Sasha came here to hide. She couldn't trust any adult. But I'm here now, and I can take care of her. Please tell me where she is. The man who's after her is close. I have to find her quickly, before he does. Please." She cast him a pleading look.

"Do you have money?"

She nodded and motioned to the small handbag she'd slung diagonally across her torso. "In my wallet." She slowly lowered her hands. "I'll get some."

She removed her wallet and pulled out all the banknotes she had. It amounted to a little over eighty dollars. She reached her hand with the cash out to him. "It's not much. But I hope it helps you."

He took it, and quickly shoved it into his pants pocket. Then he looked past Emily, and Emily looked over her shoulder. Two more teenagers, younger than the boy, were approaching. None of them was Sasha.

"Get lost!" the boy ordered, and the two kids stopped in their tracks.

"The last time I saw her she was one floor up, in the far corner," the boy now said and pointed to a spot behind Emily. "She keeps to herself and doesn't talk much. But she looks like the girl you're describing."

"Thank you."

Emily turned around and quickly exited the large room, feeling the eyes of the other two homeless kids on her back. Would they follow her, suspecting she had more money or valuables in her possession? The tiny hairs at her nape rose, but to her surprise, she heard no footsteps following her as she ascended to the third floor.

Up there, the layout was very similar to the second floor. She entered the former open-plan office and noticed that it was connected to other smaller offices at each end. A flickering light, either from a candle or small fire, drew her to the corner of the building that the boy had indicated.

As she walked closer and passed the few cubicles that were still intact, she noticed a movement. She whirled her head to her left and saw a person crouched down underneath a desk. Emily took a step toward the dark figure.

"Sasha?" she murmured.

"Get lost!" somebody growled. The accent was definitely American, though the voice was that of a female. But she sounded older, maybe in her forties or fifties.

"Sorry, ma'am," Emily said quickly and withdrew, not wanting another knife aimed in her direction.

She continued to where she'd seen the flickering light, but it was dark there now. Walking closer, Emily drew in a deep breath. She recognized the smell as that of a candle that had just been extinguished.

Slowly walking closer with the shine of her cell phone's display guiding her steps, Emily reached the entrance to another office, one that had space for four or five desks, though she could only see two desks. Both lay on their side, forming a partition.

"Sasha?"

She heard somebody breathing.

"Sasha," Emily said again in a soft tone of voice. "I'm here to help you."

She stepped around the partition. There, a dark-haired girl with blue eyes was pressing herself against the wall, as if she could melt into it and disappear. In her hand she held a broken glass bottle, a weapon that by the determined look in her face she was prepared to use to defend herself.

Emily didn't come any closer. She lifted both hands in a motion of surrender. "*Drug*," she said, hoping that she pronounced the Russian word for friend correctly. "*Podruga*." It also meant friend, but one of her music students had said it meant female friend. "*Podruga* Maddie. Maddie *podruga*."

Emily hoped that Sasha understood that she was trying to tell her that she was Maddie's friend.

"Maddie?" Tears shot into the girl's eyes, but she sniffled, and didn't allow them to flow.

"*Da*. Maddie." Emily pointed to herself. "Emily. *Podruga* Maddie. *Da*."

Slowly Sasha took a step toward Emily. Emily kept her eyes on the glass bottle in her hand. Sasha followed her gaze and hesitated. For a few seconds there was silence between them, and neither of them moved. Then Sasha dropped the makeshift weapon onto the blankets on the ground.

"*Potruga*," Sasha said.

Suddenly Emily heard a loud sound coming from the stairwell. Heavy footsteps. Sasha stared at Emily, disappointment shining from her eyes.

She bent down to pick up the broken glass bottle, but Emily was faster, and pulled her back, then pressed her fingers over Sasha's lips to keep her quiet.

A surprised look appeared in Sasha's eyes. She understood that whoever was coming wasn't an accomplice Emily had brought with her. Sasha nodded, and Emily removed her fingers from her lips.

Sasha pointed to a second door that led out of the room. Emily nodded and took the girl's hand.

Suddenly, Emily's cell phone rang. Emily let go of the girl's hand and fumbled to silence her phone, but it was too late.

"There you are!" she heard him grunt from a distance.

Emily tossed her cell phone on the ground. Sasha grabbed her hand, and together they took off running through the second door into the darkness. Emily prayed that Sasha knew this place like the back of her hand by now, and that the darkness that Emily had lived in for fifteen years would once again be her friend.

80

YANG AND JEFFERSON were already in the car, arrest warrant in hand, ready to arrest Annika's killer, when Yang's phone rang. He didn't recognize the number.

"Detective Yang," he answered.

"Detective, it's Vicky Hong," the woman said. "I think Emily is in mortal danger."

Instantly alert, Yang put the call on speaker. "What happened? Where is she?"

"She went to Maddie's townhouse and called me from there, but I missed her call. I think Maddie's killer is after her."

Yang ordered Jefferson, "Reroute to Georgetown, Madeline Bolton's townhouse."

Jefferson switched on the sirens and lights and made a U-turn.

"Slow down, Miss Hong, tell me exactly what happened."

"Emily went to Maddie's house to spray Luminol to figure out if Sasha was killed in the house, and the killer cleaned up."

"What the fuck?!" Yang cursed. "Where is the police officer that I had stationed outside her place?"

"He's probably still there," Vicky said, sounding sheepish.

"What the—"

"She must have gone out through the back where the trashcans are kept."

"I told her to stay out of this for her own good! Goddamn it! That woman is driving me bonkers!"

Jefferson suddenly smirked. "Wow, she's totally getting under your skin."

Yang raised his hand to stop his partner from talking. "How did she even get access to the house?"

"I shouldn't tell you that, I mean with you being police and all."

He sighed. "Fine. What happened then, Miss Hong?"

"She called me but I missed the call, but her voicemail said that there was no blood anywhere other than the living room where Maddie died. And then she said she now knows where Sasha might be hiding. And she was gonna go there."

"Did she say where?"

"No, but it's close to Maddie's house. I activated the find a friend feature on her phone a few days ago, 'cause I was worried."

"That's smart," Yang praised. "Send me the coordinates."

"Yeah, in a sec. There's something else. Diego showed up in Maddie's house when Emily was spraying the Luminol, because I'd told him earlier that Emily would be there. I was supposed to go with her, but my client's server crashed, and Emily didn't want to wait for me. So I told Diego to go there so she wouldn't be alone."

"Diego Sanchez?"

"Yeah, Maddie's boyfriend. He went there, but then Emily acted all weird, and when he turned his back to her, she hit him over the head. Twice! Diego said Emily didn't knock him unconscious, though it hurt like a bitch, but he said he heard the door slam after she ran out of the house, and when he managed to get up from the kitchen floor where he was, he saw a man leaving a few seconds after Emily. But he only saw the man's back, and by the time Diego made it to the door, the guy was gone. I tried to call her just now, but she's not picking up her phone."

"Fuck!" Yang cursed again. "We have to get to her before he does." He glanced at Jefferson. "Step on it, Simon."

"Detective, did Diego murder Maddie?" Vicky asked.

"No, he didn't. You can trust him. Call him and give him Emily's location. He's closer than we are. Tell him to look out for Caleb Faulkner. He's the killer."

The DNA result they'd received had not been a fifty-percent match like they'd expected, indicating a father-son relationship, but a hundred-percent match, confirming that not Mike Faulkner, but Caleb Faulkner had killed Annika. And Yang would bet his next paycheck that he'd also killed Maddie and Petrov.

81

SASHA FAIRLY DRAGGED EMILY through a labyrinth of corridors, confirming to Emily that she indeed knew this building like the back of her hand.

"Exit," Emily whispered to Sasha in English, hoping she would understand.

Sasha turned her face to her, and the dim light coming through a broken window illuminated it sufficiently for Emily to see that even if Sasha hadn't understood the word, she knew what they had to do: get out of this building.

"Emily!"

Diego's voice cut through her like a knife. It was coming from the direction they were heading in, not the one they were coming from. How had he cut off their escape route?

"Emily! I'm here to help you and Sasha."

Emily heard the sound of a cell phone ringing. Judging by the direction it was coming from, it had to be Diego's. She didn't hear him respond to it. Instead he called out again, "Emily! Damn it!"

Emily didn't respond, knowing that he wanted to draw her out so he could kill them both. Emily motioned for Sasha to turn around. There had to be several staircases in this large building. The building code required it. Somehow they had to find one of those staircases to escape. Once on the street, they could flag down a car and ask the driver to call Detective Yang.

"Damn it, Emily! I'm not your enemy. The killer chased after you. Please, let me help you!"

How stupid did Diego think she was? She wanted to tell him what she thought of him, but she bit her tongue, knowing any utterance would give away her and Sasha's location.

Meanwhile, Sasha led her through different rooms and corridors away from Diego. There was little to no light now, since they were moving away from the exterior windows. Sasha suddenly stumbled over something and gasped. But Emily prevented her from falling. She stood still for a moment to listen and heard footsteps. Diego didn't even attempt to sneak up on them. He was like a bull in the china shop. Emily hoped that he hadn't heard Sasha's near fall and gasp over his own loud footfalls.

"Emily!" he kept calling out. "Damn it, I'm here to save you!"

Emily couldn't afford that either she or Sasha stumbled again. When she'd been blind, she'd rarely stumbled, because she'd had the right tools to help her.

Of course! That was the solution! She opened her handbag and rummaged through it. Her collapsible cane was still in there, as a crutch so to speak. She sighed with relief as she pulled it from her bag and opened it up.

The cane in one hand and Sasha's hand in the other, Emily guided them forward, away from Diego. Careful for her cane not to make a sound, she let it glide along the floor in front of her, rather than tap the floor, which would have made too much noise. It worked. She'd used the cane for so many years that she could feel in her hand what kind of materials and obstacles its tip encountered without having to rely on loud sounds as feedback.

Emily and Sasha hurried through a broad corridor with many doors on each side. Some of them were open, and through those, some light filtered into the hallway. Emily pressed onward, knowing that the hallway had to lead to a staircase somewhere. She was right. When the corridor turned and she looked down toward the left, she saw a staircase.

She motioned to it, and Sasha nodded. Hand in hand, they approached it, then as quickly as was safe, they descended to the second floor. Hope finally bloomed in Emily. They would make it. They would be out of the building in less than a minute, and out on the street, where they could get help.

Illuminating the stairwell that led from the second floor to the first was a window without a glass pane letting in a little light from the streetlights outside. At the switchback of the stairs Sasha abruptly stopped. Emily was a step behind her. She felt the presence of the man before she saw him.

"*Ubiytsa,*" Sasha pressed out, her voice full of horror.

Emily didn't know the Russian word, but when she looked at the man who stood at the base of the stairs, a gun leveled at them, she knew what it meant: killer.

Emily and Sasha pivoted in the same instant, and rushed up the stairs. Emily had only seen the man's face for a second, but it wasn't Diego. Still, she recognized him. She'd seen him at Maddie's funeral.

It was Caleb Faulkner. He was the man who'd killed Maddie and abused Sasha.

The realization hit her like a punch in the gut. She'd been running away from Diego, who'd only wanted to help, and steered herself and Sasha right into the killer's arms.

"Yeah, run, but you can't get away for long," Caleb taunted them as he pursued them up the stairs.

Emily didn't waste her breath responding to him. Instead, she pulled Sasha toward the darkest part of the building, where Emily would have an advantage over a sighted person. For a moment, Emily thought of the three teenagers that occupied a large space on this floor, but as street kids they probably knew how to take care of themselves and stay off Caleb's radar.

"I'm gonna get you fucking bitches," Caleb announced from far too close behind them. "Nobody escapes me."

Emily felt Sasha shake, and understood what the girl was going through. Her abuser, the man who'd raped her countless times, who'd locked her up under whatever terrible conditions, was trying to capture her again. The fear rolling off Sasha was visceral. But Emily would do everything in her power so Caleb could never lay hands on Sasha or any other girl again.

"Come," she whispered low to the girl.

With her cane scouting out debris on the floor and avoiding it, they worked their way deeper into the interior of the building, back to where Diego had been earlier when he'd called out to her, professing to want to help her. She knew now that he'd told the truth. She hoped he'd already called the police for backup. If only Emily and Sasha could hide long enough for them to arrive, they had a chance to survive.

Emily cast a look over her shoulder and glimpsed a thin light beam that moved rapidly back and forth along the corridor. Caleb had either brought a flashlight or was using his cell phone to illuminate the space to find them.

"Come out, come out wherever you are," he said in a sing-song voice as if playing a game. And maybe for him, this was a game. A deadly one, because the loser would die.

"You know I'm gonna get you. You think I don't know what you were doing, Emily? Sticking your nose into things that don't concern you. When I overheard that you were bothering the Boltons, I knew you were trouble. You shouldn't have done that."

Caleb kept talking, inadvertently drowning out the sounds of Sasha and Emily's footsteps as they quietly moved farther down the hallway. Suddenly, the cane hit resistance. Emily moved it side to side, then farther up, and realized that the corridor had reached its end. She touched the wall, searching for a door, but where she assumed a door had once been and perhaps led to a stairwell, somebody had barricaded it with plywood and two-by-fours. She suspected the reason for it was that the stairwell behind it was unsafe.

Shit, she cursed soundlessly.

They had to turn back, bringing them closer to Caleb again. Emily could see now that the light beam wasn't strong enough to come from a flashlight, but that the light was most likely coming from Caleb's cell phone. So far, it hadn't penetrated their location. But they couldn't stay here. They had to get into one of the rooms to either the left or the right of the corridor.

Emily tested the first door they reached on their right, but the door didn't budge. Quickly, she moved to the corresponding door on the left, and this one opened. However, the hinges creaked. Emily froze.

"Trying to get away?" Caleb called out. He'd heard the creaking. Then he said something in Russian, something clearly meant for Sasha.

A shudder raced through Sasha, and Emily could feel it physically. Quickly, before Caleb's words could paralyze the girl, Emily shoved her into the room and closed the door behind them. From the little Emily could see this was another large open-plan office space. Most of the windows were boarded up, only two were still intact and let in a little light from outside. At the far end of it, Emily spotted several doors. She hoped they led somewhere safe.

Emily and Sasha made their way toward the doors, careful not to make any noise, when she heard somebody call her name in the distance. Diego! She signaled Sasha to stop so Emily could concentrate on Diego's voice.

"Emily? I'm trying to help!"

Emily knew that now. She knew that Diego wasn't the bad guy. But could she risk calling out to him so he could find her? Seconds ticked by. All kinds of possible scenarios played out in her mind. If Caleb got to her and Sasha before Diego did, he would kill them both, and his secret would die with them. But if Diego knew who Maddie's killer was, Caleb might realize that he couldn't kill them all. Perhaps he would give up, knowing he'd lost. But there was the risk that by conveying this information to Diego, she would give away her and Sasha's hiding place. But she had to take this gamble.

"Diego!" Emily called out. "It's Caleb. He's here. Caleb killed Maddie and raped Sasha."

Not waiting for Diego's response, Emily pulled Sasha with her as she charged toward one of the doors. She opened it, realizing too late that it was a broom closet. She whirled around, already heading for the door next to it, when she heard a sound.

"Big mistake!" Caleb growled from less than five yards away. "You just signed Diego's death warrant." He pointed the gun straight at Emily. "And take this to your grave: Sasha is mine, and I'll make her suffer for escaping. A little bit each day. We'll have fun, won't we, Sasha?"

"Net! Net! Net!" Sasha screamed.

Caleb smiled as if he enjoyed Sasha's fear. "Good bye, Miss Warner."

A sound from one of the other doors made her snap her head in its direction. She was expecting Diego to charge in.

"Diego, the gun!" Emily yelled, but it wasn't Diego who barreled into the room and jumped in front of her, just as Caleb pulled the trigger.

The sound of the gunshot nearly pierced Emily's eardrum. Amid Sasha's screams, a second gunshot sounded, and the man who'd jumped in front of her collapsed against Emily, knocking her off balance so she fell against the wall.

"Dad! No!"

Her father dropped to the ground. Emily couldn't see how badly he was hurt or where the bullets had caught him, or even if he was dead. But she saw that Caleb was aiming his gun again, this time at her.

Using the wall behind her back as leverage, Emily jumped forward and tackled Caleb. She knew she had little chance of defeating him, but if she didn't try, she would be as good as dead.

Together, they crashed to the ground, Caleb onto his back, absorbing the brunt of the impact. It seemed to knock the wind out of him for a second, while Emily tried to wrestle the gun from his hand. But he held onto it with an iron grip.

Caleb was strong. Emily was still on top of him, trying to wrestle the gun out of his hand with both hands now. She felt his fingers loosen just a fraction, while he used his free hand to pull her hands away. But she held on. She couldn't give in. She was fighting for her life, and for Sasha's.

"Bitch!" he ground out, his teeth pressed together.

Emily tried to shake the gun out of his grip, but realized that they were evenly matched. When she felt him loosen his grip a little, she managed to turn the gun farther to the side, thinking that he was about to let go of it. Caleb made a rapid movement, and suddenly his left hand was around her throat, choking her.

Gasping for air, Emily loosened her grip on the gun, and her gaze met Caleb's. There was a glint in his eye that told her that he knew he had the upper hand now. She couldn't take her second hand off the gun to try and pry his left hand off her throat, knowing that he would be able to point it at her head and shoot her.

Already, she felt dizzy from the lack of oxygen. No, she couldn't let this happen, couldn't fail when she'd come so far.

All she could do, was to try to shift her body, try to move backwards, when her right leg suddenly dropped between Caleb's thighs. With her last breath of air, she jerked her knee upward and plowed it into his crotch.

Caleb howled with pain and instantly released her throat. Emily took in a quick, much needed breath and used her newfound energy to grab the gun and wrestle it away from him.

The gun went off. Caleb let out another scream of pain, and Emily realized that the bullet had hit him in the shoulder.

Finally she could grab the gun fully. She slid it across the floor in Sasha's direction, when she heard somebody else's rapid footfalls.

"Emily?"

"Diego! Here! I've got Caleb. He's shot."

With his good arm, Caleb tried to reach for her throat again, but he didn't get a chance. Emily punched him in his shoulder wound, making him howl with pain just as Diego crouched next to her.

"I'll deal with him," Diego said, and Emily rose quickly.

Diego now held Caleb down with his knees on his arms and torso, and Emily saw with satisfaction that Diego started beating him as if he were a punching bag.

She turned away from the scene and rushed to her father and Sasha, while she took out the flashlight she carried in her handbag, switched it on and gave it to Sasha. Sasha understood, and pointed it at Emily's father, so she could assess his condition.

Blood gushed from his stomach and chest wounds. Emily pressed her hands on the wounds, trying to stop the blood loss.

"Emily."

The gurgling sound came from her father. He was alive.

"Dad, why did you do that? Why?" Tears welled up in Emily's eyes. "You shouldn't have…"

"I had to, sweetheart. I tried to stay away, I did for a few days… But I was worried about you…" He breathed heavily. "I followed you again…"

She could sense the difficulty with which he spoke, while fighting for air. "Don't talk. We'll get you to the hospital."

"I'm not gonna make it… Please, forgive me for what I've done… to you…" His words were punctuated by labored breathing. "…to your mother… If I could go back in time…" He looked straight at her. "I'm so sorry, sweetheart… I should have been a better father… a better husband. I failed you… You and your mother. I'm sorry…"

Tears ran down her cheeks. "I forgive you, Dad… Please just hold on… you can make it… we can start new…"

"I love you, sweetheart…" His head rolled to the side.

"No! Dad! No!"

82

Yang heard a third gunshot, just as he and Jefferson reached the second-floor landing. With their guns drawn and their flashlights pointed, they charged toward the sound of the gunshot. Yang's heart was racing. His arteries pumped full with adrenaline. He hoped he wasn't too late to save Emily from Caleb Faulkner.

Sounds of a struggle, heavy grunting, and finally a scream of pain, led them to the right location at one end of a large, open-plan space. There, Diego Sanchez punched a supine Caleb Faulkner in the face. Caleb was bleeding profusely from a shoulder wound.

"I'm gonna kill you for what you did to Maddie and Sasha," Sanchez growled and punched Caleb even harder than before. Caleb had no fight left in him. He lay there like a ragdoll, in pain, and unable to fight back.

Yang let his flashlight roam, until he saw Emily crouched on the ground against a wall, cradling a profusely bleeding man, and the girl he recognized as Sasha hugging her tightly.

Yang breathed a sigh of relief. Emily was alive. And so was Sasha.

Jefferson made a step past Yang to stop Sanchez, but Yang put his arm out to prevent him, while shining his flashlight on the two fighting men.

"Give him a few more seconds," Yang said, even though it went against everything he'd learned in his training. He wanted Caleb to be in pain.

Sanchez whipped his head toward them. "About time," he said, then punched Caleb into the bleeding shoulder wound.

Caleb howled in agony, while the sound of sirens reached Yang's ears. Backup had arrived.

"Now?" Jefferson asked.

Yang nodded.

"We'll take it from here, Mr. Sanchez," Jefferson said, and approached Caleb.

Sanchez lifted himself up, and not too gently, Jefferson rolled Caleb onto his stomach, pulled his arms back and cuffed him, ignoring the fact that Caleb's shoulder wound caused him more pain in this position.

Yang stepped closer. "Caleb Faulkner, you're under arrest for the murder, abduction, and rape of the Russian national Annika, the murder of Russian Cultural Attaché Sergei Petrov, the attempted murder of Russian embassy security guard Ivan Lipovsky, the abduction and rape of the Russian nationals Sasha and Tatjana, the attempted murder of Emily Warner, and while I'm at it, the murder of Madeline Bolton." He tipped his chin toward Jefferson. "Read him his rights."

Then Yang turned away and walked to Emily, illuminating the area with his flashlight. Emily looked up at him, and he crouched next to her. While he searched for a pulse on the man in her lap, and found none, he asked, "Are you and Sasha hurt?"

She shook her head, and he noticed the tears streaming down her face.

"Who's this man?"

"My father," Emily choked out. "He saved me... us..." She pressed a kiss on top of Sasha's head and held her tightly to her chest. "The bullets were meant for me."

"I'm so sorry... He's gone," Yang said, his chest tight with compassion for the woman who had put herself in danger to save a girl she didn't even know and avenge a woman she'd never met.

"Sasha?" he asked gently, and finally, the girl lifted her head from Emily's chest and looked at him. "You're safe now. Caleb Faulkner won't hurt you anymore."

Sasha looked past him to where Jefferson was dealing with Caleb. Yang followed her gaze and noticed that Diego was assisting Jefferson by holding the detective's flashlight. Then Yang looked back at Emily and Sasha. Sasha pointed to Yang and asked Emily, *"Drug?"*

Emily nodded. *"Drug.* Friend."

"You speak Russian?" Yang asked, surprised.

"Only a word or two."

Yang heard footsteps of several people approaching the room. "We need EMTs and Forensics over here. And lights," he called out. "Let's get you and Sasha checked out by the medics."

Several officers entered and used their flashlights to get an overview of the scene. Yang helped Emily and Sasha up, when Sasha suddenly pointed to Caleb, who now stood with Jefferson's help. She started talking in Russian. Yang shook his head, because he didn't speak a single word of the language. They would have to get a translator quickly.

"I'm sorry, I don't understand," he said to her.

She shook her head, pointed at Caleb again and continued speaking in Russian. This time he understood one word.

Tatjana. The third missing girl.

"Tatjana?" he asked, and she nodded.

"Was she with you?"

Sasha spoke again, this time she added a few English words. "Tatjana, friend. Help."

Yang exchanged a look with Emily.

"She must mean that Tatjana is still alive and locked up somewhere," Emily suggested.

Yang was guessing the same thing. He turned to one of the uniformed officers that had arrived. "Call for a Russian interpreter. It's urgent."

"Yes, Detective."

"Excuse me, Miss Warner." Yang turned and walked to Jefferson who stood waiting with a handcuffed, bleeding, and wincing Caleb Faulkner.

"Where's the other girl? Where is Tatjana?" Yang addressed Caleb directly.

Blood ran from Caleb's nose, his face was bruised, his lip split, but he forced a smile. "I'll tell you, if I get a plea deal. No jail time."

"Dream on," Yang scoffed. "So far, I'm counting four murders including Miss Warner's father. You'll serve four life sentences at a minimum. And I'll make sure your cellmates know that you raped and abused children. You know what they'll do to men like you in prison? Besides, you're a pretty boy. I'm sure someone will make you his bitch."

Caleb spit at him, but Yang wasn't close enough to be hit. "My father will fix this."

"You mean like he fixed it so you wouldn't go to prison in Moscow when you raped that fourteen-year-old Russian girl? What was her name?"

Caleb blanched.

"Caleb," somebody said from the entrance to the room. Yang glanced at the newcomer: Mike Faulkner.

To say Yang was surprised to see the Chief of Staff, was the understatement of the decade. He was floored.

"Dad, thank God you're here!" Caleb called out to his father. "They're trying to frame me for something I didn't do. You have to help me."

Faulkner met his son's gaze. "I'll get you help. The best doctors money can buy."

"Doctors?" Yang repeated. "So that's gonna be his defense? That he's insane? He killed four people, possibly five, and he kidnapped and raped three girls, and probably many more!" Yang fumed.

"He's sick. He needs help," Faulkner said. "I thought he got better, but I was wrong. I suspected something when—"

"Don't tell them anything, Dad!" Caleb cried out.

"Shut up," Jefferson growled and jerked on the handcuffs, which aggravated Caleb's shoulder wound and elicited a painful cry from Caleb.

"I'm sorry, son, I should have done something back then. I should have gotten you treatment a long time ago. I failed you."

Yang turned to Caleb. "How did you do it? How did you stage Madeline's accident? There were no signs of a struggle, no defensive wounds."

Caleb scoffed. "I didn't do anything."

Yang exchanged a look with Jefferson, then looked back at Caleb. "You must have sedated Madeline Bolton. We'll know for sure when we get Madeline's tox screen."

When Yang caught Mike Faulkner's guarded facial expression, he added, "I'm assuming you've seen the report already, Mr. Faulkner."

When Faulkner didn't say anything, Yang continued, "Never mind. The Secret Service will have to turn it over now that we have an eyewitness to Madeline Bolton's murder."

"What eyewitness?" Faulkner asked, clearly stunned.

Yang pointed at Sasha, who, together with Emily, was being led away by two EMTs. "The girl Madeline was sheltering on the night of her murder. She saw everything." Even though Yang hadn't yet been able to get confirmation from Sasha, he guessed that Sasha had witnessed the murder.

Faulkner stared at Caleb as if he didn't even know him.

"Dad, they have no evidence to tie me to Maddie's death! Nor to Petrov's or to Annika's," Caleb claimed. "You have to help me!"

More police officers entered. Jefferson handed Caleb over to them. "Lock him up."

"What about the injury?" one of the uniformed officers asked.

Jefferson shrugged, though he knew—just like Yang—that they had to provide the perpetrator with medical care, no matter the horrific crimes he'd committed. "Do what you have to. But take every precaution. He's a flight risk."

Once Caleb was being led out of the room flanked by two armed policemen, Faulkner looked crestfallen. Yang felt satisfaction fill him. Faulkner's son was still defiant, but Faulkner was smarter, he knew that he'd lost.

"We found Caleb's DNA under Annika's fingernails," Yang said. "He's going down for it. There's nothing you can do. Now might be a good time for you to cooperate. Let's start with why you're here. And don't tell me you listened to a police scanner."

"I couldn't get a hold of Caleb. I needed to speak to him, to confront him... I tracked his car to Maddie's house and when I saw police cars converge on this building, I suspected that Caleb was here."

"You suspected your son of killing Madeline Bolton?"

Faulkner sighed and shoved a trembling hand through his hair, hesitating.

"I need to know why," Yang said. "What evidence were you hiding from us? We can do this down at the station with an attorney, but if you want a lenient sentence, then tell us right now what you know."

Faulkner's shoulders dropped. "Sometime around Madeline's death, a bottle of Midazolam disappeared from my horse farm. We use it to sedate animals during procedures. I couldn't be sure that Caleb had taken it and why, but when Maddie's tox screen came back, I saw that they found traces of alcohol and Midazolam. When combined with alcohol, Midazolam acts within minutes to render the person unable to move, unable to fight back."

Faulkner dropped his head and shook it, then looked back at Yang. "They were friends, Maddie and Caleb. They worked together. They trusted each other."

Yang nodded. "So she let him into her house, and had a drink with him. He must have had reason to believe that Madeline was looking into the disappearance of the girls that were placed by the charity."

"I didn't know about any girls." Faulkner's voice was devoid of any emotions now. "But earlier today, when I received Maddie's tox screen, I realized that if he killed Maddie, it was in order to protect a secret. I just didn't know what it was."

Yang didn't quite believe that. "You knew what he did in Moscow. You covered it up, and you're telling me now that you didn't know about the girls?"

Faulkner let out a trembling breath. "I didn't, not for certain… But I was worried…"

"So where was Caleb keeping the girls?"

Faulkner shook his head. "I don't know. Not at the estate in Virginia. He barely goes there. And not at my townhouse in the city either. I would have seen or heard things."

"Does he have his own place?"

"Yes, a condo in Georgetown, but it's just a two bedroom without any storage area, or individual garage. No basement. He couldn't possibly hide anyone there. The neighbors would hear that."

Yang waved at one of the officers to approach. "Take two men, and go to Caleb Faulkner's condo." He looked at Faulkner. "What's the address?"

Faulkner recited an address, then the officer left.

"Does he have any other property in the city?"

Faulkner shrugged. "Not that I know of."

Yang looked into Faulkner's eyes. He didn't look like he was lying, but then, Faulkner was a politician, and all politicians lied. "You sure? The life of another girl is at stake. Tatjana, the third girl he kidnapped, is still missing."

"That's all I know, I swear. I don't know where he kept them."

"Fine. If it turns out that you did know about the location where he hid the girls, we'll add this to your obstruction of justice charge." Then he addressed a policeman, "Take Mr. Faulkner to the police station for a formal interview."

83

OUTSIDE, in front of the abandoned building, several police cars and ambulances were blocking the street. A policewoman was by Emily's side, while an EMT checked her for injuries. Sasha was being checked out by another EMT in the same ambulance. Sasha had insisted on staying close to Emily, still mistrustful of anybody else, particularly men. Emily couldn't blame her.

Besides a few bruises, neither Emily nor Sasha had sustained any injuries. Emily squeezed Sasha's hand, and got a smile in response. This was the first time the girl had smiled. She was a survivor, Emily sensed it. Sasha would get through this, though healing from the psychological trauma she'd suffered would take a long time.

From the corner of her eye, Emily saw two men with a stretcher come out of the building. On it was a black body bag. She knew who was inside. Emily excused herself and stepped out of the ambulance.

"You should stay here, Miss Warner," the policewoman said.

"I have to see him one more time," Emily said and walked to the coroner's vehicle, where the two men with the stretcher now stood. The policewoman didn't stop her.

When Emily reached the stretcher, the two men looked at her.

"It's my father," she said before she put her hand on the zipper.

The two men nodded and let her proceed as she lowered the zipper sufficiently to expose her father's face. His eyes were closed now, and his face seemed relaxed, though pale. She ran her knuckles over his cheek. The skin wasn't entirely cold yet. There was still some residual warmth, yet he was gone.

"I hope Mom can forgive you too. Tell her that I miss her… Not a day goes by where I don't think of her. I love you, Dad."

Tears streamed down her cheeks, and she turned away from the stretcher, only to see Diego stand a couple of yards away. He crossed the distance between them, put a hand on her shoulder and squeezed it.

"I'm so sorry for your loss," he said. "I wish I would have gotten there earlier."

She sniffled. "It's ironic that the man who saved my life tonight was one I thought for such a long time to be evil." She shook her head then met Diego's gaze. "I'm sorry, Diego. I'm sorry for suspecting you."

"And for hitting me over the head, I assume?" he said in a light tone.

"Yeah, that too. Twice. I'm so sorry."

"I've got a hard head. It's alright. Had I suspected you of killing Maddie, I would have done much worse," he admitted. "I loved her, and I would have never hurt her."

"I know that now."

"She would have liked you. You have heart. Just like she did." There was a wet sheen covering Diego's eyes, attesting to his loss.

Emily couldn't reply, not wanting to tear up again. Instead, she changed the subject. "Can I borrow your cell phone? Mine is somewhere in the building. I need to call Vicky to tell her that I'm okay."

"I don't think that'll be necessary," Diego said and pointed past Emily.

Farther down the street where the police had cordoned off the area where the ambulances had parked, Vicky was arguing with a policeman.

"Vicky!" Emily called out and walked closer, Diego accompanying her.

"See, that's my friend. She needs me," Vicky insisted.

The policeman looked at Emily and Diego.

"Please let her through," Emily said, and the policeman complied.

Vicky hurried toward her and put her arms around her, giving her a bear hug. "Oh God, I'm so happy you're not harmed." She let go of her, then glanced at Diego. "Thanks for calling me earlier."

"You called Vicky?" Emily asked.

Vicky answered in his stead, "Just as well that he did. Otherwise I wouldn't have known that the killer was after you. Diego saw him running after you. So I called Detective Yang and told him which way you were heading."

"But how could you know that?" Emily asked, confused.

"Ever heard of the *Find-my-Friend* feature on your cell phone?" Vicky smiled. "I activated it the other day so your cell shared your location with mine."

Stunned, Emily wrapped her arms around Vicky. "You're the best."

"Well, somebody had to keep an eye on you, since you wouldn't listen to reason—or Detective Yang."

Emily released her from the embrace, when Vicky pointed past her toward the coroner's van. "Tell me that's not Sasha in there."

Emily shook her head and gestured to the ambulance where just at that moment Sasha emerged, her eyes roaming until they fell on Emily.

"So it's the killer," Vicky said.

"No," Emily replied. "He's alive, but they got him. My father is dead. He took a bullet for me." Another wave of tears threatened to overwhelm her.

"Oh, honey, I'm so sorry."

Emily sniffled. "We had a minute before he passed. He told me he regretted what he'd done to my mom and me. I forgave him."

Vicky nodded, understanding. "He'll be at peace now. And you have closure."

Accompanied by the policewoman, Sasha joined them, and Emily put one arm around her.

But Sasha didn't look at her or Diego or Vicky. Instead, she stared at the other ambulance. On a stretcher in front of it, Caleb sat propped up, one hand handcuffed to the guard rail of the stretcher, the other in a sling. He stared right at Sasha and Emily.

"*Ubiytsa,*" Sasha said with contempt in her voice, sounding much stronger than she had before.

"Yes, Sasha, he's a murderer, but he'll never hurt anybody again. I promise you," Emily said.

Sasha looked up at her, and it appeared that she understood. *"Da."*

When the EMTs pushed Caleb into the ambulance, and a uniformed police officer stepped into the back with him, Yang and Jefferson appeared with Mike Faulkner, the President's Chief of Staff.

"What's he doing here?" Vicky asked.

Diego let out a grunt. "He knew what his son was capable of. And he kept it quiet."

When Jefferson led Faulkner to a police car, Yang approached.

"Detective," Diego said, "tell me that Mike Faulkner will pay for his part in this."

Yang nodded. "I'm not the DA, but trust me we've got enough evidence to charge him with obstruction of justice."

"I'm glad you got here when you did," Emily said.

"Thanks to the ingenuity of Miss Hong," Yang replied.

"Detective Yang!" a man in a dark suit approaching them said.

"Ah, Mr. Belsky, I was wondering when you would show up," Yang said with an arched eyebrow. "I thought your people were keeping an eye on my partner and me."

Emily found this to be curious. Who was this man?

"I saw that you had it under control," Belsky said with a heavy Russian accent. "I didn't want to interfere until my help was needed." He inclined his head toward Sasha, then said something in Russian.

Sasha replied in only a few words.

"Can you translate for us what Sasha knows? We believe there's another girl, Tatjana, still locked up wherever Caleb Faulkner kept Sasha."

"Certainly," Belsky said.

"Let's do this down at the station," Yang suggested.

Belsky addressed the girl again in Russian, and Sasha replied, but shook her head, while holding on to Emily.

"Something wrong?" Yang asked.

"It appears the girl doesn't trust us. She wants Miss Warner to come with her."

Emily was surprised that the man knew who she was. "I don't think we've been introduced."

"Ah, apologies, Nikolai Belsky, Chief of Security at the Russian Embassy."

Emily nodded. "You worked with Sergei Petrov. I'm sorry for your loss."

To her surprise, the Russian smiled. "Your compassion is touching, yet not necessary. Sergei Petrov is alive."

"What?" Yang blurted. "I interviewed his security detail myself."

Belsky turned to Yang. "We had to make sure everybody thought that Petrov hadn't survived the second attempt on his life. We couldn't trust anybody, not even the police, or anybody in your government."

"But how?" Yang asked.

"According to the medical staff who saved Petrov's life, he'd been injected with air, which, yes, if injected into a carotid artery will cause an embolism in the brain and kill a person very quickly. But the killer was clearly improvising and didn't have sufficient medical knowledge to understand that a small amount of air injected into an IV port rather than the carotid artery doesn't necessarily kill immediately."

"I don't understand. Caleb Faulkner would have come prepared."

Belsky nodded. "He did. The needle he used on the security guard was found in the hospital room. It contained traces of Midazolam, as did Lipovsky's blood. Caleb Faulkner used a massive dose of Midazolam on Lipovsky. In general the drug takes a few minutes to knock somebody unconscious, but the dose was so large, it rendered him unconscious in a matter of seconds. Had it not happened in an ICU, Lipovsky would have died for certain. And since Caleb used the entire syringe on Lipovsky, he had none left for Petrov."

Stunned, Emily said, "Then Petrov will be able to testify when he wakes up."

Belsky nodded. "He woke up an hour ago. I was on my way to see him when I got word that Detectives Yang and Jefferson were about to apprehend the killer."

"Got word?" Yang asked, tilting his head to one side.

"We all have our sources. Let's just leave it at that, shall we?" the Russian said with a smirk.

84

GIVEN SASHA'S FRAGILE STATE, Yang decided not to interrogate her in a cold and bare interrogation room at the station, but opted for one of the private offices that had a couch and a few comfortable chairs.

A Russian interpreter had arrived at the station, and Yang invited her to join them. Even though Belsky would be translating Sasha's answers, he wanted somebody neutral to make sure the Russian Embassy's Chief of Security didn't omit anything crucial.

Emily sat on the couch with Sasha, holding her hand, while Belsky had pulled a chair closer on Sasha's side. The interpreter sat on a chair farther away, a notepad on her lap, while Jefferson sat behind the computer to take notes.

Yang sat in an armchair opposite the couch and looked at Belsky. "We just need a quick confirmation from Sasha that she saw Caleb kill Madeline Bolton, before we talk about where she was locked up so we can find Tatjana. We'll go into more details in subsequent interviews."

Belsky nodded. With his help, Sasha told them about what had happened in Madeline's townhouse.

According to Sasha, it was evening when the doorbell rang and Maddie told Sasha to go and hide in the guest room. She did so, but because she'd left the door to the guest room ajar, she could hear that Maddie let a man in the house. She heard them talking and recognized the voice as that of her captor and rapist. The same man who'd killed Annika.

When Sasha took a short break, a sob tore from her chest, and Emily stroked her forearm gently. "You're doing great, Sasha."

Belsky continued translating for the girl and revealed that Sasha left the guest room to see what they were doing. From the upstairs hallway there was a spot where she could see down into the living room, while being hidden behind the banister. However, she couldn't understand what they were talking about.

Yang recalled the layout of Madeline Bolton's house, even though he'd only been there once, and only for a short time. The staircase that led upstairs had a switchback before it reached the upper hallway. From there, one could look down into the living room. A three-foot high partition obstructed the view of the upper hallway somewhat, making it possible for somebody to hide behind it and catch glimpses of the goings-on in the living room below.

"What were they doing?" Yang asked, and Belsky translated the question.

Sasha saw them drinking a glass of wine, but they started to argue and it looked like Maddie wanted him to leave. That's when her wine glass fell from her hand, and she tried to stand up from the sofa, but couldn't. She fell back onto the sofa. That's when Sasha's rapist stood up. His voice changed, just like it did every time he hurt Sasha and the other girls. Sasha realized that he would hurt Maddie, and she wanted to help her but couldn't.

Meanwhile, tears streamed down Sasha's face.

Everybody sat silent until Sasha was ready to continue.

Sasha saw Caleb leave the room and ducked behind the partition so he wouldn't see her. She couldn't tell what exactly he did, but he carried a stepladder into the living room. And then he grabbed Maddie. Her eyes were open, but she wasn't fighting him. Sasha described her as being limp like a ragdoll.

Yang swallowed hard. Maddie had known what was coming. He felt a shudder run down his spine, but he needed to hear the rest.

According to Sasha's teary recollection, Caleb had lifted Maddie up and then dropped her on the glass coffee table, which shattered on impact. Once he'd staged the scene so it looked like Maddie had fallen off the stepladder, and he'd left the house, Sasha took all the money she could find and ran.

When Yang asked why she hadn't gone to the police, Sasha said that she was too scared, because Caleb was a powerful man.

"Powerful? In what way?" Yang asked.

Belsky listened to Sasha, then looked at Yang and Jefferson and sighed. "Apparently Caleb Faulkner told the girls that he was friends with the President, and that *they* would be punished, not Caleb. Nobody would believe them."

Yang nodded, understanding. "Ask her whether she can find her way back to the place where Caleb locked her up."

Belsky translated Yang's question.

"She doesn't know. It was in the middle of the night, and she just ran until she stopped in front of a church."

"A church? Which one?" Yang asked.

"She doesn't know the name, but the charity had an event there a few months ago. A lot of the children were there, and Maddie and Caleb too."

Yang motioned to Jefferson.

"Already on it," Jefferson said before Yang could even voice his request. A moment later, Jefferson took his laptop and turned it so Sasha could see it. "Here are all the churches in the vicinity of Madeline's house." Slowly, he scrolled through them.

Sasha pointed to the computer. "This one."

"Holy Trinity Catholic Church," Jefferson said.

"That's a start," Yang said before turning back to Sasha and asking her the next questions via Belsky. "How long did you run until you reached the church?"

"Not long, maybe ten or twenty minutes."

"Did you turn many times, or run straight?"

"I turned a few times, but I think I ran in circles. Everything looked the same."

"Did you cross any bridges, run through any parks?"

Sasha shook her head. "No. It was just normal streets. Small streets."

"No major roads with lots of traffic?"

She shook her head.

Yang turned to Jefferson. "If she didn't cross any bridges or any major roads, then she must have been locked up somewhere in Georgetown."

"I need more," Jefferson said, looking at the map he'd pulled up on the laptop. "Sasha, how about restaurants? Bars? Any stores you passed?"

Belsky said, "She doesn't know. She didn't look. She just wanted to get away."

Yang sighed. "Ask her about the place she was locked up in. Was it in a house, a warehouse, a garage?"

"It was downstairs. A basement. It was always dark, and the air smelled bad…"

"Bad? You mean musty?"

She shook her head. "No, like food. Curry. It always smelled of curry."

Yang and Jefferson looked at each other. "An Indian restaurant."

Moments later, Jefferson said, "There are only two Indian restaurants in the vicinity."

"Show them on Google Street View," Yang said.

Jefferson zoomed in on the first restaurant, while Sasha looked at the screen. She shook her head. "No, it doesn't look familiar."

"How about this one?"

Sasha stared at the screen, while Jefferson used Google Street View to do a 360-degree turn, showing what other buildings were on the same street.

Sasha jerked her hand toward the image, and Belsky translated, "There! She saw this. She saw this when she escaped. That's the street!"

85

THE SMELL OF CURRY wafted through the air, even though the restaurant from which it originated was closed for the night. Emily looked at the building on the quaint one-way street that was lined with pretty two-story townhouses on one side, and larger buildings on the other. One such building was occupied by an Indian restaurant.

When Sasha got out of Detective Yang's car, she stayed close to Emily, gripping her hand once more. Belsky had also come with them, while Jefferson and the interpreter had taken a separate car. A police cruiser with two uniformed police officers was already waiting for them.

"Look around, Sasha," Yang instructed the girl with the help of Belsky translating, "when you ran out of the basement where Caleb kept you, what did you see?"

Slowly, Sasha turned around, glancing up and down the street. When she tugged on Emily's hand, Emily walked with her up the slight slope of the street. Sasha suddenly began to tremble, and her eyes fixated on a metal gate between two townhouses. She pointed to it.

Emily looked over her shoulder and nodded at Yang. He approached, as did Belsky and the other police officers.

The metal gate wasn't locked. It led to an area where the garbage cans were kept, but there was no door anywhere.

"There's nothing here," Yang said.

Emily heard the disappointment in the detective's voice.

"Maybe you're misremembering?" Yang said to Sasha.

But Sasha shook her head and pointed toward the oversized trashcans. On her insistence, Yang grabbed the handle of one of the cans and rolled it forward, then did the same with the second one. Emily couldn't see what he was seeing, but when she noticed Yang's expression change, she knew he'd found something.

"I need a bolt cutter," Yang called out over his shoulder.

Moments later, one of the police officers handed him the requested tool. Emily looked over Yang's shoulder to watch him as he cut away a heavy chain that had locked an unassuming steel door. When he opened it, Emily saw that behind the door, steps led down to a basement.

A dim light on the wall provided some illumination. Yang used his flashlight to peer into the darkness. Emily now saw that there was padding on the inside of the door in an attempt to make the place soundproof.

"Tatjana!" Sasha called out toward the basement. "Tatjana!" Then she said something in Russian.

"Sasha! Sasha!" The excited words came from a girl. They were accompanied by the rattling of metal.

Yang descended down the stairs, and Sasha stalked after him. Emily had no choice but to follow, not wanting to let go of the girl's hand. The room they entered at the foot of the stairs was large, but had a low ceiling and an earthen floor. In one corner was a mattress raised on a two-foot-high wooden platform. In the other was a crudely built metal floor-to-ceiling fence with a locked gate. The area looked like a jail cell out of an old Western. In it was an old toilet and a washbasin as well as several cots.

Holding onto the bars of the cell, Emily saw a young girl dressed in dirty clothes. She had dark hair and the same blue eyes as Sasha. Caleb had definitely had a type.

When Tatjana laid eyes on Sasha, who now let go of Emily's hand and rushed to her, tears streamed down her face. Sasha reached through the metal gate to take Tatjana's hands into hers. Sasha spoke fast, only interrupted by tears.

Emily turned to Belsky, who'd entered behind her.

"Sasha is apologizing to Tatjana that she didn't come back earlier to free her. She was just too afraid that Caleb would lock her up again," Belsky explained.

"We've gotta get this gate open," Yang said.

"I can do that," Emily said.

Yang stared at her, stunned, while Emily pulled her lock picks from her handbag.

"Wow, I hadn't expected that," Yang said, but stepped aside.

It took Emily only a minute to unlock the gate. The moment it was open, the two girls embraced, crying in each other's arms. Tears rimmed Emily's eyes too. She pushed them back. Tatjana was safe.

Emily turned around and walked outside the oppressive bunker-like room. When she reached the street, she breathed deeply. A sob tore from her throat, and she let the tears flow. She couldn't imagine how the girls had survived being locked up in a place without natural light, having to endure being brutalized and raped on a regular basis.

The policewoman from the cruiser put a hand on her arm. "Did they find her alive?"

Emily nodded. "Yes. It's over now. It's over."

Her words opened the floodgates even further, and Emily let herself go until she had no tears left, the policewoman providing a shoulder for her to cry on.

"Thank you," Emily said and sniffled.

The policewoman smiled at her, before she walked to assist her colleague.

Emily composed herself, then turned toward the window of the police cruiser to look at her reflection and dry her tears with a tissue.

But she didn't see her own face in the glass pane. It was Maddie who looked back at her, a smile on her face.

"Maddie," Emily murmured and reached out her hand to touch Maddie's face.

Maddie mouthed something, and though Emily wasn't adept at lip reading, she knew what Maddie was saying. *Thank you.*

When Emily blinked, the image was gone. Instinctively, she knew that this was the last time she'd see Maddie, although she could still feel a connection to her, still feel Maddie's compassion and gratitude.

86

THE NEXT TWO DAYS, Yang and Jefferson were busy interviewing everybody even remotely connected to the case with Caleb Faulkner at its center. Everybody they interrogated had a different piece of the puzzle. Together with the autopsy and toxicology report for Madeline Bolton, which the Secret Service released immediately after Mike Faulkner's involvement in the case was disclosed to them, Yang and Jefferson had everything they needed for an airtight case against Caleb Faulkner.

Only one thing remained to be done. Yang had volunteered for it, wanting to give closure to a grieving family.

An assistant ushered Yang into Eric Bolton's downtown office. The man stood looking out through the large window that had a view of the Capitol.

The assistant closed the door behind Yang, and slowly, Bolton turned to face him.

"Thank you for seeing me here rather than at home," Bolton said. "There's no need for Rita to hear all the details of Caleb's depravity. It's enough that she knows that he'll be punished for what he did."

"I promise you that," Yang said and took the proffered seat on a comfortable armchair.

Bolton sat down opposite him. "Tell me everything, no matter how horrific."

"When Mike Faulkner was ambassador in Moscow, Caleb was a teenager. I don't need to go into all the details of why he raped a fourteen-year-old Russian girl and nearly strangled her to death, but suffice it to say that Sergei Petrov confirmed that there was a sexual assault incident. Petrov only had snippets of information and believed that it was Mike Faulkner who'd committed the rape, never suspecting Caleb. After all, it was Mike Faulkner who paid off the family so they wouldn't go to the police or the papers. Everything was swept under the carpet, and Mike and Caleb Faulkner returned to the States."

Bolton nodded. "I always wondered why he'd only stayed there for two years. When I asked him once, he said that it wasn't a good environment for Caleb. I even complimented him on putting his family before his career."

Yang exhaled slowly. "I can't condone what Faulkner did for his son, though I understand that no parent wants their child to languish in a foreign prison. But he could have gotten him help once back in the States. A psychiatrist, medications, therapy, something."

"Caleb's a psychopath, and none of us saw it." Bolton shook his head. "I liked him. I even thought that he would make a wonderful son-in-law. How wrong I was."

"He fooled everybody and pretended to be polite and caring, when he was anything but. We might never know how many young girls he raped and killed, but we know of three of them. Two are still alive and have confirmed that they were lured into Caleb's car after a session with their therapist. The girls had seen him at a charity event, and thought he was a good guy. They trusted him. There's a witness, a homeless person, who told the police after Annika's disappearance that he saw a fancy car wait in the alley behind the therapist's building. He wasn't taken seriously at the time, because he was high on drugs and couldn't describe the car or the man."

"Annika is the dead girl?"

"Yes, according to Tatjana and Sasha, the two surviving Russian girls, Annika fought back when Caleb raped her particularly savagely one night. They had to watch as he strangled her. It takes a particularly heartless person to strangle somebody with his bare hands. She fought as long as she could. That's how his DNA ended up under her fingernails. He thought by disposing of the body in a shallow grave in Fort Dupond Park her body would decompose quickly and nobody would ever find her. Well, somebody did."

Bolton seemed to shudder. "The two survivors, they must be traumatized."

"They'll need lots of counseling."

"How did Maddie get involved in all of this?"

"It started with Sergei Petrov. They met at a society event. He targeted her because she worked for *No child abandoned*, a charity Mike Faulkner founded after his return from Russia. Petrov believed that Mike Faulkner was using it as a front to get access to underage girls. And since several girls who were rescued by the charity disappeared over the last few years, Petrov believed that Mike Faulkner was behind it. He convinced Maddie to use her access to look for proof."

Bolton sighed. "She wouldn't have done it to prove that Mike hurt those girls."

"What do you mean?"

"She would have done it to prove that he didn't. She loved Mike. He was her godfather. She must have accepted Petrov's request to clear his name. That's the kind of person she was."

"You may be right. But by digging in the charity's records, she drew Caleb's attention on her. We interviewed the charity staff and found out that in the couple of weeks before her death, your daughter accessed various files on a number of girls when this wasn't really her domain."

"That's how Caleb found out that she was looking into the girls' disappearances?"

"We have to assume that. Unfortunately, Caleb isn't talking." Yang shrugged. "Doesn't matter. We have enough other witnesses."

"You mean the two girls who survived?"

Yang nodded.

"How did that girl, Sasha, even escape?" Bolton asked.

"Caleb had come and picked Tatjana to take her to the cot where he regularly abused one or the other. Normally, Sasha would have been locked in the cell, while he was busy with Tatjana, but when Caleb took Tatjana out of the cell, Sasha managed to jam a piece of cloth into the lock so it didn't snap in. Caleb seemed too eager to get on with his abuse of Tatjana, and didn't notice. Perhaps he had more to drink than usual. We don't know."

"So she ran?"

"When Caleb's back was turned, she snuck out of the cage and ran out of the basement and into the street. Tatjana said Caleb stumbled when he tried to run after Sasha, because his pants were down below his knees. But when Tatjana tried to run past him to escape like Sasha, he snatched her ankle and she fell and hit her head so hard that she passed out."

"Oh my God!"

"Sasha ran and ran, until she found herself in front of Holy Trinity Catholic Church. No *child abandoned* had held an event there that many of the rescued children had participated in. That's how Sasha knew who Maddie was. Apparently they exchanged a few words with the help of an interpreter, and Sasha felt she could trust your daughter. When the event ended, a bus took everybody back to their respective homes, and the driver dropped Madeline off at her townhouse only a few blocks from the event. Sasha remembered the house, because she was wondering if one day she would live in a beautiful house like that too. It took her a while to find the house, but she eventually did and asked Maddie for help."

Bolton sniffled, and Yang looked at him, noticing that Bolton's emotions were getting the better of him. "Do you want me to stop?"

"No. Please, continue."

"Your daughter took Sasha in, but she couldn't get much out of her, only that a man had hurt her. And that she was scared. This is when Maddie must have called Sergei Petrov for help. But he was out of the country, and only got the message after Maddie's death."

"So she did call him like Miss Warner said?"

"Yes, and according to the Secret Service, they found the record of the call on your daughter's phone, but by the time you received it, it had been deleted."

"By Mike?"

"We believe so. He was the only other person who had possession of the cell phone before he returned it to you. I believe he wanted to make sure that nobody drew a connection from Maddie to Petrov, which might have ultimately led to discovering that her death had something to do with the missing Russian girls."

"He must have realized that it would lead them to Caleb."

"Perhaps. He might have realized even earlier that Caleb was up to something, because Robert Wolff, Mike Faulkner's groom at his equestrian estate confirmed that he'd called Faulkner a week after Madeline's death when he couldn't find the bottle of Midazolam that he needed for an injured dog. Mike told his groom that he'd accidentally broken the bottle, but that was obviously a lie. Caleb stole the drug, and mixed it with wine to sedate Madeline so he could stage a household accident."

A tear ran down Bolton's cheek, and he wiped it away. "At least she didn't know what was happening to her."

Yang didn't correct him. The dose of Midazolam that Maddie had received in the wine she drank with Caleb was likely not enough to knock her out completely, since Caleb couldn't risk her breathing and her heart to stop before he'd inflicted the head injury. However, the drug in her system had relaxed her muscles to the point where she had no control over them and had been unable to fight Caleb, while knowing what was coming.

"To think that I've known Caleb all his life..." Bolton said. "As if he never cared for her at all. Or for any of us."

"That's the definition of a psychopath. They don't care for anybody other than themselves," Yang responded.

Bolton nodded, taking in a steadying breath. "But why did Caleb shoot Petrov and Miss Warner? Did Mike give him their names?"

"Not on purpose, no. Rather, I think it was you who alerted Caleb to the fact that Petrov and Miss Warner had information that might lead the police to the killer."

"I? I would have never—"

Yang lifted his hand. "I know that. Your contribution to this situation was entirely innocent. When I re-interviewed you yesterday, you told me that you called Mike Faulkner, and he was in his townhouse in D.C. where he was getting dressed for a White House dinner. According to you he put you on speaker to continue dressing, while you told him that your wife had had a visit from Miss Warner in which she claimed that Maddie had spoken to Petrov. I believe that Caleb was at the townhouse and overheard the conversation, although neither Caleb nor his father is giving us any information. It doesn't matter. We have plenty of evidence to convict Caleb. We can even prove that Caleb disguised himself as a doctor to make a second attempt on Petrov's life. Though he was wearing a surgical mask and a cap, we were able to overlay the security footage from the hospital with security footage of Caleb in the charity's foyer. Did you know that every person has an individual gait?"

"No."

"Caleb and the person who attacked Petrov and his security detail in the ICU walked exactly in the same way. Their gaits were identical. A perfect match."

Bolton let out a deep breath. "So much pain, so many deaths, so many people hurt... All, so that Caleb could hide what kind of monster he is. And Mike knew. He knew all along what Caleb was capable of, and still, he let it happen."

"It wasn't just that. In a way he facilitated it."

"In which way?"

"After Faulkner's return from Russia, he must have felt guilty for what his son had done. I believe he wanted to make good on his son's crime, so he founded the charity to help abused children. His motives at that point were most likely pure, even though they were steeped in guilt. Years passed, and perhaps Faulkner believed that his son had overcome his... shall I say sexual appetite for young girls? Anyway, Faulkner would have done more good by getting his son help in the form of therapy and medication."

Yang shook his head, then continued, "So when Faulkner had to resign from the charity when he became Chief of Staff, he put Caleb at the helm. It was equivalent to putting the wolf in charge of the henhouse. It gave Caleb full reign over any of the girls that came through the charity. He had his pick. He had a type: dark hair, blue eyes. We're still going through the charity's files to figure out whether there were other girls before Annika, Sasha, and Tatjana that he may have abused or killed."

"I can't understand Mike. How could he even think of putting Caleb in that position?" Bolton asked.

"We'll never know. Maybe he truly thought that Caleb had gotten better and had repented." Yang shrugged. "But after Madeline's death, he ignored all the signs that Caleb was involved in something nefarious. Instead, he tampered with evidence, like erasing Madeline's call to Sergei, and did everything to cover up what he deep down already knew: that Caleb had killed Madeline."

"I'll never forgive him for that," Bolton said.

"At least, it's over now," Yang said. "Caleb will die in prison. And Faulkner, given his age, will too."

Bolton nodded, then looked straight at Yang. "It's ironic, isn't it? A woman who was blind half her life helped us all see the monster behind the façade."

"Yes, she did. And she led us to the only eyewitness who saw Caleb kill Madeline. There aren't many women like Miss Warner."

"No, Detective. A woman like her is a rarity. You should seize this opportunity."

Involuntarily, Yang smiled. Maybe he would follow Bolton's advice.

87

A WEEK AFTER SASHA'S RESCUE, Emily was back at the same cemetery at which Madeline Bolton had been laid to rest to say goodbye to her father. It was a quiet and small affair.

White lilies were draped atop the elegant coffin, and a priest recited Psalm 23.

"The Lord is my Shepherd…"

Emily barely heard the prayer, her heart filled with grief and regret, but also with gratitude. Her father had paid his debt to Emily with his own life. Whether his sacrifice would buy him entry into heaven, she didn't know. But she no longer felt any ill will toward him. Today, she grieved for the father she'd lost fifteen years earlier, and wept genuine tears for him. Maybe her mother could forgive him now too.

Emily stood looking at the casket, flanked by her trusted guide dog, Coffee, and her best friend, Vicky. Both had given her strength during the past week.

When the priest finished his prayer and stepped aside, the few mourners stayed and conveyed their condolences. Ambassador Pacheco was accompanied by Catalina.

Catalina wrapped her arms around Emily's waist and pressed her head against her chest. "I'm sorry you lost your dad. I don't know what I would do if I lost mine." Catalina sniffled, trying to hide her tears.

"It's okay to cry," Emily said, tears rolling down her cheeks. "I'm sorry too that I lost him. Promise me something, Catalina."

The girl lifted her head. "Anything."

"You make sure you tell your dad every day that you love him." Emily met Ambassador Pacheco's gaze and held it. "Because that way you'll never lose him."

"I will, Miss Warner," Catalina promised.

Ambassador Pacheco's eyes moistened. Emily could sense that he was thinking of his wife. She smiled through her tears. Pacheco reached for Catalina, then offered Emily his hand. When she shook it, he suddenly clasped it with both hands. "If you ever need anything, Catalina and I will be here for you."

"Thank you," she said, knowing his offer was genuine.

The ambassador took his daughter by the hand and walked to his security detail.

Diego Sanchez, who'd stood on Vicky's other side, turned to her. "I'm sorry for your loss, Emily."

She took his hand and squeezed it. "I wanted to thank you for everything you've done—"

"That's not necessary," he interrupted. "From what I could see, you had it all in hand, before I managed to jump in. I only wish that the police hadn't arrived so quickly, and interrupted me beating the crap out of Caleb." He sighed. "But it is what it is. I'm the one who has to thank you. Without you, Maddie would never have gotten justice. And Caleb would have continued hurting even more innocent girls." Then he said to Vicky, "I'll wait at the car."

When he was out of earshot, Emily looked at Vicky. "Are you dating him?"

Vicky blushed. "He invited me for coffee. That's not really a date, you know."

"Of course not," Emily said and smiled. "But I'm sure you can turn it into one."

Vicky leaned in. "I sure hope so." She giggled.

"You're incorrigible."

"I know. Isn't it fun?"

"Don't let me keep you. Have coffee with Diego. I think he likes you. Just remember that he's still grieving. He loved her."

"I know."

Emily motioned to a spot at the other end of the cemetery. "I need to say goodbye to Maddie."

Vicky hugged her. "I love you."

"I love you too."

When Vicky walked to where Diego had parked his car, Emily took one white lily from the flower arrangement on her father's casket.

"You won't mind, Dad, will you?"

Then she looked at Coffee and said, "Come, Coffee."

Together they walked across the cemetery. As she got closer to
Maddie's grave, she could already see the two people who were waiting
for her: Maddie's parents.

When Emily reached the grave, where a white gravestone had been
erected, Rita Bolton put her arms around her and squeezed her tightly.

"I'm so sorry for your loss, my dear," Rita Bolton said amidst tears,
before she released Emily from her embrace.

Emily felt a new wave of tears come on, but tried to suppress it. "I'm
so grateful to you." She looked at Eric Bolton now. "I could have never
given my father such a beautiful resting place if it wasn't for your
generosity."

Bolton took her hand and held it for a moment. "It's only fitting that
we paid for it. What you did to get justice for our little girl, for our
Maddie, can never be repaid."

Rita sniffled. "We had no idea how depraved and how cruel Caleb
was. You think you know somebody…" She shook her head.

"We severed all ties with the Faulkners. I could never be friends with
Mike again, knowing that he tried to cover up Caleb's crimes…" Bolton
moved his head from side to side. "The President made him resign the
moment he heard the news. Mike will be prosecuted as an accessory after
the fact and for obstruction of justice," Bolton said.

Emily had heard about the resignation on the news. "I wish I could
say I'm sorry to hear that, but I'm not. Caleb is a monster. And his father
knew and did nothing to stop him."

But she didn't want to be bitter. She laid the lily on Maddie's grave,
before smiling at the Boltons. "I wish I would have known Maddie when
she was alive. I know we have nothing in common, but—"

Rita put her hand on Emily's forearm. "You do have something in
common. You both have a big heart."

Emily smiled. "I know she's at peace now."

Rita nodded. "Thanks to you." Then she looked past Emily. "I think
somebody is here to see you."

Emily looked over her shoulder and was surprised to see Detective
Yang approach.

"Goodbye," she said to the Boltons, then she pivoted and walked to
where Yang stood.

Coffee walked with her, his tail wagging when Yang crouched down
and petted him.

"I didn't think you would come, Detective," she said.

"I didn't want to intrude on the funeral," he said. "But Vicky called me to let me know that you might need a ride home."

"I could have gotten an Uber back."

"Sure you could, but I figured maybe you wanted to have dinner with me?"

Surprised, she stared at him. "You want to have dinner with me?"

"Yes. Unless you have plans already." He motioned to the main road that snaked through the cemetery. "Maybe the Argentinean ambassador asked you out?"

"So you finally believe me that I know the Argentinean ambassador, Detective?"

He shrugged. "Sometimes you need to see it to believe it. Sometimes you believe it even if you can't see it."

She chuckled softly.

"So is that a *yes* or a *no*?"

"Can I bring Coffee?" She cast a quick glance at her dog.

"The dinner invitation *is* for Coffee. Did I not make that clear? You can accompany us two bachelors if you want to, but only if you stop calling me *Detective*."

"What should I call you then?"

"Adam."

For the first time in fifteen years, Emily felt carefree and knew that her future would be happy no matter what happened from here on out, because she had Maddie in her corner, watching from above.

~ ~ ~

BOOKCLUB
DISCUSSION QUESTIONS

Q1

Emily is bitter about the past. Which events contribute to her being able to let go of her anger and pain?

Q2

Emily takes great risks to get justice for Maddie. Is her fear of losing her eyesight again the only thing that drives her, or is there something deeper at play?

Q3

Detective Yang has a strong sense of right and wrong, and follows his gut. What makes him believe in Emily's stories?

Q4

What in the killer's past contributed to him becoming more brazen and believing that he would never have to pay for his crimes? Could an early intervention and therapy have halted his psychopathic nature, or was his progression inevitable?

Q5

Several of the characters in the book have lost somebody they loved: Emily her mother, Eric and Rita Bolton their daughter, Ambassador Pacheco his wife, Catalina her mother, Diego his girlfriend. Discuss how everybody deals with their loss in a different way.

COMING SOON

Gated
A Thriller

After losing her husband in a home invasion, a young widow moves into a gated community to feel safe again. But what if the gates aren't meant to keep the evil out? What if they are there to keep the evil in?

FEBRUARY 2023

ABOUT THE AUTHOR

T.R. Folsom is the pen name of a New York Times and USA Today bestselling author. T.R. has a background in accounting, taxes, and screenwriting, and has written over 40 books in the vampire and paranormal genre under the pen name Tina Folsom.

T.R. lives in a beach town in California with her spouse and goldendoodle.

Website: http://trfolsom.com
Email: tr@trfolsom.com